One Man Dancing

We gratefully acknowledge the support of the Canada Council for the Arts and the Ontario Arts Council for our publishing program. We also acknowledge the financial support of the Government of Canada.

Cover design and illustration: Val Fullard

Library and Archives Canada Cataloguing in Publication

Keeney, Patricia, author
         One man dancing / Patricia Keeney.

(Inanna poetry and fiction series)
Issued in print and electronic formats.
ISBN 978-1-77133-273-6 (paperback). -- ISBN 978-1-77133-274-3 (epub). -- ISBN 978-1-77133-275-0 (kindle). -- ISBN 978-1-77133-276-7 (pdf)

         I. Title. II. Series: Inanna poetry and fiction series

PS8571.E4447O54 2016   C813'.54   C2016-904857-8
                                                C2016-904858-6

Printed and bound in Canada

Inanna Publications and Education Inc.
210 Founders College, York University
4700 Keele Street, Toronto, Ontario, Canada M3J 1P3
Telephone: (416) 736-5356 Fax: (416) 736-5765
Email: inanna.publications@inanna.ca   Website: www.inanna.ca

MIX
Paper from
responsible sources
FSC® C004071

One Man Dancing

a novel by

Patricia Keeney

inanna poetry & fiction series

INANNA PUBLICATIONS AND EDUCATION INC.
TORONTO, CANADA

ALSO BY PATRICIA KEENEY

FICTION
The Incredible Shrinking Wife

POETRY
Swimming Alone
New Moon Old Mattress
The New Pagans
The Book of Joan
Selected Poems of Patricia Keeney
Global Warnings
Vocal Braidings (with Penn Kemp)
You Bring Me Wings (with Ethel Krauze)
First Woman
Orpheus in Our World

TRANSLATIONS
Selected Poems of Patricia Keeney (Hindi)
Engenderings: Selected Poems (Chinese)
Swimming Alone and Other Poems (Bulgarian)
Nager Seule (*Swimming Alone*) (French)
Le livre de Patrick (*The Book of Patrick*) (French)
Le livre de Jeanne (*The Book of Joan*) (French)

For Charles,
for Abafumi

Charles Tumwesigye and Patricia Keeney

TABLE OF CONTENTS

PROLOGUE: **THE ROCKIES**

*T*HIS IS CHARLES' STORY. *The story of an African man told by a North American woman. What he asked me to tell. What he let me see. What I saw.*

I don't pretend to understand it all. Or know it all. I cannot reveal its meaning in an easy phrase. As though any phrase can express the meaning of a life. Can explain why some of us are allowed health and good fortune while others suffer every kind of physical and social assault. Why some of us are spared. Why some of us are singled out to be victims.

Like Job, tested again and again.

Why some of us keep struggling in the face of existential indifference and caprice.

Like Charles. Always believing in some ultimate purpose.

He stands alone. A man marooned on a mountain. Frozen in shock. Staring out. Swaying slightly.

Time is his god here, keeping him rigorously attentive to the shifting of glacial moments. On top of this treacherous mountain Charles is a martyr to his own rigid limbs.

Extreme exertion put him here, outrunning fear. Every morning he climbs the same mountain of ice, clawing at its hard face, willing himself up, desperate not to fall down.

Again.

A small-wheeled machine whirs below him in this cold, impersonal meat-packing plant. It is fast, darting at the great glinting rock, attacking it block by block, biting off chunks, chewing, swallowing. Relentless. Shrinking his mountain.

As he pounds and splinters with axe and spade at the top of ice mountain, black against white, he dances and slips, drops. His sleek dark body churning, frigid, hurtling down a giant slide into frozen whiteness.

Bound for refrigerated rooms.

No.

Packed cold around the bodies of dead animals.

No.

After a few months, he is moved to the other side of the mountain, chopping frozen carcasses free, wrenching and exposing the blues and reds of stopped life. He carries this cargo to room-temperature work stations where women clean and section. This they do methodically in their white coveralls and heavy hairnets, threads of gossip knotting and fraying and twisting as they extend, examine, and discard.

Arranging death now as surely as they have arranged life.

He admires women. Loves them. Superior creatures. Guardian angels who first taught him the joy of dance.

His ancestors — slim, herdsmen clad in leopard skins and sandals — wandered among the curved horns of grazing cattle. Their wide brimmed hats casting great shadows against the sun; staffs resting easily on their shoulders. The whole scene, with its conical hills and puffy clouds rising pleasantly from plentiful grasslands, pastoral serenity.

This ancestral Uganda is an image Charles continues to hold against the slaughter that now shunts along this brutal, bloody assembly line in this vast warehouse of animal sacrifice. Watching the line move, he is relieved that each carcass is "shrouded" in cloth, emerging smooth and lustrous into the light. Born again, he thinks.

On the other hand, Korean Jim admires the efficiency with

which the killing is carried out, fascinated even by the pistol that stuns the cattle as they enter.

The two immigrant workers watch a carcass swing, hung on a hook by its hind legs so that arteries and veins can be severed and drained. Sure as a surgeon, thinks Charles, knowing the animal has long gone.

Jim regales Charles with stories of his own sovereign ancestors in leisurely extravagance beside garden streams, drinking wine from precious cups, reclining on stone, beguiling time with poetry and song.

Charles tells Jim about cows very much alive, cows both sacred and profane. One cow fell in love with his father. Followed him everywhere. Charles describes the special milk bowls. Carved and polished. With beadwork, patterns of waves, lightning bolts. "Animals are meant for use, not sentiment," Jim chides.

After work they turn their energies from friendly feuding to the serious business of pleasure. Charles is often invited for a meal cooked by Jim's wife Angela. In his home, Jim plays at being *yangban*, the privileged noble to her *kisaeng*, the aristocratic concubine.

On other nights Charles has a quick drink at a local bar with fellow workers, followed by supper with Beth — a Ugandan actress with whom he shares much of his life these days — and then goes out to the dance clubs, arriving in his battered black Ford, built like a tank. How he savours its cracked white vinyl seats, its miniature of St. Jude framed in fur dangling from the mirror. He caresses the knobbed steering wheel or whirls it flashily with one slender ringed finger to impress female passengers.

On the dance floor he is mambo king, samba king, king of the twist and the monkey. Beer flowing, lights flickering, Charles jumps and spirals, catches every beam, twirls the most daring girls, watching skirts fly.

Dance is his speaking.

Once long ago, he wanted to be part of the King's dance troupe, to be a court dancer, a *bakisimba*. In their village house, his mother and his aunts would gather to eat, drink and sing.

Charles would begin to dance, arc himself into the air, his body defying space, tracing unexpected angles. Swaying gracefully from the waist, dissolving and beginning over and over. But rooted, always rooted to the earth. Charles' body radiating effortlessly from that centre of his being, that irrefutable pull of gravity.

Dancing was his passport. To the women's rooms. Beyond the walls. To the king, the *Omugabe,* who appeared in his glaring white robe brandishing a beaded oxtail. Striding through his archway of reeds investing them with strength, magical power.

Omugabe rode in a silver-finned Buick, swimming along the dusty road. Stiff and strong, glistening in blazing sunlight. And always the drummers pounding. Then Charles danced for the sovereign and was given a small drum that travelled with him everywhere. Girls were dazzled by his instrument. Then. Now.

Even white women were dazzled. Like Polish Malgosha with skin the colour of blanched bone, with her red lips and glittery blue eyes. Or Swedish Ingrid whose hair shone bleach bright around her pale salty face, like a ghost from the sea. These were the women he first mated. Happily and exuberantly through his free-wheeling nights. These white women with their openness, their flirting, their kissing and caressing in public.

Charles loved his women of the world and was loved by them — in their tight denims with blouses that plunged thrillingly over soft full breasts. In their flimsy, clinging dresses that drew his eyes over every curve causing him to imagine each secret perfumed place. Exotic brazen creatures walking half naked in sunlight, displaying for him, put on earth to please him.

And the women of the world loved Charles back. Because he adored them.

"You should be where you are," Jim admonishes Charles this Friday afternoon as they rumble in Charles' old car towards the Rocky mountain playground where, with Angela, they will spend a weekend. It is hot as they move along the road into flatlands, the sun turning dry stubble fields the colour of tangerines. Foothills thunder deeply among mountains named for natural forces. They cruise along smooth asphalt, a reassuring baseline under the extravagant scenery, slowly climbing, rising gradually as clouds.

Charles dreams past the signs: "Raindrop Lake" and "Whirlwind Casino."

Jim flicks on the car radio and listens intently to a station filled with strange music and an unknown language. "Is that Korean?" Charles asks.

"It's actually Chinese," says Jim. "Not as good as Korean." And laughs out loud.

The remark sets Angela off. "There's nothing wrong with Chinese," she admonishes. "Our language is based on it."

Jim just nods, patronizing her. "You should hear a soccer match in Korean," he tells Charles. "A header through the goal is unforgettable."

"Did you know," adds Angela, "that the first written reference to soccer can be found in a *Chinese* military text!"

"Who really cares," cries Jim. "I can kick a soccer ball better than any Chinese."

As they banter on, Charles watches the sky turn a thick, yellowy green. Drop lower and lower.

Rain attacks their car. A sudden and violent barrage pelting from every angle. Pooling on the windows.

The world is suddenly rattle and blur.

They slow to a crawl, a tank in a battlefield, completely surrounded, seeing nothing, knowing nothing except the sounds around them. A million spears, thinks Charles, piercing everything in their path.

"What's happening?" shouts Jim. "It's pitch black"

"I don't know," yells Charles, frozen behind the wheel by pounding water and sudden wind. "But we are stopping."

There is nowhere to go. They are in the middle of it, whatever it is. Unable to see. They have crossed some invisible border into this country of storm, broken some law. The wind screams.

Charles goes back. As a child, he saw lightning fry cattle in the fields. Once, in a village, fire bolts turned the ground to charcoal, striking again and again. A charred world of farmers and herdsmen. He heard the terrified stories of lightning, celestial fire, its essence speed and power, creation and destruction, illuminating, annihilating. He knows lightning can sear the earth to a dead husk, bald and empty. Now it is all around him.

He thinks he hears someone whisper and then shout.

"It's a tornado!" screams Angela. "We're in a tornado!"

Suddenly the rain begins to bounce off the car like rocks. In Charles' panicked mind, it is thunder flints, silver axe blades, glinting missiles. He lets out a cry. "It wants to come in. It wants to come in." His demon drama has begun.

The car is completely under attack. The storm flashing and growling, targeting them, following them, interested in no one and nothing but these three figures, exposed and helpless, determined in its blind blast to destroy them, send them scurrying into oblivion like squashed insects.

Death must be chased back by Kyikuuzi, thinks Charles, back through the cracks in the asphalt, through the crust of the earth. Charles waits for the ground to open wide and swallow them now.

Air tears up the valley. Wild air, air on the move, churning forward, slashing, grinding. They perch precariously, directly in the path of the oncoming whirlwind.

Like the distant slitherings of a giant snake, ripping and pulling everything into itself, this huge cone of maddened air sucks violently, until viper becomes dragon, a lowering mass undulating across the sky, striking down and swallowing whole. A great deadly stirring of malevolence with furious winds belching out smoke from its belly. Surrounded by eerie white light.

The black sky demon drops chunks of itself as it rotates, flaps and bangs, and crashes. Without a road, the car slides, amphibian, on water. Thunder explodes, the clapping hands of malevolent force, cosmic anger. Charles tries to think what he has done. Is it because he has ceased to believe in his old gods they have stopped believing in him as well? He knows lightning makes no mistakes. Seeks its target precisely. Aims and brands with accuracy.

Charles reaches for the medal of St. Jude. Swinging crazily, his little silver saint is attached by a flimsy chain to the glass and mirror that stands between him and annihilation.

The pounding of the rain continues.

He tries to pray. St. Jude, the saint of hopeless cases and hopeless causes has always helped him. Charles has developed a special bond with St. Jude whose shrine glitters before his inner eye, willing him to stop the rocking and slithering of the car. Even the soldiers of Idi Amin solicited St. Jude for funds, calling him the Chairman of the Bank of Heaven. But St. Jude cannot hear him.

Wind screeching and rain drumming everywhere.

Like a child, Charles keeps repeating "please, oh please, father, please."

"Try the radio," cries Angela. "Turn it up." Static.

The car is being bombarded now by missiles, crashing through the windows, bouncing off the doors. Shuddering intensity. Electric shocks through three rag doll bodies, their minds paralyzed in panic.

Rain. Wind. Thunder. Lightning. All the elements unleash their fury.

"What are you saying?" he cries out to Jim.

"Free us, free us," shouts his friend, his voice rising and falling in waves of hysteria. But Charles is alone with his own terror, unable to share his fear with them.

Then he hears other words, fuzzy and uneven, surging and receding randomly. The car radio has clicked on. Alarm is the base note. In and out. "A tornado ... destructive rotating wind ... massive storm clouds ... dangerous only if it touches the ground."

Then, clearly, "Meteorologists don't know a tornado has arrived until an eyewitness reports it."

The car twists madly now in cloud — a dense, inky pummelling mass that won't let go. Are they really in the air?

Simultaneously they realize that the sky has picked them up and is hurtling them in a circle. For a moment, he feels weightless inside a stillness that carries, almost cradles, him. He is a bird soaring, floating, gliding. Untouched within the wind.

Looking out, he sees barbed wire. A bucket punched inside out in a jack-o-lantern grin. A calf charred by lightning. A barbeque, flapping open like the jaws of hell.

Charles is suddenly calm, serene as rain cuts into him like knives, slashing through the windows, filling up the car until it is a boat pitching frantically before the smash of a tidal wave.

All four doors tear off simultaneously.

With enormous strain, he raises an arm to shield his aching face. Something to his right. Coming at him. A boulder. Through the window. No. Charles looks over and down. It is not a boulder. It is Jim. His head sliced by glass from his body.

Pouring blood. Eyes open. Angela screaming.

Charles is thrown against the roof. Upside down, he flails in an ocean of murky turbulence.

Watching his soul leap out of his body. Lost.

All goes silent.

1. UGANDA

LANDLOCKED UGANDA STRIDES across the equator five hundred miles from the Indian Ocean. Sloping gently downwards to the north and more steeply to the south, ringed by mountains and valleys, Uganda's Mufumbiro volcanoes reach over four thousand feet and to the east, Mount Elgon — the cone of an extinct volcano — rises mightily from the plain, with ridges radiating thirty kilometers out from its gaping crater.

In the late nineteenth century, Arabs, Indians, and Europeans joined the land's indigenous population and settled in the territory creating a mix of religions and cultures. Hindus and Sikhs were later enticed to the country by money to build railroads. From other parts of Africa came Kenyans, Rwandans, Congolese, and Sudanese refugees fleeing violent conflicts in their own lands.

The most ancient were those from the Ankole Kingdom, composed of two different nineteenth-century groups who shared the same language: the Bahima, who were cattle herders, and the Bairu, who farmed. The two fought many wars over territory, and the antagonisms between them were deep and real. However, eventually an uneasy truce evolved with the Bairu farmers emerging as the military protectors of both groups, an arrangement that endowed the well-protected cattle-herding Bahima with a sense of special status. As the decades passed, the Ankole Kingdom grew and expanded to establish political control through its king, its Omugabe, over other areas including the contiguous land of the Buganda people.

The Buganda had their own traditions and language and called their royal chiefs Kabaka. In both Ankole and Baganda traditions, royal blood was traced through the maternal line and kings were traditionally chosen by clan elders from among the eligible princes, always assuring that the throne was never the property of a single clan for more than one reign. It was through the Omugabe and the Kabaka that these two kingdoms interfaced.

Buganda soon became the wealthier and more powerful of the communities, a well-armed kingdom. Yet the Ankole kingdom also flourished despite its own ethnic tensions. The Omugabe's palace stood between the two communities, on a hilltop, surrounded by kilometers of privileged space filled with grass-roofed dwellings, meeting halls, and buildings whose agricultural and military stores were legendary.

At the entrance to Omugabe's court burned the royal fire, the *gambola,* which would only be extinguished when the Omugabe died. Thronging these grounds were many foreign ambassadors seeking audience, chiefs assembling for the royal advisory council, messengers running errands, and a corps of young pages who served the Omugabe while training to become future leaders themselves. For communication across the kingdom, there were runners and personal messengers. But mostly there were the drums. The drums of the Ankole spoke with their own gravity and sovereignty.

In 1891, Buganda disturbed the established order by signing a treaty with the British, allowing incursions into the land the foreigners would call Uganda in return for British recognition of the Kabaka's ultimate authority. In 1894, the British went even further and annexed Buganda. Two years later the name Uganda was adopted for the territory.

Ankole and Bunyoro territories came under what the British began referring to as Baganda control, further inciting ethnic tensions. Indeed, the historic heartland that had been transferred politically contained numerous sacred burial grounds. Eventually these "lost counties" became the source of ever-deepening animosities between the Baganda, the Bunyoro, and the Ankole.

The British — by way of thanking the Kabaka — appointed mostly Baganda as political administrators and tax collectors. To know the Baganda Kabaka was to know power. It remained the way to power right through the first half of the twentieth century. The Baganda even insisted that everyone they dealt with — except the British — use the Baganda language and wear *kanzus*, their own version of traditional cotton gowns. They also actively encouraged (with the aid of British missionaries) religious conversions to Christianity among both those who practiced traditional animistic beliefs and especially among those who followed the tenets of Islam.

Buganda was also home to the country's political capital, Kampala, and the city grew wealthy. Cotton and coffee flourished as exports and international trade with Europe increased. Baganda families spent their burgeoning incomes on imported clothing, bicycles, metal roofs, and even automobiles. Baganda chiefs spent much of their income on their children's education, and a number from the best families were sent to England on scholarships for university training. Within the region as a whole came the rise of a young and literate elite, many of them graduating from new Baganda schools in Kampala such as Mengo High School. These schools placed emphasis on skills in English, translation, and typing, among others.

One eager member of this vibrant new generation was Charles' father, Kanyunya, who, though Ankole, managed to ride the coattails of the rapidly spreading British colonial officialdom. As early as high school, Kanyunya spoke not only his own language but also English and even Swahili. Because of such useful skills, and because he was somewhat faster than others in math, and because he knew typing, he was one of the first in his class to obtain a much sought after job as a clerk at a

Baganda County office when he graduated. Here, he busied himself with filing reports, making tea for his superiors, and ensuring that the huge overhead fan remained dusted so as not to float its finely sifted dirt down on the gleaming head of the District Commissioner. Kanyunya quickly evolved into a disciplined civil servant.

When the reigning Ankole king died and the new Omugabe turned out to be a family relative, Kanyunya found himself in an exceedingly fortunate political position. The British knew and respected the family connection. It allowed him to move easily between the Ankole and the Baganda communities and to rise in the hierarchy. The British had no problem when the Omugabe drafted Kanyunya for service in the royal household.

Kanyunya had a small bed in the men's quarters and an office that he shared with other royal clerks. These buildings occupied a tiny plot in a much larger compound with separate dwellings for palace employees including bodyguards, entertainers, and praise singers, the custodian of the royal graves, and many others. There was even a whole building set apart for the ceremonial drums. Kanyunya always sensed the drum pulsing through him, like a heartbeat, and the air he breathed.

For holy days, royal virgins smeared their skins with white clay to show purity and goodness and celebrate the fertility of Ankole cows. Kanyunya watched these pale young women array themselves around Omugabe while an attendant knelt, proffering the ceremonial bowl brimming with fresh milk. The bowl itself was large, carved from dark wood and polished smooth. A delicate chain of coloured beads encircled it. Omugabe lifted it and time stopped for Kanyunya. Utter splendour — Omugabe's long royal robes, animal pelts draped over the richly carved throne — held him in thrall. Overhead shone a chandelier constructed of beaded bowls from the previous year and above the throne, a crown and crossed spears. Rich carpets and zebra skins covered the floor. Walls gleamed with spears and photos of the royal family.

It was at the palace that Kanyunya also met his future bride, Kekinoni. She was one of the youthful beauties brought in to attend Omugabe's mother and sister. Kekinoni in her turn was obliged to maintain a virgin state. As it happened, the clans of Kanyunya and Kekinoni were among those allowed to marry. The two young people first became shy friends and eventually fell in love. They sought the privilege of matrimony that only Omugabe could grant. In time, he did.

The wedding took place before the magnificent doors of the palace and was presided over by the monarch himself. Kekinoni wore a white lace dress. With her bouquet of white gardenias, a sparkling tiara on her tight black hair, precious pearls glistening from her neck and ears, she glittered resplendently as a Queen of England. Like many brides, however, Kekinoni felt fear and apprehension. But those flanking her — grinning ladies-in-waiting, draped in vivid reds and greens, with polished leather handbags hooked securely over bangled arms — held her up.

Kanyunya — in blue and gold robes and a tall decorated linen hat — gazed at Kekinoni amazed. She was his wife to be but what did he know of husbandly duty? He also felt uncomfortable, the uncertain centre of a joyful celebration by important people, all of whom he was convinced understood more about what was going on that day than he did.

Both, however, survived the wedding day and the wedding night. Shortly thereafter Kanyunya was invited to step up the government ladder. His new posting took him to the village of Buhweju, a Baganda community two hundred miles from Kampala.

Kanyunya was one of four sub-chiefs who jointly administered the village of some fifteen thousand people scattered over more than a hundred square miles. He was given a well-protected concrete house complete with wooden doors and closeable shutters. It consisted of a large living room, a master bedroom, a security room where a single guard slept, a guest room, and a huge children's room meant to accommodate as many off-spring as the young couple could produce. All on a four-acre compound with garden areas suitable for receiving petitioners and hosting public events.

Kanyunya and Kekinoni felt rather important within this imposing symbol of British power. So different from the village huts of mud walls and thatched roofs.

Quickly realizing that in this place he could not be part of normal village life, Kanyunya went to work with enthusiasm in his small official world of tapping typewriters and inky reports, of clerks and messengers who scurried around with sheaves of paper at his slightest bidding. He only knew he needed to keep them busy, to create a sense of important activity.

With the efficiency his distant superiors expected, his office issued beer-brewing permits and prepared monthly memos on such matters as food production and vermin destruction. When it came time for the annual tax collection, Kanyunya could be found flanked by his clerk and a policeman, sitting behind a broad table — often under the fanning canopy of a soaring teak tree — at a cotton market or a tobacco post, accepting and registering payments from the local people.

Clearly, it was not Kanyunya's place to make things but to manage them, to be a protector of power. Calm, dignified, and polite. Reducing real life to neat numbers in a great file that he had to keep updating, revising, and sending for approval.

Eventually a child is born. A girl they call Debra. Kanyunya waits for a boy.

Their second child does not disappoint his hopes. Holding his joy in check, Kanyunya sets about the serious business of naming. He searched for their daughter's name in ponds and small lakes, in the sunlight playing on watery surfaces. But for this son, he wants something special. And so Kanyunya undertakes a pilgrimage, wheeling away from the villages on his bicycle along the red track that ribbons through verdant savannah. He needs something strong for his son, something daring.

And suddenly it is there. The flame tree. Stunning him with its elegance, its feathery leaves and scarlet flowers, its long waving stem and its fierce thorns. Tree of death and life. Amarykiti. The great flame tree. He would call his son Amarykiti. A true African name. His soul name.

That night, Kanyunya takes his child outside. They are alone. Kanyunya speaks the special name into his son's ear. "Kiti." The forest is silent. "You are Kiti." His voice is sombre and serious. "This is who you are. This is who you will be. Always. The lightning tree, the fierce. My Kiti."

Kekinoni has also whispered a name into her baby's ear, a good Christian name. And when the pastor at his baptism calls out, 'What shall we call this child?' she answers without hesitation, "Charles. His name is Charles. Charles Mugume."

Charles Who Stands for the Lord.

But Kanyunya knows better who his son really is.

Charles is a baby on the move. His mother must watch him constantly, for unlike his more placid sister he is never still. At six months he is weaned from breast to mashed bananas. He learns to sit up. To stand. With a body that obeys some great physical will, he spurts forward on invisible springs. At eight months he perches alone, alert on his little mat, tapping always with a small stick.

"Our son is a talking drum," says Kanyunya. Indeed, rhythm becomes his speech.

When Kekinoni walks into the glaring sunshine and deep shade of the thick banana plants to chop off bunches of fruit, Charles rides on her back with obvious pleasure, mesmerized by the rolling movement of her body, delighted as she bends and straightens, rocks and laughs.

Inside the house where it is cool and busy, Charles is equally absorbed. Joining the family for a meal, Kanyunya lines his hand with a section of leaf and scoops out portions of the food for each of them. For Charles, he is careful to dip the glutinous goodness into a little salt or gravy so that the baby becomes used to stronger tastes. And at a year, Kanyunya announces that the baby has accepted his true name.

"Kiti," calls Kanyunya clearly. Charles turns to him.

"Charles," whispers Kekinoni. The child turns again.

Both parents smile.

The two children see Kanyunya late and early. His life is official and busy. Family times must be found outside the normal day. Extraordinary times, appropriate to the extraordinary presence he occupies in their young lives. It is always dark in the morning, when he wakes them and they come stumbling sleepily, often tearfully, out to greet him. These progeny are his flesh and blood, the family of his loins. He must be with them and they must know him. They are also the Sub-County Chief's official family and each other's most important community. On such mornings, the drowsy dynasty shuffle around scrubbing their teeth with cleaning sticks, dabbing cold water on faces still warm from dreams and waiting patiently while Father showers and dresses, emerges from these ablutions looking like a sovereign being.

Tall and shiny, Kanyunya sits at the table with them smelling clean, smelling like the man who goes away each day to do important work, smelling of a world beyond the thick green shield of their garden. He eats the meal brought to him by servants while the children sit in silence and watch. When he has kissed them goodbye and left, Mother hurries in from early morning household chores and shoos them back to their waiting beds for the rest of their sleep.

Father doesn't observe the difference between day and night. He orders the hours according to his needs and expects his family to adapt. He often comes in late and wakes up the children, demanding deference and entertainment from them. First, they must kneel in greeting and, as in all good families, wash his feet with warm soapy water in a large, badly scratched porcelain bowl. Charles is allowed to rub his father's rough skin, cleaning each nail, always amazed at their thickness, hardness, size, and toughness. When the children touch a ticklish area, Father roars with laughter, kicking paint-chipped suds onto the floor. 'Now sing for me,' he demands. And the Sub-County Chief's house rings with the chanting of songs he has taught them in Swahili.

As they grow, Charles and his best friend Samuel — another Ankole in the official circle — notice that most of their Baganda playmates are thinner than they are, that they are not as fast to kick the soccer ball, and that they always seem hungry, always taking special interest in Mother's kitchen. The boys wonder why; they want to ask Kekinoni but dare not.

Nevertheless, in Charles' young life, difference slowly begins to matter.

At night, more often than not, Kanyunya turns to his beer, trying to drink away the tensions of the day. He does not turn to his wife now. He has no energy left for her.

Charles is allowed to invite Samuel to some official parties during which Kanyunya sits in his special carved wooden chair receiving gifts — beer and chickens and goats.

When Kanyunya drinks too much, Charles knows that the dancing will soon begin. On cue, out come all the instruments, drums, and strings. People begin swaying and chanting. Slowly at first. Dusk settles and cool air brushes in from the graceful fronds floating their high green light around the compound, allowing ease.

This is the moment Charles begins to bounce in front of his father's grand chair. As drums thunder, he and the grownup dancers vibrate ever more frantically, their hips rolling. Charles soon becomes one with the sound. His body obeying without question the thunder and tap. The unpredictable, complex, changing rhythms enter him, make his heart beat and his body speak. As he moves, Samuel grins and laughs. Kanyunya is overjoyed seeing his son so animated. Compensation for all his toiling in colonial offices among applications and reports. Validation.

"One day, Kiti will be among Omugabe's chosen," he roars out to the throng and they answer him fervently with the music of their very being, louder and faster than ever.

Kekinoni also has parties in her own special part of the house. To these events — always during the day — relatives and women of the neighbourhood often come. Here, she serves tea and treats and there are always stories.

"My son is a great dancer," she also boasts. In fact, she and her women friends have been coaching him closely, so that his performances in the grand yard at dusk for Kanyunya are not entirely spontaneous. Indeed, Kekinoni has formed a dance club of sorts for the women of the village, especially those with young sons, interested in having their offspring learn traditional dances. On occasion — and with Kanyunya's approval — she organizes children's dance competitions for the district. Charles and his friend Samuel are budding stars.

While Debra and the young girls and women learn to move from a seated position, their arms swaying gently to imitate the horns of cattle, the boys practice the more masculine gestures. Stomping and reaching, grabbing and running — movements of power, strength, agility, and skill, involving swiftness and stealth — necessary to a way of life visible now only in the dances. Seen only in the local competitions.

Charles wins these competitions more often than anyone else. Privileged as well as talented, he dances longest. He never tires. He moves to the colours of the flowing robes, the sky and tall savannah grass, the sun and bananas, the deep rages of tropical storm and the swirl of road dust. They are his world.

Charles' other best friend is the family cow, Suna. Cinnamon in colour, she seems to carry the sun in her body, heating her. When Charles touches her flank, she feels as hot as a cooking pot. One of two hundred cows in the official herd owned by his family, Suna grazes over the rich savannah land controlled by the Sub-County Chief. Cows belong to Charles and his kind, to traditional herders. Not to the Baganda farmers in whose midst his family lives and whose lives his father manages. Charles learns a balancing act, separating cultural identities but remaining deeply connected to the stately bovine creatures he comes to love.

Transfixed, he watches servants squeeze Suna's assortment of sacs amidst tufts of hair. He also wants to touch and pull but Mother warns him that Suna is not a toy to be played with. A cow — especially a cow like Suna — should be treated with respect.

"You must talk to her kindly, tell her what's happening, why you need to do certain things."

Charles is finally allowed to milk her. He floats into the dim air of Suna's underside brandishing a bowl with one hand and groping for her udder with the other. At last, he makes contact, pulls on her soft furry teat. "Be gentle," warns Mother.

"I love Suna," he says. "Suna is my cow!"

"Yes, Suna is your cow," she reassures him. "But you must be still and calm around her or she will give no milk."

And when he looks deep into Suna's big eyes, he sees that she, too, knows things very old and deep, things that never change. She knows about the green taste of grass and the blue sting of rain, about the flies at her nostrils and the sun burning her back, about dirt and tree trunks and deep snorting sounds, about smells in the air, about the magic way the oven in her body turns all these sensations into the rich white liquid that flows directly from his ancestors.

Suna knows how she and Charles' people began the world together. These tall graceful people of the cow. People who prize the milk of their cattle and all its products. People who help their cows make more milk, when the animals have difficulty, by playing tunes on the flute.

When Charles looks at the deep folds in Suna's neck he wants to make a song for her. Dance with her, for her.

Was there really a time, wonders Charles, when Suna and his people truly lived as one, wandered together over the hillocky streams and swamps, stretching themselves in the fine grasslands, grazing under quiet clouds, moving toward water holes, with the slow tolling of bells?

Within the fertile garden and busy compound of his parents' home, Charles feels the ancient force. When he is with Suna. When he drums. When he dances.

Charles watches his mother prepare for her spirit church — laying out the glistening white dress and turban in which she will sing and pray.

"Luli, Luli, Luli," she intones softly, her eyes looking far away.

"What is Luli?" he asks.

"It means the mercy of Jesus Christ," she says. His mother's wisdom glows in white.

But the moment is shattered by the sound of excited voices and the roar of a car humming along the road. The whole village has quickened. Women stop their busy garden work. Men look up from the dim depths of the pavilion where they have been absorbed in a board game. Charles runs from his mother's bright stillness to his front door. He peers through shadow into the dusty glare. The sunlight hurts his eyes. He is watching his father's official car drive slowly through red dust towards them. As the vehicle slows to a stately pace, thick fumes spiral up behind it, demanding attention. Charles and Debra fight for the door, excited at the possibility of a visitor.

The car stops a little distance from the house, in full view of the people so that everyone can witness the ceremonial disembarking of the guest. Kanyunya steps down first, his official robes billowing out around him. Then he turns and extends his arm courteously towards the seated figure, still somewhat obscured by the windscreen and swirls of dusty air. What uncoils slowly out of the vehicle is a long, lean being in a suit the colour of sun and a broad brimmed hat over shiny yellow hair. He is lavishly introduced to the assembled villagers as the District Commissioner. A man with skin the colour of elephant tusks and eyes like blue sky.

Terrified, Charles and his sister immediately run off into the bush. As far as they are concerned, the most important man in the village has driven up with a ghost. A "white" man.

Charles has had nightmares about such creatures, dreaming of death, dreaming that they will eat him if he's bad, capture him if he leaves the house alone at night, if he fails to wash his feet before bed. The District Commissioner could well be the man-eating monster, Kitinda, in disguise, whose time had perhaps come for appeasement, who needs human flesh. Charles' fantasies are now filled with pale blood-sucking demons, loose wet things of foul-smelling air and green eyes looming out of the night, attaching themselves to him, sucking out his life, draining his body's colour, leaving a ghostly mist, an evil spirit who will relentlessly wander the village terrifying family and friends.

"Of course you are afraid of white people," says Father that evening. "They do strange things. Some come here to study our snakes. They don't know enough to run from them as we do." And everyone laughs. Kanyunya has safely deposited their visitor in the guest house.

But the five-year old Charles puzzles over it all. Do white people not know about Magobwi, the snake demon? Have they not seen how chickens must be thrown to Magobwi in his great ravine down in the belly of the earth where he slides through the endless tunnels of his dark kingdom? Do they not know that when he is hungry, he can appear anywhere — at night when you are sleeping — and attack you? Magobwi moves below you everywhere. The very ground you walk trembles with him.

Mother does not refute any of this. She merely adds her own practical observation. "Don't be afraid; the Commissioner is only a man. He is staying here for a couple of days."

The next morning Father brings the District Commissioner into their house. The children have eaten breakfast and now kneel before him mumbling greetings. As the son of the household, Charles is pushed forward to touch his hand. The boy hesitates only a moment, seeing a snake looking hungrily out at him from behind the Commissioner's blue eyes. Magobwi curled in yellow hair, ready to strike.

Then the District Commissioner begins to speak in their own language. From his lips it sounds different but Charles recognizes what he is saying. Familiarity is a relief. The District Commissioner moves towards him, enthusiastically clasping the boy's shoulders. "I understand you are a fine dancer," he declares. Charles beams.

The Commissioner eventually invites the children to feel his miraculous blonde hair, later taking them for a ride in his official car. Charles brings Samuel along as well, the two boys now achieving celebrity among their peers, connected to a white man who brings marvels and beneficence to the village, a wondrous figure from another world.

By the time Charles is eight and Debra ten, Father has begun to take him into that other world. Proud of the son who looks more like him every day, Kanyunya wants him to know life beyond the village. These adventures are full of surprises for Charles, and they never cease to thrill him with their perilous hints of the unknown.

One day Father announces Charles will go with him to the Catholic District. This pleases Kekinoni who wants her children exposed to Christian things. Her husband's motives, however, have less to do with religion than bravado. He would like his son to see how far his influence extends, how he is received in other areas. He would like his son to know him as a benefactor, one whose wide fame reflects also upon his children. They will visit when the Bishop is there.

Kanyunya knows what a picture they make on his grand motorbike. He and Charles pluming ochre dust as they speed by green plantations, roaring and laughing. Charles loves to feel the machine throbbing beneath them. It shudders through his whole body. It is the sound of energy, the sound of father and son. As they go, they are joined by children on bicycles, swirling out of the bush and pumping to keep up with them, ringing their rusty bells along the road.

"*Hujambo,*" shouts out Father in Swahili. "How are you?" Some of the children shout back greetings. The women wave, beaming in their sun-splashed cottons. Father points at a flash of black and white plumage rising out of the dense bush. "A hornbill," he says. And Charles giggles at its low *cronk,* thinking of Suna's wail when she needs milking. He looks up and sees two grey parrots, gone before the sound of their rapid wing-beats leaves his ears.

Kanyunya and his son are welcomed with food and drink and dancing at every stop. "This is my partner," Father says. "He is my official aide. I rely on his opinion." There is laughter and Charles feels important.

The women are particularly attentive at these stops. In their rain-cloud dresses, in their green-lake dresses, in their dresses scarlet as sunset, they come out to greet Kanyunya and his special son, offering sweets and soft drinks, beer and melon. For Charles, it is like having mothers wherever he goes, mothers who pet him and fuss over him. Mothers who always say without fail, "We love you Charles." Then they look at Father with a little question in their eyes. Wordlessly he answers them and they leave, smiling.

Several miles from their destination — from what Charles

has called "the Catholic kingdom" — he spots a spire, glinting in the distance. "Father, look. A spear waving at us from the hill."

"It is the Catholic church, my son, and it is waiting for us."

Charles cannot contain his excitement. "It is not mother's church, is it?" he asks.

"Not at all. Hers is just an open porch where people go to speak with God." Kanyunya knows he should not be talking like this to his son but he resents Kekinoni's spirit church because it takes her away from him and makes her strange. Reports of her visions make him uncomfortable. Reports of people — mostly women — so overcome with rapture in their singing and swaying that they begin to speak in unknown tongues. It is witchcraft disguised as church-going.

Into the church precinct wheels the delegation of two, just in time to join the official parade. Cars are honking and bands playing. There are decorations everywhere — Catholic decorations for the Bishop visiting from Kampala — bright yellow streamers, blue robes around the statue of the Virgin Mother, banners with strange words.

What impresses Charles most, however, is the church itself, soaring and huge. "Why is it so big, Father?"

"Because Catholics believe God needs a big house," comes the reply.

They are walking with the official party now up the front steps. As the Bishop enters softly into the gloom, an electric generator whirrs into action. Lights blaze up brightening every corner, every statue and picture, each gold leaf. "Did God do this?" Charles asks. "Is this all God's?"

"Of course," whispers Father.

The very floors make the young boy dizzy. They are tiled in colours and patterns, squares and triangles and curls. He sees leaves and flowers. A whole forest is growing beneath his feet. The chandeliers that bloom are clusters of stars dropped down from the sky, just for him.

"God must be very rich and very powerful," he says.

With the other dignitaries, father and son proceed slowly up the aisle to a row of benches. Each is as beautiful as Father's judging chair, carved and shiny. They sit with others who are dressed in their best. Men in suits and ties. Men in their finest *kanzu* attire. Women tottering on high heels, wearing short dresses with buttons and zippers. Women wearing the bright flowing colours of the Baganda he is now used to.

"You see the congregation is very respectful," says Father. "They believe you must always wear your most expensive clothes in God's house." Charles hears the solemnity of the word "congregation." He understands its meaning: jewels and finery. Great celebration. God's mansion.

Holy pictures intrigue him, their figures in softly hued robes, their faces gentle and smiling or sad and serious, telling stories of Jesus and the kingdom of God. He has never seen anyone like the white people in these pictures. They move through their silent lives with a light that seems to come from another place. "Where do they live?" he asks.

"In heaven. It is a place where very good people go when they die. They are saints."

"Will we go to heaven?"

Charles looks at all the saints in the windows of the church, blue and gold against the sun.

Suddenly, stern-looking men in long gowns of green and deep pink have begun to mutter strangely. They are swinging a large glittering lamp from which smoke puffs up around them.

"What are they doing?"

"They are priests and they are saying Mass."

"Where are the drums?" Is Omugabe coming?"

"No drums!" Father smiles down at him. "No Omugabe. No Kabaka either."

After the service, Father and Charles walk over every inch of the church, accompanied by one of the white priests. About to leave, the priest gives the boy a little card, a picture of a serious-looking man with a grey beard. "Here, my son. Take this and keep it in a safe place."

When they are alone, Charles asks Father, "Who is this?"

"St. Jude. He will be your personal guardian now, your helper."

Charles is unsure why he needs guardians and helpers. What could possibly be a danger to him? "Who is *your* guardian, Father?" he asks.

"I think you are, Kiti. I think you are."

"Are *you* afraid of anything?"

Kanyunya's mind is a shield for Charles, a round silver shield. Shining. Blazing in the dark. It will help him grow strong.

Father is regularly called in the middle of the night to "investigate" things. Charles cannot even imagine what this means, nor is he allowed to ask questions or speak in any way of these adult matters. But ethnic enmities are a continuing fact of life in Uganda. Raids into other villages. Attacks on farms. Often on government compounds. When Charles hears of such things, he thinks of dead animals, chickens with their necks wrung or their heads chopped off. He cannot yet connect such events to human beings.

Sometime later, though, a black truck appears with a white Chief of Police, to inquire and make a report. One man has killed another. A jury will be selected. A trial. A sentence of death. His Father never disagrees with the verdict. And it is Father who must pronounce the death penalty. His own Father who smiles and waves at everyone, who kicks up dust and laughs with well-wishers. Father, the blustery force, sweeping in and out. Kanyunya, never leaving anything quite the same, like a strong wind that settles for a while on its own mountain, huffing and puffing before it whirls off again.

By now Charles takes for granted their huge home. He is accustomed to its rules. He is not allowed into the guest area, a space kept immaculate with white bed covers and blue curtains for official visitors. Indeed the compound, surrounded by its woven reed fence, has grown to include a police station, a clubhouse, a nursery school, and a jail. Even a special room for the live-in guard.

Charles spends a lot of time in the kitchen area at the back of the house. Opening into a shelter for the goats, it is a welcoming place with pungent smells. Here Charles and Samuel play among the millet bowls and water pots while Debra, engaged in helping with food preparation — shaping steaming mounds of millet into loaves between tin plates — constantly shoos them away from hot stones piled around the cooking fire. Charles laughs when it rains on the cooks stirring their large pots, dances through puddles and squeals as drops pelt bare skin, the cooks' big wooden spoons working the hot mixtures rhythmically in the coolness that showers down.

"Go and play with the goats you crazy boys," says Debra, now pretending to be Mother. "The goats like you. Go and be their friend." Charles and Samuel leave and then send one of the skittish animals careening among the serious business of meal-making while Debra yells again in protest.

Charles knows from Debra that large sums of money are kept in the guard room extension of the house, in a steel wall safe with a combination lock. The money is watched over by a tall man with a ceremonial spear and a gun in his pocket. Soldiers and policemen intermittently come through the compound and take away the funds in an armoured truck. Only after a pick-up is there no guard. That is the day Debra and Mother sweep the room clean.

Long wanting to investigate, Charles follows Debra and her broom, seeing for the first time that the room really is quite bare — a bed, a chair, and a small red curtain covering a section of the wall. Charles introduces the room to Samuel and over several secret months they get to know its special character. Indeed they can recognize every guard but they do not understand why these men are always so nervous.

"Why don't other families have guards?" Charles wonders.

"Because," says Samuel disdainfully, "their fathers are not chiefs like yours."

Kanyunya is away overnight on official business when a sharp sound shatters the quiet night. Mother slips into their room, her face as stiff as a mask, her eyes wide and staring. The children make no sound. "Thieves," she whispers. "If we are still, they will ignore us." She huddles with them behind the bedroom curtain, looking out.

Intruders are now inside their home. The guard cries out before a single shot silences him. Unable to open the safe, the outraged thieves charge through the house smashing anything in their path, frantic for someone who might know the combination.

Kekinoni's grip on her children is like iron. She holds them close. The three of them are trembling so violently Charles fears they will fly apart. She keeps them still, pushes back the whimpering that rises out of them.

Fearing wholesale slaughter, Kekinoni suddenly jumps up, runs to the bedroom window and begins roaring for help. Chaos erupts. Husbands and brothers and sons living close by rush in, knives flashing, clubs flying.

The compound runs blood. Bright and sticky, staining the ground, smelling like rust.

For days, no one talks about it. Not even Father. Ultimately, every trace of carnage disappears. And from that night of knives, Charles knows the meaning of fear. A piece of his childhood sliced out.

A piece of himself brutally taken.

At school Debra is a model student but Charles remains a reluctant one. To him, school always smells of wet plaster and burnt candle wax. He hates sitting on the reed mats covering the hard mud floor just waiting for class to begin. He and Samuel are constantly in trouble for making jokes.

History is moderately interesting. His ancestors, the prim teacher tells them, were connected to the Masai of Kenya, to Ethiopians and even to Nubians.

Samuel and Charles — an aristocracy of two — stay to themselves at breaks but this day are surrounded by some of the bigger boys. The two stand frozen, trapped in fierce sunlight through whose rays they can barely make out the figures laughing and leaping towards them, backwards, forwards, menacingly. Shrinking the circle. Closing in. Taunting and brandishing sticks. It has happened before to this privileged pair and today there will be no escaping the taunts, their schoolmate's eyes saying clearly "you are not like us."

Samuel is the first to go down in a circle of sticks. As he is tripped, Charles sees blood. He runs for the shelter of high reeds concealing three wooden toilets. But there too, he is surrounded. "Does the chief's son have to piss?" He can hear Samuel crying.

In a moment, they're on him. With sticks and kicks. His face is cut. Blood runs. "Oh look," they shout. "The fancy dancer has pissed himself. Didn't your bitch mother teach you not to do that? Special people should know better."

Stiff with shock and rage, Charles slowly stands. Twisted now into knots of hatred, his mind slams against hard walls that won't let him move.

The attackers run off. Charles and Samuel walk slowly home to their incredulous parents.

No one is ever punished for the incident.

Now hating school, the pair decide one morning to miss it entirely. Truants in the bush, sweating out noon heat. Lying in what shade they can find, alerted by the desultory snarl of a nearby animal. Wary of snakes that curl in the underbrush. Spied on by monkeys.

At the end of the day, Charles arrives home. His teacher is already there talking to Father about educating him elsewhere. Charles knows his parents want to defend him but they cannot refuse to send their own son to the village school. Kanyunya knows that he himself is better educated than most of these so-called teachers.

When the teacher leaves, Charles is sent to his room.

Nothing is said. Then he hears Mother slamming her hands on the wall. The air filling up with her soft sobs.

Father realizes that his son is now paying for conflicts he himself has with those under his jurisdiction: families on the questionable side of a law, families whose children he might have imprisoned. Charles understands now that Father cannot help him.

The physical attacks on the two friends continue. Walking home from school one day, they find themselves trapped on a bridge. Tied up and dangled over the railing by their ankles. Yanked up and down. Down and up. Tormented by ten bullying boys.

"Your mother's a fat cow. Your father's a thief. If you don't give us some money, we will make both of you crooked cows with broken noses. And drop you into the swamp."

Charles feels blood rush to his head. He feels his shins scraping. He thinks he can see into the murk and imagines being devoured there. Terrible tales will be told of his disappearance.

Bitterly, Charles and Samuel agree to comply with the black-mailers. They are hoisted back and warned not to tell anyone, "Or you will die next time."

The two friends run. Shame scalding their eyes.

That night, Charles commits his first crime.

He cannot turn back.

He peers out the window into the moonlight and thinks of Father holding court. Parties. Feasts. When life was a fearless dance of royal drums.

His eye roams further to the reed fence, eerily shining. At the far edge of the compound he makes out the small police desk and the jail. Will he be sent to jail he wonders? Surely his father would not do that. His father who rules over roads and housing in eight villages, who rules over children and criminal cases.

Charles knows the inmates of the local prison are brought from their cells every morning to help harvest and plant bananas and yams. Is Charles now to join them in lonely exile beyond the compound walls? If caught will he too be squeezed, six to a cubicle? No air. No light. Nothing to lie on.

If caught, will his crime be announced by a blast of drums? Every passing second might be the one that thunders his doom, sending villagers with machetes to hack him to pieces. Could Father allow this? Would he have time to stop it? In the darkness would Father even be able to see that the intruder was his own son?

Charles sways softly, raising his arms and pushing the air with flat hands. He imagines Mother sitting there, smiling and shuffling her feet, watching him dance with her serious eyes and her special smile.

It is almost morning and his father will soon come to shake them awake. Charles moves into his parents' bedroom. They are both sound asleep. He can hear their regular breathing and just barely make out their bodies, rolled comfortably around each other. Touching their dreams. Quick as cloud over moon, Charles insinuates a hand into Father's trouser pocket. Finds coins. They would not be missed.

On another night too, they are not missed.

And another.

And another.

Charles has become an expert thief at the age of ten, a stealthy burglar, lifting only small amounts of money at a time so as to avoid detection. No one ever knows. Except Samuel. And the village boys who eagerly take the money from him. Charles' life as a criminal continues, unnoticed at home.

Eventually, he tries his techniques upon a series of unsuspecting official guests who, when they finally discover that they are literally out-of-pocket, feel the matter is too minor (not to say politically delicate) to pursue with Kanyunya.

Then a white man comes to visit, to sleep in the guest house. Having heard his pockets jingling, Charles enters the man's room along a shaft of moonlight, looking carefully, trying to think clearly. Is this man more important than others? Must be. His money is also in bills. Should Charles leave some in the pocket? But why? Here is a chance to buy greater good will with the bullies. Maybe this is the haul that will end his torment.

Unfortunately, Father — informed of the robbery by his guest — must take action. He knows it could only have been his son.

Mother and daughter retreat to their part of the house. This is clearly going to be men's business. Charles is called in.

"You have been taking money. Am I right?" he demands. "Answer me."

"Yes Father."

"You are nothing but a common thief." Ordering Charles to drop his trousers, Father swings into his rhythmic punishment. Ten slashes with a wicked little whip that whistles through the air before it strikes his son's tender buttocks with fury.

"They made me do it," Charles screams.

"They?" says Father.

The same question Father now insists be answered at the school. 'Who are they?'

The story rolls out. A bunch of boys from the poorest families wandered into the tea terrace of a hotel and ordered a whole cake for themselves. The suspicious owner, striding purposefully towards them, demanded to know where their money came from and whose it really was. This caused the boys to rise up, toppling over wicker chairs and parasols in their wake, race down the road and disappear into the swamp.

It was the owner who reported the incident to the school. But the school never responded.

Now Kanyunya opts for a public hearing, his authority so

unchallenged that even his officials, thinking he has gone mad, say nothing.

He publicly accuses the offending boys of blackmail and violence, insisting they admit it openly. One by one, the deeply frightened miscreants stand to take their punishment. Charles watches, flinching at each whistle of the whip. Until it is his turn again.

But Kanyunya too is punished for all these misdeeds. Less that a week later, a letter arrives giving him official notice that he and his family are being transferred.

Only Charles is delighted. He sees in this the hand of fate cooperating with the power of righteous action. Like an animal from a trap, he will spring free.

But Charles' life will change only in stages. There are not enough places at the new school in the new town. His parents and Debra will, therefore, go first. Charles will finish the term at the old school, staying with Samuel's family.

During this time, the two boys return regularly to the empty house that was Charles' home. The rooms now are only shells. His mother's favourite chair and cooking pots, his bed — all were loaded on trucks and carted away. His life has gone somewhere else.

Father's old desk has been left for the new Sub-County Chief who will not arrive till the end of term. Charles stares at the large green ink blotter, cornered in leather and scrawled with figures. He wills Father's special symbols to speak to him, longs for a secret sign. Opening a drawer at one end of the desk, he runs his hand inside while Samuel watches in awe. Charles strikes metal. Cold and hard. He gasps and pulls. Then yanks the drawer quickly to full length and stares down at a gleaming black pistol.

Did Father forget it? Or was Charles supposed to find it?

He and Samuel decide that this is Father's gift to him. Armed, they will now really be safe. Indeed, the gun has the desired effect. Whenever they are threatened, he produces the weapon and the other boys scatter. Charles begins to understand authority. What it is like to be feared.

In recognition of his new-found status, school gossip elevates the notoriety of the Sub-County Chief's son from that of petty thief to fearful killer, Samuel being the whole of his trusty gang.

Such is the power of an empty gun.

When a place in the new school is finally found, Charles makes plans to leave. Samuel will travel with him and return after two weeks.

At the end of the ten-hour ride they discover new liberty in a harsh and isolated semi-desert. A new village. A new school. Overnight, Charles becomes a model student. Boyhood heaven is all before him.

Until Shakespeare comes along.

At twelve, trying to memorize Hamlet's "To be or not to be" speech, makes him hot and irritable. Charles fights the complicated language of the text, the concept of suicide, and he can make no sense at all of Denmark or castles as he sits sweating under a broiling sun.

Mother, by this time, has created a new spirit church for not only the family but for their friends and the women of the community. It is a simple pavilion on a public square. In this flat cool place Charles finds space to breathe.

He comes here to be alone, reinforced by the sturdiness of poles and roof beams, carved into unique shapes. Hidden behind thick walls, he peers out into a stream of light, feeling like some ancestor guardian who can see but not be seen. Sometimes he stands in the vast dim circle, turning slowly, a huge bird with large shady wings hovering against the sun. Protected.

Deeply lost in this reverie, one day he is suddenly aware of another presence in the pavilion with him — Debra, whose task it is to keep the place clean. Startled to find him there, she brandishes a broom at him, "Get out. Get out with your dirty feet. Go dance somewhwere else."

"I'm studying," he says.

But Debra takes her duty seriously. She wants to become a keeper of sacred places. One day she will care for the *ekyanzi*, the ceremonial bowls and the transforming milk they will hold. Even now she holds forth knowledgeably on their *omuheina*, the magic designs that decorate each one.

"Take your fantasies out of here," she threatens. "This is a holy place."

But Charles, intoxicated by his own visions of ease and completely undeterred by the protests of a mere sister, yanks the broom out of her hand. In doing so, he scrapes it against the roof. "Don't tell me what to do. You are not Mother yet," he snaps at her.

Suddenly they hear a commotion above them. A rustling menace of hornets that are nesting in the spaces between the walls and the eaves. Now dislodged and angry. "See what you have done," Debra screams, "You have disturbed the mother hornet. The mother is upset. She will sting us."

An aroused advance guard of hornets, fat and annoyed, traces a track deliberately above them. Droning louder and deeper and closer. "I'll get her," says Debra, instantly grabbing a ceremonial spear off the wall and swinging wildly at the giant hornet. But Charles has already stepped in the same direction. As he throws up his arms to shield his face, his finger is sliced by the sharply angled point. Pulsing freely into open air, blood spurts from his mutilated finger hanging by a thread of skin thin as an ivory disc.

Debra begins to scream hysterically. Panicked, she scrambles out through the gap and onto the roof, causing her badly aimed weapon to lodge in a particularly grizzled old pole, where it thrums angrily.

Now the world is truly aroused, Mother's spirit church becoming a frenzy of hornets and flying implements, anarchy in motion. At its centre stands Charles still as a pole, staring down at his dangling finger.

Dizzy with shock, he is disconnected from his own pain. He sways on his feet, his mouth opening and closing, silent as a fish. Then it all hits at once — the cause, the result, the searing sickening sensation. The howl that rips out of him terrifies Debra who watches, stupefied. Panic takes hold. Charles breaks into a run, blood pouring, finger flapping. Howling. Forgetting to breathe. Vigorously wailing after his hurt hand, loud as a parade, Charles and Debra streak home.

But Mother is entertaining a group of women — chatting about Charles with several, including his new teacher — when she hears the unearthly cries. A servant enters trembling with terror, sobbing for her to rush out.

In the glaring day, Kekinoni sees blood everywhere. And Charles about to faint. Shouting orders at those around her, she takes command, gathers up her gangly boy and runs to the infirmary with him sprawled and moaning in her arms.

Shock sets in, numbing him. Suna ambles into his mind and he falls asleep watching her graze and chew, her horns almost scraping the ground.

"Where is the doctor?" demands Kekinoni of the attendants. Everyone looks awkward, knowing that the only medic in the village is out back indulging his own hopeless addiction to strong gin. While she is grimly examining this filthy ramshackle excuse for a clinic, the doctor himself bursts through the dispensary doors — drunk and roaring.

He sobers enough to staunch the bleeding, rubs disinfectant on the wound and wraps it. When Charles screams, the doctor barks at him to be quiet. At this, Kekinoni yells back and the two shout at each other even louder. Charles, suddenly awake, is in both physical and mental agony. He feels guilty. He knows he has caused this battle scene, caused Mother to be badly treated by this awful man. Comfort lifts away from him like a vulture from a stripped carcass.

The doctor's voice drops to understanding. He speaks to Charles. "I had to put the stinging solution on the wound or you would die of infection," he tells his patient in a pathetic attempt to make amends, adding absent-mindedly, "You should really have stitches." Charles' imagination cannot conceive of anything worse that sticking needles into the torment of his poor hand. He is not a piece of ripped sacking that some needle and string can repair. The doctor winds more bandages around and around his finger.

Then Charles throws up.

"Oh God," yells the doctor. "Look at this stinking mess."

"It's your fault," Kekinoni lashes out. "You've terrified him."

A moment later, Kanyunya himself is at the dispensary door. "I've called for the ambulance. If it's not here in ten minutes, we'll drive the official car."

"Where are we going?" asks Kekinoni.

"The missionary hospital, St. Jude's."

"But it is five hours away," protests Kekinoni.

"Yes," Father snaps. "It is the only way to save his finger."

It is midnight when they arrive in the official car and Charles rouses, as the car snakes its way through the hospital grounds. He hears the rush of water. In his reverie, they have arrived in a holy place an infinite river of wellness swirling him away.

"They have everything to make you better," says Kanyunya softly.

Charles drifts off again while disembodied human parts jostle in his head: red hearts like angry fists, spidery grey nervous systems, small pink figures hunched over with cramp or irritated by rashes.

"Will they put my finger back on?" he whispers.

"Yes, Kiti, yes."

The next time Charles opens his eyes, he is lying on glistening sheets covering a narrow bed that tilts him up slightly so that he is almost level with the face of a smiling white man, Dr. Scharf, an intelligent and sensitive professional — with a particular talent for calming the hysterical. He chats easily, asking questions to distract the boy. What are his favourite games? What does he like to eat? His sister's name?

There is comfort in this, a safe, secure feeling in the quiet gleaming room. Charles relaxes and lets all the anxiety drain out. Kekinoni stares quietly now at her boy, her son: a shrine she will always pray to.

Between waking and sleeping over forty-eight hours, Charles struggles to understand the hospital while the doctor administers sedatives that release him into a state of cooperation and agreement. Charles' entire being relaxes in its new home. This pure white place.

He is taken to surgery and put out with chloroform. A professional anaesthetist covers his face with a mask. Dr. Scharf talks Charles through to peaceful unconsciousness. Kanyunya listens for any sign of danger that might send their son out of reach forever. Indeed, after the procedure is complete and the finger re-attached, Charles stays unconscious long enough for his parents to believe him dead. They have never seen anyone put to sleep before. Kanyunya, trance-like, murmurs again and again, "My daughter has killed my son, my daughter has killed my son."

But Charles is only on a journey. His chloroform dreams are vivid and joyful. He laughs and bounces on tree branches with boys his own age, carefree and weightless. No danger. No gravity. He floats on a beam of sunlight, high above the river that he sees right through to fish and frogs. Spies animals in their dens and birds in their high balanced nests. Visits and plays. Feels no fear. Excitement is in the very air he breathes as he floats this way through wavering treetops.

Kanyunya is very grateful to Dr. Scharf and, after two days, returns home without bravado, where he gradually loses all focus, becomes unkempt and uncaring, soon looking like a soft over-ripe fruit dropped from the lean limbs of his sturdy children. He stops riding both his bicycle and his motorcycle. Becomes increasingly sombre and taciturn. Wanting his son and his wife back. But they remain at the hospital for over a month.

Charles, on the other hand, enjoys the luxury of having his mother as a personal nurse, cook, and caregiver. He sleeps on a bed and she on a mattress on the floor next to him. What young boy wouldn't enjoy this special status?

Mother has brought her *sigiri*, a portable oven, along with charcoal and kerosene. When lit, it produces hours of heat. Charles feels he can go anywhere. As long as he can bring Mother and the *sigiri*.

Kekinoni works her small oven tirelessly in the hospital, producing excellent meals both for Charles and many of the security people who take grateful advantage of her generous culinary presence. St. Jude's — with its pristine staff, its manicured lawns and ornamental "rapids" and "falls" — has become host to an important man's wife and son. And it is Charles' own private amusement park. There are workers in the grounds and gardeners with huge mowers. The hospital's many acres appear endless and open with no fences holding in or keeping out.

But the pain is real. Even in such a luxurious environment. Dizziness for a week after the chloroform, one hand stiffened by a metal plate, held in place with a sling. All the while, Dr. Scharf, the high priest of healing, remains vigilant and kind.

Dr. Scharf, Kekinoni learns to her delight, is also a religious man. He prays. And encourages his patients to do likewise.

"Why is the hospital called St. Jude's?" Charles asks him one day when they are wandering in the little chapel together. The doctor does not hesitate in this still white place of high arches and tiny crosses.

"Because St. Jude is the patron saint of hopeless causes, my boy."

Am I a hopeless cause? wonders Charles. Am I supposed to give up now? Is my life really over?

In the weeks that follow, Charles realizes he must somehow get home. Dance his way back. Sing it out, flash fire all the way home.

Find the flame tree inside. His deeper light.

2. MASKS

WHEN HE ARRIVES HOME, Charles finds the whole village alight with its own small fires. He feels their intensity. Bright and hot. A restless reckless burning all around him. Everything is unsure. Flammable. Dry tinder about to ignite.

Fierce little scrub fires of what people are calling "national independence" flicker everywhere. Smouldering sullenly. Flaring dangerously. Uganda, they say, is ready to burst into flame. And such talk. A federation of Britain's three east African territories bringing Kenya, Tanganyika, and Uganda together under one flag. Even the racist whites in Kenya are being challenged by the Mau Mau under Jomo Kenyatta.

Everywhere villages tremble in anticipation. The Kabaka, however, keeps refusing to cooperate with the national independence movement, being more interested in a free and independent state. Other leaders watch Kabaka's every move.

Kanyunya, like all colonial bureaucrats, supports Kabaka but sees trouble whichever way he turns. Suspicions grow daily. And at home, Kanyunya has also overstepped his borders announcing that he will take a second wife. Not a Christian thing to do but legal within traditional structures. Kekinoni knows of her. She has been his mistress for years. He had already set her up in her own house. It is an open secret and now — as unrest boils up all over the country — Kanyunya's open secret festers inside the family. A new and younger woman.

Charles and Debra are torn and hate having to share Father this way. In the house, Kekinoni stays silent. But as the political debate roars on outside, Kanyunya finds his family unwilling to deal with a second wife. Nevertheless, he marries her, brings her home, gives her a room in their house, and insists the children call her Stepmother.

Kekinoni suggests to Charles and Debra that this new woman is a witch casting spells under their roof. Her chanting in the shower rattles their nerves. It is part of a curse that could kill them all or make the family's next generation infertile. She suggests that items Stepmother leaves around the house possess an evil spell: beads, small calabashes, coins. She cautions Charles not to touch these things: "A witch can transfer her power to objects."

"Do you really think Stepmother is a witch?" Charles asks Debra one day. "She can't be a real mother," he reasons. "Father quarrels with her all the time. I've also seen the shrine she brought with her, the black pot with bloodstains. And the staff she carries is magic. I've seen her shake it."

And so the children secretly but regularly burn or bury a constantly replenished collection of tainted, harmful objects that represent the animist world they also believe in. A non-human world that they are convinced Stepmother inhabits. A monstrous unnatural place of uprooted trees and disfiguring disease. Their own world turned terrible by the witch who anwers Father's needs.

Even the priest wags a finger at Kanyunya, saying he is being un-Christian. After eighteen months of internal warfare, Kekinoni finally challenges him directly.

Stepmother must go.

In front of the whole family, the woman is told. Kanyunya can no longer fight the opposition. Stepmother, too, threatens. Then cajoles. Then bargains with Father. Finally begs.

Driven to the limit, Kanyunya grabs her by the shoulders, shoves her towards the door and literally throws her out. The children toss her possessions into the dust after her: keys, clothes, the dreaded black bowl.

Mother sits down quietly and prays. Sings a hymn.

Charles watches Stepmother on the road. She is pounding a stick on the ground. Calling down curses. What surprises him now is her appearance. Suddenly she bears no resemblance to the witches of his nightmares. He sees defiance and strength in this real woman with her head flung back and arms stretched wide. He watches Stepmother move slowly away, wrapping her glittering garments around her and striding off, staring straight ahead. Like an offended queen.

But if she is not a witch, who is she?

National chaos crackles dangerously inside and outside their village. Independence is the cry everywhere. Religion, politics, and economics fuse and contest fiercely. Protestant parties emerge. Catholic parties. Islamic parties. Marxists. Capitalists. Some blame merchants from India for Uganda's economic troubles. Some blame Kabaka. Others attempt to raise Kabaka to national power but are met with hostility in several parts of the country.

For Charles, however, the most important thing is graduation from junior school. Nearly fourteen, tall and handsome, still the best dancer around, he has completed his coursework and is almost ready for middle school. Proudly he attends his graduation ceremony, with Kekinoni and Kanyunya present.

Next morning, before the sun has fully risen, he walks slowly back to the school for the last time to collect his diploma. Facing the building that has held him captive since he came to the village, he studies the hot concrete box with metal shutters, still baking under a tin roof. He cannot make sense any longer of this space that held him sweltering over numbers and names. The dates of important events. The dilemmas of Hamlet.

The air is damp with morning mist. Far off trees wave like clouds, lifting early walkers lightly along with their bundles at the edge of this vast dusty patch. It is hazy, the light soft and grey. Under a huge fanning tree, Charles' reverie is broken by a woman's gentle voice. Very close.

"Kiti. Why are you back? You have graduated. There is nothing more to learn here."

He turns, sees a woman's shape in the shadows and sun. Tall, shimmering with colour. A dark purple skirt rustling jaggedly against indigo. Etched contours of moon and stars hover like dimmed ghosts of some long past night. Her shoulders shine in bright yellow. She is the sun before it rises. The sky after storm.

Stepmother.

Months have passed since her leaving. Now with her gleaming hair and firm round face, she is looking at him anew with sad eyes and questions. Who has she become? This tall woman whose ancestors walked with the same herds his did. Had she followed him this morning? Does she live beneath a tree? At the school?

"Come and sit, Kiti," she says to him softly. "We haven't spoken in such a long time."

She studies him. Vulnerable but almost a real man.

"You are so much like your father," she says. Her smile is smooth as ivory, soaring high into the complicated weave of her eyes. She is amazed at the long legs on this slender stem. She touches him and he is spellbound.

"Where... ?"

"I live nearby," she says. "Beyond."

He has no idea what she means by "beyond," but she has mesmerized him, and when she begins to walk in that direction, he wants to go where she is taking him. Birds chirp around them. A dog barks somewhere near. The morning is a soft cottony curtain. Together they walk into a small shack, her place beyond what he knows.

She sits on her bed, her long legs uncovered as her skirts part casually, caressing him now as she did his father. Springing him awake. He comes alive.

He has touched himself there before but nothing like this. His body feels like water. He is scared. Has she bewitched him after all? He cannot think clearly. He cannot think at all. He is flooded with feeling and fear.

"Kiti, don't be afraid. I will not hurt you."

"But you are a witch," he says

"No," she responds. "I am a woman."

She puts his hand on her breast. Pulls his lips down to her as she would a nursing infant. He suckles while her hand rubs him into hardness. Rubs him and pulls him gently. Changing him. Then he explodes. There is a fountain in the middle of him.

"It's okay. Yes. It's good. You are singing now like your father," she says. "You are bursting open like a flower for the sun. Always remember it was I who set you free."

Charles is wet. He is terrified. He pushes her away. He doesn't know if he can stand. Or should.

She smiles, waving before his eyes glistening hands, hands that have just squeezed his own juices out of him. "Yes, Kiti. Just like your father."

He leaps up and runs. He hears her laugh. "I have your soul, now, Kiti," he hears her say. "I have your soul."

He feels suddenly invisible. Is it really his own feet ripping through the undergrowth, tearing vines and creepers? Is this really his heart pounding? Where has she taken him? Where has he been with her?

Wherever it is, he senses there is no turning back. He stops. Smiles. Likes this new sensation. Wants to know this experience. To wake up again. And again.

Independence comes to Uganda with Kabaka as the new national ruler. The Baganda have taken ultimate power. Is that better than the British? he wonders. He reads of Milton Obote, independent Uganda's first Prime Minister. What will they do with the big portrait of the Queen of England at primary school? Will they still have to sing "God Save the Queen"?

Life is changing more than he knows. When he thinks of middle school, a door opens in his mind through which he is more than ready to walk.

Since he will have to travel a distance now, why not go all the way to the best middle school in Masaka, a large city over twenty miles away, just across the equator. He could eventually live in his own half of the globe far from the family. But the Masaka School is full.

Charles' next choice is the even more famous Mengo Collegiate in Kampala, the far away capital. Built on the edge of Kabaka's own territory in the Mengo district, begun by the British as a mission school and therefore attached to the Protestant Church of Uganda, it is old and impressive and equated with the success of its graduates, from Kabakas to film stars, from politicians to international football heroes. Even dancers. Could he really get in? After all, his own father went there. When things were very different.

Charles has seen pictures of the main building at Mengo surrounded with graceful date palms, a swimming pool, many white teachers — all bald with spectacles and trim moustaches — their Ugandan assistants in handsome hats with tassels and school crests looking serious and satisfied. He applies on his own. Father grudgingly agrees to sign the forms.

In midsummer, the news comes. Mengo will take him.

"Impossible," roars Kanyunya. "I cannot afford that boarding school. I went along with the application because I believed you wouldn't get in. If your grades were not good enough for Masaka, how could it be!"

For the first time, he realizes Father has alternate plans for him — to take up the paternal torch, work for the government, be transferred from small village to small village. Care for the people under his control. Bear responsibility and worry. He no longer needs the very British Mengo.

Uganda is independent now.

But Kampala is too exciting a possibility for Charles. With

its huge population. With its big cars and lights and roads. Life is fast and dangerous in Kampala. There are even grand restaurants. And people from everywhere in the world.

Charles is obsessed with his own vision of future now. He thinks of it day and night, filling his fantasies with what facts he can glean from teachers and visitors, from pictures.

The great city of Kampala flung out over fifty red hills. Curving summits twisting and swerving with churches, mosques, and cathedrals. Makerere University spreading across graceful grounds and colleges of learning, its sculpture gardens designed in fantastic forms, its exhibition gallery filled with vases that almost hum to the painted rhythm of dancing bodies twirling tirelessly around them.

He studies every aspect of the capital.

Kampala, glowing prosperously through electric nights, buzzing with light. Kampala billowing down to its elegant and charming bay, its botanical gardens and its glorious parks and lily ponds. Kampala, its handsome crowned head held high over dense rain forests that heave and sigh around its many-coloured feet.

Charles and Kanyunya use the whole summer to fight it out.

One day, Kanyunya announces that he and Charles will visit Mengo but only after he also visits Masaka where he has some government business. Charles is sceptical but has no choice. The next day, since Kanyunya's official car has been forfeited to independence, they walk in silence as far as the bus stop on the main road. Father and son have lost their ease with one another. Kanyunya is no longer his son's only link to the world. Charles has his own ideas now. He knows what Stepmother gave Father. And what she took from him. There are no secrets left. Kanyunya's star has shifted in his son's heaven.

Once on board the bus, they sway and doze to the incessant snorting and lurching of the awkward rusting conveyance. Charles thinks of Suna and how it would be to sit on her back all the way to Kampala if Father won't pay for transportation. He wonders if he could ride her. She could be no more reluctant than this bus.

After a long silence, Charles looks up at Kanyunya and suddenly sees an old man. For a moment, he feels guilty for quarrelling about schools. He misses the Father who parted dust with his motorbike and hailed everyone in sight, who made and gave gladness. But this is the same Father who now stands in his way. Suddenly weary and disappointed and angry. And disinterested in his British alma mater. Still the master of his own strong will.

It is the rainy season. The bus drops them on the outskirts of Masaka, just as big drops begin to spot the red murram of the road. Broad green leaves shake and shine with the rain. It drums on the tin roof of a small bar, a plaster shell of pale yellow with a blue awning, open to the street. Father and son duck in quickly and seat themselves on stools. Kanyunya orders beer for himself and a Coke for Charles. There is no one else in the place as the rain pounds down. Chickens squawk and wander through.

"Can you imagine this boy not wanting to go to school here? Masaka is a great town," says Father to the bartender.

"It certainly has schools," the man agrees, glad of the business. "Four collegiates and one technical institute. Which one will you attend?" he asks Charles.

"None," comes the flat reply.

They walk a little further along the Masaka Road, pause at the Uganda Company Limited Store with its broad wooden verandah and tiled roof whose wrought iron filigree curls fancifully into the sky. The rain has stopped. As the door squeaks open, they are almost blinded by the sun bouncing off polished wooden floors. There is a sharp smell in the air.

"I know the manager here," says Kanyunya. "He is a very smart man. He has made a lot of money from dry goods."

Charles stares amazed at the rows of bottles and jars, tall

cans and flat tins. There is a ladder on wheels that climbs the walls up to the roof. He is fascinated by the many spools of coloured thread — every shade imaginable — arranged like stars shining from their deep dark shelves. Now he knows where the rainbow women of his childhood come from, moving in their bright robes. And Stepmother's vibrant cottons. Maybe Father is right. A man who sells such things should be listened to.

They talk with Father's friend about football for a short time. Then father asks the question. "Amoti, what do you think? Kiti wants to go to school in Kampala. Wouldn't Masaka be better?"

"I'm sure it would be cheaper," says Amoti. "But Kampala is special. My son went to Kampala. Did it against my better judgement. And he has a very good government job now. Unfortunately, I never see him anymore. Didn't you also go to school there?"

This was obviously not the answer Kanyunya wanted.

"The boy will do what he wants to, Kanyunya. You know that. Even on your money."

Once they are out on the street again, Kanyunya pleads with his son. "You are making problems for me, Kiti. I will have to spend too much on you in Kampala. Go back to the primary school and get better grades. Then attend middle school here. It is better for everyone."

Charles has never heard Father plead. Still, he remains silent. They visit the middle school but the Headmaster is away. An assistant says very little and they leave unimpressed.

As the sun begins to set, Charles walks behind his father, seeing Kanyunya at a distance, now such a small man against a giant road, vanishing into fading sky and dense foliage. Kanyunya's shout suddenly cracks the air like thunder as he turns back to Charles. "You are a crazy boy, Kiti. You will put me into poverty."

Offended, Charles sits down in the middle of the road while

Father slowly walks back, the menace of him growing and growing into a huge shadow glowering over him.

He knows Charles' mind is made up. "I want Kampala," says his son finally. "I want a bigger world. Just like you did. I want to know more. And most of all I want to dance."

They are both sitting on the ground now, Charles running his hand through the dust. The silence is long and terrible. Father finally understands though. "Perhaps," he says "we can see if money is available. A scholarship. Maybe for children of alumni. But even if that is possible, don't ever forget how you are pushing me. I will have to spend a lot. And I don't have a lot. Times are changing. It is not the way it used to be for me."

Two weeks later, they step off the bus in Kampala. Take a taxi to the school. Kanyunya and Charles sit solemnly. Stiff and abrupt against the harsh bright walls of the Headmaster's waiting room. Mengo sits near the top of one of Kampala's central hills. Here, the young minds of some of Uganda's brightest and most well-connected young men are trained in a quiet garden city of its own.

The sturdy lower half of the room rises to pale latticed plaster, allowing cool air to flow through. Carved mahogany doors separate them from the Headmaster's office located beneath a tiled balcony. At the bottom of Mengo Hill are dozens of shopping stalls, lottery ticket sellers, and taxis jostling together for space in a chaos of sound and movement.

The taxi driver — clearly looking for a big tip — mutters about what a lucky boy Charles is, going to Mengo and that his father must be an important man. Liking the sound of that, recalling his power days, Kanyunya pays him well.

The British Headmaster treats his guests with civility and respect, ordering tea and saying little at first. He wants his visitors to feel at home. Charles studies his bristly white hair that runs around his cheeks to meet at his chin. His eyebrows rise on his forehead like two arching caterpillars.

Headmaster Hermitage speaks directly to Charles in a way that also includes genuine respect for Kanyunya as a former Mengo student. While smoking a British cigarette, he acquaints Charles with the school and what it offers. He refers to famous graduates and fulfilled students. He talks of proud parents. Sports teams. Plays. Even Shakespeare.

"It hasn't changed so much," says Kanyunya who smiles broadly. Shuffles in his chair uncomfortably. Charles has never seen father so nervous.

"There is a scholarship fund," says Headmaster. "I have looked into your application. Your Father — one of our successful graduates — has worked hard for the government. I think support can be found. We can certainly use good dancers and tall footballers."

Charles is ecstatic.

"Leave it with me," says Headmaster. "I'll have the financial people write to you with details. For now, let me just say that I think you should formally accept our offer. Charles you will enjoy yourself at Mengo. And I think your father will be very pleased with your accomplishments here."

Few words are spoken when they leave. Over lunch, however, Kanyunya suggests that they should probably get Charles his school uniform before returning home. Charles, holding back tears, says simply, "Thank you, Father."

In the nearby shop — very British, very formal — Charles is most thrilled with the required leather shoes, his first pair. So stiff. His toes have disappeared. His feet have become other creatures, resolutely pointed. He will never be able to dance in these shoes. Nor play football

Later, in the tailor shop, Kanyunya — becoming his old Mengo self again — watches with pride as Charles is fitted for the blazer. In this house of cloth and humming machines, the walls vibrate and sway to the whirr of frantic sewing. Scissors and tape measures quiver on worktables. Shiny wheels spin, treadles pump, needles thread, and swaths of cotton and linen are shaped into men. Near the ceiling, side by side like a procession, sport jackets with brass buttons hang below bright purple shirts. Each finished outfit carries Mengo's rose in its lapel.

In the middle of this whirring industry stands Charles now in khaki pants and white shirt. A tall dignified warrior full of self-possession, he has unwound from the loose robes of his ancestors and spun easily into the geometric complexities of shiny western propriety. In a moment of self-recognition Kanyunya also realizes that Charles is both repeating and completing him.

Father and son treat themselves to dinner and a comfortable night in a tiny rented room. The two know a natural line has been crossed. When they arrive home, Charles is anxious to show Kekinoni what he has become. He tries on his blazer for her.

Kanyunya smiles at her.

She weeps in pride.

Summer passes. Day one of his new life begins. At Mengo Collegiate School. He sits, trying to find himself in his new clothes in his new classroom. Cool air shifts through cantilevered windows. The quiet is broken only by a fountain gurgling in the garden. He is surrounded by important looking volumes lined up at attention on sturdy shelves. At his feet lies a new briefcase in which to carry books and papers. He feels very, very important. But he knows no one.

The class is composed of boys and girls from many communities and ethnic origins — Bahima and Baganda, East Indian and British. They are easy and polite. They include him. An unknown equal among unknown equals. He is one of the tallest.

The teacher enters. Writes his name on the blackboard. Then each is asked to stand, say their full names, where they are from, what they do for fun. Charles emphasizes the fun part and gets a warm laugh.

"I dance," says Charles shyly. "I talk to my cow Suna."

The girl seated next to him smiles. Then whispers, "I love to dance."

Mid-morning the classes all break for a snack in the high ceilinged dining hall, pillared like a church, under photos of Queen Elizabeth and Prime Minister Obote. They talk of sports and clothes. Charles realizes that his new friends believe Father to be rich. He does not dispute this and goes off happily with them to wander in the town.

Charles collects an official allowance from the school each week. But he also has a bit of his own money, given to him before going away by Kekinoni and Kanyunya.

Some of the boys head into a sporting goods store. Charles has never seen so many jerseys. He is fascinated by a display of many-coloured belts, all carefully coiled like dead serpents over and through one another. Some fastened by shiny silver buckles, metal mouths wide open like snakes with their sharp tongues sticking straight out. Some are calfskin making him think of Suna and the velvety creases in her neck. Her inward looking eyes.

His eyes light on other piles of belts. More expensive than snakeskin, the costliest made of crocodile. Charles knows crocodile. Remembers seeing a crocodile once. A nesting crocodile, sleeping in a pool of sun, but rigidly attentive.

"She has eggs," Father had told him then. "Down in the sand underneath her. She will let them bake for weeks until they are ready to hatch. And she will look ferocious for anyone who comes near."

Charles recalled so clearly the gaping mouth with its pointed teeth and its long raised head. An attitude that said "Stay away." The creature's tail curled behind her, leaving scale marks in the sand.

But he also knows about the skinner's hut. Dead crocodiles piled on shore waiting for the knife.

Father's next words followed the track of this thought. "Hunters kill them for their skins. They make shoes and belts."

"Like Kitindi," Charles recalls saying.

"No," explained Father at the time. "The real Kitindi is all powerful and would not allow himself to be taken."

"The snake," Charles says suddenly to the clerk. "I'll have the snake belt," committing in that moment every bit of his spare money. His friends quickly gather around him to admire the daring purchase. As do the girls when he is back in school.

Charles is intrigued by the girls. They are not like Debra. These girls laugh and tease. They enjoy looking pretty. Especially the white girls in the school. And they are always eyeing him. Nearly six feet tall. Slim. Handsome. A young dancer with the playfulness of a puppy.

The headmaster's two daughters — Julia and Dolores — especially seem to delight in his company. For Charles, they are pale, floating spirits. Their eyes wandering and enticing. Smiling in ways that Ugandan girls do not. They flirt.

What amazes Charles most is that Headmaster Hermitage doesn't care in the least that his daughters flirt, even with the Ugandan boys. Charles knows that Father would punish his children severely were they to dare such behaviour: touching in public, blowing kisses.

Headmaster Hermitage is clearly a free thinker. Whatever that is. Charles soon realizes that white girls also apparently tell their parents almost everything.

Other than girls, Charles dreams of football. He makes the freshman team and quickly becomes its most valuable player, breaking records and receiving special mention in the school newspaper. He loves the attention this brings him, the unquestioning acceptance of others at the school. He fantasizes about playing in the national stadium.

As the year passes, Charles grows more confident with each success. The effort he puts into things he enjoys actually yields results. His achievements even go beyond him.

In his second year, the Mengo football team plays against

the King's Collegiate team, a school perhaps more famous than Mengo, in the Nakivubo National Stadium. It is a dream come true.

When Charles sends his parents a copy of a newspaper story about the game and the goal he scored, Father only advises him to pay attention to his studies. Nothing will satisfy Kanyunya now except straight As. Charles wavers around C. So, there are things he must keep from Father. How he spends his money. Who his friends are. And his growing skills as a student actor and dancer.

Father would probably not approve of Charles having so many willing dance partners. He waltzes like a silk ribbon blowing through the wind. He coils and lunges and angles to tango, rolls to rhumba, glides and skips to cha-cha beats. His British ballroom dance teacher loves his lithe, effortless grace and enthusiasm. So rare in boys of his age.

The headmaster's daughters giggle and gossip with him as he leads them across the floor in his flared pants that float around long slim legs. Their arms cross his chest leaving tiny trails of girl on his satiny shirt. His soft leather boots shine and his hands curl the air.

"You are as pretty as a girl yourself, Charles," the dark-haired Dolores tells him, when they take a break, the three of them standing together in a shadowed corner.

"Yes," chimes in the fair-haired Julia, "as pretty as us. And as good a dancer. How can we ever know for sure that you are not really a girl?"

They smile mysteriously.

In third year, having won most of the school dance competitions, he volunteers to help run and judge them. When Mengo's best dancers are invited to the local television studios to compete with schools from all across Uganda, the tension is feverish. Charles leads the Mengo dance team to victory. The lights bright and hot. The cameras moving. Directors. Sound.

Charles suddenly understands why he is on a stage and knows he never wants to leave. His audience loves him. They sing his praise and applaud him on. He has found his place to be.

In his last year at Mengo, Charles also takes drumming lessons, somewhat depressing news for Father who knows drummers are community born. "You don't learn drumming," Kanyunya tells him, "You inherit it. If your father is a drummer, then you will be a drummer." Kanyunya does not understand drumming as a school subject. He does not understand drumming for fun or money. "Maybe they will throw coins at you, like a performing monkey."

Charles learns the Ankole drum, cylindrical at one end and tapering at the other, composed of two skins. He watches older drummers tune the skins by heating them over fire and moistening them. He hears their deep drum voices that can imitate human speech.

Charles learns the Baganda drums. The big drum and the little drum — made from hollowed trees and the skins of rams — that resound in the night calling townspeople who move in a circle with burning lamps of clay and palm oil. He learns the talking drums of West Africa — the *gangan, dundun, omele* and *djembe* — used to announce importance and respect.

But if Charles' drumming lessons depress Kanyunya, Charles knows that his study of acting with Mr. Makuba, the Ugandan English teacher, is probably driving Father to tears. "The stuff of childhood," Father rages. And it is true. Theatre is not taken seriously by anyone Charles has ever known. It is considered showing off. Tawdry. Cheap entertainment. But Charles is drawn to it.

His first experience of a real play is a special visiting performance by a British troupe at Kampala's National Theatre. When Charles learns that it will be *Hamlet,* however, his heart sinks. He does not like Shakespeare. He has never understood the words or the situations. On the other hand, he has never watched a Shakespearean play performed by real actors so perhaps it will make some sense.

He dresses for the occasion as if for a visit to church. The group enters the theatre building in awe. Nearly filled to capacity, the National is a huge rental hall, the largest indoor space he has ever seen, with a facade open to the air.

"That is so the spirits of the play can drift out when they want," Mr. Makuba tells the class with a wink. "They are hard to catch," he continues. "They come to life only on the stage or, if you are lucky, in your imagination."

Mr. Makuba is thirty, an age that sounds very old to most of the students he teaches. They feel close to him but know he himself has touched the magic. They fear that part of him. The rumour is that he has also written some plays.

He ushers the students through the entrance and they find their numbered places. The group is excited and whisper enthusiastically as they settle themselves in the plush seats before a huge red curtain. What marvellous thing is behind it? they wonder. Is it safe? The mainly student audience holds its collective breath.

The theatre goes dark.

When the curtain opens, Charles is sure he is in a waking dream. His eyes are transfixed on the large square of light in front of him. A castle. Night. Guards.

"Who goes there?"

He is looking into another time and place. The story of Hamlet has come vividly to life. Its people talk and laugh and curse and cry. Others are watching too, but the dream is his alone and he is lost in it. At the intervals, he remains in his seat, only once daring to walk toward the stage where he looks down into the empty orchestra pit. As swords are drawn in the play's last scene, he is somewhere far away. When it is all over, he leaves the theatre dazed.

Charles knows he has been transported. Transformed. But he has also been allowed to return. Was he ever in peril? Has he changed? He must have. Something raw and magnificent touched him. Delivered in whirls of smoke and unearthly screams. Delivered through sound and fury and flooding colour. Unbearable moments of want and fear, hatred and hopelessness. Nothing has ever spoken to him like this. So directly.

The next day they speak in class of the experience with excitement. Now they all want to be actors. Near the end, Mr. Makuba announces his wish to put on one of his own plays with the class. "And if you do well," he adds, "it will be recorded. And perhaps played on the national radio station. You might all become famous right across the country."

Charles can't believe his ears. He hadn't even begun to consider where actors come from. What kind of people they must be to turn into others the way they do. Was it witchcraft? Or magic? How do you become someone else? And stay yourself.

"Acting is like putting on a mask," says Mr. Makuba, as though reading his thoughts.

Charles conjures up masks. Ritual masks, with their huge features and fixed grins, connecting to the dead. Whole body masks of grassy swirls in which dancers spin and leap. The fixed wooden faces of otherworldly spirits carrying the essence of the ancestors.

"But Sir," says Charles, "those actors we saw last night were not wearing masks."

"We all wear masks," responds the teacher, cautiously. "You have been wearing masks ever since you came to Mengo — the school blazer and tie, special pants and shirts. The girls too in their knee socks and skirts. These are your masks, not the masks of village children. You are playing another role now."

"But does the mask change you?" asks Julia.

"Has it changed you," asks Mr. Makuba "being here?" Before she can answer, he hands her a man's felt hat from a hook on the wall. "Here, Julia, put this on." Charles watches her tuck her sunny curls under it. Then she puts on a stern frown and puffs out her stomach.

"There you see," says the teacher with a flourish of his arm, "now you look like gruff old Polonius!"

Charles looks at this old man Julia and laughs. Julia can never be anything but a perfect girl for him.

"I want you to try reading certain characters in my play," says Mr. Makuba. "Charles, you will play the Sub-County Chief. You should be able to do that well."

"But, sir, it is disrespectful. I do not want to mock my father."

"Why would you mock him, Charles? Acting is respectful. It is a way of honouring people if it is done seriously. And it is not your father. My character is only one example of a Sub-County Chief."

"I'm not sure I understand," says Charles, "but I'll try."

"If it makes you uncomfortable, then I will not insist you do it, but you know best the world of a Sub-County Chief and I thought you might enjoy the role."

"Yes sir," he repeats. "I will try, sir."

Charles begins to sense that acting, as Mr. Makuba has told them, is more than just pretending, more than just learning lines and avoiding the scenery. Rehearsals begin. Improvisations.

"Imagine," says Mr. Makuba, "that the Sub-County Chief is holding audience and one of his petitioners comes with a complaint about a neighbour's cow which has been trampling on her garden."

Julia, as the complaining woman, pleads that her husband is ill and she cannot repair the cow's damage. The cow's owner says that he does not have time to watch the cow. The garden is very close to his property. The petitioners turn to Charles, the Sub-County Chief. He must decide what is to be done.

Charles creeps his way into the character, timidly at first, slowly trying on the idea of control, of making decisions for others. It is new to him. It is what adults do. And not even all adults.

"Imagine you are sitting on your special judging chair," says Mr. Makuba, pushing his own teacher's chair towards Charles.

Once seated, Charles feels different, taller, more visible. When he opens his mouth to speak, he realizes he is someone else. "Your people are listening to you," whispers the teacher to him. Charles likes that.

Sub-County Chief Charles makes a decision that will benefit both petitioners. Everyone in the village will be asked to help build a fence to keep out the cow. How could the village not want to help Julia? Both neighbours are satisfied with Charles' improvised decision and Julia's character, before backing away, sends a special little ray of thanks from her angel face, directly to her benefactor. A light that only he can see.

"That," says Mr. Makuba," is effective performance. You both used your heads and your hearts. We all have instincts. They can help us in our improvisations, in our role playing. "

The possibility of playing anyone, of living any kind of life, thrills Charles.

Mr. Makuba now brings them the play itself, the first in what he says will be a weekly series about young people growing up in Uganda. The Drama Club is excited. Radio Uganda agrees to broadcast the student performances. Charles is now heard from one end of the country to the other. For many Sunday nights.

Everyone in school listens to the radio sitcom — based on the life of a Sub-County Chief and his endless tribulations, his struggles to keep the younger generation in line.

Kanyunya and Kekinoni listen as well and laugh at the comic comings and goings of the petitioners and their problems. They recognize themselves in the agitated voice of their son and raucous arguments, in the songs, in the drums.

With this work, Charles also begins to make money for the first time in his life. The equivalent of what would be a month's pay for most people. Honoraria the radio station calls it. He sends it back home in the form of gifts — an expensive shirt for his father and a Swiss watch. A special pot for his mother.

For thirteen weeks, Mr. Makuba's plays are done live from the stuffy studios of Radio Uganda in downtown Kampala.

The group is so absorbed in their paid acting, that they barely notice how the dark blue walls of their protected sound booths are quickly disappearing behind dozens of political posters. The Uganda People's Congress has a key as its symbol. The Democratic Party is represented by trees.

Charles does not follow the political arguments himself but, living in an overcrowded city, he knows instinctively he wants trees and so he paints trees on his bicycle. He has often ridden through the muddy streets of Kampala after a downpour, through dirt and poverty, his wheels thickening with muck.

As he peddles now, unintentionally splattering people who do not know he is a radio star, he shouts at those he passes "Fight for trees. Fight for trees."

Charles is beginning to learn the names and the players in Uganda's first political struggles. It has been almost six years since the British left. Obote, a socialist, is running the country amidst growing opposition. Foreign governments watch with keen interest.

At school, Charles and his class are given one of Obote's speeches to study. It has come to them directly from the Ministry of Education. It talks about African Socialism for Uganda. The speech advocates free education. Charles thinks of the many sacrifices Father has made for the education of his children, sacrifices he is still making. If education had been free....

The speech also refers to free medicare. And to the nationalizing of certain businesses.

In drama class, Charles asks Mr. Makuba what he thinks of it all. His teacher is, evidently, not impressed. "Obote has his hands in everyone's pockets just like every politician," says the impassioned teacher. "Look at nationalization. He has given control to the millionaire who has been bankrolling his own party. Is this the kind of socialism we want?"

Charles listens, unsure of his responses. He thinks of his own people and how they share cattle within the extended family where wealth and position are based primarily on the size of the herd. How would this socialism work in a village like his?

"You are right Charles," says Mr. Makuba. "There are cultural and community concerns to be considered, not just economic ones." Then after a moment, he adds, "Why don't you join the National Union of Students and fight for the changes that you think are more appropriate."

"Join a union? I don't know, Mr. Makuba. I've never really thought about politics. I'm more interested in doing plays."

"That's okay. But be aware, even plays are political. You may not want to be in my plays for too much longer. You have to be sure before you take certain steps." He adds, almost as an afterthought, "Anyway, think about the problems that Obote is causing. There are other ways to be a socialist. There are some alternatives out there."

"Out where? Who?" Charles asks, genuinely baffled.

"There's one in particular. He's a little crazy."

"Who is he?"

"He's an army man from the north. His name is Idi Amin. He's advocating a Uganda run for and by Ugandans, a Uganda where foreign influence is reduced. That can be dangerous, but if we are careful it might be a direction to follow."

"Isn't he the one who wears the funny T-shirts? Everyone knows about Amin's clowning."

"We should look at him," says Mr. Makuba. "He is strong. He inspected his troops wearing a T-shirt with Obote's picture on it. That's a piece of theatre right there."

"But what does it mean?"

"I don't know yet, Charles. I don't know."

The conversation drifts away from the political to the upcoming Mombasa school trip. "You will love Kenya," says Mr. Makuba. "Truly. But the political has seeped in there too, altering the very air they breathe."

For Headmaster Hermitage, education means life learning as well as book learning, trips and experiences that one cannot get at home. He brings his whole family on this particular grand excursion. Along with sixty of his senior students.

This is Charles' first trip outside of Uganda. He has travelled from village to town to city. Now that he is about to leave his country, he cannot contain his excitement.

They set out in slanting late afternoon sunshine to begin the twenty-four hour, eight-hundred mile journey. Overnight by train. For Charles it is a house on wheels with its own indoor toilets, a dining car, foldout beds, small shiny sinks, and running water.

He is enraptured by this long writhing metal snake, chugging down a steel track, windows wide open, trees and houses flying by, sloped fields flattened in a rush. Headmaster has booked his students second-class passage with meals so that when they stop at stations, they are not bothered by the food vendors but can simply watch them swarming against the third-class carriages — plastic buckets, blue and green bowls, garbage bags tied up tight around goods to sell.

Charles watches passengers spill out, arms flailing, shouting orders for food. Or, more often "Hey, you forgot me, you forgot me" at each stop. So many hungry people clinging to doors and window frames, balancing one foot on the movable step, over brick sidings, skimming precariously above puddles.

This class of eighteen-year-olds is truly graduating.

Mombasa itself is a coral island lying on a bay, its waters spinning out goods from east Africa to India, to China, and even to Europe. As Mengo's high-spirited party train winds slowly into the city, the students notice a different architecture, one that seems to hover in wind and water, causeways packed with lorries and cars. In the port are huge metal ships and slow wooden dhows, the latter floating like thick shadows under gentle beige sails breathing with the current, looking like giant birds landing to rest after long flight. The whole city, thinks Charles, feels poised to lift off and fly away.

The group checks into a student hostel, utilitarian but clean, one set of bathrooms for the boys, another for the girls. There is excited talk among the boys of spying and sneaking into the "forbidden" dorm. But it is only talk. There are sufficient adults on hand — including Joro, Mr. Makuba's young assistant — to insure that nothing untoward takes place. They have enough time that first night only for a dinner in the next-door cafeteria.

But in the morning, Mombasa lies all before them, humming energetically. As their rented tour bus drives under white concrete half moons in the shape of elephant tusks that arch over its main traffic artery, Charles begins to understand difference. Past and present. Country and city. Uganda and Kenya.

"You cannot ignore the Kenyan elephant," says the Headmaster, "even in the city."

Mr. Makuba adds, "You can't trample down the ancient ways just because you are in a hurry to get to the future."

In the old town, narrow and intricately winding streets intrigue Charles. If he weren't with the group he would get happily lost. "This maze of shops is the Arab style," says Headmaster. "The old medina, the market. It has grown up over the centuries. It is living history. It just keeps adding to the pattern, increasing the complexity as it goes."

Charles follows Julia's mass of golden hair, lighting his way through a labyrinth of older women rustling by in their long *bui-buis*. Suddenly she stops. "Look." Julia is pointing up, her eyes fixed on the elegant shuttered balcony and fanciful railing of a *mashrabia* house. "It is like lace."

"I want to buy it for you," says Charles, suddenly the teenage braggart.

"And if it isn't for sale?" she queries with a smile.

The next day, they visit fine old mosques that gleam white and green in the sun. "I can breathe here," Charles remarks.

"Yes, Allah seems to need a lot of space," agrees Headmaster.

They are peering through a small opening in the medina that reveals one of the holy places, like a garden of tiles and quiet light in the middle of a jungle. Old men are praying. There is hushed whisper.

Headmaster has booked a bus and ferry trip for them one hundred and twenty kilometres outside the city to a place called Fort Jesus. On the ferry, he points toward a pile of rock as the boat splashes forward and announces flatly, "It is officially known as Malindi."

"Essentially a Portuguese stronghold," explains Headmaster. "The oldest fort in Africa. Fort Jesus was constantly fought over. It changed hands between the Arabs and the Portuguese many times."

Charles rolls the word "Arab" around in his head and realizes he knows very little of its meaning. He asks Headmaster.

"The Arabs brought many important things to Uganda and Kenya," says Headmaster, "including firearms and Islam, a whole new religion, but they were also responsible for some of our early martyrs. Boys about your age." The students are all listening now.

"You remember Kabaka Mwanga from your history book?"

They do because Kabaka Mwanga, it has been joked widely, bears a striking resemblance to the very fat General Idi Amin. And Amin has even named one of his own sons after him.

"Well, Mwanga had rather a liking for young boys and so he persuaded the Arab traders to bring village youths to him so that he could inspect them and select some for himself to keep as a sort of harem."

"Isn't a harem for women?"

"Usually, but not always."

"Did he treat them well?"

"Oh very well. But in return, they had to do certain things for him."

"What kind of things?"

"Pleasing things. Love favours."

"You mean like husbands and wives?"

Headmaster knows their giggles. "Indeed many boys objected to this treatment and refused to cooperate."

"What happened?"

"They were thrown into a pit for days and finally asked to choose the Kabaka or death."

"Did they all die?"

"The strongest boy, Kizito, defied Kabaka. He inspired the others to refuse. Kabaka had them burned alive."

They stare up at the flat, crenellated wall. Walking around inside Fort Jesus, Charles is struck by its angles and might. Soaring up from the harbour, it boasts gun turrets and battlements and houses within.

"Who owns this?" Charles asks Headmaster.

"The State owns it," he is told.

"Ah, but who owns the State?" asks Charles, not quite sure himself what he means.

"No one," says Joro.

Headmaster brings him abruptly back. "Malindi, which many call Devil's Island, is a part of Fort Jesus that nobody talks about because it is a place of shame," he explains, "where many actually were kept in chains before being sent on ships to be sold as slaves to Arabs at auction."

The word "sell" is terrible to Charles. It conjures up the marketplace, full of fruits and vegetables, pawed over, squeezed and prodded and thrown back. He hears their laughter and loud voices. "Look, this bunch is bruised. These are too thin, too green." Slaves?

Saleswomen sit among baskets, squinting in the sun, their eyes alert for a customer. He recalls bargains made over cows or goats, a staff pointing to flank and legs, a finger feeling nostrils and gums.

People selling people?

For Charles, this is another new beginning. Black history. Arab history. This part of the island is crumbling stone, tumbled and dark on white foam the sea throws up. Water rinses and drains here, again and again. Like the women of his village washing clothes, never satisfied, never able to get the stains out. And what about those people who were being sold? Charles wonders. Were they told to be careful or did they just slip and fall? Were they rescued?

They scramble up over jagged outcroppings, panting audibly and chilled by spray. Then they see it. Like the entrance to a palace with a wide painted porch and steps curving up, pink in sunshine. Other steps plunging blindly down. But what is it?

"This nice shaded house is where the Arab slave traders lived," explains the guide. "The slaves themselves were kept in dark cells underground," he says.

As they descend the stone stairway, the students breathe in dampness and dimness. Mr. Makuba shines a flashlight on the wall of a tiny cell, picking out a hand scrawled sign: "Who will write of our holocaust?"

Charles walks by disturbed and unsure.

The bars divide darkness from darkness. "These tiny rooms held thirty people each," continues the guide. "They had to take turns sleeping. Some were chained to the walls." Charles observes the iron rings in the plaster, their rusted loops dangling heavily. "They had nowhere to relieve themselves." He goes silent for a moment before adding, "They probably thought they were going to be killed here.

"Outside the door, you will find a list of all the slave centres like this in Africa, the number of ships carrying slaves each year, and some of the tribal groups that were preferred. From this part of Africa: the Kikuyu, the Acholi, the Masai."

People like me bought and sold, thinks Charles. *Weighed and inspected like bunches of bananas.* He looks at the shackles that bound hands and feet, the empty necklaces of heavy iron and feels them tightening around his own body.

"A teenage girl was worth a barrel of oil; a strong man two barrels; a child, a mirror."

"Why didn't the new government destroy this place?" someone asks.

"So we can remember. History must not be destroyed. It is our only saviour."

Outside, fiery heat thickens the silence that has grown among the students now, as they labour slowly back over rocks to the waiting ferry. Mr. Makuba has one more thing to add, stopping for a moment on drenched stone. "You are walking where they walked," he says. "Where they walked onto the slave ships. But you are also walking where some of them jumped into the sea."

They wanted to die, thought Charles.

"They would rather be eaten by sharks than leave their homeland in chains," says Mr. Makuba.

Their ferry speeds away from Malindi, from Devil's Island, cleaving its urgent track through the sea. Teacher and pupils lean over the rail. Happily pulling away. Then drawn back.

"This is the last glimpse of their land the slaves would ever see." A pile of jagged black rocks.

Back in Mombasa, a Sound and Light show tells the city's long story. Five centuries of triumph and tragedy with history and religion all mixed up together. Fine steeds speeding around the sturdy walls in front of them; cannons firing and swords flashing; singing and drumming, crescendo and crash. Blue and scarlet robes lighting up the arena, whirling with victory, writhing in defeat.

Charles sits next to Julia under the stars. He watches the wonder of her small white face through flickering lights.

The students visit the public beach the next day. There Charles sees the marvels of Julia multiplied. She is in bathing suits of every style and design. How can so little material appear in so many different forms? Some garments have middles like fishnets. Or no middles at all. Some have peep holes like bubbles in a fish tank. Some have no backs, plunging down below the waist with just the thinnest of straps to hold them up. Some have soft see-through wings and look like wet moths when they come out of the sea. Some have short skirts and very skimpy tops.

He sees these multiple Julias — black and white — stretched out on blankets. They are running into the sea, laughing and carefree. They are oiling themselves, caressing every inch of their bodies with slow loving fingers. They are lying, seductively cupped, to catch the sun. They are smiling and half naked, self-absorbed as cats.

Charles has never seen so much exposed female flesh. He has never seen so many white women. He is amazed at the paleness of white flesh, like morning sky before dawn or between rains when clouds still form a canopy overhead. Some girls appear to crackle in bronze, like meat before eating and some are, astonishingly, spotted like the coat of a leopard.

It is these young women who show him the fullness of breast and thigh, the delicacy of nipple and navel, the gently rotating stride of girls in their primary flourish, each step a deliberate corkscrew into the sand, boldly marking their trails, knowing they will vanish the instant they move on.

And they always move on.

Out. Over the horizon.

He watches the setting sun copper the waves and then sink. He wants to go where it goes. Where they go.

The trip home to Kampala takes them through Nairobi where the group stops for two nights. Even more eye-opening than Mombasa, Nairobi — the Kenyan capital — seems like sin city to them.

"Kenya is a country of many colours," remarks Headmaster on their first excursion into the city. "The Masai called this area 'place of sweet waters,' and they would let their livestock graze and drink freely. Now, it is full of parks and restaurants and museums."

The Masai. Tall, slender bodies billowing in red cotton, bright under the sun, staffs swinging slowly beside cattle. Charles is amazed at how wide the world of Africa is. When they enter Nairobi, however, he feels small. Invisible. The harsh light glancing off concrete high-rises blinds him, cancels him out. Even when he sees a traditional Masai sipping coffee.

"There is a colour Headmaster forgot to mention," says Mr. Makuba to a handful of students sitting around him. "And that is the colour white. The British Government set aside the most fertile areas for their own settlers and called it the White Highlands."

Charles hears and nods but says nothing. He is caught up in the clicking pace at which people walk and traffic signals change, the impersonality of stores where money seems to flip back and forth, where clerks do not smile. There is no softness here. Only efficiency and organization. Palm trees and street lamps bend the same way, spaced and placed in exact order.

They visit City Park and the Arboretum where acres of grass stiffen behind fences, where the bursting flora of the land is preserved under glass or arranged precisely in ornamental tree gardens.

After dinner, they are free but they are warned not to go more than a few streets from their dorm. Mr. Makuba wanders off with some of the male members of the Drama Club, including Charles and Joro. An hour later, Charles drinks his first beer — which tastes sour — and smokes his first cigarette, which scrapes his throat.

An hour after that, he sees something he could never have imagined even existed. "We are going on a secret mission," Mr. Makuba says with a smile. "You must tell no one of this excursion, especially Headmaster." The senior boys savour the prospect of this extracurricular visit. Whatever it is.

It is dusk as they thread through the glittering back streets. Humming, the city lights up for the evening. Putting on spangles and bangles. The sinuous music of Tuareg bands pulses from tiny restaurants and bars. They stop now before a black door framed by the painting of a nearly naked woman. A giant white female who curves up, over and around the entrance with the circles of her soft body. The boys all have one simultaneous thought. To touch this vision whose flesh seems to glow like a lightbulb from deep inside.

"She is truly a naked goddess," says Charles appreciatively.

"You might say that," replies Mr. Makuba. "But let's keep religion out of this tonight. Would you like to see the real thing?"

The real thing?

Mr. Makuba presses a bell and the boys stare in awe as the goddess winks a big blue neon eye at them. The doors of her arms open wide and they file in.

They are led through a smoky blue haze by a tall young man to a round table directly under the stage. The women they look up at now are encased in sparkly nets, winding themselves around poles, caressing themselves under mauve spotlights. Drinking their second beers, the boys stare amazed. When some of the dancers flick gauzy scarves at them, Mr. Makuba catches part of one and, laughing, wafts it in the faces of his boys. When the dancer comes a few moments later to claim it, she bends her oiled naked breasts over the table. Mr. Makuba carefully places a bill between them and she smiles. Her fullness so near. Smelling of flowers.

Fragrant female bodies torment Charles the next morning as the group strolls through Nairobi's Museum of African history. Mr. Makuba whispers to the group, as they stand before cases of skulls in the National Museum of Kenya. "We all come from the apes. These are humanoid skulls from more than a million years ago, skulls found right here in Kenya. Even older skulls have been found in Ethiopia."

Charles stares at the empty eye sockets staring back at him. In most cases the lower jaw is missing, so that the forehead

— the thinking part — is prominent. Homo Sapiens. "What do the words mean?" he asks.

"It's Latin," says Mr. Makuba. "First there was Homo Africanus. African Man. Then Homo Erectus." The boys giggle. "Standing Man" he says, ignoring the joke. "Then Homo Sapiens. Thinking Man. Man with knowledge."

As Charles gazes through another glass at the squashed skull of an actual ape, images from the previous night appear through it. Julia's features waving in green fluorescence. He looks around quickly and blinks. "Julia?"

Reality intervenes when they start the long train ride home. Relentless as the sun, the round smiling face of Idi Amin beams out at Charles from the front page of a newspaper held high for all to see by Headmaster. Threats. Boasts. A new heaviness hangs in the air that is more than heat and humidity. It sits in big black headlines stabbing out stories of Amin's meteoric rise to power.

"If he really gains authority," says Headmaster, "we might get our Olympic-sized pool."

"Will he really have the influence to do that?" Joro asks.

A recent graduate of Mengo, Joro has impressed Charles as being smart in many ways. Now a student at Makerere University where he is studying theatre, Joro is like a younger Mr. Makuba. He also writes plays, and seems very political as well as being a wonderful actor and dancer. Mr. Makuba has invited Joro back to the school on several occasions in the last two years to assist him.

"He wants to have that power," says Mr. Makuba. "But he is still a deputy. President Obote is in Singapore right now at a Commonwealth Conference, so Amin is making a lot of noise back at home."

"Perhaps," says Joro after a long pause, "we had better get the pool order in quickly."

Headmaster holds up another full-page photo of Amin

dancing at a village festival. In his hand is a ceremonial spear. The general's head is down, covered by a huge brimmed hat, as though hiding the grin that they know is there, as though concentrating on the heavy stomp of his feet, exactly where and when to place them.

"He's wearing a John Wayne hat," thinks Charles who, like most of his classmates, has long been addicted to American westerns. On the same page is a photo of Amin playing the royal flute. The paper is passed around. The general is shown in another photo laughing heartily.

"He looks jolly," comments Julia turning her attention to the next photo. "Not like President Obote."

The conversation stays on Amin. How strong is this general really, who looks as solid as rock and rooted like an old tree?

"Here is an interesting fact," says Mr. Makuba, "General Amin was raised a Muslim."

Charles looks at Amin's glowing face and wonders whether he also likes little boys. "Where did the general go to school?" he asks.

Mr. Makuba tells them that Amin never completed school and, according to rumour, cannot even read very well.

"He has friends in high places," says the Headmaster. "Like Obote, he is also a northerner. And he helped Obote when he came to power. The British military also likes him. For the army, he was always a model soldier."

In fact, Amin is change itself, a big blustering wind of change blowing a sandstorm through Kampala, through Uganda, through East Africa.

At midday, the train chugs slowly back into the Kampala station. But someone has connected the wrong dots.

Soldiers are everywhere. At every exit. In the station itself. Occasionally they emerge pushing someone before them. Or, they emerge smiling and smoking a cigarette. Charles raises a window and thinks he hears screaming. Sees a man bleeding on the ground. Sees a young woman on her knees before a soldier, with her hands tied behind her. He quickly closes the window and prepares himself.

Soldiers guide them to a waiting bus. Normal. The driver explains to Headmaster what has happened. "The military has taken over. It's a coup. Amin is now in charge."

"Get us to the school," says Headmaster.

As they start to drive he tells them that all will be well. Joro is dropped near his parents' home. The tension on the bus is thick. The ride is slow. Unbearable.

The road up Mengo Hill is blocked. Headmaster steps outside and speaks to someone with a gun. A moment later, he calmly instructs his students to get out. Soldiers with guns separate Headmaster and Mr. Makuba from the rest and put the two of them into waiting jeeps. The students are told to get back on the bus that immediately turns in another direction. A soldier not much older than Charles now stands at the front. With a machine gun.

Charles focuses on the caked rubber boots of the many peddlers outside pushing tires through gritty puddles, wobbling rickety wheels beneath the wide wet trees, digging deeper and deeper into the clay ruts that suck them down. No one is smiling now. They are almost too intent on their tasks: cleaning windows, folding fabric, piling fruit, cutting up tires, trimming hair before mirrors tacked to trees.

It is deathly quiet he realizes.

The bus passes the radio station. It too is surrounded by soldiers, a tank rumbling on chains outside, roaring as it prowls around the perimeter. Like king crocodile, with a gun. Kitindi with a monster metal head and eyes that never close. "What could they be doing at the radio station?" Charles wonders, concerned now about the place of his first theatrical success.

The senior students are installed in small hot huts in a wooded area just outside the Kampala city limits. A dozen in each hut. They all hear the occasional blasts and yells and crashes.

Like the movies, thinks Charles. Real and not real. Flattened pictures on a screen.

They are fed military meals. Sent back to the huts. Boys here. Girls there. Told nothing. Restlessly they squirm on wooden seats. Clothes sticking. Flesh squeaking. They try to absorb the words they hear. White fluoresecent lights hiss at all hours.

The next morning they are marched out of the sleeping area, past the awful smelling latrines. They have no idea where Mr. Makuba is. Or Headmaster. They are given old books and told to read. They whisper. They wonder. They eat and they sleep.

On their third morning, a military figure arrives. There are now more than two hundred private school students in their group. He addresses them all politely.

"I am sorry you have been inconvenienced. There have been changes. You will return to your schools now and carry on as usual. There is no bus available at the moment, so you will have to walk. Leave your bags here. We will send them later." And then he adds, "Long live the revolution. Long live Idi Amin."

Smiling oddly at the frightened students, he dismisses them. Obediently, they follow instructions. Because this man has a gun, the new authority.

They begin the long walk towards Mengo.

Headmaster Hermitage is at the school when they start arriving. Fruit and drinks are waiting.

"Where is President Obote?" Charles asks. "Where did the army come from? Who are all these soldiers?"

Headmaster puts a warning finger over his lips. "Too many questions are not good right now Charles. I have been told to tell you only that General Amin is now in charge."

They head to their rooms in a daze, hearing only the occasional burst of gunfire.

Two days later, Charles and some of the older boys decide to find out for themselves what is really going on. They walk down the hill into town, into the choking grey cloud that is now Kampala. Charles cannot see and he cannot breathe. There is a stink of rubber. A scorched acrid haze that makes him cough.

Smashed glass spikes the road as they move out from the school. Tin roofs in the town have caved in. Metal lampposts twist through thick haze. Wires coil over the road like dead snakes, some still sparking. Trees loom suddenly, then veer off. Not trees but the ghosts of trees, their green life gone, their shadowy shapes straining.

The destruction seems accidental, desultory evidence of a stand made here and a battle lost there. Resistance easily overcome. A city briefly, fiercely defiant, then easily defeated.

The town has been conquered in warlike fashion. Perhaps the war is still being fought. The few people who are outside sit silently. A few crouch in alleys or scurry along walls like frightened insects. Holding small transistor radios to their ears, listening for some signal, some instruction that will explain, tell them what to do.

What they all hear, however, is music that wants everyone to move, not think. Martial music, good for a soldier swinging his gun. Music that will not allow anyone to pause for even a moment. To wonder or doubt. Just to keep going.

The boys see a blasted car. A burned hull of metal and roasted upholstery. A shrivelled black lump at the driver's wheel. They stop and stare. A soldier tries to move them on. But they are frozen to the spot. Transfixed by a corpse with a sign around its neck that shouts "Traitor."

"That was a priest," the soldier finally says to them. "He spoke against the revolution. Let that be a lesson to you."

A priest?

Charles remembers a tall handsome priest from childhood. Met in the Catholic kingdom with Father. A man who helped so many get an education at Mengo. A man of God. A man who preached what Kekinoni herself believed. That Jesus died for everyone. That he was nailed alive to a giant wooden cross and left hanging in humiliation and agony while the sky turned dark.

Charles also remembers a cross in a large church with Jesus twisted on it. He remembers studying Jesus' foot. The rest of the cross was so high, he had to look up to see anything. But the foot was at eye-level, its delicate bones and fine nails, its ivory colour. The skin punctured by a square nail poking through, peeled back a little, the way his fingernail did when he bit at the quick. Bright blood painted on. A blue vein ruptured.

Had the boys' combined sins helped make this happen? Their sins of flirting, swaggering in new clothes, beer drinking, cigarette smoking? Their sins of vanity, dancing, acting, playing football? Feeling his legs weaken beneath him, he looks around and sees horror on other faces. The group is gradually shooed away, leaving the dead priest to turn slowly into ash and Kampala to melt in the acrid haze.

Far away, Kekinoni stands numbly over her daughter Debra, who had been caught in it all. Pain keeps Debra unconscious. Asleep for two days now, entwined amidst the pink and blue flowers of her bedsheets, cradled among the stems like a small seed that won't open. Sunlight beams white on the gauzy curtains billowing at the open window of her room that rain turns blue. Debra lies in her bed of dreams. Draped with mosquito netting.

Ripped. Raped. Now in a witch's spell.

Don't worry," the doctor tells Kekinoni. "She is still breathing. I am sure she will be all right." The doctor can tell life from death. Can give injections and apply bandages. But he has no idea how to deal with the damage inside Debra's head.

Kekinoni creeps through the house in the starched white cotton dress of her spirit church. Calling Raphael the Healer, softly intoning hymns of praise and supplication from under her white turban.

When classes across the country are suspended indefinitely, Charles makes his way home. His close friend Samuel arrives too, his own house burned to the ground. The boys are in shock. "How can it have happened to her?" Charles asks his parents over and over. "I don't understand."

"They attacked her when she got off the bus," says Father. "Here, not far from home."

"Soldiers."

"Two of them. They offered her a ride home. Her mistake was to take it. She thought they were there to protect her."

Charles remembers her smile. How she was unable to control it when teased by her brother. Once the smile began, she couldn't stop it. And it made her so angry.

"They dropped her off afterwards. She was full of blood. They said she had been in an accident. She was hardly moving. And then they drove away. As if nothing had happened. I'm sure they thought she was dead. But people saw. Heard. Now they are gone. Sent to Kampala. We'll never find them."

Kanyunya is bereft. No power left to help anyone.

Charles feels the ice of anger in his veins.

"They did their dirty work and crept off into the forest like hyenas," says Kekinoni.

Silence.

"She will never be Debra again," mumbles Charles. "I know she will not."

"Part of her has died and has gone to Jesus," says Mother. "We must take care of what's left."

Charles has never seen Father cry like this before.

In the dusty compound behind the house, Charles and Samuel watch the cows, their ragged tails twitching at flies under the dry, gnarled branches of winter trees.

"Is that all cows can do?" demands Charles, seething. "Can they think? Or feel? Or figure things out? Are they happy or sad? Do they only move when they are prodded? Squirt milk when they are pulled? Bawl when they are hungry or thirsty? Are they half dead or just stupid?"

Samuel has no response.

Cows used to give Charles comfort. He could tell Suna everything. She seemed so wise, taking it all in through her big brown eyes, absorbing it into her bulk, through her eyes and hide. But they now seem so useless, expressions blank as wooden posts.

He wonders what good it has done him to descend from the people of the cow. We have no long horns curving out of our heads, no crowns of strong white bone to part the air. We cannot even produce milk. Cannot nourish. We cannot help anything, change anything.

"She misses you, my son." It is Mother in her white robes pulling old Suna towards him. Dust puffs up around them filtering sunlight. "Milk her. Let her know you are here again."

Samuel stands and pets her.

Charles is soothed by Suna's strong smell, the way her great head rolls towards him, as if acknowledging his presence, still listening to him.

"Suna, Suna," he whispers, "what do you know?"

"Whatever she knows," says Mother, "she will not tell. She will keep your secrets."

Over her shoulders, Mother balances a slender rod dangling two precious milk bowls at either end. They rest easily in the rope netting. She bends to lay them on the ground the way a servant would.

Shiny and black. He looks at the bowls' design, shooting beads of white fire through him. Debra's bowls. Suna does not move. Under her, feeling the pulse of milk and blood, Charles finds his strength.

"Confide in her," Mother says. "I have already told her that Debra is not dead. Somehow, Suna is keeping her alive. Let her do the same for you and Samuel."

A week later, Debra wakes up. Broken and fearful as she will be for the rest of her life. She cannot speak to her brother, or even look at him, recalling mutely the shameful way she was used.

The next day Charles returns to Mengo. Before he leaves, he and Father hug. Kanyunya says nothing.

At the school, classes remain suspended. A few teachers come by. Charles meets Joro near the Headmaster's office. Joro looks around and then whispers, "There is something I must tell you."

Charles will listen carefully to anything Joro has to say now because Joro has proven himself smart. One who is always right. He admires Joro. Perhaps not yet a real teacher but, as an assistant at Mengo, he is much more than a student. Helping those doing important things. Adult things. Like Headmaster. Like Mr. Makuba.

Joro seems to know so much. And it makes him strong. Charles trusts what Joro knows. "Amin and his army are starting to kick out the Asians. All those Indian business people. The ones who run so much of the country. 'Africa for Africans,' he says. 'Uganda for Ugandans.' It's nonsense. He has already named a Supreme Council which will re-allocate Indian property to the army."

"Can he really do that?"

"I just saw it on television. The Indians are already leaving. I saw them boarding buses with their baggage. Some of them have lived here a hundred years. Can you imagine? It's a huge mess at the airport."

"I suppose," says Charles in confusion, "I suppose it's right somehow that Uganda is for Africans. Isn't it? You know Indian students. Forever being picked up in fancy cars. Never give us rides. They always felt they were better than us."

"They went too far, but Amin has gone even farther. Uganda needs their money and their expertise. You can't just throw business people out of a country and take their property."

"What about the British? Can't they stop it?"

"I don't think the British are safe either. Headmaster and his family are preparing to leave."

"Leave? They can't leave."

"Well, they are. And it's not just foreigners who are in trouble. Yesterday, a handful of soldiers came to the school and shoved everyone who was here onto a bus. We argued. Screamed and pushed back. But they had guns.

"On the bus, they told us we were going to see what happens to people who question Amin."

"Who was questioning him? Where did you go?"

"A public execution," says Joro. "They took us to an execution."

Charles barely comprehends what he is being told.

"When we got to the main square, someone was already tied to a tree. His arms handcuffed around it. His back to us. Other buses were arriving with students on them. Teachers too."

"Who was it?"

"I couldn't see his face at first. But they were beating him. He never knew when the next blow was coming. They kept hitting him and shouting that he was a traitor, a traitor to Uganda. That he had been speaking against the general. That he was infecting students with his words."

"Was he an Indian?"

"No. He was one of us. Very much one of us."

"Who was he? Did you find out? Did they kill him?"

"The soldiers said he was harbouring guerillas." Tears were rolling down Joro's face now.

"Just when I thought he had already given up his life, his knees buckled and his whole body sagged as though each single bone had been broken. The soldiers came with ropes and tied up every part of him that was dangling or drooping. Then they allowed a Muslim holy man to pray for him. Another mockery. He was an Anglican! I watched the blood pour down his arms and legs.

"Suddenly one of the soldiers said something about a black hood for his head."

"Why did they need a hood? "

"Because they were going to shoot him. That's how they do it. Well, they couldn't find a hood and so the soldier in command grabbed some young guy in the crowd and ripped his shirt off. When he struggled, they started hitting him too.

"They tied it over their victim's head and ... and they shot him. Each bullet stood him straight up. Then someone started screaming. Ran straight toward the same tree yelling like a maniac. The soldiers clubbed him with their guns before they finally understood what he wanted. His bloody shirt back. It was the guy with the shirt. So they tore it off the face of the executed man and threw it at him. That's when I saw who it was." Joro stops, overcome.

"He must have seen that tree every day of his life. He lived on that street. When he came to school each morning, he could never have imagined he would die there."

"When he came to which school Joro? Here? To Mengo? He came here? Who was it Joro? Tell me. Who was it?"

"Mr. Makuba."

"Mr. Makuba?"

His teacher. The man of masks.

"Yes. Mr. Makuba. Our friend."

"But he was just a teacher. Wasn't he?"

"Was he, Charles?" The two young men stare at one another. A new question hanging in space.

Who was he when he died?

3. ABAFUMI

"**I** KNOW HOW YOU CAN HONOUR Mr. Makuba's memory."
A week has passed. Charles and Joro have spent time in each other's company. Talking. Sharing. Trying to understand what has happened. These two young men stand together now, looking up at a blank sky where they once read their future.

Charles feels uncomfortable. For some days, Joro has been watching him closely, almost testing him. Slowly they are becoming friends but also something more. They talk of art. "Do you love your theatre classes as much as football," Joro asks him one day.

"As much, yes," says Charles.

"Will you become a football star?"

"Not now."

"Then I shall invite you to honour Mr. Makuba. Come with me."

"Where?" asks Charles.

"Just trust me. We will walk together."

It is a month since the coup but Kampala still lies in ruins around them as they head down the big hill into the town. Past squawking chickens. Past charred trees and torn lives. They are silent.

Suddenly Charles recognizes their destination. It is the large shady portico entrance to the National Theatre. After days of harsh heat, cool shadow engulfs them. Charles has not been back since Mr. Makuba took the class to see *Hamlet*. Joro is right. His beloved teacher is now a spirit in this house of plays. This is where they can come to find him, to honour him.

They enter the building and creep quietly into the back row of the huge theatre. A rehearsal of some sort is going on. Charles looks at the polished wood and velvet all around him. The air crackles with a magic. It buzzes and hums. Something is happening.

"Do not come in here empty," booms the director's voice from the house. A Ugandan voice. "Don't just take. Bring me something. Find it inside yourself. Find who you are. Don't tell me. Show me. Show me how you move. Show me how you walk. Show me how you love."

The actor tries again. And again the director is not satisfied. "Everything you are doing is on the outside. Show me who you are from inside your skin. This is not a European television show. Be African. Be who you really are. Show me the mask behind the face I see. Tell me your real name. Show me what is really going on outside this theatre. In your life."

Such passion, such anger rivets Charles. Mr. Makuba, too, believed in what he called the interior mask. Believed it protected and revealed you. But he was gentler, kinder than this man, this director.

And Mr. Makuba was dead. This man was very much alive.

"This is the Abafumi company," whispers Joro. "They will be great. Mr. Makuba recommended me to them. And the director is Robert Serumaga. He came back from Europe last year to make money for his family business. But his family is starting to realize that this is his business. That theatre is his business. They will be great."

Charles looks up at the stage and studies this Robert Serumaga. Solidly built and very sure of himself, Serumaga clearly comes from money and privilege. But the things he is saying are extraordinary. Masks. Dance. Inner self. Africa. Drums and colours and chanting. Charles is thrilled that Joro has brought him here, to Abafumi, to Robert Serumaga.

They sit silent for many hours. It is a Baganda story that Abafumi is telling with their bodies, with their bead skirts and elaborate hairstyles, with their headdresses and knives. It is a story Charles knows. The story of Nakayaga, demon of storms and whirlwinds, who demands the limbs of many victims before being appeased. The story of a victim who pleads for mercy, pleads with his song and his drum to be spared, pleads because he is a father and a husband, because his family needs him.

The intensity of the rhythms stops Charles cold. His heart hammers and he breathes hard. This is not an imitation of life. It is larger than life. Not just a story, but the imaginative inside of a story. "Where understanding begins," Serumaga is saying.

Charles and Joro have moved closer. When they take a break, Joro introduces Charles. "Robert, you said we needed another player. This is Charles. The young man I told you about."

Serumaga's eyes quickly turn, beam deeply into Charles. For a moment their gazes join and lock. Robert recognizes sleeping strength in this tall intense young man. Unmasks him silently.

Charles staggers back from the fire of Robert Serumaga. It is not random, this burning. It wants to scorch him.

"Tell me Joro, tell me everything about this man," whispers Charles urgently when they are alone in the clammy coolness of the theatre.

"His father was rich and served the British as County Chief."

"An official, like my father," says Charles.

"His father died early. Serumaga went to university in Ireland. Learned his theatre there. Became a playwright."

"With the eyes and that voice," says Charles, "he could have been a priest."

"Except that he loves women too much."

"Why did he come back to Uganda?"

"To run the family business. Make money."

"So he's really a businessman," says Charles admiringly.

"He finally realized how he could use his commercial connections to make theatre."

"What kind of plays did he write?"

"Angry plays," says Joro.

"What was he angry about?"

"Injustice. Victimization. The abuses of colonialism." Charles rolls these words around in his head. Small sharp rocks, they tumble and scrape.

"Eventually he turned away from realistic theatre and began a professional group which he called Abafumi. The Storytellers."

"They've given a few performances around Kampala, performances with dancers and drummers."

"He writes the scripts?"

"No real scripts in this work. It's improvised. They enact it mostly through movement. Serumaga calls it 'total theatre,' because it uses everything from stillness to frenzy, from silence to screams."

"But no dialogue?"

"No dialogue."

Charles stops to consider. Sound. Movement. The world is composed of sound. Moving sound. The pounding of grain in wooden bowls. The bawling of cattle. Mother's crooning at night. Rain.

"How much time do you spend rehearsing?" asks Charles.

"He wants sixty hours a week. I give can only him twenty because I really want to write plays. But I've learned so much from Abafumi. And I help him find talented young actors and dancers right in the high school. People like you."

"Like me? You think I can do this? Really?"

"Make no mistake, Charles. You are talented, but this is not a game for him. It is hard work. And know you cannot deceive this man. He demands commitment."

"Yes. I want to give myself," says Charles.

"It has to become your life. He will accept nothing less."

Somewhere in the depths of his being, Charles needs that.

To be pulled by something larger, moving and changing, unstoppable. Like the dance. Achieving his own shape. "Yes," he says to Joro again. "I want Abafumi."

Charles is determined to remain in Kampala. Abafumi, he is told, is a communal venture. Room and board are offered. His first workday starts at six a.m. He has not yet eaten. His wide eyes are red and tired. But his mind is on fire, his nerves and his heart, taut with apprehension. Hotter than morning sun.

He is given a tracksuit by Beth, one of the company members. Silver. He puts it on and joins the others. Serumaga leads the pack as they jog around a steaming oval at Makerere University. Charles sprints up to him.

"Good morning Robert," says Charles. "Thank you for inviting me to join you."

"No speaking during exercises," says the director without turning to him. "Save your energy." And he speeds effortlessly away from the apprentice.

A bad start, thinks Charles.

But soon, he is racing, unable to stop. Controlled by another force. Yet, he feels free. Free of guns and violence, free of guilt and responsibility. And pain. He sprints over gravel and brick. Around bend and curve. Alcoves and arbours encourage thought. Low buildings entice him with their woven arches and vine-covered porches, calm and soothe him.

Four miles. Around and around. With Joro and Kasa, with Kiri and Beth and Obusi, with Bita, Mara, and Susi, with Willy, Joseph, and Monday.

And Robert. In black. Silvery black. Shining like the night moon over water. Older by ten years than most of them, he keeps up a fast pace not allowing even one to fall a step behind.

"Sweat!" he cries. "Sweat. Clean out the poisons." The regimen is intense.

When the run is finished, they huddle together in the still early morning sun, panting and glistening, bending and dripping, their bodies stretched and thrumming. At some invisible cue, after breath returns, they execute a communal leap, accompanied by an awesome shout of a word unfamiliar to Charles.

"Sardinia."

After showers in the gymnasium, the group scrambles into the van and charges toward breakfast — a Chinese restaurant across from the National Theatre that knows them all. Its name, Charles comes to understand, is Sardinia.

Sudden as a dust storm, they whirl in, scraping chairs up to a large round table. The waitress, a small Chinese woman named May, greets them familiarly. "The usual today, my dear artistes?"

"Of course," says Robert warmly. "We had a fine workout this morning. We'll devour everything you throw at us."

"I know," says May. "Eggs. Bacon. Bread. Onions. Potatoes. And you'll follow that with meat and Chinese vegetables." Robert, her favourite customer, looks every inch the proud and generous father here, beaming beneficently at his hungry brood.

Happy to attend her faithful clan of precocious performers, squat little May shuffles into the back on her red and green satin slippers, barely noticing the blue and white mural of Mediterranean waves which ripple through her apparently Italian-Chinese dining emporium.

In the streets after breakfast, Kampala is another story. The watchful soldiers — arms braided with insignias, chests clanking medals — are still everywhere. But here, near the university, this gang of civilians is allowed.

Charles is wary as military eyes ogle them. Are they looking at the women? Or the men? He knows he too is a fine physical specimen. They all are.

Robert walks his theatre family briskly through the armed camp that is Kampala — through its jittery streets, past its strained faces to their home at the National Theatre — with an air of genial defiance. He knows his children are safe. As their wealthy and influential prime guardian, he guarantees it. And pays daily for the privilege.

In regular classes — held at the National — Charles struggles with many of the exercises led by various specialists Robert has found. Both European and African. All are trained experts who stretch him to breaking point, wind him up tight and then release and relax. Over and over. Until he turns to water.

"Your body is your instrument," Robert tells them afterwards. "It is your means of communication. You must know and control every inch of it. Work it every day."

Charles eventually finds the courage to ask about time off. Robert is offended.

"An artist has no free time. Your experience is your only true teacher and does not grant holidays. Learn from everything. Learn from dreaming and making love. From eating and puking and shitting. Learn from anger and fear, from envy, lust, and desire. Don't let any of it go to waste."

Robert's words make Charles feel as though he has been unconscious until now. As though he has understood nothing. And he loves Robert's easy assumptions about his sexual life.

"There is no inner experience without external physical expression," says Robert another day. "Study people. Learn to read them. Know what they are saying."

Charles thinks of Debra and her long sleep after trauma, wanting never to wake up. He thinks of Mother swaying to the hymns of her spirit church, moving to music, rocking all the way to heaven. He thinks of Father, kicking up dust on the motorbike. He thinks of winking women. How all these images provide keys to the people who inhabit them.

Forced to focus on his own body, he becomes aware of toes and toenails, of ankles and fragile bird bones; he realizes the density of hip and thigh: how they root and how they fly, feels the sockets of arms and the hair on skin, the knotting complexity of knee joints. After hours of straining to the farthest perimeters of his newly discovered body, Charles suddenly ceases to believe it exists. He floats in another dimension.

Where the master's mesmerizing voice lures him forward. "The small truths reside in physical actions," says Robert. "It is physical action which stirs the great truth inside, the truth of emotions and imagination. That is how you convey truth. It is in your body, not your words. You construct truth physically, draw it, colour it in."

Robert has flung him far out and now draws him slowly back, sleek as a fish on a hook.

So Charles thinks about body again. The one he lives in. So happy dancing, finding rhythm in drums. So completely unaware of itself when running on a football pitch. His body has always used him. Now he is being asked to use it. But in a natural, instinctive way, like an animal. He is being turned inside out and upside down in order, says Robert, to sing a human song and cry a human cry. "Sometimes you just barely indicate what's inside. A gesture so small, it is almost invisible. But the audience must see. They must be attuned to you, trust you. You must make them see the familiar with fresh eyes."

"COW!" The word comes out longer. "CAOWWW!" And longer still. "CAOOOWWW!"

The voice coach dances through it, elongates the bridge of vowels across the chasm that separates the sound he wants from his inept pupils. In a frenzy, he flings the word up, hurls it down, lays it out flat and round, with a thud on the floor, pungent and oozing as cattle dung. The group jumps back in awe. Not knowing what is expected. What to do.

"You must say it almost the way the cow does when it cries out. We should hear every letter, as long as your longest breath. Big and slow. Open your mouth wide. Let the creature in. Let the whole cow wander through you. Let her graze and munch and chew, taking her time. Let us see how lazy she is. Keep the cow inside you. Fill yourselves with her."

Charles feels himself give way, feels his body succumb to the loose, hanging frame of the cow, to Suna's hairy flank, warm with the business inside her bulk, to the sideways slide of her jaw, to the soft teats, rigid-ready for the hands of the milker to squeeze loose.

"COW! COW! COW!" they all continue to repeat in the streets after the session.

Those walking by turn and cluck their tongues. "What is this noise? What are these people doing?" they wonder, "wasting their time when they should be in the fields or in the market or, at the very least, studying something useful. Like economics." The group hardens themselves against these mutterings because they know they have been chosen. They know that Abafumi can somehow give them the power to overcome the differences of their ancestors: Acholi. Baganda. Rwandese.

They all love lunch. It is brought into the theatre by a large cinnamon woman in a silvery turban and a long dress, the colour of leaves after rain. She is their envoy from the outer world. Gathering at an upper window, they watch her come to them with determination and purpose, vanishing from the market crowds between columns into the black interior of the National. There they know she slips nonchalantly past the young military guard who stands aside to make room for the huge basket she carries on her arm. It swells with appetizing aroma under an immaculate white cloth. Ravenous, they listen for the guard's question. "And what have you brought me from your kitchen today?" And the woman's tantalizing description of one dish after another.

"Welcome Mama Africa," says Robert inside, always the first to greet her. As she wafts in, she sings out "Food for Abafumi!" and watches with satisfaction while they shift eagerly in the big leather chairs of the boardroom waiting for the feast to be set out.

"Before we eat, we make our weekly confession," explains Joro to Charles.

"What do you mean?"

"The boardroom is a confessional in this church and Robert is our priest."

This surprises Charles who simply asks, "Does everyone have to?"

"Well, if you are a member of the company, then the company is your life and you must confess on a regular basis. We have to respond to the exercises. We have to say how we feel about working together."

Joro pauses for emphasis.

"If any one of us believes we are not adequately fulfilling the company's mission, it is up to that person to come forward. In being responsible for ourselves, we are responsible for one another. But you will never find one member accusing another because, for Robert, self-knowledge is the key." Charles listens intently.

"If one of you is not true to the vision," Robert continues, picking up the thread of his own mission statement, "we will all suffer until balance is restored. The well-being of the company comes before any personal need."

His probationary period — three months — is finally up. That lunchtime, Charles' fate will be decided. Maybe it already has been. Maybe that's why they're having a party in that stern boardroom where self-evaluation is practiced so rigorously. Maybe they're all celebrating his failure among the warm smells of cassava and fresh cooked fish, bananas, yams and ground nuts. The conference table is transformed into a feasting place, each laden bowl a dance and each dish a drum beat.

Charles sits in silence, waiting to hear his fate. Hoping.

"You have all agreed by secret vote," says Robert, riveting each Abafumi member with his gaze. "It is unanimous and I bow to the majority." They all know the subject.

Charles looks down, wishing to disappear. If his future is to stop here, then let him burn out on the spot.

"Welcome Charles," says Robert grandly. "You are one of us now. Welcome to Abafumi."

Charles beams.

Robert fondly embraces his newest protégé, his youngest member, trembling in his arms. Women cry a high-pitched ululation, moving Charles to hug and kiss new sisters.

And he knows that this is right. It is where his life wants him to be. With these people who are his family now.

Charles finally feels included as actor and dancer.

"What you are is what you can give," says Robert back in the rehearsal room. "If you are the only one of your kind, you are rarer still. You must be protected. Because you are the end of the line. After you, there can only be the ancestors. It is your responsibility to save the line from extinction.

"Our ancestors cannot see this world without us," he continues. "And the world cannot know us without our ancestors. We carry them from their eternal place to our living one, as we carry our terrors, our joys, and our pride. Our bodies carry all, they are the temples that carry both gods and demons."

Like the women of Kekinoni's spirit church — bare feet sounding on the floor, hands raised in salute — the group answers every poetic image Robert calls out to them.

"You are the leopard's fire, *Mayanja.*

"You are the rainbow, *Musoke* and *Muwanga*, the future.

"You are *Kibuka,* the war god.

"And the god of earthquake, *Musisi.*

"You are the plague of *Kaumpuli* and the snake demon, *Magobwi.*

"You are the man-eater, *Kitinda,* and the god of thunderbolts *Kiwanuka.*

"You are *Abafumi,*

"Keeper of the stories.

"You are Abafumi."

Robert breathes deeply and gazes at each one. He speaks their names. Deliberate as though trying to unlock unseen doors.

"And I want to go with you to the place where you live," he says. "Take me to the home of your soul."

"Joseph," he says without smiling. "Where will you take me?"

Joseph is Acholi. Tall and strong. Not willowy like a herdsman but firm and compact. Like a rooted tree. A warrior. Charles is aware of their reputation. Valued fighters who wore old British military uniforms — especially the braiding and medals. The Acholi could never be bought.

"My ancestors were powerful and independent," he tells Robert. "They wore brass around their wrists and ankles so that their bodies shone like evening sun when they moved, rich with the colours of day after tending crops."

Charles learns that Joseph's own father, a chief of police, was also a dancer travelling the country, telling Acholi legends. What would the Sub-County Chief think of that, wonders Charles? What would Father think of actually combining the nonsense of "entertainment" with the real work of a civil servant? Since schools are on permanent hold, it makes sense.

"I will take you to the labour of the fields," says Joseph softly to Robert.

And he begins a muscular movement of digging: bending and pushing and rising; bending, pushing, rising. Wiping sweat from his face. Beginning again. Moving to the percussion of a small Acholi drum, singing a mesmerizing phrase over and over. At every gesture, an ostrich feather plumes up, tickled by the slightest air current, a floating crown as fine as mist. Like the green invisible rain high in the tea plantations of the Rwenzori Mountains.

"Charles!" The name snaps around the room, tumbling him abruptly out of his own deep reverie. Robert looks at him without emotion, his expression neutral. But Charles feels a rope about to snare him. It has been thrown casually enough and lies loosely coiled on the ground next to him. Will he step around it and walk away, or will he pull it up and begin to weave magic.

"Take me where you live."

Suddenly it is out. Sound and animal all at once. Charles mouths the word loudly, hugely. "COW."

He is in panic but "COW!" calms him. "COW!"

"Good," says Robert. "Show us your cow. Sing us a Bahima story."

Charles begins to sing. Softly at first. And the song brings him movements that are both gentle and stately, a celebration of birth, a song of sacred moment. Of new things. Of future. Of a time when people were blessed by the cow, when a new child was anointed by butter from the cow's milk.

Charles' hands and eyes move seductively, enticing the cow forward. Calling the cow by name. Luring her forward. Dancing her name. Changing tempo. Signalling a new rhythm for the stomping of bare feet on the hard floor, feet that keep pace with him as he dances his special story.

The cow blesses the child and slowly moves away once again, grazes once more in the field, filling its stomach with the nourishment that will tomorrow again feed the baby.

A cycle of life. Ensuring the future of his people. Proud People of the Cow.

The van hurtles along through early morning mist and sunshine. They are on the familiar dusty red road out of Kampala. Yellow grasses bristle at its edges. Tall trees stretch into the new day, their leaves quivering in upper air. Well-tended fences of wire and wood mark off farmers' fields and grazing plots. But it doesn't prevent two Ankole cows from ambling along the road, their horns in high arc, as though anticipating some royal procession. Fixed on their path, they make cars swerve because, as Charles knows, if you don't make way for cows bad things happen.

It is a relief to see a road without soldiers. They are not needed out here, although there are still occasional roadblocks and checkpoints. Here, nature takes its course through days and seasons, and village life beats on in the timeless heart of the bush. Without Amin. Without politics.

"This is where we have all come from," says Robert to no one in particular, steadying himself in the bouncing van. The remark provokes a deeper silence. They all know where they have come from and most don't want to go back.

"You have all torn away from your roots. I understand that. I am not asking you to go home casually. But those roots will die if you leave them totally. They are the circuits of your being. Without them, nothing connects. You need their soil and sun. You and they need nourishing. You can provide that by understanding what they live on. By recreating that. Each in your own way. That is our collective work."

It doesn't make real sense to any of them yet but they trust him. He has given them important and interesting things to do in a city under siege. Though very few have seen their work yet, he has protected them, provided for them, and made promises to them. How can they doubt? Yet, they can't reconcile the prestige they now dream of with this ride into yesterday, this trip back to childhood when they had no power.

Joro, with the company for nearly a year, speaks up first, articulating what the rest are afraid to say. "We don't understand why you are taking us back here, Robert. We don't want to be killing chickens again or kissing goats. We are city people now."

"You must return to go forward, rediscover what it means to live in the old way. You must consider it consciously, remember it so that you can call it up when you need it in performance. From soul level."

Soul level. The phrase stays with Charles. He wants to find his soul level.

"There is," says Robert finally, "sacrifice involved. And I am not, my dear friends, talking about chickens and goats."

They do come to see village life in a new way. In Kilembe and Kaabond, in Atura and Namasagali, in Yumbe and Kumi, they watch and listen to the instrument makers. See how the *omuteze*, the royal flute player with his white turban, leads a solemn procession of Bahima in honour of the chief. They learn Luo words and they recognize its rhythms in drums, the pitch, and the melodies of their own speaking. The same drums also send Ikoci dancers into great leaps that they accentuate when their bare feet pound down on the ground. Charles is stirred by this combination of urgency, rhythm, and intensity. It banishes tangos and foxtrots, rhumbas and waltzes into some remote part of his being where they fade like scratchy movies running out of reel.

With Joseph's people, the Acholi, the group is introduced to a dance called Orak. Robert's actors provide vigorous accompaniment with handclapping, rattles, and calabashes that are thumped on the ground for maximum sound. They watch an instrument maker construct a *nanga,* a zither, hollowed and carved into a wooden bowl. They learn how to notch it at both ends, how to take the single string and zigzag it seven times over the bowl, how to twist it so it is thicker at one end than the other causing the separate segments to produce different notes. Its polished boat-like body glowing and its long neck — strung and pegged — straining forward only to be pulled back by tight strings where the music waits.

"It could sail away on a cloud," says Charles.

"When you play it, that is exactly what happens," adds Robert firmly.

The long journeys continue. Days. Weeks.

They watch a man who speaks the Iteso language play his *arigirigi*, a tube fiddle, amazed at how he stops the single sisal string with fingers and not frets.

They spend time in the South, hearing legends of the people of Masaba Mountain, listening to them speak Lumasaba, one of many Bantu languages. Their chief musician plays a *litungu*, covered with hide and fitted with a wooden yoke to which strings are attached. His songs are of migration and dislocation, heavy with foot-stomping and the jingling of small crotal bells at his ankle, reminding his people again and again not to forget who they are, words bubbling up out of him, splitting his face into smiles.

The company is invited to join in these songs of aging and beer, of farming and poverty, of love, sung by vocalists in an urgent falsetto. As they sing and sway, Charles feels the humiliations and fears of childhood abolished, adolescent rebellions settled somewhere, content and quiet in this new sense of belonging.

They learn about Kabaka's great traditions of courtly music and study the Baganda xylophone, the *amadinda*, with its twelve keys played by three musicians simultaneously. Its repertoire coming from the music of royal harpists — complex — with fiddles, a flute, and the refined *ennanga*. Long and slender, it produces a buzzing that reminds Charles of the frantic hornets in his village pavilion. He hears their complexity and profundity in the rings around the neck of the graceful eight-stringed instrument. In this intricate music, Charles finds sounds of himself, presented and repeated and re-assembled in a thousand different ways, constantly creating new patterns of possibility.

"This is our sound," says Robert to them after the playing has stopped. "Africa's sound. The sound of our cultures. We can give it to the world. No one else can do this. If we don't, it will vanish."

And on it goes.

From the Jopadhola people, they learn the intimacy of dual singers and dual harpists, vocalists alternating call and response in an animated conversation that ripples along to the deep watery notes of the bow harp, the *ntongoli*, that each plays with precision. "Instruments that speak to one another," says Robert.

Added to the harps are percussion instruments — two *teke*, pieces of wood played with wooden sticks; the *fumba*, a long narrow cylindrical drum with a skin at one end only; and the many bells the dancers wear twisted around their legs. Charles is intoxicated as the singers begin chanting and the women ululate, as the drums pound and feet stomp in rhythm.

A female dancer motions to Charles to join in. Now, he sways backwards and forwards from the waist to the shoulders as though he has been doing it all his life. And he has. Undulating like rain and wind in trees. Like a running river or the swimming of the crocodile. Skimming over savannah like the leopard. Roaring like storm. Crackling like night fires.

It is around such fires in front of village huts that the troupe also hears stories and legends. These tales invade them: stories of night dancers who walk over graves calling dead bodies by name, bodies of those who have practiced witchcraft and so must be punished. It is the night dancers who pull them out of the ground, drag them to a place of desecration. Then walk through the village whirring like bats roused up and swooping.

Charles watches them in a village near Yumbe. While the bush settles itself thick as fur, folding close its night creatures, they focus on the animated face of an Acholi woman who tells of twins. She addresses her words directly to Joseph. After all, he and they are the same people and she will rely on Joseph to convey her tale to others.

Twins are a fearful event for them all, combining heaven and earth in a single being. Twins with two fathers — one spirit and one material. Perhaps they are an incarnation of Wuo — the wild bush cow — mad with twitching and jumping, moody and capricious, to be handled with caution. Kill them. Better to be safe.

Charles watches the dancers' masks with their bold black-and-white sectioned cow heads, their startled eyes, huge horns and black skirts completely covering the body. Twins have always meant danger to the community.

"If you are the father of twins," says the lead singer to Robert, "you are not allowed to fight in tribal wars. You are not allowed to shed blood. For if you do, then your twins will turn on you. To prevent this, they must die by spearing. And you must be purified. So is it spoken."

Silence. The words take root.

"Now I will tell you the story of Renga Moi, the Father of our village, the Father of twins."

Gathered back at their rehearsal room, stretched out on mats that cover the polished wood floor. Robert recalls *Renga Moi* for them.

"He painted his skin with red dye, the colour of blood. He called himself the Red Warrior and he was renowned for his bravery. He is the leader. He is the first into battle. The other warriors only fight because he is among them."

Now the whole company is contributing, eager to show Robert they too remember a place existing long ago.

"There is also a Priest who leads the village in religious matters, settles disputes, and makes sure that rituals are properly observed."

Charles listens carefully. "It is the Priest who decides when to fight. It is from him that Renga Moi derives his power."

Robert leans into the group. "But we have also learned that this man's wife, Renga Moi's wife, Nakazzi, has given birth to twins. What will happen to the village if they are attacked and he can no longer lead the warriors into battle, can no longer draw blood? What if other villages know as well and they attack? What if he goes into battle anyway? Can the village survive?"

"If Renga Moi does fight, the twins must be killed," Charles says solemnly. "The rituals must all be observed."

"Now," he whispers urgently, "Let's dance this through. Begin with morning, the morning the twins are born."

Leaping to their feet, they move in unison. Give birth in unison. A passage through legs sturdy as trees. The drumming intensifies. Only when a second child emerges is the danger felt. Faces carved in fear. Strained and secret. Impending calamity. With the first assault on the village, Renga Moi steps forward to fight.

"But he cannot break the taboo," says Charles. "He cannot."

"Yet he must save the village."

"Then the twins will die. Must die."

"Protect the village now or lose it. Some action must be taken." Joseph stands on one side of the room as Renga Moi, the Red Warrior, the Father. On the other side, stands Robert as the Priest warning him — warning the whole village — that divine edicts must be obeyed.

Abafumi's first original play is being born.

"Renga Moi is a warrior before anything," says Joseph. "He must defend his people against invasion. He has no choice." Defiantly, Joseph beckons his warriors, and marches across an invisible border. He does not look back.

"Renga Moi is doing what he is trained to do. Does he have a choice?" asks Robert in a steady voice.

"The original story ends there," says Willy. "If Renga Moi fights, the gods will bring famine. People will starve. He may save the village but at what cost? His own twins will be the first to die."

"Nakazzi suffers most," whispers Beth mournfully, "because she knows her babies are in peril."

When the village is attacked, an enraged Renga Moi fights back.

"He has broken the law," declares the Priest. "The twins must die."

"Hide, Nakazzi. Hide your children."

A hunt begins for Nakazzi's children.

Robert, the Priest demands unquestioning faith. Kill them.

Renga Moi will not beg.

Though the villagers return without the children, the Priest will still be obeyed.

A tale hundreds of years old, re-lived in dance and sound. Sacrifice reborn in Kampala's National Theatre. The world outside has stopped as well. Amin, like the maddened Priest, demanding the blood of innocents.

Faint, fearful bells strum at the nerve endings of the group.

They have arrived at a hanging point in time. A convergence of history and heart. Robert has brought them here. To whom must they listen?

From the floor, Nakazzi's arms shoot up. She collapses in a shapeless shroud of grief. The Priest touches her shoulder. "Be proud."

Her eyes are black. "My children must not die"

Spears cross. Strike home along a beam of silver. Pierce and stab. A shriek wounds the air. Silence.

Slowly, to the hypnotic sounds of drum and bell, two tiny bundles of black cloth appear. Held high on the ends of weapons.

The Priest has had his sacrifice.

At the next rehearsal, a new tack. Renga Moi — not knowing his children have already been sacrificed — tries to warn the village of further danger. Then he finds Nakazzi. She is softly weeping.

"Where are the children?" he demands. The villagers crowd in, close the space between husband and wife. "Where are my children?"

Nakazzi motions feebly and lifts two mounds of cloth. Like a wounded animal, Renga Moi roars his pain, shaking and mad with grief.

The Priest enters, raises his arms as if to stop the storm that is Renga Moi.

Warrior and Priest face one another in a power struggle that will determine the very continuation of this community. Joseph and Robert locked in conflict before the waiting company, which is improvising half sounds, cries that could tip them into oblivion.

"You have brought pollution upon us," accuses the Priest. "My laws had to be followed."

"I have saved our land," retorts Renga Moi. "We are free."
Faces go stiff, eyes and mouths gape wide with shock.
"You cannot challenge my power," roars the Priest.
"You cannot challenge the people."
Renga Moi allows the purification ritual but reluctantly.
He is led to a teeming mound of earth, a tower of termites.
A fantastic weave of arches. To be purified, he must climb
through it.

Robert walks Joseph through the crawling insects played
now by the actors. Speaks him through it. "Renga Moi is no
longer the warrior," says Robert. "He must become a human
sacrifice to survive this torture chamber and emerge newborn,
knowing this supreme test shall not destroy him."

Each actor now also follows Renga Moi, taking their own
turns in the suffocating mound, squirming through its horrors, hunching against the swarming, biting, stinging insects.

A complicated choreography. Drums building slowly. One
by one, Renga Moi and the people return to sunlight, blinking
and disoriented.

When it is over, Robert asks each where they were, how they
experienced this agony.

"I was in a slave house," says Charles "waiting for a boat to
take me far away. The stings were the tips of swords prodding
me along."

"How did you feel?"

"Ashamed. Terrified."

"Good."

Asked where he was, Joseph, naked when he finally crawls
out of the giant mound just sings. "*Zibo ko-ko-ri....* Bring my
children back."

Joseph demands their bodies. Nakazzi, rigid as stone, eyes
closed, turns away, keens for her dead babies. Suddenly, Renga
Moi runs at the Priest and, with one prodigious blow, kills
him. The play is finished. The dictator is dead.

But in that same moment, equilibrium has been destroyed,

the balance between past, present, and future. All will perish in the failing earth. The ancestors!

Is redemption possible at all? Even for those with right on their side?

The actors continue their work, continue to change and multiply ideas.

Dawn. Renga Moi towers above the body of the fallen Priest. He draws the bloody cloak carefully over his own shoulders.

He himself has now become both warrior and priest. Saviour. Dictator. As the play ends.

"What will happen," they all ask Robert. "Will Renga Moi succeed?"

"We don't know. All we know for sure is that he has sustained loss. We all have."

"Why does one always have to lose so much?" asks Mara, the angry gadfly of the group.

"He has learned," says Robert finally, "the cost of upsetting divine balance."

"But why couldn't someone less important than Renga Moi be sacrificed?" Mara persists.

"Because then the value of the knowledge gained would be less."

"What knowledge?"

"Real knowledge."

"We do learn from it," says Charles, in rapt silence until this moment.

"Great tragedies," Robert concludes "always end in knowledge. Yes. We do learn."

A new Kampala also begins to take shape. Slowly the ministries re-open their doors. With a general in charge of everything.

In order to get the company out, Robert has requested support for touring abroad. A small amount — barely enough to cover daily expenses — is granted. Robert reaches into his own bank accounts for the rest. He tells Abafumi he knows where to get more.

He has also asked for new housing to accommodate the company in Kampala. Empty homes of Indian businessmen are offered and, after much debate, accepted. With barely enough to eat, the company suddenly finds itself in luxury living quarters.

Charles stares at the ornate ceiling of his new flat. Sky blue and gold. Bright tendrils curling around a crystal chandelier in sunbursts. Elaborate. Ornamental. Shiny hardwood floors reflecting it all. Pure white walls blind him, fill him up, drive everything from his mind.

Draperies hang in unexpected places, hiding secrets. Oil lamps glow coldly. Archways intersect, each painted with a different scene: miniature crowned elephants, peacocks and flowers, their nodding heads alive as snakes. Veiled women dance in the bedroom, their starry saris intricately entwined.

A maze of delights, the compound boasts an inner garden, flowers, and a mango tree with plump mauve fruit ripening over high walls that block off the angry streets.

He feels guilty. They all do. Like usurpers. As though they have killed a king and taken over his wealth, usurped a ruler. But no one declines these free and sumptuous spaces.

Military transport is also available to them any time they wish. But they wish they did not need, so often now, to be stuffed into army vehicles and hurtled away like convicts. In open jeeps they roar through the sights and sounds of this new Kampala, a loud humming, a speeding ring of unpredictability. Trying not to see just beyond the urban buzz, people hurrying out of sight, slipping into doorways and down alleys. Trying not to be seen.

Abafumi gathers at the Serumaga family's own compound in the "big shot" section of the city, a rambling estate, long owned by his family, which has become the new artistic command post. A pale palace, with many rooms immaculately set on green grounds. Perfect for their own dictator. His personal White House.

Guest rooms display grand chairs — supple leather and carved wood — that remind Charles of Father's judging chair, chairs that tell everyone how important the people are who own and occupy them.

Robert has an imported sound system and tape recorders. Music of all kinds that can be used in the service of art.

But tonight, Robert wants to party. He knows he cannot do this on a regular basis because his wife and children are not part of the company and they would not understand so easily. Tonight, though, they are away. His wife, particularly, would misconstrue the rather special attachments that her husband has developed for two of the beautiful young women in the group, Kiri and Mara, who casually accept Robert's regular attentions. All in the interest of art, of course. But can Robert's theatre wives be so easily accommodated in his own home?

If this a double standard, it is never questioned by any company member. Especially in Robert's presence. Especially on a night like this, when strong spirits conspire with joy. Robert loves his women almost as much as he loves his company. Almost as much as Charles loves them. Robert's youngest and most avid student, Charles watches him constantly, learning his every move.

Joro, an inspired musical improviser, begins to play his own version of Santana. Mellowed by beer, by a sense of accomplishment in their daily work, temporarily exalted in some sort of diplomatic exclusivity, all join in the music — Kasa on bass, Willy on bongos to praise their Chief, their Main Man, their Leader. It is he who has shown them the way and it is he who is now able to lavish some modest luxury on them, making them one.

Kiri and Mara now sing his praises musically as fervently as any griot. They improvise and embellish, growing louder and more outrageous. Robert sends back his own greetings until they jointly exhaust voice and energy. Through the long evening, Robert drinks and sings, sings and drinks, letting go the ascetic in his soul. Disappering for long stretches of time with his two favourite women.

So many secrets still to learn.

Ways of being in the world.

Word is out. Abafumi wields influence, is becoming a force to be reckoned with. On an increasingly regular basis, Robert is seen meeting foreigners. At his home. In hotels. American dollars appear in abundance.

Internationally, however, Amin's Uganda is a pariah. So who are these contacts Robert speaks of? What is their business together?

A tour is quickly announced. Abafumi will go to Europe and perform.

Tickets are booked.

Charles will now fly. For the first time.

On the plane, Charles shivers like a new baby in a cold bath. The shock of water. Air. Airborne. Free and trapped, He huddles in the long dim tunnel, praying. He is certain this great shuddering and vibrating steel womb will split wide open and spew him out. As the wheels leave the ground, he shuts his eyes and prepares for death.

"It's okay," says Beth softly, seated beside him. "We are safe. You are safe." She takes his hand.

Now, the metal beast roars like thunder and the ground falls away. Charles sits frozen in his seat, watching Entebbe Airport recede from sight. Watching it turn into a tiny map and then, incredibly, a pinpoint of light before clouds enshroud him.

Abafumi is en route to Amsterdam for a major international

engagement. A festival of experimental theatre. Accommodation and meals. Modest money in their pockets.

Slowly, Charles relaxes. Everyone starts talking now, joking. Turning to one another, kneeling over seats. There are only a handful of other passengers on this plane heading first to Cairo and then on to Europe.

Willy pulls out a small drum and his nervous fingers fly over the skin. It is a cue. Joro and Kasa begin tuning strings, plucking at songs they all know. Robert joins in. Soon the whole plane is alive, rocking its way to an opening night in a strange new playground that tantalizes them all.

Dinner is served. They return to their seats. Robert announces that the plastic food they have before them is edible. "But just barely."

A Dutch passenger — impressed by their artistic credentials — offers to buy beers for everyone in the company. But Robert politely refuses the offer, explaining that it is strict company policy not to drink alcohol or use drugs.

The facade must be maintained here. Robert is good at facades. They have all come to understand that.

"You are dedicated," remarks the businessman. Robert smiles broadly. He winks at his actors, remembering the enormous amount of beer they had been drinking just nights before.

They eat. They do not drink. Some sleep. But not Charles. He is alive to every new sensation. Hanging in space among so many possibilities.

It is announced they will land soon in Cairo. A forty-five-minute refuelling stop. But they cannot get off, cannot see the pyramids. Charles is disappointed.

"Another time," says Beth.

With touch-down, there is a mighty thump and then a huge roar. Beth tells him to raise the window shade. He is sure they are still careening through the air and will tumble to earth any moment. He is sweating when the plane comes to a stop.

The scene is repeated as they leave Cairo. And again when

they arrive in Amsterdam. Charles lifts his shade and sees Europe for the first time. All cement. So many planes. So many men in orange suits. Lights.

Europe is truly amazing.

The company files into the immigration building, show passports, have them stamped. Signs glare. A wait for their bags. Then onto the bus that will take them to their hotel.

Charles feels homeless under the overcast skies, in the chill October dampness. The air smells of rain. But not African rain. This is concrete rain. Big city rain. Old rain. Rain that has fallen for centuries on pavement.

As they enter the city, he is fascinated by the maze of waterways around them and the large number of small boats on the water, some glass covered. Railings rising symmetrically from the dams and bridges, directing the water, turning it this way and that, around corners and under houses.

Everything is so ordered, Charles thinks. The tall buildings, their wooden tops curling and draping into fanciful shapes. He watches the autumn leaves flutter restlessly between the buildings.

Beth points out the large hooks on each floor of the skinny houses. "To get furniture up," she tells him. "I read that the staircases are too narrow." He tries to imagine living in one.

The bus edges forward, past a flower market. A little further on, stalls sell coats and combs and socks. Not so different from Kampala. He sees a barrel organ making relentless circus music, and a tame monkey grinding along.

In their tall, skinny hotel, Charles has a room to himself. And a bathroom in the hallway. Exhausted, he sleeps and sleeps.

They are to visit the theatre the next afternoon. Then in the evening there will be a technical rehearsal.

Breakfast is odd. Meat and cheese, bread and coffee. They have all slept fitfully.

Only one street away, they are told, is Holland's most important theatre museum. Charles wonders what could possibly be kept in it. They trudge off to see what Dutch theatre tradition is about. Mostly costumes and sets. Devices for sound effects. A sign invites them to create their own storm. They shake a wide hunk of metal. Thunder. Beth adds rain, her voice pattering like drops on parched leaves.

"And I am wind," bellows Charles, his cry released like pain through a body, screaming then fading.

Photos and promptbooks and programs. Charles is assaulted by a history not his own.

Lunch is *rijsttafel* in a small Indonesian restaurant where dish after dish is placed before them. Tangy tastes of many colours. Some sharp like real food.

They have two hours off before a rehearsal at the strangely named Mickery Theatre — Amsterdam's premiere experimental venue. A few company members decide to have their own look around the town. Charles is delighted to escape Robert's rigour for a bit. He takes Beth's hand.

She guides him through cobbled streets, keeps him barely afloat so he does not drown in his wonder. He stands transfixed by a naked wooden angel smiling at him from under an awning. He is fascinated by a delicate birdcage in a window worked into a tangle of levels and areas as complicated as the dense foliage of high trees. He is enchanted by a wooden rocking horse in an antique shop with wheels and bright eyes, ready to take him anywhere.

When he finally looks around for Beth, she is nowhere to be seen. He is surrounded by extravagant strangeness. And entirely alone. Lost.

He comes to a narrow maze of streets buzzing with nightclubs and large bold signs that remind him of Mombasa. He realizes how revealing clothing can be when it is a scrap of material strategically placed, a satin ribbon or a gauzy scarf. One club advertises "erotic live shows" and displays over its door a red fringed curtain with the legs of a woman. She is upside down, the rest of her falling into a yellow pillow. On her legs are black net stockings studded with stars, garters that plunge down into the billowing material, and shoes as long and sharp as daggers.

Charles stands in front of another shop window looking directly at a woman in a bikini. She moves. She is not a mannequin. She is real. She is all red sparkles and he cannot tell how anything stays on. She is smiling at him and turning this way and that. She is available to him. Like merchandise on display. Under a red neon light.

He sleepwalks past window after window of many such powdery bare-limbed girls, all white and wiggling and winking. But he must not be late for rehearsal. If only he had a watch.

He begins to walk faster and then faster. Out of this maze of streets, as confusing as bush tracks. He doesn't want to be fondled or eaten or attacked. He only wants out.

Totally lost now, he steps in front of a vast complicated church with high spires and long windows, larger than anything he has ever seen. Looking for someone to direct him, he enters by a wooden door and disappears into the grand gloom. He sits alone in a pew, allowing the pillars and arches and vaults — the secret, sacred corners where the angels and apostles of Jesus live — to comfort him.

"We don't know where he is," chorus the three young women simultaneously. Robert is furious.

"You are responsible for one another," he says. "Check the hotel again. He could get robbed. Or worse. Was he carrying his passport?"

"He doesn't let it go," says Beth.

"Tell me next that he is carrying his whole month's per diem."

"He is."

Having missed the rehearsal completely, Charles finally creeps into the hotel with his haul: a pair of new shoes, two blue shirts and a knock-off watch. He sees Robert in the bar. Worse,

Robert sees him. "Stop!" comes the imperious voice. "You think you are invisible?"

Charles freezes, his whole being concentrated in guilty apprehension. "I'm sorry Robert, I was exploring the city with the others and I got lost."

"You didn't come here to sightsee. You came here to work. Even if you are not on the stage, you have responsibilities — like showing up for rehearsals. You deserted us."

Charles melts under the erupting volcano.

"I am not paying you to be a tourist. You are an actor in a theatre company. Doesn't that matter to you?"

The company has gathered around, witness to his public humiliation. "Go and pack. I will arrange for a car to pick you up later tonight and take you to the airport. You will return to Kampala."

"No," says Charles. "Please. I'm sorry. I got lost."

Looking around at his fellow company members, he realizes what a shambles he has made of his first foray into the big world. But most of all how he has failed Robert.

Staring pointedly at his delinquent, Robert says with finality, "Didn't you hear me? Go."

No-one — including the director himself — is sure how serious he is.

"Give him another chance," interjects Kiri, speaking for everyone. "He has been a good worker except for today. He is a good actor. And he makes us laugh." Kiri has become expert at wooing Robert, teasing him with her imprecations. He can rarely resist her but even she feels his steely edges at this moment. "Give him some time. He deserves another chance. And we need him in the show."

"He is stubborn," the director finally says. "But so easily seduced."

"Just like you," she purrs, leaning into him. The others have drifted quietly away. This night, Robert does not even try to resist.

Charles is given a reprieve. Probation until the end of the tour. He is ecstatic.

Expectations fly high for Abafumi. The Festival has arranged numerous interviews for Robert. He wants to speak of art, total theatre, Antonin Artaud. But the journalists only clamour for the politics of Africa, the real news of Idi Amin and the chaos he makes.

The theatre is sold out for all eighteen performances of *Renga Moi*. The director of the festival has already spoken with Robert about extending the tour. About Belgrade, Brazil, and perhaps even Tokyo. Even the Ugandan Embassy will be attending the opening. A reception afterwards. They must all come. Meet the officials. First company from Uganda. Africa. Interviews. Charles is slightly bored with all of Robert's public relations.

Although the opening performance is a huge success in the press, it is only passable for Robert. He lectures the whole company late that night on what he calls the discrepancy between popularity and artistic relevance. In the light of their positive reviews, however, Charles finds his dissatisfaction ungenerous.

Although careful, he finds himself occasionally challenging Robert lately. "The public and the journalists are too easily pleased," is all Robert will say.

"But the audience…"

"Audience response is no indicator. Crowds also react to sex and circuses. You know that."

"How can we be responsible for audience tastes as well?" asks Charles.

"Artists are also teachers. Teaching is hard work."

"But you are the toast of Amsterdam," pleads Kiri, "An African theatre magician. They compare you to Peter Brook, to Grotowski."

"False flattery," he shoots back. "They don't know what else to say. And if merely prancing about in feathers and loincloths is enough, then we might as well go back home."

"Maybe we should go back," says Joseph soberly. "Have you seen Amin's latest edicts?"

"Every day we hear news of more gruesome deaths," Beth adds with a catch in her voice. "My cousin…"

"Right now we can do more good here," Robert retorts. "We would probably be thrown in jail at home like everyone else who speaks out. And we would die there."

Robert wants to extend the tour. There is agreement.

"Only when Renga Moi is as sharp as a spear can we go home with confidence," he finishes.

Robert has even suggested playing in the U.S. He meets often with Americans. Government people too. But there are no invitations from the States and no American performances scheduled. Still American money is the coin of their realm. Each week they are paid in crisp U.S. bills. Where does it come from? Charles wonders.

He asks Beth about the currency. "Don't stick your nose in too far," she cautions him one day. "Don't ask questions about that sort of thing. If he pays in U.S. dollars, it's fine. Okay?"

Charles agrees to bite his tongue. But the question remains. For weeks. For months. For years.

In a flurry of activity, new agreements are reached, contracts signed, visas obtained for everyone. Who is opening these doors for them?

From Holland, they move on to Bitef in Yugoslavia, then to Tampere, a small city in Finland. Similar successes. Similar interviews. Similar talk.

On a cold Sunday afternoon, the actors have toiled up a long steep path to an old-fashioned sauna deep in the Finnish countryside. Mingling easily with the local people at this shrine, they breathe in sweet honey wafting up from clover. A wooden tea-shop on top of the small mountain creaks like a ship at sea. Charles is gaining confidence each day. In a photo, he stands next to Robert, beaming. The caption on the picture reads "Africans Find Finland Bracing."

Charles is appreciative of his new celebrity status, enjoys being introduced to reindeer meat, lingonberry jam, and lakka berry preserves. In this rewarding fashion, weeks flash by. But he needs to speak with Robert before they leave the Tampere Festival.

He peers through the steam of the hotel's sauna trying to find his director. It is hard to see as water hisses off heated stones. The glistening forms of Joseph, Joro, and Willy sitting in rough white towels on wooden benches look like holy men.

Uganda seems so far away. Dark and hot and lost.

He looks through the mist and recognizes Robert seated close by. He suddenly hears the strike of birch on bare skin. "It is good for the circulation," booms Robert's voice. "Beat out all the sins. Sweat them out." Charles feels the sting of the branch on his own back.

"Have you learned your lesson yet, Charles?"

"Which one is that?" Charles asks in response.

"How to use a sauna of course." Robert laughs. "You know you remind me so much of myself. When I criticize your shortcomings, I am criticizing my own. You realize that."

Charles is surprised by this sudden candour. It is hard for him to imagine what similarities the maestro sees between them.

"You have my weakness for the good life. Pleasures of the flesh. Food, clothes, drink. And women."

Charles has certainly sampled a few of the items from Robert's list of delights. And knows he is attracted by all of them. He has been caught in flagrante once with Beth.

"I created this company on group loyalty and self-discipline. If I personally indulge in 'mistakes' once in a while, it is my privilege. You have to earn those privileges. That way lies freedom."

"Yes, sir. I understand."

Charles is determined now not to lose his place in this pantheon of pleasure. He's heard talk of other exotic places. Jamaica. Brazil. He is in awe of Robert's abilities to find them venues, his connections and power.

"How, how do you do it?" he asks Robert hesitantly. "How do you know so many people in so many places?"

Beth has told him more than once that this is none of his business. And he knows it.

"Too many questions, Charles."

"Why do we always get paid in U.S. dollars?"

Robert now heads out of the sauna. "Not so much thinking. Enough for today. Let's try the lake. Maybe it will wake us up."

"Yes, sir. The lake."

His smile brittle as ice, Robert winks at Charles and veers off.

The American government. Could the rumours be true? Why would they be paying Robert? His head full of questions, Charles plunges after his director into the freezing lake.

3. ON THE MOVE

IN JAMAICA CHARLES MEETS AFRICANS for the first time outside Africa who call this land of palm trees and beaches home. Who call him and his fellow actors "the Africans." Who call themselves the chosen people. "Why don't they want to return to Africa?" he asks Joro. "Why would they want to stay here in permanent exile?"

"Because Africa sold them out, sold them as slaves to the whites."

"The Arabs in Kenya. They were the ones who sold East Africans like us as slaves. They should blame the Arabs," says Charles.

"But it was black Africans who were complicit with the Arabs. And with European slavers. Without African cooperation in slavery, there would be no blacks in Jamaica. It started with us. We have to take some responsibility for the slave trade. That's how they see it here. So why should they go back?"

Charles is fascinated by the political anger and aggression he finds among these Africans he meets in Jamaica. He listens carefully to the English and even the Creole spoken — with its mix of Spanish and French — and hears traces of his own story in it. Echoes of languages the whole company speaks, as though it had been forgotten in some remote time and then re-discovered, syllable by syllable, achieving new patterns, fleeting ensigns from different cultures fluttering on many tongues.

And he sees what isn't Africa.

Cruise boats plying back and forth in their prescribed patch of ocean between the invisible fences that separate one "whites only" hotel resort from the next. Bright sun umbrellas shading nearly naked bodies stretched out on blankets all over the beach. Canvas chairs spread flat to match, each hotel marking its spot, assertively planting its own special tourist flags along the shore.

He sees the striped awnings and the white painted steel drums of reggae bands while Joro continues to share with Charles his recent readings on the politics of the African diaspora. "Some of the slaves who were brought here escaped," Joro informs him as they sit watching pale green waves whisper over white sand. "My book said that they became known as maroons"

"Why maroons?"

"It's from a Spanish word for untamed. That's how the British saw them."

The British. Charles does not know how to think about them anymore. They were everywhere.

"They started coming here as slaves in the 1500s. They were mostly from West Africa — Senegal, Benin, Nigeria. Many Yoruba. Mandinke. But once here, some escaped to the mountains. Then they began raiding the plantations, stole cattle, burnt crops, and freed other slaves. The British could never catch them. They believed these Africans possessed witchcaft."

"Why?"

"Because they were so clever and because the British needed a reason for never being able to catch them. There are all sorts of legends about warriors disappearing into rocks or turning themselves into trees before slitting the throats of British red-coats marching through the forest."

"I like their jerk cooking. Spicy, like our food."

"Pure West Africa. But still Africa!"

"So we are at home," says Charles, smiling broadly at the concept, smiling at the women admiring him, knowing how much the local men also admire their women.

He feels calm when he looks up and sees cows and chickens moving lazily among a handful of shacks, or at a woman with a suitcase full of strung shells that she will sell to tourists, telling them the names of the various coral: brain, finger, staghorn.

Two days later, Robert is waiting at the university residences where they are staying. He has given three press interviews already and a lecture at the Creative Arts Complex on the evolution of *Renga Moi*. The entire three-week run is already sold out.

But Robert is angry again. He hears that some of his actors have been strutting around the university like movie stars. Now he gathers them all but speaks most directly to Charles. "You are not Bob Marley."

Kiri laughs out loud. "That's true. We're not paid enough."

"And you won't be," he snaps at her. "If you want to be real artists you have to live truthfully. Real artists don't show off that way. Even here."

"We're just having a bit of fun," says Beth.

"Hey mon," quips Willy. "I be Bob Marley. Me great."

"You don't know what it is to be great. You want real greatness then look at Derek Walcott. There's greatness." At rehearsal the previous afternoon, they read Walcott's poetry out loud.

Charles knows Robert's gaze at these times. Can't look at him when he gets so serious. When his mood is dark.

"Smoking pot and wiggling your bums on the beach to bongos is not how you become great. I don't want to see that, especially when my own kids are around. It's not acceptable."

Ah, Robert's children. That's what it's about. Charles and Willy have seen Robert's pubescent daughters on the moonlit beach on more than one occasion, cold beers in hand, watching limbo dancers and fire-eaters, listening to the sea heave and sigh.

"I don't know why you brought the family here," says Kiri. "They get in the way."

For several in the company there is even a bit of jealousy

around this situation. Robert and his own family are installed at a four-star hotel while the actors are made to bunk in with students at a dormitory. The family's presence is an issue for them all.

Robert has targeted every company member at some point for one misdemeanor or other. Now it is Charles' turn. Again.

"We had better find you more to do Charles. You seem to be spending really excessive amounts of time with the local women. I have been given a list of several girls already by university security who have suggested to me that you are compromising them."

"They're compromising me, Robert," says Charles to general laughter.

"And you can't say no?"

The truth, of course, is that Charles doesn't want to say no. In fact, the first night, he actually found himself involved with one of the security women who had initially shooed him out of a student's room. Ten years older than Charles, Safety Sue, as he calls her, turned imperiously on him under starlight and he found he simply could not refuse her command that he kiss her. The next day they were spotted driving together, careening through Kingston on the creamy seats of her father's convertible.

Charles admitted to Joro that he was still seeing images of her body in front of his eyes all the time, naked in the sea, naked when night dropped down and the crickets sang. Naked while the screen sucked wind and curtains billowed like white sea ghosts, urging them roughly on through thick blackness.

Only onstage is Charles able to recover his primary focus. Robert has to stop being his parent. After all, Charles is now nineteen.

That evening, Robert continues the attack. "You realize," he says calmly to Charles, "they are writing about us in the press. They say that they love our theatre because we are expressing their stories. We are heroes here and we must act like heroes."

"That's exactly why this woman wants me," reasons Charles. "She wants you because you are good looking. You are just another scalp in her belt. Don't you know the difference between real and fake? She doesn't love you, Charles. She doesn't worship you. You are just a prize. In Trenchtown at the Marley house, you saw the real life of this island. It is crumbling concrete like at home, gang wars and deserted schools, rusting tin roofs and barbed wire fences, garbage gutters and broken bridges. That is the reality here too. Not just resorts. Not this policewoman. She could be a spy."

A spy? For whom? Amin? This stops Charles cold.

"We have a responsibility here, Charles. You simply cannot parade around like a playboy. That is not on. And you are driving me mad with your antics. You really are."

"It is not my intention, sir, but it is you who have given me that strength. Anyway, Why would Amin or the CIA care what we do in Jamaica?"

"Both of them are watching us." Charles is stunned.

"I'm giving you a week's notice."

"Notice of what?"

"Show me you can behave for a week and you can have some of your social life back."

"What does that mean?"

As it turns out, Robert's idea of proper behaviour means that after each performance, Charles must return directly to the residence. What Robert does not know is that Safety Sue meets him there each night. After almost every performance, with meals and high quality pot — all in the service of the pleasure that is their nightly ritual.

She even puts on her own very private performances for him, swinging and swaying breasts, with wisps of clothing, a wave of red and yellow, a gold turban piled high on her head, her long thick lashes hooding a sexuality directed only at him.

He sees her everywhere, moving under blue sky, against waxy green leaves. He watches her like a flower found in grass.

Even under house arrest, his daytime schedule remains the same. The whole company are up at six, run three miles, have breakfast, do warmups and vocals for an hour, work on text and improvisation.

The second morning after his talk with Robert, he is disastrously late, kept up most of the night by Sue-induced pressures of the flesh. At nine, he realizes he has slept in, jumps into a cab — still pulling on socks and shoes — in a frantic attempt to get to the rehearsal hall and insinuate himself into what is happening. Robert sees but opts to ignore Charles, staring resolutely past him, as though he is not there. He is lecturing the group about interviews and whether they should be speaking out on social issues, political issues.

Amin, Robert tells them, has decided to invite a delegation of Jamaican film stars to Uganda to exchange views about "self-determination in black societies." Given that Amin is destroying Uganda, should they try to discourage the visit? They will be asked, says Robert.

"Surely we do not support Amin's policy of Uganda as an anti-Asian state," remarks Joseph who, like Joro, is always probing the political edges, a custodian of the group's higher purposes.

"We are not politicians," declares Robert after a pause. "Many artists have said that it is the purpose of art simply to raise the appropriate questions. It is up to others to answer them. Personally, I think we do need to know our political position on this going in."

That evening, Robert is watching from a distance as Charles enters the dressing room. For a change, Charles is early. When he sits down in front of the communal mirror to prepare himself for the performance, Robert's deep voice booms out. "You cannot sit there Charles. Your place is gone."

Charles is stunned. Staring straight ahead he responds firmly, "This is my place. I am part of this group."

"No longer."

"Robert. You cannot kick me out. This is my life now. You can't just take it away. You are not God. I'm sorry I was late this morning. I was not feeling well."

"If you stop cavorting all night you might feel better in the morning. You cannot continue to break our rules. I will not allow that. You are good on the stage, Charles, but you have to be as good off the stage. And you are not helping things."

As the others arrive, they listen to the debate. Whatever Robert is going to do, they know he has his reasons.

Charles stands up. He bows his head before Robert's gaze. Before the rest of the group. "I know I have put you through hell and I am sorry. But…"

"But what, Charles."

Charles looks at his leader. "I have never seen a woman so beautiful. I love her."

Robert asks the company to wait outside. Clearly, Charles is the devil himself. Robert no longer resists.

"Tell me about her."

"To look at this girl naked, Robert, would drive you crazy. Her breasts are round milky moons. Come out with us. You will see. I mean really see. She's watched you onstage. She'll agree."

After the performance, Robert drives with Charles and his lady to a beach pavilion where the moon bronzes a sea undulating like silk. There, the three of them get drunk. As the island breezes blow and patio peacocks shudder colour into the air, as small sharks cruise in lights shooting off the pier, Robert's gaze drinks her in. Jointly they toast the glories of Jamaican women and the treachery of beauty. Then all three swim naked in the sea. Charles sleeps alone that night. His woman is on loan to the hero of his life.

The next day Robert says simply to Charles, "I want your energy on the stage. You are dissipating your force. You are performing in too many places and in too many ways. We have to find out how to channel that energy.... And she is extraordinary, Charles. I'll give you that."

Charles tries to call Mother from the hotel. There is only one working phone in Mother's village and no one is picking up. He then tries Samuel who has been staying at Charles' house in Kampala for the week.

Samuel describes the city as hell. Streets clogged with beggars. People missing body parts. Hands. Legs. "The whole place is crippled and deformed," his friend says over a crackling connection. Like somebody fondling a phantom limb, Charles cannot believe so much is gone. Amin's security people are everywhere.

"Is my place okay?" Charles asks.

"Two windows have been broken," he is told.

"Also, the lock on the front gate was badly dented from hammer blows."

He imagines the rest from Samuel's careful words. Furniture hacked by vandals, bright fabrics torn, the immaculate white walls gouged, paintings taken, the chandelier smashed.

"Thieves had broken in before I arrived," Samuel finishes, almost apologetically, "and they were thorough. Nothing of value was left untouched."

"Before I left home, I did go over to your house to see your family," Samuel says. "Debra is recovering slowly. Returning breath by breath. But she is only a faint semblance of your sister. Your father is away more and more. Your mother is always sad. And seems so much older."

"I should be there, Samuel," he moans urgently into the phone.

Charles has no argument when his friend tells him to stay out of Uganda.

His only hope now is Robert and the work that is Abafumi.

A few weeks later, they are off again. This time their plane floats over Brazil, a ring of foamy sea nuzzling against dark rounded hills called the Moros that herd Rio's stately white buildings into a glistening phalanx on the edge of the sea. All blue and green, netted in pearly humidity.

"This place is large and generous," Robert tells Charles. "Like a fine woman who flaunts herself because she knows she is irresistible. This woman, this Rio, is the soul of Brazil."

At the airport, the company is met by a handful of enthusiastic hosts. Charles watches Robert separate from the group for a few moments to speak with yet another white man in dark glasses. Joro mutters "CIA" under his breath. Charles sees Robert take a bulging envelope from the stranger and quickly put it in his pocket. Robert passes a brown envelope back.

Clearly their tour now has many agendas. Is the CIA involved? If so why? What can Robert possibly be offering them?

The actors take an official "artistic" walk around the city. They are to observe and absorb. Robert is the only one near the guide. If Robert thinks it important, he informs the others of some place or thing. They hear Portuguese for the first time.

"Some of the roots of Brazilian Portuguese are African," says Joro. "Did you know that, Charles?"

As they walk, the heat reminds them of home. But the Spanish and Portuguese influences do not. Robert leads them toward what looks to Charles like a mountain of rubbish. As they get closer, he sees roofs stacked one upon the other and then realizes he's looking at shacks, each flimsy lean-to balanced precariously in a house of cards. *Favelas*.

"Our village huts are better built than these," Charles comments without thinking.

"Yes they are," agrees Robert. "Because our village huts are built for rural living. These are thrown together from scraps, never meant for a permanent urban world. They are without water or proper sewage. These slums of Rio are an open sore. You remember the socialist reforms of Obote? He wanted proper housing for all. Socialism thinks about things like that."

What's he trying to tell us now? wonders Charles.

Robert has really taken to speaking in riddles lately. When he is with the group, he can no longer say anything directly. He implies everything. He is not free here, thinks Charles. In fact, Robert always seems to be looking behind, anticipating eyes upon him by someone unexpected.

"We are artists, not politicians," Joro says to no one in particular. "We can't make these decisions in our art. But in our lives, maybe we can. And if we need more help maybe we should ask the CIA."

Everyone takes a deep breath. The word has been spoken aloud.

"As artists," counters Robert, "we might be able to influence decisions. Let's leave the CIA out of our vocabularies."

Is this a direct command or the slightest indication of uncertainty?

Charles looks up over the sweltering hotbox *favelas* that culminate in a high hump-backed rock, rounded and hardened by wind. Then, before them, rising from the middle of this unforgiving shape called Corcovado is a three-story statue of Jesus Christ, arms spread wide — in despair or hope or supplication — looking straight out to sea, the ultimate icon of Rio. Cristo Redentor. Christ the Redeemer, breathtaking and disturbing. Watching them.

To Charles, the city seems self-assured. Elements in harmony. He walks past windows spilling light onto dark gardens alive with fireflies. Rio is elaborate. Blue bays lacing tight the extravagant rock cones that frown over it day and night.

For the first few days of their visit, the main topic of local newspaper headlines is the kidnapping of a baby girl. Will it affect the audience? They find themselves discussing the fate of the child — Isobelita as everyone calls her — over meals and during their walks. Inflation and the cost of living, the usual political crises, have been put aside to focus on the fate of the child. Joro tells them that Brazilians actually have a special name for dead children. They call them "little angels." And the coffin-makers do a booming business in tiny paper-trimmed boxes. Blue for boys and pink for girls. Strange.

"They are poor," says Robert. "They die of malnutrition or bad food. In the *favelas,* parents spoil their kids with all the wrong things because they cannot afford the right things. They can kill their children out of love with bad medicines and sweet syrups."

The idea that love can kill stays with Charles.

The opening is one of the strongest performances yet of *Renga Moi.* The death of the twins brings an audible gasp from the packed audience. Real tears flow from the balcony. The orchestra floor is filled with less emotional viewers, mostly the wealthy of Rio who have come to get a dose of culture. And politicians. And ambassadors. Eyes everywhere.

The opening night party prances, struts, and shimmers with style and verve, lavishing rich Brazilian food and drink on its high society guests. *Churassco* in its appetizing variety and *caipirinhas,* the alcoholic fantasy of sugared lime and ice. The celebration is especially solicitous of its visiting artists in their traditional dress.

Robert adopts an ironic stance, observing the sharply tailored tuxedoes and seductively flowing gowns that corner and curtain his brightly African troupe of vulnerable young performers. He fears he has let them loose to the lions, blinded by faith, their gaze resolutely on heaven while their flesh is torn to pieces.

He knows even better who is watching.

Tonight they will suffer in ecstasy. Time enough to resurrect, he decides, after a day off.

The Ministry of Culture asks if the company would like anything special. Some want to go to the ballet. Charles, however, knows he is in the country of Pele, the great footballer, and asks if it would be possible to get seats to the match on Sunday with Argentina. When you are a star, apparently, anything is possible. Though the game has been sold out for months, four spaces are found. "Not the best seats but pretty good," they are told.

Charles and his companions couldn't be happier as they join 130,000 Brazilian football fans in the national stadium. They are perched high enough to see everything but close enough to the field to get a sense of the personal dramas unfolding before them. The sea of people roars more deafeningly than crowds in Kampala. When a sure goal is missed, players and spectators weep theatrically. When a goal is scored, the stadium bursts into ecstasy, players kiss and fans hug. When Pele himself scores, the somewhat inebriated Brazilian man next to Charles grabs him by the shoulders and plants two wet kisses on his cheek, yelling over and over, "*Coitado, Coitado!*"

"It means 'poor thing'" shouts the translator beside him. "He is lamenting for anyone not on the Brazilian side."

"And because his team is victorious, he loves you." Joseph laughs. "He has given you a Brazilian embrace. And you know what? He also loves you because he thinks you are beautiful. I believe the secret ingredient of beauty in this country is to have a drop of real African blood in you. That's why they adore Pele to such a degree. He is truly African."

The final score pleases everyone:

Black Brazil: 1. White Argentina: 0.

Charles soon learns that there is much African blood in the soil of Brazil. In fact, oceans of it.

And the press hails *Renga Moi* as enthusiastically as it does Pele.

The next performance venue is Bahia, home to the colonial capital, where their Africanness is greeted even more eagerly by the press and by audiences. They are pursued everywhere they go and photographed as eager tourists. They are shown visiting sugar mills, the engine that helped to create a powerful European empire. They are seen following the steps of African slaves who laboured in the mills and on the enormous plantations that operated the mills. They are photographed among graceful hills and colonial facades, in the Citade Alta of Salvador with its ubiquitous wavering palms and peeling plaster buildings. They are shown the spot where a church was built by slaves in the eighteenth century.

They follow the twisting and winding streets. They see where slaves were auctioned and publicly punished, tied to a post, stripped almost naked, and whipped with rawhide before the assembled Europeans and their own people. Fellow slaves did the whipping.

Charles gazes at a peaceful square, barely breathing in Bahia's noonday heat, trying to understand this land's bloody African-linked history. Listening for the faint echoes of screams shuddering back through the still air. Seeing blood. Flesh torn. Brothers and sisters falling.

Robert tells them that anyone trying to escape was hung by a hook through their ribs and left outside until they died.

They pass a woman cooking at a street stall. Charles notices the jangling collection of silver charms she wears around her waist and asks about it. It is a *balanganda*, he is told, used in the old days to show off the wealth of a slave owner. He watches her hands busy among gleaming aluminum pots and spattering pans, vibrant with their orange, yellow, brown foodstuffs. He knows she is the mistress of her business and her life. She smiles at him. Then asks him to taste something from her cooking pot.

"*Acaraje*," she explains. "Fried bean stuffed with peppered shrimp," she announces in halting English, her eyes glinting in the sun.

"A little Africa in Brazil," he nods appreciatively.

Performances each evening. Tourism most days. Robert has arranged for them to see a *capoiera* performance one afternoon in the fort of San Antonio da Barra. Part martial art, part dance, part song, the actors leap in the air and scream their music. They soar high, eyes wide and muscular arms spread like wings. The sort of acrobatic work that Robert is trying to develop in his own actor-dancers.

Charles studies the musical instruments that are played so brilliantly in the centre of the arena: the drum-like *atabaqu*; the *berimbaus*, stringed, bow-shaped and graceful; the *pandeiros*, punching the air like tambourines; the double-headed *agogo bells*; and the rough scrape of the *reco-reco* with its corrugated surfaces.

"We could be back in our own villages at home," he says, "The music and stories are not so different."

"Except those stories were born of liberty and prosperity, triumph over adversity. These crawled out of captivity and torment," Kiri counters.

In the circle, the rhythm begins slowly, played first on the *berimbaus* and then on the other instruments. Soon the soloist begins to sing his heart-rending story.

"Listen," whispers Joseph, "A Bantu word."

This is a zebra dance, prototype of the Brazilian *capoeira*, they are told, and for them another connection to Africa. The piece increases in complexity and intensity as other players repeat phrases of praise after the solo singer. Then the voices swerve into call and response.

Two performers have now cartwheeled into the arena. They mirror one another in a rocking side step, teasing, taunting, challenging. As the dancers pace around, they vault suddenly into attack and defense. Carefully choreographed. Nothing left to chance.

Their bodies are tying knots in the air, thinks Charles, transfixed by their discipline. Yet they barely touch as they hurl themselves around with dazzling invention.

"Some say," whispers their guide, "that this was all the original invention of Ganga-Zumba, King of Palmares, the greatest of the *quilombos*, the escaped slaves. It was so successful that all such communities adopted its name."

Charles is eager to know more about Ganga-Zumba, the King of Palmares.

"*Capoeira* is really a form of self-defence disguised as a dance," says Robert. "Art can trick. It can reveal while it hides."

"In the seventeenth century," their guide continues, "there were many *Palmares*. Begun as bush hideouts where palm trees grew, these developed into communities of escaped slaves. One of the largest had over two hundred huts, a church, smithies, and even a counsel house. All surrounded by lush stream-watered fields. The escaped slave kings of these communities ruled with extraordinary wisdom and fairness. They also occupied splendid jungle palaces with fine accommodations for their families, attendants, and public officials. In their presence, subjects had to kneel and strike palm leaves with their hands. The kings often had many wives and children."

Charles travels easily back to such kingdoms, the storied palaces he has heard of since childhood.

"The *Palmares* have become one of Brazil's symbols of freedom and fairness. All contemporary African-Brazilian social movements — and there are many — acknowledge those roots."

Robert sees his young actors begin to glow, blooming visibly on the rich fare he's offering them. But he saves the best for last — tickets for the entire company to see *Maria Maria*, a controversial sold-out production that has been playing to admiring houses. Abafumi are to be guests of honour at this performance. Robert has spoken about abstraction in the theatre. He says that this is one of the great examples of how it can work.

As Charles watches, he is filled with many Marias. He lives all her lives.

On stage, the familiar shacks that crawl one over another, up dark hills, stretching away to places where only vultures hang. Maria waits in long lines of women to fill her water bucket. She moves from rural poverty, isolation and boredom, to urban poverty with its greater dangers of disease and crime.

He goes back in time with her. Maria becomes a female slave taken two hundred and fifty years ago. The slave vessel arrives on the African coast. A barricade is placed above the upper deck. Cradling her first-born, Maria is led in shackles to the ship. She turns to look for the last time at her homeland. The vessel trades for beads, textiles, and gold while filling the lower decks with more and more bodies in chains, each sharing tales of terror in other languages, some overcome with panic and grief. Mime. Music.

As the middle passage begins, Maria sings a song of loss. Writhing bodies in mournful rhythms create her agony. She is a rainbow whirling through childhood. Her manacled hands move only in pain. Chained to a rod with other slaves, the chorus staggers and weaves as the whip comes down.

Maria is now a puppet on a stick, poked and prodded to perform. The actors arch and bend, trapped in the music of their story.

Maria, in billowing white, throws back her head, lifts her arms, and rolls her eyes. In the grip of her special *orisha*, her spirit self swaying and singing; when she transports herself, Charles goes to his own place, with Maria. Dancing and singing her life.

At the end of the performance, the two companies embrace. Their bond is artistic, visionary.

"You have understood. You have understood," says Robert.

"No," says their beaming host, "you have understood."

Over drinks, they all agree that *Renga Moi* and *Maria Maria* belong to the same family.

"They are brother and sister," Robert says enthusiastically. "Power and misery danced. All of our history danced. All of the contradictions danced. Making love and finding liberty, danced. Life, the dance of our own truth. May we always dance together in joy," he shouts in his heartfelt toast.

There is one more thing Robert wants for the company in Brazil. It requires an extension of their tour, along with the complications of visa renewals, many trips to the police station, and the passing of generous gifts of cash to officials.

But Robert believes that Rio's Carnival — only an extra week away — is an essential experience for Abafumi — as a popular and multifaceted art form, as a highly indigenous eruption of cultural energy that is both tempestuous and disciplined. He wants them to understand what it is and why it is. To feel its fire.

Charles and Beth spend days in anticipation stretched lazily on Ipanema beach. They spend evenings making love, their newly-awakened relationship heralding Carnival itself. Festive. Wild.

And it is all around them. Headdresses and veils, bangles and billowing silks vie with each other while musicians spin tambourines on their fingertips.

The air is jittery with streamers and confetti. Unfurling, floating, spinning. Charles breathes in the sweet scent of tropical flowers squirted incessantly by "perfume shooters" aiming their fine spray onto his hot skin.

They are startled by a large beaded ox head in black velvet with blue eyes and golden horns towering over dancers who mime the animal's story: how it prances, grows sick, and returns to life amidst great rejoicing. Bush Cow masks rise up before them in black and white squares, faces hard and sharp, rough fibre bodies shaking furiously.

"The square where we are standing, Praca Onze, was called Little Africa," one of the actors from the *Maria* company tells them. "It was a centre," he shouts, "for the African community. Today there are attempts to give it back to the black community. But the government is a bit nervous. They think this will encourage protest."

"Are they right?" asks Robert. Mara, Robert's constant companion now, presses in to hear.

"Probably, but our group is supporting its development. We want to find the political centre of Africa in Brazil once again. But we must do it carefully. The government is always watching us."

The way Abafumi is watched. And watches.

That night Charles and Beth observe Robert and Mara exchange documents with another stranger in the hotel lobby. Quickly. Slyly. Almost unnoticed. Charles will keep the secret to himself. He knows that Robert knows this. Without words, power and responsibility have been conferred.

On Charles.

Riding the chaos of Carnival, Charles and Beth whirl into Brazil's hot hedonistic heart. Still shy with one other, they bear the burn marks of passion awkwardly. It is love they talk of now.

"Robert should not have brought Mara into his life," Beth says one evening. "He was asking for trouble. And now he has it."

"Every couple quarrels," says Charles. "And it is obvious how much he loves beauty. Beautiful women. As I do. Women like you."

"And his wife puts up with it," says Beth disconsolately. "Mara just wanted to shine for a while, have a few nights with someone powerful. Then Robert fell in love with her."

"I didn't see that," says Charles curiously.

"No, men never see those things. She is selfish. She just doesn't realize what she's doing to all of us. They snapped at each other in public this afternoon," she finishes angrily.

Abafumi was supposed to be above all this. Petty squabbles. Jealousies.

"Perhaps," says Charles, "extending the tour wasn't such a good idea."

"No," says Beth. "Giving us time off was the problem. Taking time from his wife for Mara."

"What can he do now?"

"I think he should send her home."

In the morning, the company flies to São Paulo for another run. Robert sits quietly with his wife at the front of the plane. Neither one speaks.

But Sao Paulo cannot hide Robert's tumultuous affair with Mara. It is spinning them both out of control. They miss workouts, warmups. But Robert has to consider his wife. Mara taunts him. Robert tries to ignore her but she is a lion in heat. Pacing now on stage and displaying. Nudging and pawing. With Robert picking up every cue, playing the superior alpha in a pride of fine physical specimens. Tensing for a last preening lick, trying to turn his chosen female glossy and languid.

While the rest of the troupe bristle and squirm.

Robert has re-cast Mara as Renga Moi's wife.

Kiri, whose role it was, is livid.

But Mara is good and everyone recognizes it. In her stage agony she hauls up jagged moans of despair from a cold dark cave. Edgy, dangerous. Robert, like everyone, is impressed with her work.

There is a qualitative difference between his two actresses, both women who have enthralled him. Kiri, rooted in tragic sorrow, rocked by her grief. Rolled her deep sleepy voice up from some dark place, like the very spirit of the underworld itself, like a tree sighing in strong wind, like grass hissing in rain. Kiri was Robert's best student. His best advertisement. His creation. Kiri's solemn face shines like fine carving, a perfect female form sculpted to timeless serenity.

Kiri's eyes bore into Robert now while his appraise the volatile combustion that is Mara. Kiri will not allow herself to be relegated to the status of occasional mistress. She has seen the parade of Robert's beautiful women come and go. She will not be merely one of the pack. Petted and sent off. Like a wife.

Outside the theatre, Kiri cultivates other admirers. In and out of the company. And then suddenly decides to step out of the ring entirely. Into the arms of someone else.

The company follows this new drama with uneasy curiosity.

Lorenzo, Abafumi's official tour guide in Brazil, is Italian. Slick as a grass snake, he is especially watchful of his female charges. With the practiced smoothness of a Venetian gondolier, he slides up and down his practised scales admiring clothes, makeup, the way skirts flutter as his women walk. Slithering along the street like ribbons in the wind, his charms intrigue Kiri and, she notices, deeply irritate Robert.

In extraordinary Brasilia where they spend two days. She giggles as he shows her buildings floating on colonnades, ramps swirling from one level to the next, massive concrete bowls — congress halls, conical cathedrals — flung up into the air on concrete slanting beams and looking as fragile as spider's webs. She doesn't stop smiling at him.

He makes a special stop for the group before two huge bronze forms: women seated on a bench in a clear pool, washing their hair before the presidential palace.

"You see," says Lorenzo, "you women tempt kings and presidents and poor Italian tour guides."

Lorenzo does his work with cheerful efficiency, eventually ending the tour at the theatre where they begin to prepare for the evening show. Kiri thanks him on behalf of the company. He publicly invites her to dinner after the show.

While Robert fumes.

And fights with Kiri. "You are wasting yourself on that cheap gigolo. He will destroy you," Robert barks at her when Lorenzo leaves.

Charles stands with several of the others in uneasy silence listening to Robert and Kiri spit fire at each other.

"I will love him," says Kiri defiantly. "And I don't need your permission."

She is challenging him to a duel in the arena of the erotic. Ranking them equal and opposite. Robert knows she is right, declaring war on male privilege that, until this time, only Robert's wife has ever questioned. Robert storms out of the theatre and Charles, fearing the worst, follows him into the street.

Lorenzo is there waiting for Kiri.

"You are finished working with us," Robert shouts. "If I catch you here again, I will kill you. I will kill you."

"Is this because of Kiri?" Lorenzo asks coolly. "If so..."

"Don't come back for Kiri or for any of us."

"You must be crazy," says Lorenzo baffled. "No woman is worth this!"

Robert pauses for a moment. Then turns away. Screaming at the sky. Hating all women.

In the theatre, Mara and Kiri are together, whispering, crying. Robert is back.

"You two," he thunders at them. "You have caused all this trouble." They turn from him, walk into the women's dressing room and slam the door. "You are the twins," Robert rails. "You have split Priest and Warrior. You have robbed them both of their power."

"No," says Kiri from behind the door. "You are the problem. You and your ego. And your appetite."

"Kiri is right," adds Mara. "You are the problem. I am sorry." Her voice breaks, shallow water over splintered stones.

"Just know," says Robert, "Lorenzo is gone."

Everyone is nervous about that night's performance.

In darkness, the onslaught begins. A flash of spears and a flurry of drums. The Village of the Seven Hills is attacked. Renga Moi takes up arms. Ignores the taboo.

And on this night, Robert begins adding unfamiliar text. Scowling and muttering, he shrieks out, "You will all perish at my hand. I will kill you, personally, one by one, because you have defied me."

"We have not defied you Priest," says Charles, growing before his comrades, improvising lines.

Mara and Kiri stand frozen in fear.

The Priest rises, perilously waving a flaming torch in the frantic search for his children. Scattering the rest of the cast. The audience is enthralled. Theatre and life merge though they don't know it.

Flames. Weapons. Anger and argument.

Nakazzi is suddenly pulled to the centre of the stage by her husband. Kiri stays rooted in one spot. Robert swings at her, knocking her arm roughly as she steps back. Another line is added. "You will be the downfall of us all," she tells him.

The audience is taking sides, shouting their support or their condemnation.

"You are drunk, Priest!" yells Charles in full fury. "You are not going to kill anyone because we are stronger. We do not need you the way you need us."

Robert suddenly stops, looks around, returns to character. Somehow the play finishes.

In the Green Room, there are accusations. Embarrassment. Charles cannot look at Robert who is sitting in silence. Beth adjusts an ice pack on Kiri's arm where she has been bruised by Robert. It is black and blue.

Kiri sobs quietly. Mara has raced away.

Charles cannot bear to see the fine kingdom of Abafumi in such trouble. But the king is down. And now the king exits the room without another word. They are left to face their admiring backstage public alone.

"He cannot do without us," says Joro. "It will be all right."

"We cannot do without him either," says Beth. "He is this company."

Next morning in the hotel, their tension is palpable. Charles and Joseph have called a meeting. Robert is edgy but agrees to come. Everyone is waiting for him when he arrives.

Robert's gaze sweeps the room. Pouring himself a coffee, he sits down. Waits. "Talk to me," he says finally. "What do you want to tell me?"

Behind beige blinds, the streets roar and sweat. Charles, in his capacity as company manager for the São Paulo portion of the tour, will speak for them. He tries to articulate the humiliation of the previous night's performance, how they witnessed their beloved founder and director debase himself and give in to personal rage at the expense of the play. How this action has devastated them all. "You have broken your own rules, sir," concludes Charles. "We don't know how to continue now."

Robert's eyes are small hard pellets. Charles looks around at the others, knowing what comes next.

One by one, each Abafumi member stands and looks directly at Robert.

"I am Beth. I am Baganda. And I resign."

"I am Susi and Muganda. And I resign."

"I am Willy and Muganda. And I resign."

"I am Kiri and…" She stops, unable to look at anyone. She starts to cry. She sits down. The others continue.

Robert is stunned into silence. He did not expect this response. Their names. Their roots. Their decisions to leave him. So profoundly taken.

Charles speaks last. "I am Charles. I am Bahima. And I resign." These are the hardest words he has ever spoken. He doesn't mean them at all. Nevertheless, he knows that only unity, now, can help change anything. Robert has taught them that focus is the power of theatre. And this is a piece of theatre. No doubt.

They need Robert to know what it is like to live by rules he himself invented. And then break them. How dangerous the breaking of those rules can be. They want him to know he is responsible for this. They want him to know consequences.

Mara stands and apologizes to them all.

Kiri stares at the floor but says softly, "It is not you Mara. It is Robert. He has put his own selfish needs before the company. Robert, you have compromised me personally and all of us artistically." She speaks haltingly to this king of kings, this magnificent man whose turbulence, whose love of female flesh has taken them all down.

He watches. He listens. He has avoided all their eyes but now he stares straight at Kiri. As though the others are not there. As though this is only between the two of them. But it is not.

"We are willing to continue," she says, "but only if you resign. We will be Abafumi without you."

Robert takes a moment to absorb this. Almost in a whisper, he begins his response. "This is my company. I have control. You don't dismiss me. I dismiss you. All of you. I'll form Abafumi again with others. I am Abafumi. Not you. I do not accept your ultimatum. You can all leave."

"All right then," says Joro. "We have our answer. We also have our plane tickets home. You perform tonight by yourself. We are leaving."

Slowly, they file out.

"Robert..." Charles hangs by the door, hoping for some last minute reversal of his fate.

"No more words, Charles. It is finished for now." Adding a moment later, "How could you turn against me too? How many chances have I given you?"

"If I have betrayed you, it is by remaining loyal to your own principles," Charles says reluctantly.

"Go home then. Take your treason and find another director for it."

Numbed by Robert's accusation, Charles embraces his treason, takes firm hold of it, insists that it give him something. Decides to change the plane tickets and return to Uganda almost immediately. When he informs the others, they agree it is the only course.

They all hand in their tickets. That afternoon, Charles and Joro trudge morosely along to the airline office, determined to take charge of their own fate. Determined to take the company home. Not knowing what awaits them.

But treason doesn't come cheaply. They are appalled at the cost of changing flights.

"Charles, it's a sign," says Joro. "We are not meant to do this."

Standing before the counter where a clerk smiles mechanically at them from behind his official forms, pen ready to sign away their money, their loyalty, and their future, Charles needs no persuasion.

Every instinct tells him this is wrong. You do not walk out on family. You re-group. You discuss, argue, and debate. But you never break the circle. So they retreat.

Robert sits alone in the hotel bar. It is late afternoon. Those who walk by him see a stone man, stiff and solid. Inside he is a volatile mix of disgust, pride and frustration. Bouncing through space. Rapidly losing light. Tired and scared, he is almost ready to let go. Let the solar winds blow him out.

Charles announces to the actors privately that they cannot return home. It is too expensive. "We must perform."

They are all in the theatre when Robert arrives. He surveys the traitors as they file past. Watching as they get into costume. Framed. Caught. They all squirm in their turn. The mocking make-up mirrors flash everyone's misery. A wall of masks shunning the sun.

Their performance that night is abysmal. At low energy, they stagger through one *mea culpa* after another. Beat the drum of contrition. Renga Moi, no longer a hero, is transformed. A pig-headed opportunist. Nakazzi, a tiresome whiner. The Priest, a vindictive bully. And the villagers a shrill chorus of complainers.

At the end of this travesty of their masterwork, it becomes

blindingly obvious to Charles and perhaps all of them just how much the power of Abafumi is the power of ensemble. The multiple and often simultaneous sparkings of the group into a blaze that Robert may ignite but that, only together, can they fuel. And keep alight.

It is cold ash, however, that piles up in the Green Room. Robert sits before them in silence, his mind frozen. He has killed their spirit. Can he raise them up? Does he have any right? Is he worthy?

Charles feels plagues dropping. Judgement. Hatred. Blame. And bounties. Love. Hope. Need.

Robert finally speaks. "I was wrong to let my personal life interfere with our work. I was wrong and I'm sorry."

The pause is eternity.

"But you were so right about the results," says Joseph at last, putting the whole tangled problem into perspective for them. "It is devastating for the work. We cannot let it happen again. The work is primary."

"How do we avoid it, though?" asks Charles, feeling responsibility. "Especially on tour. What if a critic had been there tonight?"

"I think we must refuse interviews from now on," says Joro. "Those puff pieces distort everything. And we should be very choosy about participating in the roundtables. Even though they are part of every festival, they can turn nasty."

"I think we need some time to heal," says Mara in a childlike voice, looking wistfully at Robert.

"Let's cancel these last performances. I want us to get back to basics, our regular routine of running and working," Robert says finally.

Their days, however, are still tentative, floundering now between wish and reality. They struggle with the realization that fame and, inevitably, politics have sucked purity out of them, creating expectation, making them demand things. That they have been competing with one another for spotlight, celebrity, recognition.

They all know they have traded wonder and excitement for aggression and acquisitiveness. How can they protect their art from this contamination? How do they nourish it again?

Numerous new invitations shimmer before them, a fluttering of indulgence.

They agree to go to the Caracas Festival — one of Latin America's most prestigious experimental gatherings. There they will regroup, play for a full week to a formidable battery of international critics including, for the first time in Abafumi's career, American critics. One from Miami and another from New York. The festival is the wealthiest in Latin America and will help cover various extra costs they've now incurred.

Robert's negotiating ability is back in top form. He continues to revise his life for them. In the interests of professional and dramatic peace, he has even sent his wife and children back to Kampala. Where he hopes they will be safe.

Yet the company remains wary and suspicious. They see Abafumi's substantial house of theatrical reflections thinning to glass. An intricate geometrical space, brittle and transparent. Revealing and exposing them. Randomly. Hazardously.

In Venezuela, unable to hide, they shine reluctantly in a light they cannot extinguish. Fine artists whose fame has travelled before them, even overcoming rumours that their country is dying. That they have abandoned their country after so many months away is transparently clear. But the company's future is not so clear.

Beginning with the increasing presence of people who now seem to be watching them even more closely, grey-suited strangers, always in sunglasses, alone or in pairs. Regularly they see Robert in fleeting conversations with these figures in the hotel lobby where he sits, expressionless, before murals of seas and mountains, while messages are passed to him, from him. Envelopes that show up later when their payroll is due.

Among themselves, the actors whisper questions to each other. Privately. Nervously.

They are uneasy in their new Hilton home, bristling amid the stiff white forest of highrises in Caracus, a dazzling city. In this American bastion of comfort, they can almost forget the city's barrios erupting sullenly on the hillsides. But here Americans are everywhere.

Robert, wanting to make amends, has booked them in this luxury intentionally, ensuring they are splendidly arrayed across several private suites, so they may take their ease on plush couches, behind thick brocade curtains, ordering room service on wheeled tables covered with snowy linen, gleaming glass, and delicate china. Money flows so easily.

After a series of moderate hotels on the tour and good intentions notwithstanding, they warily accept privilege again. His apology to them all. Signing for everything. Watching him buy drinks for the world.

A company of internationally famous African theatre professionals. Adored and afraid.

In the luminous lobby Charles catches Robert's eye — stern as a gargoyle scowling out of stone — and they start a conversation.

Over whiskeys in the bar, Robert asks simply, "How is it with everyone? Are they still angry with me?"

Charles feels flattered to be asked. "I think Kiri is hurt."

"Yes she is." Robert admits he offered her jewellery. A pearl necklace. "I told her I would dive among sharks to find them. Practice abstinence until I have the perfect pearl."

"That's quite a line, Robert," says Charles smirking. "Did she believe it?"

Robert smiles. "It is a good line but it's not mine. You know the Spanish colonizers used to forbid their pearl fishers any sexual activity until they had recovered their quota of pearls because they believed that sexual gratification made their divers more buoyant, preventing them from penetrating deeply enough into the pearl beds."

"Did she believe you would save yourself for her?"

"She told me I was trying to buy her."

"Were you?"

"Of course."

Robert shows Charles a lustrous set of black pearls. They glow in the palm of his hand. The colour of the sea in deepest sleep. "I know what is truly valuable. I was very proud of how you all stood up to me when I failed you."

"We failed you too."

An older woman, shimmering in recognizably Ugandan cottons, suddenly strolls into their view. She looks at Robert, at Charles, and then quickly turns away. Robert is about to excuse himself when Charles, suddenly emboldened, asks the unaskable question. "Who are these people you are always meeting? These men?"

"Forget you ever saw them," says Robert in sudden anger.

"Who are they?"

"They can help our country. That is all I can tell you."

"Are they Americans?"

"Don't ask, Charles."

"Some of the others think they are CIA. Are they CIA?"

"Stop," Robert commands.

Charles takes a long breath, searching his mind for a less controversial subject. "So who is that woman who just came in?" he finally asks.

"She is our safety here. She is one of us. On our side."

"What does that mean?"

"She keeps me informed. She tells me things that will protect me, protect all of us. Think of her as a good witch."

"Why do we need protection? Is she Ugandan?"

"President Amin has been asking about us. Concerned we are spending too much time abroad. He has also told the Ministry of Culture that unless we return immediately, we will not be given a licence to perform at home. I am, however, afraid that if we do go home, we will not get out of the country again. That is why I have been extending the tour."

"That woman told you all this?" Something stirs in Charles. A tall woman of regal bearing. A strong woman with gourds and beads.

"She has also given me a stone. In a special iron box. She brings it to me everywhere I am. It is my shield."

Was it not a woman like this who once called Charles Kiti? Who still hovers at the edges of his dreams?

"She is never out of my awareness. She protects us all."

Suddenly Uganda floods into Charles once again.

At the opening night party, the Ugandan ambassador is smiling. As is the Director of Uganda's National Theatre who has made the long trip from Kampala to be here. Government and cultural officials appear everywhere. All eyes are on Abafumi. But why?

Perhaps, Charles thinks, the whole show is just national public relations. After all, this is the biggest festival they have yet played. So many companies here from Europe and America, from Asia and from all across the Caribbean. But they are the Festival's first African company.

The press badgers Robert's actors constantly with political questions. "Are reports of Amin's brutality true? Can rumours about his cannibalism be confirmed?"

"No comment," they have been told to say by Robert. "We are only actors. Perhaps you should ask our director." And Robert always deflects such inquisitions with grace and style. But when they are out of journalistic range and with people who might really know, Abafumi seethes with the same questions.

They corner the director of the National Theatre, Byron Kawadwa. Robert has spoken of him many times as a cultural leader, as someone who can be trusted. A playwright, Kawadwa is precise with words. He cautiously hints at what is happening, beginning sarcastically. "He evicts the Indians yet advertises Uganda with their good food," he sniggers to Joro.

Later in the scented darkness of the garden where, one by one, they have inconspicuously joined him, his soft voice continues. "Amin has turned on the Christian community as well now. Only Muslims have rights these days."

"We have heard that," says Robert. "How bad is it?" The group gathers round him, shadows among flowers.

"He announced on the radio that Allah came to him in dreams one night declaring women should not wear short skirts. And if they did not cover their heads, they would be imprisoned. Oil money is coming in to support him from Libya. Gaddafi wants to see Uganda as an ally. Perhaps it's because of his money that Amin is going this route.

"Even buying a car is difficult," Byron continues. "Or getting a good apartment unless you have a Muslim name. It is ethnic war. That is what is really happening. And he is violent. Cruel."

"We heard that western dress is no longer allowed," says Joro.

"Oh, it's allowed but not if you want to be safe. You will not recognize your friends when you return. Amin has put everyone in *jellabahs*. We all look like Gaddafi's people. We must also eat rice with our hands now. He has banished forks, everything modern and western."

"But we are a country of Catholics and Protestants too," states Joseph. "How can he abolish these religions?"

"Of course. Everyone protested. And then he started murdering the protesters."

"It really began with the priest," says Joro, looking pointedly at Charles. "You remember that?"

The priest. Charles will never forget that day, the torched car, the charcoal body slumped in its seat.

"Maybe it is time go back," says Robert.

"Not right now," Byron cautions. "Stay away as long as you can. Unless you want to convert. Amin has built a giant mosque high on a hill overlooking Kampala. So now we can all hear the *mezzuin*'s call to prayer, like a siren through the air. At regular intervals, we all have to stop what we are doing and bow to Mecca."

"Do they?" asks Joseph. "Does everyone stop?"

"At first, they all laughed at the order. Then people started disappearing. We heard of shootings and bodies dumped in Namanve forest. So now, everyone obeys the call to prayer."

"How about food? Can people still get what they need?"

"There are queues everywhere," says Robert. "Salt, sugar, kerosene are all in short supply. These were all things managed quite efficiently by the Indian businessmen. Without them…"

"And now he's left the running of the factories to people who know nothing about it," says Joro. "He is trying to nationalize all the big companies. Only the Americans and the British are stopping him."

"He can't quite figure out where artists fit in. In any event, you are still good advertisements for Uganda and therefore for him," Robert adds. So stay at the biggest hotels, eat the best food. But say nothing. Amin's spies are following you everywhere."

"Even here in Venezuela?" asks Charles incredulously.

"Even here."

Every day stories from home circulate secretly.

Screeching in the dark. A small mound squirms and squeaks, softly at first, then like the tearing of tin. Again and again. Agitated. Excited. A thump against bars. Flesh hitting metal. Over and over. A cage flies up. And rats run out, packs of them. Leaving the intricate organs of their victim lying bloody and distended. Decorated in red ribbon.

While a man dies.

And stories circulate.

A former boxer, now in military uniform stands there flexing his muscles. He is handed a hammer. Swings it, back and forth,

*up and around, gathering speed and momentum, as though
it will carry him off. A line of men forms in front of him. All
swinging hammers like windmills.*

*"Now!" rings out the command. Hammers come crashing
down on heads. Pound down simultaneously as the bodies
fall, gently, soft as melons.*

The last man stands with his bloody hammer.

Slumps obediently when the gunshot rings out.

And circulate.

*A refrigerator door is opened and in the harsh cold light,
human heads stare. A hulking shadow of a man takes them
out one by one, places them on a golden tray. And holds them
up for everyone to see. Laughing his deep red, roaring laugh.
Like molten lava from a volcano. Unstoppable. Deadly.*

And do not go away.

*Two men saw desperately at leg bones. Trying to fit some-
one's long bullet-ridden corpse — the president of an American
company — into the back of a car.*

Abafumi does not risk returning to this new, this horrific Uganda yet. There are theatre festivals in Poland where they have
standing invitations. They beckon to Robert. For reasons he
cannot quite fathom, he decides to bring *Renga Moi* to Eastern Europe. He senses there is some truth waiting for them in
Poland. Something they have been avoiding.

They have also begun rehearsals for a new production —
Amarykiti: The Flame Tree. It will unashamedly cry out the
martyrdom of their country. It is what they can do now:
paint the picture, tell the world. *The Flame Tree* will be
both the pyre of Uganda and the fire under Amin. A wound
in the earth. An image of ending and beginning that must
be understood.

They leave the Caribbean behind.

In Warsaw, their searing images burn into the imagination of audiences. *Renga Moi*'s visually raw allegory of suffering seems to be working well. It is understood and solemnly embraced. Those who have seen rehearsals of *Amyrikiti* are also moved.

Walking the old Eastern European city as tourists, Abafumi learns why.

"Your Flame Tree parallels our Jewish Ghetto," says Marek, head of the very political student theatre festival that has agreed to host them. "Even though Poland's Ghetto Uprising was a failure and we lost, we also won. And you will win too."

Marek shows them photos of the Warsaw Ghetto Uprising: Soldiers crouching behind blasted pillars. A solitary woman hurrying along, a human form slumped in her arms. An old man limping through broken glass. An impromptu street burial: two men crouch, their backs to the camera, obviously pawing at the earth. Two women watch. One with her hand to her face, still capable of shock and grief. The other, a mask of stillness. At the edge of it all, a small boy looks on, bundled up in cap and boots and scarf, his face, impassive.

Charles tries to read the boy's mind, back through time to a place so different from his own. But so eerily similar in these days of Amin.

A third photo: The final desperate battle for Warsaw's telephone exchange. "Hitler hated Poland's resistance. That's why he bombed Warsaw just before the war ended. Spite. There was no military point."

"They look so fearless," says Charles, scrutinizing the two clearly visible faces so resolutely close to hopelessness, bodies tensed to take back what is theirs.

"It would have been their last moment on earth," says Marek. "This picture keeps them alive."

"Hitler reduced Poland to rubble," he continues, "a burning ruin. But we rebuilt. We reconstructed our capital, brick by smoking brick. We wanted the city to look exactly as it had been before Hitler bombed us. The rebuilding began in the first moments of liberation."

Marek shows them another photo of a Polish flag waving over ruins. He points to scraps of paper, notes wedged into window frames of burnt-out buildings — from those looking for lost family members. "Like mail between ghosts," he says. "And look, here's a restaurant in a demolished tram car."

Charles studies a large metal cooking pot and a wooden kitchen table piled high with loaves of bread.

"If you look closely, you'll see a bombed out church behind it all. Empty arches where stained glass should be."

It is a merely a facade, flooded with dusty daylight.

"A theatre set," says Robert.

"That's right," agrees Marek. "One didn't have to imagine anything after the war. Reality took over. Look at this. A flower shop in a blasted street. In the theatre, you would say, 'This is too obvious.' But it is what life became here."

To Charles, it could be a market in Kampala, with its flimsy awning and plastic bins of bright blooms. Though a watery sun plays on their faces, the women wear heavy coats and shoes. In photo after moody black-and-white photo, the craggy, gaping ruins of Poland rise up to meet them.

Abafumi stays in one of the city's huge old Stalinist-style hotels. Officially, this is a privilege but it makes Charles feel like a prisoner. Every time he rides the clanking elevator cage, grinding up to the highest tower, he panics. He imagines winter in the cold streets, where slow cars rumble along, blowing up wisps of stinging snow. He feels so alien.

It is spring but he never sees faces, only hunched figures. Somewhat cheered by the red lamplight of cafés, he longs for music but finds only secretive whispering groups, huddled over drinks, as though hiding.

In front of the city's largest church, he watches the sun glow white fire, bleaching fine pillars and filigree behind the stern figure of Jesus bearing his cross, his right arm raised and beckoning. Encouraging, rallying.

Heaven. This way.

They are one of a dozen foreign companies in Warsaw. "The only Africans again," remarks Willy with a smile. "We are really quite exotic."

Abafumi's physical theatre — seen in two productions now — is widely praised. Its music and drumming an audience favourite. Every company member fights the temptation — even here in a truly sophisticated theatre environment — of easy celebrity.

Joseph is not happy though. "The audiences are always enthusiastic. But you just ask them about the images we project and the politics they contain. Noboby has a clue."

"It's not true," counters Charles. "Look at how *The Flame Tree* is being interpreted here."

"Over and over again as the cross," says Robert. "Suffering is the message. Sacrifice. They do understand."

Kampala is where Abafumi needs to play, thinks Charles.

But Poland grips Charles now. Including its women. They are sophisticated works of art, paying attention to every detail of their appearance from earrings to handbags and belts. They are the most fashionable women he has ever met. With their heels and their stockings and their smooth clinging dresses on fine chiselled figures. He loves their jaunty hats and their fiery red lips. Even communism has not thwarted these beauties. They way they look at him, hearing drums as he walks, aching with him, yearning, struggling to be Amarykiti.

The women are, somehow, both old and new, full of the secrets of their city. They are Gothic and Renaissance like the Old Town, with its café tables and long-stemmed parasols fluttering before archways. Formal, elegant, but fragile. Modern, but restrained conservative.

There is so much complicated history here. A city and a

country so often bargained over and sold. Used and bought back. Fought over. Defeated and restored. German and Polish. Enslaved and empowered. So much to learn from their example.

The company moves on to play in Krakow with its colonnaded courtyards of pale pink stone and delicate balconies. The domes dazzle them, green conical roofs spiralling into crosses, tiny bronze banners and whirling weather vanes, airy towers embroidered in stone. Peaceful over sun-reddened flowerbeds.

"In 1945, the German governor set up local headquarters in the university here. He executed the university's teaching staff and then sent thousands of Jews to Auschwitz," Marek tells them.

Charles looks at Joro and Willy. Then at Kiri and Beth. They all seem as dazed as he speaks. They know about World War II. They do not really know the truth about concentration camps. Or Jews being tortured and killed. He looks at Joseph whose face has gone blank. And Robert who is frowning.

Amarykiti is again hailed in the press. On their first day off Robert herds them onto a bus. Only then does he reveal they are bound for Auschwitz, ninety minutes away.

His voice is very quiet as they speed through farmland. Charles and the company have been so distracted with the tragedy of their own country that it is almost impossible to imagine anything remotely as bad happening anywhere else. They have come abroad to escape. To be praised and admired. To share damage that they cannot repair. To bring news of their disaster elsewhere. The enormity of what they are losing. So that some part of it may be saved. Any part of it.

They have not come abroad to be plunged into someone else's pain. To weep and cry over past human destruction on such a scale that they will never be innocent again.

"This Auschwitz," says Robert, his voice emotional, "is what is happening today in Uganda. It happened here three decades ago. Genocide. The wiping out of a people. I am telling you so that you know. It is not enough that I know. You, also, must know. When I am gone, you will carry the message."

Gone?

Where is he going? wonders Charles in the heavy pall that has slowly settled over them. Like that thick political cloud that leaked slowly into the train from Mombasa, when Headmaster showed them the newspaper coverage of Idi Amin. The cloud that tipped up and poured down on them, its gourd full of poison, once they had returned to Kampala.

"They brought the victims to Auschwitz in boxcars from all over Europe," Robert begins. "The Nazis deceived their victims by saying that they were part of a workers' resettlement plan and that transportation costs had been taken care of. Those being 'deported' were given pre-paid train tickets. They were treated worse than cattle. When the big doors clanged shut on the trains, there was no light or air, food or water. Nowhere to relieve themselves."

The slave boats, thinks Charles. *The middle passage.*

"All they knew was the rumbling of metal towards an unknown fate."

They had each other. At least they had each other, thinks Charles uncertainly as the bus rolls alongside an intricate network of track, crossing and criss-crossing, in gleaming grey rain.

Each other. What does that mean? Charles has not thought of his family in so long. Mother and Father. Debra. Their faces fly in and fade before his eyes. How are they? Where are they? How can he help them? What has he been doing all this time away from them?

As the bus enters the gates of Auschwitz, he begins to panic. They glide under deserted watchtowers.

"How calm it is now," muses Robert. "But then, there were machine guns ready to cut down these people for the slightest reason. Searchlights picking them out like bugs crawling, one by one. Tramping sentries. Boots at the changing of the guard. Boots that would kick them to death for the merest infraction."

They have begun walking. Every few steps of the way, they encounter signs with crossbones, that say: "*Halt-Stoj*," a grim reminder of the electric current that used to run along endless fences of spikey barbed wire, assuring death at a touch.

"Once the boxcars unloaded, a selection process began. Each prisoner had to pass before the camp doctor for medical inspection. Those fit for work were sent one way. The unfit — the old and the children — were sent another."

"Where did the unfit and the children go?" asks Willy.

"Extermination," says Robert bluntly.

The group is now joined by an official Auschwitz guide. He is dressed in a black and white striped uniform. Like pajamas, thinks Charles.

"I was here and saw everything," he says. "I am going to show you. This is how we had to dress."

They walk through room after room. One chamber filled with a mountain of human hair. Another filled with tumbled suitcases. A third, a landslide of boots and shoes. Whole warehouses of clothes. A huge room — a gas chamber behind glass. Lit and still, except for the insidious hum of neon.

"After selection," says the guide, "people destined to be gassed were taken to the bathhouse. When they looked up, naked and crowded together, some already broken and bleeding, they saw shower fixtures. A few knew there were no showers. Then the door was clamped shut. Poison gas billowed in through special vents."

The horrors they hear separate them.

Charles finds nothing familiar. Isolated in a reality he instinctively rejects.

In a photo, a single child with hands held up. A gun pointed at him.

Robert does not allow them to avoid the connections. "Amin," he says, "has recently called Hitler his model for racial purification, for the Africanization of Uganda. Well, this is Hitler. This is what that means."

They are outside now. Beside a pond still as a mirror. Where human ashes were thrown.

"At least Hitler was original in what he did," says Robert. "No one had ever worked toward genocide on such a massive scale before him. Amin has a perfect example to follow."

The guide stands with them. "Many ask why we keep this alive. I tell them that to forget is to repeat."

Charles stares into the water. All he sees are trees growing down through the glassy surface, their leafy tops plunged into darkness. The scream of trains remains. He hears it. Through the night bringing human sacrifice. He sits and weeps. For himself. For all these deaths. For the ladies of Poland.

The bus trip back to their hotel passes in total silence.

Gathered together in the Old Town, Abafumi searches its soul. But the company is completely distraught in the shady colonnade. Fanned by breezes they don't feel, oblivious to the chat and clatter of tourists, they look past each other, each angled differently in thought. Only Robert sees what he has created: a new group sculpture, shiny and stiff, inappropriately erected in an old historic market square. Robert breaks the silence. "As artists, we can tell the world what we see. It is all we can do. Even if our own government might not want us to. We carry the images and spread the word. I am resolved." He pauses, measuring precisely how much information to share.

"So we *are* working against them by doing what we do," states Joseph, wanting wilfully to clarify.

"Are we?" asks Charles. "Are we really working against the government? Do they know we are working against them?"

"Some of us more than others," counters Joro, now looking directly at Robert. Suddenly they are all looking at him. Auschwitz has become Kampala. Hitler is Amin. A troupe of wandering African artists have suddenly become Jews.

"I can tell you nothing else," Robert states bluntly. "It would endanger your lives."

"And what about your life?" Kiri aims her dart directly at him.

"No one can guarantee any life in times of war. And there is definitely a war on. No, I cannot guarantee my safety any longer," he replies, calm once more.

The foundations of Charles' very being are shifting yet again. Moving beneath his feet.

"What will keep me going longest is your faith in me," says Robert.

They reach the inevitable conclusion. Finally, it is time to return to Uganda. But before they leave Europe, Robert has arranged two last performances. In Rome.

Guided as ever by his master plan, they wander Warsaw's Old Town in search of their last Polish supper. Gather near their hotel, fitfully whispering fears and questions to one another. Nobody sleeps that night.

Groggily they check into the airport for the night flight to Italy. Beth and Charles are inseparable now. Beth tells him, "We will be all right if we stay together." Holding hands, she and Charles sleepwalk through the formalities.

Charles watches the moon come into view, remembering another moonlit night when he defended himself against thugs.

It is so bright that he wonders whether Amin's spies can see him even up here? Perhaps the general himself, with a huge telescope, has the plane in his sights right now and is peering straight into their minds. Reading traitorous thoughts. Is Amin already preparing extravagant punishments for this precocious tribe of artists who have taken themselves and all their privileges just a little too far, for just a little too long. He drifts off to sleep against Beth to the rumble of engines.

"I can get you guns."

A loud whisper invades his dream. He awakes with a start to see, just ahead of him, a white man speaking softly to Robert.

"And why would we want guns? We are actors."

"I know who you are," he says. "And my name, for the

moment, doesn't matter. What matters is that I have several businesses in Kampala. Amin needs capital and wouldn't dare throw me out or close me down. More important, he would never suspect me." The businessman sits down in the plane seat next to Robert. Charles picks up as much as he can of their conversation. And Robert knows Charles is listening.

"Let's get serious, Mr. Serumaga. I know you and I know your company's reputation. I am aware you have your own contacts and your own business dealings. I believe I can speak freely here. These are your people."

"I have no idea to whom or what you are referring to," Robert responds.

"I think you do," says the white man quietly. "There are not so many of us lately who can fly in and out of Kampala as easily as you and I can. Here's my card. In the next few days, you will know more about what I can do to help. What I will do to help. You'll have to excuse me now. I believe they are starting to serve dinner."

"There's no dinner being served," says Charles.

"In First Class," says the stranger getting up, "dinner is always being served. Nice to meet you young man." And then he adds, "Forget everything you heard. It will be safer for you."

What can Abafumi do, Charles wonders, except put on productions? Why would they want guns?

The fact is, he realizes, the company has the freedom to travel. Clearly, they are good publicity for Amin. Before they left, in fact, army officials and the actors were photographed together many times. The general himself even showed up in one. Grinning broadly. His arm around Robert's shoulders.

Charles is at the mouth of a cave, a gaping hole in a mountain where ferocious beasts prowl, a lair roaring out warning from the depths of its belly.

Guns?

5. AMIN

JUNE 28TH, 1976. ABAFUMI STEPS off the plane into the summer sunlight of Rome. A representative of Africa House greets them, ushering the group into a cramped minivan. With news they cannot avoid. Absorbed as they breathe, seeping in through their pores.

By the time they get to their quarters, they know the essence of disaster, how Uganda's own national tragedy is affecting the world. An Air France flight has apparently been hijacked and has landed at Entebbe Airport. The details emerge from television and radio.

Robot-like, Abafumi gathers in Rome to rehearse. But now they cannot concentrate. How do they justify this play-acting? In Rome, this indulgence in make-believe while real events in the real world are wreaking such havoc, events taking place on a bloody stage in Uganda.

Even Robert seems distracted.

June 29. *Details are emerging from Entebbe. The flight had set out from Israel's Ben Gurion Airport for Paris. During the flight, German hijackers took over the plane and rerouted it first to Athens, then to Benghazi, Libya, and then to Entebbe. Idi Amin allowed the plane to land. At the airport, the passengers were taken by the hijackers to a hangar where they were separated into groups at gunpoint.*

Visiting the wide square of St. Peter's Basilica, Charles gazes up into the stony eyes of divine shepherds and saints with crosses and staffs who study him from the high, round dome of this Catholic world.

Inside the huge church, Charles studies what Robert has called God's "Centre of Operations."

June 30th. *In Tel Aviv, a retired Israeli Defense Force Colonel named Bar Lev, who had spent some time in Uganda, is led into a sterile military planning room. He makes an international call through to Kampala. This is the first of several calls that the Colonel makes to his old acquaintance Idi Amin, massaging his ego, reminding him that Amin had received his paratroop training from the Israelis and eliciting every scrap of relevant information while Defense Minister Shimon Peres listens in on an extension.*

At that same moment, forty-seven of the hostages — all non-Israeli — are released as a goodwill gesture. They include the captain, his crew, and a French nun. The captain refuses to go. The crew joins his protest. As does the nun. The Ugandan military forces the nun to cooperate but allows the others to remain behind with the Israelis. Paris, Tel Aviv, and Washington are in close contact.

In Israel, three possible plans emerge: a parachute drop at Entebbe, a large-scale military crossing from Kenya, and a direct landing at Entebbe followed by a quick assault and a fast removal of the hostages by air.

Inside St. Peters, Charles sees himself arched splendidly over everything. Glimmering in bronze and gold and ivory, ruby and emerald and deep polished wood, carved and majestic. He towers and twists, streams holy pictures in flowing patterns.

It is what he always wanted to do. Send rays of light.

The church radiates pure light on him. A sunburst beams into the dark. His art will take him there.

July 1. *Israel's highest military personnel burrow through blueprints of Entebbe's airline terminal, a terminal built by the Israeli construction company Solel Boneh.*

The first freed hostages are now being debriefed in Paris.

A full-scale model of the Entebbe terminal is erected in the Israeli desert. Rehearsals begin for a landing in a Hercules aircraft.

A flight plan is drafted that will secretly bring the Israeli soldiers to Entebbe Airport. There is concern. What about the element of surprise? A white Mercedes limo is delivered to the Israeli desert.

By the time it arrives in Entebbe, the car will be black, a painted disguise.

Abafumi visits the Sistine Chapel. They all strain their necks to take it in. God Creates the Sun and the Moon, The Creation of Man, The Original Sin and The Expulsion from Paradise. In pulsing colour. Naked muscular forms that live and breathe.

These are not the pious painted saints and idols that Charles remembers from his first Catholic Church. These are real people, he thinks. They are strong and they are struggling to understand, their bodies animated with effort.

"God brought us here," says Robert, "to give us strength."

"You brought us here," says Kiri.

The members of Abafumi want to scatter and hide, dissociate themselves from the news about Uganda that is happening without them, that they cannot control. Terrible events that accuse and blame. They consider once more their return. They know they must go home.

It is late evening on July 3rd when they board their Air France flight. They will arrive in Kampala the next afternoon.

That same night a camouflaged Israeli plane commanded by Lt. Col. Yoni Netanyahu of the celebrated Sereyat Makhtal brigade flies into Ugandan airspace. Touching down at Entebbe undetected, the plane — still rolling, its rear ramp already open — sends vehicles and assault teams speeding across the tarmac. By the time the rescue is over, forty-five Ugandan soldiers are dead. One Israeli soldier — Lt. Col. Yoni Netanyahu — is dead. Six of seven hijackers are dead.

The hostages — all but one — have been freed.

When the Abafumi plane arrives, they are immediately surrounded by reporters in the VIP lounge who bombard them with questions. They are the first plane allowed to land at the airport since the Israeli's surprise attack.

"Did you see anything as you were landing?"

"Did you have any idea what was happening when you were in the air?"

For a moment, Robert and his actors seem dazed, believing the brace of journalists are there to interview them. But once it is clear that the commotion is a result of what is already being called by Israeli commandos "the raid on Entebbe," he concentrates on getting his company away from the press. But they follow Robert and continue to ask questions.

"We circled the airport for a long time. That was the only unusual thing."

"Why didn't you stay in Europe until this was over?"

"We felt we needed to be back. We had been away long enough. And President Amin has always ensured our safety."

Amin's soldiers do surround them now and roughly escort them onto a bus, then downtown where they are dropped, as always, at the National Theatre.

Suddenly their old space seems emptier and more silent than usual. This house of work and pleasure where all their stories begin and end. They cannot resist going inside for a moment.

"It is silent, but it is still ours," says Robert. "I don't know whether we can bring it back to life but we can try. We will begin our work again next week. This will be our refuge."

But their theatre now seems a tomb. Can they really revive it? Will anyone come to see their work? What will they be allowed to perform?

Robert is determined to spend some time with Byron Kawadwa, still the National's Artistic Director. They have not met since Brazil. Robert wants to make sure that all the arrangements for use of the National remain as they were. He is also hoping that Byron will allow the company to play both of their shows in the main space.

"I'll let you know next week how my meetings go," says Robert in a low voice. "For now, return to your homes. Stay low. Stay out of trouble. The fact is that we really don't know what's going on with anything. I will be in touch. Go now. Help each other."

Nobody wants to be alone. Charles, Joro, and Willy gather for dinner the next night. In his borrowed Indian house, Charles hopes they can all relax in the bright tranquility that has become home. Damaged though it is.

Fear is palpable around them though. Soldiers are truly everywhere. Stores shuttered. Schools closed. As though everyone is waiting for some Armageddon.

Charles knows they are between worlds — one disintegrating, the other yet to be made. They sit secluded in his square of Hindu heaven.

Over the garden wall, gunshots and sporadic shouts are heard. Like snapping foliage, wrinkled and brown, from over-ripe trees. Dropping to the ground and churned into mud.

Charles fiddles with the radio. A station crackles into their dusty sitting room like a gust of stormy wind from behind curtains. The president's voice. Amin's voice. "I want to tell you that Hitler was right about the Jews." So Amin is not dead. Or is he?

"What has happened at Entebbe Airport proves that the Israelis are not working in the interests of the people of the world and that is why they were burned alive with gas on the soil of Germany. People everywhere now agree with me that the Israelis are criminals."

Fresh from their experiences at Auschwitz, the three artists stare at one another. "What did he expect Israel to do?" asked Charles. "He has really gone mad."

"It seems he is not dead," whispers Willy, his eyes narrowing as the radio booms on.

"We must work with our Muslim brothers now," Amin drones on. "General Gaddafi and I have already had many talks. He agrees with me, with the people of Uganda. Libya and Uganda will work together for a greater Africa, an Africa for Africans."

"Gaddafi!" exclaims Joro. "Another devil who swaggers around in gold gowns."

"Who speaks in riddles," Charles adds.

"Apparently, he hates the Jews too. Gaddafi can supply arms and help Amin kill everyone who isn't a Muslim," adds Willy, tapping softly on a drum.

They sleep on sofas. The next morning they are again assailed by shouts from the streets. Throughout the day, the reports from Entebbe continue to change. First they hear that the Israelis killed all of Amin's soldiers who were guarding the terminal. Then they wander outside to try and gather information.

"The Israelis apparently had huge planes," says Joro later, who heard the story from a soldier. "One plane was rigged up as a hospital. They flew in at night between other flights when the runway lights were still on. One of the planes had cars and jeeps."

"A lot of people were killed," he continues, "but in the end the Israelis got the hostages out. All of them. It was amazing."

A few hours later they hear on the radio that one hostage still remains in Kampala. An old woman, now hospitalized. The Prime Minister of Israel had been on the phone to Amin demanding that she be returned.

They all knew, however, that this one would be sacrificed as payment for Uganda's butchered military pride. Some days after, the confirmation comes.

"Amin had her killed in her hospital bed," they hear from Mara. "They took her body to Namanve. My soldier friend told me. It hasn't been announced yet."

Charles puts his head in his hands. It aches with bad news. Mother is also ill. Debra continues to languish. He cannot help them. With almost all the phones down, a storm of guilt and anxiety pounds at him constantly. And fury.

Namanve, the forest of the damned. The dark place into which Amin's victims disappear, never to be heard from again. Dumped into shallow jungle graves, pieces of them scattered so families can never mourn properly. Souls not free.

"What did that one sick Jewish woman have to do with Uganda's troubles?" asks Joro. "It's perverse."

Charles walks the city that afternoon under darkening rain clouds that touch the ground. Black shapes begin to move. Growling through the streets towards him. Big guns now churning ahead on metal wheels. Ready to shoot thunderbolts. Tanks.

Two young soldiers from his home district recognize him. Whisper fiercely to him. Trying to save his life. "The country is under attack. Amin has gone mad. Run!"

Charles turns and runs. Streaks into a garden where mangoes hang like hand grenades. He lies down in the scented darkness of this refuge breathing slowly, gulping in its rare air, clenching and unclenching his jaw, his fists, his whole being. Hardening into readiness.

When it is quiet again, he creeps home.

As the new week begins, they all meet again at the National that now seems secure. The company shelter. They sit in silence. Robert has not yet arrived. Unusual.

Gunshots. They wait. They eat lunch near the theatre. When

they return, there is noise on the stage. A rehearsal is apparently starting. They walk in quietly. A stage manager tells them they are welcome to watch. It is a new play by Byron Kawadwa. Byron, they are told, is supposed to be directing it but he has not arrived yet. One of the actors is directing in his place.

"We were told," says the stage manager furtively, "that the play has not been approved yet by the censor. We think Byron must be meeting with them."

The rehearsal begins.

Soldiers wander through the auditorium. Sit silently. Watch. And leave.

Joro and Charles have often spoken of Byron's plays. How honest his work has been. How blatantly political as compared to Abafumi's work, which is disguised in myth.

"What does the title mean?" asks Charles.

"What do you think *Song of the Cock* means?" blurts Robert suddenly from the row behind. "It's about greed and ambition and too much sex. It is also," he adds in a loud whisper, "the title of Uganda's entry to the pan-African theatre festival in Nigeria later this year. A great honour for Byron."

"And us," asks Charles. "Will we be there?"

Robert is unlit dynamite with all his secrets, thinks Charles. *Soon something will ignite him and he'll explode his mysteries high as the sky.*

"Who knows?"

Charles shrinks down into his seat, feeling fire move closer.

The rehearsal continues. Scenes of palace life, royal extravagance. The story weaves like coloured twine on royal baskets, around the larger than life figures of prominent kings. Monarchs like Mtesa, Causer of Tears. Who roasts bodies. Mutilate them with knife-sharp reeds for the slightest infraction.

And Mtesa's son, Mwanga, who butchers students. Hacks off limbs and burns them in front of his victims just before their merciful release into death.

Drumming booms a signal for revolt. Chaos.

When the play finishes, the stage goes dark and lights come up in the auditorium.

Suddenly the theatre doors swing open and the military swarms in. "What is your name?" a young soldier with a Kalishnikov demands of Charles.

"Hajib. My name is Hajib," says Charles. Robert has told them to use false names if they are ever challenged by military people.

The others are challenged as well. Robert answers to Omar, Mara to Layla. Muslim sounding names are best.

The soldiers are from the State Research Bureau, Amin's most-feared henchmen. They are searching for Byron. The excesses of royal power in the play have not gone unnoticed. The actors feel their insides turn liquid. Then one of the soldiers strides to the centre of the stage pulling along with him a little boy.

"Your father is somewhere in this theatre," he tells the boy. "He is hiding. It's a game. I want you to find him."

The child is hesitant but the soldier reassures him. The boy walks into the aisle. "Are you here Father? Are you here?"

"Where are you Byron?" says the soldier loudly. "Your son is calling."

Suddenly a voice is heard from the balcony. "I am here. Leave him alone. I will come down to you." In a moment Byron is on the edge of the stage hugging the boy.

He says softly to his actors, "I have been watching everything. You are doing wonderfully. The play will be fine. But I think I may miss the opening."

Two soldiers now stand on either side of him. Guns pointed. The boy holds his father's hand.

"Take him away," says the officer. "Leave the boy with these actors." Byron and his son are separated.

Mara takes the boy in her arms. "It will be all right," she tells him.

As he leaves the theatre with the soldiers, Byron's actors set up a rhythmic chant. They drum from the stage. The rhythms speak danger to everyone who can hear.

"Where are you taking him?" they ask. "What are you going to do?"

"Shut up," they are told, "or you can join him." No one makes a move. The drums continue.

An actress runs to the bar, grabs an empty pop bottle and hurls it at the soldiers. Others follow her lead. Abafumi and friends send a barrage of glass toward those leading Byron away. One draws blood.

The youngest soldier turns and fires. One of the actresses screams, hit in the leg. The others duck. Byron is led out.

Everyone rushes to the lobby.

Soldiers thrust him into a car while the actors curse and shriek at them. The soldiers then turn back, grab the wounded actress and, to everyone's horror, throw her, screaming, into the trunk of the vehicle.

They have all heard soldiers brag about chopping people down to size in order to cram them conveniently into conveyances. Into coffins.

They all know their tall graceful actress is doomed. And Byron with her.

The National Theatre sinks into silence.

Amin is on the warpath.

Robert is with them again. He seems to know more than anyone. He speaks to both groups of actors with no expression in his voice. "You were very brave."

"They will give him urine to drink," says one of Byron's actors, distraught. His eyes glaze over. He cannot look at them when he says it.

"They will burn his body in Namanve so that no one will recognize who has been destroyed. And so his soul can never return," another actor adds.

Robert's head is down. He is in tears.

"Why are they doing it to artists?" barks Joseph with disgust. "Byron is only a storyteller. Like us."

"Byron has spoken the truth more than once," Robert answers. "Truth is dangerous in Uganda."

"So are we now all in danger?" asks Charles.

"Yes," says Robert gravely. "And I am not so sure anyone can help us anymore. Not Byron. Not me. We must try to continue our work, all of us, but you each have to decide for yourselves. It is dangerous. It will be dangerous."

The next day, they arrive to find a lock on the door of the theatre. A small item in the newspaper announces that the National has been officially closed until further notice. Lower down in the story is an announcement that Byron Kawadwa has been relieved of duties as Artistic Director of the theatre.

No word about Abafumi. Yet.

The wider national theatre of Idi Amin is just beginning. And Abafumi is drawn into its deadly melodrama.

Amin has decided to invite the presidents of the Organization for African Unity to meet in Kampala. He wants to show off before them. Abafumi is told to prepare one of its shows as part of Uganda's contribution to the evening's entertainment.

Robert makes the announcement and then leaves them to talk among themselves.

"He trots us out for the dictators but he won't let us perform for the people," Joro says.

"He is afraid we will contaminate the public," Charles agrees.

"He's right," says Joseph. "We would shine a light through this nightmare."

"I remember," adds Joseph "at another official performance in freer times, the Nigerian writer Chinua Achebe telling us that theatre goes beyond language. He said mere talk gives us the lie of certainty. But the song and story travel like thought, without boundaries. There is the spirit of redemption in every moment. You can make artists of the oppressed!"

They agree to play *Renga Moi* for Amin and an audience of kings and prime ministers — dictators mostly — from across the continent.

Robert remains tight-lipped and tense through the rehearsal period. There is no joy in the enterprise. They have been allowed to use the National again. But walking through the dark building is like walking through a cemetery.

The performance, however, will not take place at the National but at the massive Nile Hotel a few streets away. Abafumi will be one of three companies performing that night, the only company from Uganda. Each troupe has an hour or so. *Renga Moi* is 80 minutes. They must cut it down to time. "If we don't cut the play," grunts Robert, "they will cut us." They agree on a shortened version.

They will be sharing dressing rooms at the hotel with artists from other countries. Robert objects and gets permission to have Abafumi dress at the National and walk the two blocks to the hotel in costume and makeup. Robert cautions them more than once to be careful what they say backstage, even to other artists, especially to other artists. They can expect police and military everywhere.

"There will also be spies in each company," he tells them. "Some forced to report under threats to their family. They will ask you questions. Say nothing. It is safest."

As the international event approaches, headlines report who is withdrawing: the few democratic leaders. It seems the only leaders coming— the ones who will attend their show — are the worst of the butchers, men who have opened fire on students during demonstrations, who have killed dissenters and now rule from thrones set upon the mountains of corpses they have made, burnished with gold from property and possessions they have appropriated.

"Amin loves these men," Robert warns gravely. "Be on your guard."

"How can we perform like that?" Charles explodes.

"Perform as though your life depends on it," Robert advises simply. And then adds, "Because it does."

Performance night. The cast of *Renga Moi* walks majestically from the National Theatre through the street in leopard skin robes, beaded caps, and ostrich feather headgear, carrying swords and drums. People on the street stop, stare, and applaud.

As a body, Abafumi enters the hotel Conference Centre to more applause and ascends the stairs towards what has become a communal Green Room for all the artists. At the door, the other artists start applauding. The applause grows as they step inside.

"Bravo," says the director of the troupe from Zaire standing to greet them. "We honour you. We know of your success abroad. We have been asked to entertain here so we will sing and dance as they wish us to, in the traditional ways. But we know that you are the real creators, the brave ones, and that you do something very different from us. And the world has understood. We admire you and we wish you luck."

But Robert is suspicious. What is it that these people know? Are they sending a message? What have they heard?

In the chilled hotel air, Charles feels his skin contract. Everyone in the group is now sure that Robert is involved somehow with the anti-Amin resistance movement, based in Kenya. Such secrets needle them, sharp as sudden showers.

But direct confirmation never comes.

In the dressing room, Charles sits gazing into glass trying to read the future, decipher the meaning of it all. Others lie on the floor beneath racks of street clothes — white shirts, beige pants, pretty ruffled dresses — for the official party afterward. Several stand, arms over chests, listening to the presentations already going on, boom through squawky soundboxes above them.

The auditorium is full. Fifteen hundred people. Charles hears clapping. And laughter. The stomping of feet. He knows this audience is primed for entertainment.

Will they accept *Renga Moi*?

What will Amin think? Does he have any idea what it is about?

Extended clapping wakes him from reverie. They now have twenty minutes to get the stage set.

Robert rises, resplendent in his priestly regalia, stern and severe. "It is our turn. Play the piece as you never have. Play for everything you've ever believed. Perform this sacred duty with all you've got."

Charles does not quite know what Robert means by this but he does know that he cannot pretend. That what they will dance and express over the next hour must be nothing but truth.

And so it starts.

A high altar surmounted by a cross with the Priest bowed before it. A body beneath him held in chains.

The audience gasps audibly. Not the image the assembled heads of state expect.

Charles looks into the darkness. Is Amin frowning already?

The cast whirl and dance their way into the story. The stage is ablaze with colour, chanting and stomping, eyes rolling, sound everywhere accentuating the violent emotions of this ancient allegory. The village of the Seven Hills trembles on the brink of disaster. Now it is held together by the machinations of the fearful Priest and Renga Moi. Glory shrinks and darkens before the village can be saved.

Charles assumes that Amin is focused on the women. He knows that all the attractive females in Uganda belong to him merely for the asking. His Beth, Kiri, Mara, and Susi. Gleaming in their beaded skirts and tops, their strong bodies taunting him, their inner concentration irresistible.

What must Amin be making of Nakazzi, brimming vessel of double life.

Renga Moi prepares to perform the necessary rituals. They must be observed.

But Renga Moi must defend his village in battle before he is able to complete the rituals. He must shed blood before purification is finished. The Priest's dreadful decree.

The bereaved mother makes a special point of falling to her knees before Sese Seko Mobuto, the dictator of Zaire, begging him to save her babies. He chuckles down at her.

"You are a beautiful woman," he whispers in her ear. "I will do anything you want. You do not need to suffer this way." And brushes his hand across her chest.

She leans forward and whispers in his ear, "Do not touch me." He is surprised.

But not as surprised as he is after the impaling of her babes on spears a few minutes later. Mobuto stands. The audience goes silent. The actors suddenly freeze.

He glares at Amin and says, "I do not find the murder of children entertaining. I am leaving." His delegation quickly follows.

Charles expects the soldiers in the theatre to open fire on them all. The company has flaunted the sins of power-mongers. Surely this is the reason for Mobuto's dramatic exodus. Should they continue?

President Amin registers surprise for a moment. Charles tries to imagine what he is thinking. Maybe he sees that Renga Moi, the warrior, is the people's hero. Maybe he thinks that he is Uganda's own Renga Moi. But Amin is not. He is the dictator. The Priest who holds pure power.

With a broad grin, Amin motions the actors to continue.

In a breath, the hysterical spectacle of grief returns to life. Renga Moi sheds his own ritual blood. The Priest comes forward, like vengeance itself, exhibiting to the great warrior the corpses of his infants.

And Renga Moi strangles him. Kills the dictator. The play ends. Then, ominous silence.

Applause beginning slowly but defiantly. Continuing hesitantly for some minutes. Then Amin stands. And disappears behind the curtains of his elevated box, reappearing in a moment on the stage. There, he shakes the hand of each cast member.

"Your actors risk everything for you," he tells Robert. "I remember supporting your first tour with state money. I thought your work was just fine gymnastics. But I see now that you are being ... what is the word ... provocative. We must speak further about all this. You must explain it more to me. You know I don't understand such things. In any event, you must come to the reception afterwards. Oh yes, do bring all your theatre soldiers with you. I will arrange for a bus outside the National to take you over to the palace."

In the showers following their performance, Charles, Willy, and Joro exchange nervous words. "We'll probably be assassinated for dessert," says Willy, trying to laugh. A rush of water muffles his voice.

"Maybe we shouldn't go," says Joro as he steps out of the shower. All three stand in white towels peering at each other through cloudy air.

They stride to the changing room. Clang doors. Gaze at press shots of themselves. Slick back hair with small flicking wrist actions. Put on confidence with their clothes. Crisp shirts, perfectly creased pants, shiny shoes. Aromatic aftershave wafts around them.

"C'mon," says Charles. "Let's party. We will be the toast of the town." They head to the Green Room.

It is in this cocky attitude that Robert finds them, along with the others, squeaky clean, expecting accolades now and flowers. But Robert is not smiling. He is a thundercloud. Behind the rumpled scowl, they catch flashes of lightning, crackling sporadically. "We are going to be killed," Robert says flatly.

"Killed?"

Firing squad? Bomb? Poison? The questions hang in the air, visible to everyone.

"I thought he liked the play," says Willy. "I thought he liked us."

"You thought wrong," says Robert hotly. "Because we

embarrassed him, criticized him publicly in front of his peers, he cannot let us go free. There is more but that is enough for now. Our bus to the reception will meet with an accident. I have been told so by a friend, a soldier. If we get on that bus, we will all die. If we stay in the country, we will all be dead by morning. One way or another."

"What do we do?"

"Leave. Leave Uganda," says Robert. "Leave now."

"Where?" asks Charles.

"Wherever you can. It will not be safe for your families if you go home. You must each take your own route out. I will meet you in Nairobi. In a week. When you get there, go to the offices of the Ford Foundation. They will tell you what to do."

"The Ford Foundation?"

The actors stand motionless. Robert takes a large wad of U.S. dollars from an envelope. Fifties. Hundreds. He counts out a thousand dollars for each one. When he has distributed sixteen thousand dollars there are still many thousands left.

A thousand dollars, thinks Charles, is four months salary. Where did Robert get so much cash? So quickly? Is he really leaving them? Or are they leaving him?

"This money is for travel, yes, but it is also for bribes when required. Do not take risks. There will be more money for you in Nairobi. Hitch rides where you can. Don't take obvious routes. Get across the border any way possible and quickly. Godspeed. I will meet you there. Now go. Go."

Susi and Willi ponder chartering a private plane. Mara, Kiri, and Beth decide to take buses right to the Kenyan border and will try to walk across. Joseph and Kasa will travel by bicycle hoping to leave without detection.

Susi and Willy quickly run through the stage door, hand-in-hand. Charles watches them leave. They are immediately stopped by soldiers. Within full view of the theatre, they are shoved into a police vehicle.

Charles and Joro head out a back door. Their home villages

are near one another. They decide to try and walk home. They will say goodbye to their families. They will borrow bicycles and they will cycle away from Kenya, go in the other direction, to the Rwandan border where they will try to leave Uganda.

Charles arrives home two nights later. Kekinoni and Kanyunya offer to hide him with friends, insist he remain nearby. They are looking so old to him now. Father is without energy. Mother is without spirit. Debra sits silently. They eat together before he leaves, knowing finally that he must, for their own safety. He will not divulge the route he is taking out.

It takes him two torturous days, slinking through forest heat and insects, avoiding cars and the many military checkpoints. Nights, alone on the forest floor, tormented by animal cries and his own bad dreams.

He arrives at the Rwandan border at dusk the third day. Joro has been there for several hours waiting for him. Their escape plan seems to be working.

But the Rwandan guard — a Hutu — is suspicious of these young men who look more Tutsi than Ugandan to him. So many Tutsis had moved there in the early 1960s. Could he have found not one but two of the hated enemy? A supervisor is called. He, too, suspects they are Tutsi. More so, when he makes them empty their pockets and sees how much money they have.

The cash is removed and put into a paper shopping bag. The guards roughly dump the rest of their belongings into another bag. Six hours pass in a locked, stuffy little room where the two are held and given only a cup of water and some stale cooked rice to eat. They have already despaired of ever leaving this airless prison, when the door crashes open.

"Stand up and follow us," they are ordered. Charles is hurried off one way. Joro another.

They are jailed as Tutsi spies.

The makeshift prison wall against which Charles crouches

glares yellow, from a severely angled sun. It is like cold fire on him. Flies swarm the light. Sweat beads his skin. Suddenly the wooden door bangs open and the two guards haul him to his feet. "Where are we going?" Charles asks.

"Shut up. We ask the questions, not you."

He is thrown down in the yard beside a stone fireplace. And kicked in the ribs. Again and again. Clutching his side, he vomits onto what he realizes is a charred football left lying in ashes.

"Sick like a girl. You even look like a girl."

After an hour lying in the hot sun, they bring him to another room, empty except for two wooden stools. He is ordered to sit. He does so, painfully. The door opens again and they drag in Joro. The moment the two men are alone, Joro says gently, sadly, "They've hurt you."

Charles winces each time he breathes in deeply. "I think they have broken a rib," he says.

"And you, Joro?"

"I'm okay. Probably because I have a face like theirs. You look to them like the enemy, so they abuse you more."

"What do they think we've done?" asks Charles, anger and frustration straining his voice. But the protest has taken all his energy and he sways on his perch like a lame bird.

"I'm not sure what they know or don't know," says Joro. "There is such hatred between Tutsi and Hutu, it could just be that. Or maybe Amin is involved in it. We should play dumb and say nothing. If we want to live, we must not reveal anything. Only that we are actors on our way to Kenya."

For another two days they are interrogated, several hours at a time. Alone. Together. They are given one meal each day. They are made to eat in the hot sun. To stand for hours in its glare.

On the third morning, the guards return, now all smiles.

"We have had a call from the American Embassy in Nairobi. You are free to go. You have been arrested by mistake. Sorry."

Sorry? They have been sadistically mistreated. Nearly starved.

"I would like something to drink, please," says Charles.

The guard leaves instantly and returns with a glass of juice, all bubbles at the brim. Charles wonders for a brief, fearful moment whether it might be poisoned. Then he takes it and drinks it down. He has never tasted anything so good.

The guards laugh. "So who are you really? Why are the Americans calling our government? Why are they interested in you? Why were you trying to get out of Uganda so badly?"

The guards want to sit and gossip and joke now.

Joro asks if they can get their money and papers back. Their passports. Two hundred dollars is returned to each of them. They had arrived with eight hundred each, having left some money with their families. "And the rest?" asks Charles.

"That was all you had," says the older guard. "But we can let you shower and give you fresh clothes. A good meal. What would you like?"

"We would just like to get out of here," Charles says, his voice subdued but firm. "Right away. We would like a drive to the airport."

An hour later, they are taken by jeep to a military airport and left in a hangar. They are told that the American Embassy is sending a plane for them. How are the Americans involved? Charles wonders. He and Joro stare stonily ahead.

The driver of the jeep is silent for most of the ride from the border. Just before dropping them, he suddenly speaks. "You must be important. You must be some kind of spies. Are you CIA? Why don't you stay in Rwanda? We could use some good spies." They remain silent.

In the empty hangar, they wait for their plane. Another guard — who looks no more than sixteen — stands casually at the entrance holding a rifle. Then the ancient phone on the wall near him rings. He answers, says a few words and then calls them over.

"You speak," he tells them. "Not a good line. Nairobi."

The line crackles and groans as if a ship were rolling over it. Charles says a hesitant hello.

"What the hell are you doing in Rwanda?" It is Robert's voice. "Rwanda is the other way!"

"Joro and I thought it would be a safer place to cross," says Charles apologetically.

"There are more efficient ways to die than taking a wrong turn. Use a compass next time. Meanwhile just get your sorry selves on the plane as soon as it arrives. We are waiting for you in Nairobi."

Charles looks at Joro wanting to laugh. "Robert is waiting for us in Nairobi." Tears fill his eyes.

He is getting used to planes. But this one is small. A flimsy toy plane controlled by a child with a string, he thinks nervously. The flight itself is less than two hours. They both remember that first dazzling, terrifying school trip they took together not so long ago. "When I went to Nairobi with Mengo, the city scared me," Charles admits to Joro.

"Well now it will save you. No more of Amin's cutbacks here. In Nairobi things actually work: electricity, sewage, running water."

At Embakasi Airport, they have their passports stamped by a Kenyan official, younger than they, who asks why they are here.

"For work," says Joro.

"What kind of work?"

"We are artists."

The uniformed guard is suspicious and makes a call. Moments later, they enter Kenya as free men.

"So many refugees must be fleeing from Amin," Joro whispers.

Charles, tries to find a place for the term "refugee" in his head.

"Ugandans on the run are flooding in here. Taking up jobs and houses. Kenyans like to control things. They can't control us."

At the end of a passage of blue-carpeted walls, doors suddenly swing open revealing Robert, Kiri, Beth, Mara, Joseph, and Kasa. "Where are the others? Susi and Willy? Obusi?" asks Joro.

"We don't know," says Robert. "We're still waiting to hear."

Despite this anxious cloud thickening above them, Robert smiles like a father whose prodigal sons have returned home. "Here," says Robert. "Let me introduce you to our friends from the American Embassy. They have money for you."

Effusive embassy officials shake hands in the limousine simultaneously giving Joro and Charles each two thousand dollars in cash. "We want you to feel better. We want you to know who your friends are. This is a grant that had been applied for."

The Americans are generous, thinks Charles. But Robert never mentioned a grant. Why are they doing this?

The welcoming committee also includes a Kenyan police official and Uganda's Deputy Minister of Culture, a gracious woman who flourishes flowers under their noses. "I am so glad you made it here," she says.

Charles is skeptical of these new connections.

A police cruiser leading, they drive the nine miles from Embakasi to the city centre. Charles watches the new housing estates fly by, industrial parks, railway sidings, access roads, highways. They are taken to a hotel.

"This will be home for awhile," says Robert. "It's a little like a small amusement park, but we will be safe here and the Americans are paying. Charge anything you eat to the room."

They thank their saviours again. The company — most of them — is once more together and everyone wants to hear their story.

That evening, Charles asks Beth what has been going on. "We are in a state of ignorance," she says. "We don't know who we are any more. Or who these Americans are. Only that we cannot return to Uganda. Our lives have changed completely. Our families have no idea where we are and we cannot tell them. We are like orphans."

Charles takes it as his personal challenge to comfort and reassure Beth that night.

A week later, Robert moves them to a slightly better hotel

in the English residential area of the city, once exclusively European. Here they sit in the soft lamp-glow of wood-panelled pubs having afternoon high tea.

"You would probably have to be a member of the House of Lords to afford this in London," says Charles. He is admiring the polished brass and shining carved mahogany, the plush velvet seat cushions, and inviting nooks and crannies of the pub. For several afternoons in a row, they take tea like this, served on silver. Dainty sweets and crustless sandwiches on a three-tiered tray. Black waiters in white gloves.

In an affable fog of cigarette smoke and laughter, conversation turns away from the missing members of the company to discussions about their plush luxury beds, the problems of adjusting thermostats, and the pleasures of room service.

During this period Robert comes and goes. Sometimes he is amiable. Mostly he is tense. They all agree he's not getting any sleep. When he is with them, he is depressed. He finally opts for work and books a rehearsal space at the Alliance Française, charging Charles with the task of heading warm-ups. Kiri does vocals. Beth leads improvisation exercises.

They are thirteen now instead of sixteen. But they are still Abafumi. They talk of a new production amidst posters of French wines, food, and bathing beauties whose breezy bronze bodies offer the flowery languor of Nice in return for learning a few fundamental French words.

Eventually, they begin rehearsals of *Ekinke-kenke* under Joro, now the new Assistant Director, and Charles, their Company Manager. "*Ekinke-kenke* is the cry of the refugee," says Robert. "The cry of fear. The ultimate demon of destruction."

The actors learn to shout their anger, their fear. Their speeches now spin around the invisible tower of a curse: strong words soaked in bloody event. The power of terrible taboo forges separate meaning into a thick wall of threat.

But who or what is the enemy? In this new work, there is no recognizable creature. It is something amorphous. Without head or tail or legs: Ekinke-kenke. Invisible, ubiquitous, Ekinke-kenke squats on the stage, an actor with a crooked face.

Once it enters the scene, dreadful things happen. Vegetation shrivels, huts are raided. There is sickness and death. The people run, seeing the source of their torment, its size.

But it is sound only. A signal from another world. The next desperate chapter of their own story. Abafumi's reduced company now plays out a Ugandan tragedy it knows it cannot really alter.

Villagers prowl around their dwellings with machine guns, in pursuit of Ekinke-kenke, blasting it out into the darkness. The dancers become tanks rolling through jungle. The villagers put their own people before the firing squad. And so the village is reduced to a pile of smoldering garbage. Fed upon by flies. Implacable. Droning.

In their own strange new lives, the Abafumi faithful go limp as unstrung puppets, deserted for days at a time by Robert. They flounder in an alien French context, struggling to find meaning in a world they no longer understand.

The Deputy Minister of Culture, Lucy, now appears. But they soon learn she is no longer the Deputy Minister of Culture. Why? No answers. She is now just Lucy and she has a plan for them. As she begins to talk, her hands arc and dip like petals in the wind. "I have a friend from Stockholm who works for the UN here," she tells them all. "She can get you to Sweden. Kenya is no longer safe for you. Amin's people are everywhere. Even here ... in our own government."

She continues. "You will be welcome. They can provide funds for you as refugees. The Ford Foundation will arrange another grant for all of you to get there. They are simply awaiting your application. You have to decide though whether you are willing to leave Africa. If you don't go, I think your lives will be in real and constant danger. If you do, I am not sure that the theatre company will survive. It has to be your choice."

"What about the three of us who are still missing?" says Joro.

Robert is reassuring. He urges them to take the offer. "It is a way out for you," says Robert. "I must stay here. There is an active anti-Amin underground in Kenya. I am already part of it."

"How can we go so far away without you, Robert? It will definitely be the end of the company," says Charles.

"You carry me with you," Robert replies evenly. "You are everything we have accomplished together. We can all be killed any moment here. You know I am right. Amin wants us dead. We are not the same today as we were two months ago. We have to survive as people first of all. If we do not survive personally, Abafumi cannot survive. I will join you when I can. I will send my wife and children to be with you."

"Why did this happen so suddenly?" asks Charles.

"Amin found out that one of our sources of funding was the American government," says Roert after a long pause. "I'm sorry. I should have told you earlier."

"So it was CIA money," says Charles. "We thought so."

"You *will* be killed," Robert repeats. "I have not wanted to tell you this. But you need to know. I only just found out that Susi, Willy, and Obusi were all caught by the police the night we left. They were taken to Amin's palace." Robert pauses. "Their bodies were identified later. I'm sorry. Every artist in Uganda is suspect now in the government's eyes. Especially us."

The company is inconsolable. For their friends. For themselves.

Charles wonders if word of Abafumi's American support will get his Father in trouble too. Wonders whether he can still get money to his parents.

The next day, Robert makes arrangements for Abafumi's departure. And quickly disappears in the underground.

"And where is Mr. Serumaga?" asks the Ford Foundation

official who has been sent to their hotel to collect full names for identification papers and visas.

"He will join us later," says Charles, following Robert's precise instructions.

A week later, Charles and Joro are called to the Ford Foundation offices. "There is a problem with Stockholm," they are told. "But we can send you all to Rome. I am sure that it will be sorted out reasonably quickly. There will be temporary accommodation there. Ford officials in Italy will be in touch with you as soon as Sweden is cleared."

No one knows how to reach Robert now, not even his own wife. They bring the offer back to the group. Unspoken fears pass between them. From Beth to Mara, Joro to Charles, Kiri to Kasa. They have always taken decisions with Robert. Now they are about to act on their own and they are not comfortable.

"I am sure Robert will contact us there. He will know where we are in Rome and he will know what we should do," says Joro.

"If we get into trouble, we can always visit the Pope," adds Charles with inspired timing. His joke breaks the tension in the air.

Three days later, air tickets to Rome are handed out.

"These are one way tickets," says Beth.

"You're only going one way for now," the Ford official says.

Twenty-four hours later, Ford Foundation officials escort them to the airport. Each is given an envelope with another fifteen hundred dollars in it. They are told that they might be able to perform if they are in Rome for any length of time. They are told that the Italian press has been informed that the company is rehearsing a new production in Rome. Hesitantly, they board the Alitalia flight.

Charles is the last to climb the portable stairs shoved against the plane on the tarmac. He stops half way up, turns back and gulps in a last breath of African air. It is filled with nasty fumes that quickly bring him back to reality.

6. LEAP OF FAITH

LIKE THE ACTORS THEY TRULY ARE, they once again assume their role as an important theatre company.

At the Rome airport, bustling officials in shiny suits jostle before them, impatient as jousters in newly polished armour. In the VIP lounge, they are confronted by journalists, some from the Vatican newspaper, all very excited at the arrival of major artists from Uganda.

The next day they are hailed as Christian heroes who have tried to save Uganda from the perils of Amin's Muslim autocracy. Large print blares their arrival: "Holy Warriors Seek Asylum."

"Spearing the Infidel. "

"Africa Exiles Its Artists. "

"We don't need this kind of publicity," says a worried Joro. "What we need is anonymity."

"Well, we are in the bosom of the Catholic world," answers Beth. "Their embracing of us as artists and Christians is hardly surprising."

"Let's hope Amin doesn't read Italian," says Charles, prompting laughter.

The stories themselves are political and religious. Very little is written about Abafumi per se. Everything they had so carefully stated about the theatre company is omitted.

"The press writes what they want their readers to hear." Joro is irritated. "Why do we even bother with our version of things?"

A day later a telegram arrives from Robert: *I have told the* UN *of your plight. You are to be recognized as political refugees prevented from performing your art in your homeland. That is the reason for the publicity on your arrival. I requested it. Please believe I am watching and always working for you. Have faith.*

"He is still pulling the strings," Kiri tells them with some pride. Her words seem to Charles both triumphant and fragile. He sees how alone she is, hovering and hesitant in the plant-filled hotel lobby, green shade dappling her through flimsy lace curtains. A bright, timid fish in a decorated bowl.

A week later another telegram from Robert: *Abafumi has a contract to perform at Teatro Tenda, a huge tent in a park. I have promised them* Renga Moi *and* Amarykiti. *Rehearse as best you can. Recast the plays without me. You will be contacted about rehearsal space.*

Indeed, the maestro is still watching over them, giving them this chance to be professionals again, instead of fugitives.

With a reduced cast and a mere ten days before they are to open, Charles, Joro, and Kasa spearhead a valiant effort to recover the essence of their art. To find it with so much of their theatre family missing: Willy, Susi, Obusi. To recover without Robert who is clearly now living in danger. They rehearse a truncated *Renga Moi,* but it lurches without limbs. Too many significant lines, dramatic moments have been surgically removed.

Kiri makes Nakazzi's agony her own. Then starts to cry. The rehearsal stops.

Charles watches in silence as the women all throw arms around one another and begin a long, loud keening. Like ancient fates, drawing in the rest of the company to grieve with them.

They need to mourn, he knows, but they also need to move on.

The park they perform in pulses with drums and chants, the variously created rhythms that push the audience into unknown territory. When Nakazzi's babes die each night, there is always a collective gasp. When Renga Moi executes the Priest, audiences register shock.

On alternate nights, *Amarykiti* sears them with anger and sorrow.

At every rendering, the emotional core of their stories deepens, forcing the reduced company to accept that it can still make a difference. And that somehow Robert is still with them. They hear that he might even appear for the last show. But he does not.

The day after their final performance, the company gathers for a meeting. A worried-looking Italian in a dark suit also arrives, saying, "Robert has sent me to take care of you."

"Take care of us," says Charles. "How? Who are you?"

"My name is Gianni. I am a local employee at the American Embassy. I can't tell you any more. Only that in an hour, a van will be waiting for you all downstairs. Please, I must ask you to pack your bags. You are being moved to another hotel. Believe me, it is for your own safety."

When Gianni leaves, the company erupts.

"So what's this about?" sputters Joseph. "I'm starting to feel like a puppet yanked this way and that. Robert just pulls strings when it suits him."

"I'm sure he's looking out for our future," Kiri insists.

"We must trust him," Charles says, trying to wrestle down his own doubts.

An hour later, they are all in the lobby with their bags.

Disgruntled in the silence of the van, they feel like criminals being punished for someone else's crime. The mood worsens as they bump along back streets through one slum after another. Noisy, narrow alleys hung with balconies of shrill housewives and flapping laundry. When the driver finally stops at their new hotel, the Villa Gloria, they hesitantly step out and into the musty foyer.

The manager, short and sharp-eyed, answers questions in a rudimentary English. He points up a flight of worn dark steps and, whistling through two gold capped teeth, reads off their room numbers, adding that they will be using shared baths on their floors. And that they are now two to a room.

"Life among the ruined," Kiri says to no one in particular.

"We are stronger than this," Charles urges. "Fire up your imaginations. Think of our suffering brothers and sisters. We are their messengers in the world now."

Living in a weary, weathered building that promises blistering summer sun and pelting winter rains, with no place to meet or rehearse, depressed under the pall of Robert's silence, Abafumi is deserted.

Three times a day, they traipse two blocks to a tiny restaurant for their set meals This is all part of another Rome for them, a gabble of women in windows high over narrow streets.

At Trattoria Gloria they take their free meals with beer or red wine. And yet they feel like prisoners. Despite the plentiful food, they all feel morosely that each meal will be their last.

The novelty of their celebrity fades and they grow quarrelsome with each other. Dancing as fast as he can, Charles calls up every resource he knows to keep them together. And to keep himself and Beth together.

Gianni comes by every other week with cash. But the amount decreases as regularly as the meals shrink in size.

A month into their stay, Robert's wife arrives at the same sad hotel with their two children. Everyone gathers around her, eager for new information. But she knows as little as they do. She has been in Nairobi she tells them, where her husband made sporadic, anxious visits. Then he told her that she would have to leave and join the company in Rome.

"I know nothing," she assures them, her face shut tight, her children's eyes glancing from one familiar portrait to another of Robert's other family, his extended family. "Nothing."

At meeting after meeting in the hotel's tiny sitting room,

Charles tries to develop a work strategy but the encounters quickly degenerate into complaint sessions. Finally they arrive at the same conclusion. Abafumi is dead. They are on their own.

Joseph is the first to say it. "Until our situation improves or we hear from Robert, we should find work that pays." The idea sits in the air like heresy.

Charles, Kiri, and Joro visit Robert's wife to discuss their predicament.

"We can barely keep ourselves going. Can you help us contact Robert?"

"I leave messages at the U.S. Embassy but I cannot contact him directly." Wanly lit by a square of dirty window, Robert's wife perches, for this inquisition, on the edge of frayed velour in the sitting room. She answers their questions through tears that seem, thinks Charles, to roll helplessly out of her.

Can she help them generate some extra money?

"I have none," she tells them. "I have nothing. Not even for the children's education. I want the children to go to school. But they are not Italian and they don't speak the language. We are stranded here like you. I don't know if I will ever see him again. I don't know where he is. I don't know what will happen to us. Truly."

It's a lament that makes them feel like intruders into her small space, her tiny Italian refuge. In the tense silence that follows, their eyes fall on a white lace doily that has floated onto her shoulder from the back of the sofa, as though sanctifying their collective hopelessness.

This is how they leave her.

"She is in worse shape than we are," says Charles as they walk down a street sliced cleanly in two by late afternoon shadow. "We will have to do what's practical."

In the next few weeks, they sell themselves to the Italian Ministry of Tourism. And the Ministry rents them out as African drummers and singers, to shimmy and shake, as Joro puts it scornfully, through Rome's vast parks. "We are performing chimps," says Joseph.

"Don't make it harder," Charles chides him. "We are doing this to survive."

Joseph is bitter. "This is our demise as artists."

They array themselves over the moss-covered shell of a fountain, where Joro gyrates comically in a vain attempt to keep the ostrich feathers of his headdress dry.

At the Trevi, designed to commemorate the founding of Rome, they situate themselves beneath the allegorical statue of the She-Wolf, mother of all Rome, to render a sad little homesick song.

They chant and drum down the avenue of The Hundred Fountains, lurching and jumping jets of water that gush from stone carvings of small boats, obelisks, mouths of animals, eagles and lilies. Down the cypress-studded slope they slide and twist, lighting the faraway fires of equatorial Africa among Italian waterfalls.

Four tipsy maidens spray water at them before an elaborate chapel at the Fontana dell'Organo. "They want to wash us clean of everything African," quips Beth.

When they finish each performance, Kiri walks among the purple rhododendrons and the bemused crowds to collect money.

Charles takes particular care of Beth. They have grown close again, comforting one another in a shared room and a shared bed, such exchanges being easier now among the company. Together they watch themselves in the shining mirror of each other. One night, during sleep, the mirror shatters.

It begins with a soft thump at the window. Beth wakes and makes out the upper rungs of a wooden ladder angling itself against the sill. Or is she dreaming? The shadows of two men slide into the far end of the room. She drifts off once again

Some hours later, she jolts awake. Screaming. Looks around.

Charles leaps up to comfort her. "It was real. Charles, it was real. Look. Look." She is nearly hysterical.

The open window gapes wide. Winding themselves in bedsheets, they survey the room then rouse the others. Call the manager. Their bags have been taken. Wallets. Clothes. Passports. Gone.

The Italian police are no help, confirming that the thieves were primarily after passports and cash. "Why would they take our bags?" asks Beth. The best police guess is that they just happened to be near the window.

"We can no longer stay at this hotel," says Charles over coffee.

Joro suggests it is time for the group to split up. They have not received funds for two weeks. The hotel manager is getting irritable. No one at the U.S. Embassy seems to know Gianni.

It sounds so callous and cold to Charles, so logical. But he knows Joro is right. It is time to go.

Along damp cobbles they walk, careful steps merging with Joro's quiet words. "Abafumi is over Charles. We all need a fresh start. Mara too. She has never recovered from Robert's treatment of her in Brazil and I want to take care of her. The way you look after Beth. We've made up our minds. We're going to Morocco."

"Morocco!"

"At least it's Africa."

Charles looks stricken.

"You stay here, Charles, if you want. You be leader now. You can still help them. You believe in Abafumi — and Robert — more than anyone."

Beth and Charles inform Robert's wife of the decisions and urge her to tell Robert everything. The last of their old reality is vanishing quickly.

Applying for political refugee status, Joro and Mara prepare to leave. Charles knows they are glad to be escaping.

Should he and Beth go too? But where?

Others in the group are turning into street people, drifting away as well. And apart.

Charles and Beth stay for a time but know they need to find new lodgings. They have all been given two weeks notice. They are offered a series of temporary homes by various emissaries of good will – first, a Ugandan studying in a Vatican seminary for the priesthood, then a Zairian attaché who takes a particular liking to Beth and invites them to use a spare room at the Embassy. But the attaché soon loses interest when Beth does not satisfy his many requirements, among them entertaining groups of his male friends.

Furious at what she has been asked to do, Charles roughly hoists their very modest luggage on his head and marches them both off, like the exiles they are, to the railway station. This vast glass and iron house of arrival and departure becomes home for a week. To the sweaty chuffing of trains, to the wailing of porters and cries of vendors, to the bumping of luggage, to the faraway look of scurrying travellers, they huddle together in dark grimy corners. With drunks cowering under filthy overcoats.

They are propositioned by pimps to make some money with their bodies. Their only defense is staying awake. Heads resting on their one suitcase, they become sleepless fixtures in the railway station like gargoyles on a Gothic church, warning the unholy. Ugly. Hated as the devil himself.

The Ugandan Embassy is their worst enemy now. The American Embassy is totally closed to them.

Someone tells them of unused trains that can be opened quietly at night. Here, on soft dusty seats, they find refuge for a few hours, until the police come with flashlights, harsh words, and a few well-placed kicks to rout them out.

Another habitué of the train station tells them of a place to get free food from a priest called Castelli. "But be careful," he says. "Castelli expects payment."

They protest they have no money.

"Still," they are told, "you may be able to give him what he wants."

The next morning, Charles and Beth ring a corroded doorbell beside the iron gate of a closed churchyard. An old woman in black opens the door, hears their story of woe and ushers them into a study, full of angels.

Charles is soon extending his hand to a fleshy middle-aged priest with a watery smile whose voluminous black cassock rustles as he moves.

"We have come to ask you for food tokens," says Charles. "We are actors…"

"It is all right. I do not have any need to know who you are right now. You are children of God. That is enough."

Father Castelli opens a drawer in his wooden desk and hands them two days' worth of tokens. They are immensely appreciative. "Go to the address on the envelope this afternoon. They will take care of you. Come again when you and your beautiful lady need more."

The priest's complexion is as florid as the angels in his study. Red on white. He sits spreading out on a sofa before them. Studying them silently, he drinks his tea. "You say you are actors?"

"Our company is in exile because of the political situation in Uganda."

"Ah Uganda… What kind of plays do you do?"

Charles says they are based on myth. "No words. A lot of movement and music. The company is called Abafumi, The Storytellers."

"Can you describe the movements you do?"

"Group movement mostly," says Beth. "Like a Greek chorus."

"Ah. The Greek chorus." The priest is studying them. "Do you know," he says finally, "that there were no women in the Greek chorus. No women at all in the Greek theatre."

"I didn't know that," says Beth. "There are women in our company though."

"So I noticed." Suddenly, he rises. "I hope you will come and visit me again. I wish you good luck."

The priest holds out his hands. Beth and Charles each extend theirs in response. As they say goodbye, Father Castelli draws them close and, with a little laugh, kisses each on the forehead. As he says goodbye, he presses their hands against his crotch. "Go with God. Return in love."

Beth and Charles move briskly back from him. Race over the broken tiles of his private chapel, its rough-hewn saints smirking at them as they flee.

"I thought at first he wanted you," says Charles in a whisper. "Then I realized that he wanted me as well. No man has ever looked at me quite that way. I didn't like it."

"But we have what we needed. Two days' worth of food. Maybe we can make it last four ... until we find jobs. We are finished with Father Castelli. For now."

As late afternoon shadows lengthen, Charles and Beth scurry along shuttered side streets with high round windows and small arched doorways until they come to a small house whose walls are covered with votive offerings. Drawn to a fork and spoon flickering in neon, they enter a dingy cafeteria lit by bright bare bulbs. Uncertainly, they make their way towards a glassed-off area behind which nuns are taking the church-given tokens through a lower hinged portion of their transparent wall and handing back trays of food.

The clatter and clash of porcelain and tin is muted by thick windows. Like insects swarming over a dead cow, thinks Charles.

Speaking through a small grille in the glass they order all they can: spaghetti, lasagna, steak, beef stew, rice.

"We need to ration this out," she reminds Charles.

They take their heaping plates over to the empty table noticing, uneasily, that they are alone in the middle of this large room. Sitting down warily to eat, they expect to hear a lecture or a sermon.

Then it comes.

"*Bastardo, bastardo!*" They look up and see a filthy figure in rags lurching violently towards them.

In a flash, the nuns pounce. They have rushed out from behind their cages, a female force of robed righteousness, to scold and berate. Through the door and into the street, they firmly usher out the foul-mouthed man, telling him not to return until he can behave in a civilized way. Then, demure as they were indignant, they quietly apologize to Beth and Charles and return to their silent duties.

Charles thinks about nuns. The black widows of Christ. Catholic heaven. Caught between sacrifice and salvation.

The agreement, before everyone separated, was that they would check in at the Villa Gloria once a week for messages. On their regular stop at the hotel bulletin board, Charles and Beth find word at last.

"New accommodations found. Meet Sunday with your bags at St. Paul's Church, Vatican City." It is signed, "Robert."

On the appointed afternoon, bedraggled and weary but nonetheless pleased to be together again, eight members of Abafumi stand before the high holy stones of St. Paul's, staring up. In awe, they wander through the huge Corinthian columns and lean protectively together on gleaming floors inside the wide central nave, a tight dark knot of apprehension, studying paintings on the panelled ceiling that seems to drop straight down from paradise.

Charles scrutinizes medallion portraits of the Popes on thick walls arranged around a series of small portholes. Leos, Innocents, Gregorys, Piuses, all fixed in red and ermine robes under glittering caps turned towards something only they can see from a place where only they can be.

Far into the apse, Charles strains his eyes — high above an altar dense with black marble, lacy with alabaster, topped by arches and towers of gold — a mosaic of Jesus giving blessing. In blue and red robes, enthroned in oriental carpet, his white face beams serenity, while from his raised right hand, assurance flows.

"I believe him," says Charles quietly to Beth. "He will look after us."

Rita and Monday arrive together with their few belongings. As the two company members who have been perhaps least faithful to the group during Robert's prolonged absences, they are greeted with muted enthusiasm. Ultimately, though, it pleases everyone to see their numbers increasing.

"So do we get to bunk inside this palace?" Rita heaves a plastic bag filled with clothes.

Beth unloads her battered suitcase. The women hug and whisper together.

Charles explores the side chapels.

They circle the rose garden, sit between columns, like a tribe of holy nomads, share stories of where they have been. "Perhaps we could rehearse here," says Beth.

"More likely," says Kiri, "we will start having holy visions if we stay long enough."

"My mother's spirit church was like this," Charles says to no one in particular. "But it had wasps," he adds, unexpectedly thrown back to the past.

Talk of Robert joining them grows in the quarter hour they are there and then fades quickly as a young priest arrives to bring them in.

"I am Brother Vittorio," he says. "You are welcome. Your new home is here under God's protection. But I am afraid it is also underground. Please follow me."

"Pluto's domain," mutters Kasa as they descend a series of massive stone steps to a cavernous and cavelike cellar aglow with huge chandeliers. Rooms opening into rooms. Walls like wandering vines, extending, curving stopping, starting.

"Entering Purgatory," Beth sighs.

"It's more like the underground lair of Magobwi," says Charles, steeling himself to the absence of sunlight.

"Even more like a slave house," declares Joseph. "Everyone kept in cages and pens before the ships took them off."

"Actually," says Brother Vittorio, "early Christians hid here."

"Before they were buried alive I would assume," says Kasa. "Is there any natural light?"

"Anyone buried in the catacombs is quite dead, I can assure you," says the good Brother without a smile.

"Why should I live with dead bodies?"

"Because you want to stay alive. That's what we're all trying to do." Charles is quickly losing his sense of humour.

Water gurgles from an underground stream with a small, carved bridge that they step carefully across.

"There used to be huge cisterns down here," explains Vittorio. "Now it is part of the city drainage system."

"Great," says Joseph ironically, "So we are sewer rats."

"How could Robert do this to us?" asks Kiri bitterly.

"I think he's just getting back at us for all the trouble we've caused." Joseph is not amused.

Through a murky tunnel they wind, one after another, pressed down by an atmosphere clogged with unused light. They have descended onto another level past a small archway leading to a games room, complete with card tables, checker boards, chess sets, and a ping-pong table. From here they walk past a large kitchen and storage rooms into a great hall. High white walls and ceilings sparkle with electric light. People sit against pillars on cement floors, chatting or reading. They smile as the group passes. Some shout out, "Welcome to St. Paul's."

Vittorio stops and points out two large rooms to them, dormitories. "One room is for boys. One for girls" he tells them awkwardly. "I know you are actors but it is the only way here."

Charles and Beth look at one another. No sex in St. Paul's.

"These rooms are not our deluxe models but it is what we have available right now. You will find a kitchen further down this hall. But your meals will be taken two levels up, in the dining area with some of the Brothers who live here. Good basic food. You will not go hungry."

The group tries not to let disappointment show as they examine the cracked concrete and sit timorously on thin threadbare mattresses.

Without breaking rhythm, Vittorio picks up a scorpion and drops it into a tin cup he carries around for the purpose. "They are night creatures. Not usually out at this hour. This one obviously can't tell time."

"That means they emerge when we're sleeping," Charles says with a calmness he doesn't feel.

"They don't want you. They're after insects. And they prefer the open air."

"How many other insects live here?" asks Kasa.

Vittorio laughs. "This is a very old building. We have to share it with the local residents. After all, they were here first." Smiling, he adds, "we can give you paint for your rooms if you want. Orange is best. Scorpions don't like bright colours."

They choose beds. The rooms are on either side of a wide dimly-lit hall. They drop their bags and race up and out into the sun again as quickly as they can. Charles and Beth clutch hands and charge, as though pursued, into the eternal city.

In a public area of the Vatican, Robert is waiting. But not for them.

Standing before salmon pink columns and the blinding dome, among small white gates that mark St. Peter's Square now empty of crowds, he is imagining the blood red canopy streaked with gold. The carpeted stairs and glittering throne, crowned and polished for heaven by invisible angels. He is preparing himself for a visitation. Anticipating his own audience with the Pope.

His single chance to explain who these actors are, who he is, what Idi Amin has done to them. His hope for redemption

and forgiveness. His hunger for blessing. His need to get his
families even farther from Amin's long and violent reach.

Gradually, St. Paul's reveals itself to Abafumi in its true and
myriad colours. It is an ecclesiastical highrise, divided — mostly below ground level — into floors full of apartments for a
mixed population of students, artists, and assorted refugees
from around the world. Ringing with song and animated
polyglot conversation, on any given day it might be the centre of a political debate or echo with rehearsals and musical
performances. In this heaven-haven, many of Rome's more
adventurous citizens come to see and hear refugee artists and
would-be presidents.

Father William is in charge of it all. His door is open day and
night for the benefit of his protegées who are welcome to come
and converse at any hour. Invitations issue from the rectory
regularly for afternoon tea, morning coffee, sandwiches, and
Brio in the cloisters.

Father William is especially interested in this theatre troupe
from Uganda, his own housekeeper also being a Ugandan refugee. Fully aware of the political situation that drove them out,
he is always avid for detail, conferring with the Abafumi actors
outdoors, indoors, and even in the Great Hall of the crypt.

Soon Abafumi become veterans at the crypt. It is they who
direct newcomers to the location of the piano, the best accous-
tical niches, and vaults of the highly theatrical underground
catacombs, for vocal exercises and improvisation sessions,
for wailing saxophones and exuberant drumming. The vast
caverns now ring regularly with music, throb for hours each
day with drums, dance, and dramatic readings.

In Father William's personal paradise of the performing
arts, classical music students practice in the exotic chambers
of the crypt, then join impromptu jazz sessions with Abafumi,
clapping and stomping and chanting with the drums of African tradition. In turn, they coach the African theatre troupe

in the quivering coloratura filaments and deep bass sonorities of Italian opera classics.

As payment for the privilege and pleasure of artistic freedom, these denizens of the crypt also donate a portion of their talents to Father William for his above-ground activities, happily chiming like bells through the notes of the Latin Mass in St. Paul's glowing Sunday services.

This turn of events eases pain. Once more, Charles and his theatre family know that, though wounded, they are still members of a superior species.

They discover that Father William has also had his share of the theatrical life. He was once a song and dance man in British music hall before he became a cleric. He could, he tells them with pride, shuffle and soft shoe, wield a top hat and cane, and play the spotlight. His whole body recalls that past.

Charles asks him why he joined the church. "When I raise the host, intone the Latin words that change bread and wine into the body and blood of Christ, when I am in my long satin robe with incense and little tinkling bells filling the air, then I am still in the theatre. Much better than the one I was in before."

One day, Father William gathers them over a glass of red wine in the cool garden shadows of the cloister and, with grave enthusiasm, broaches a subject dear to his heart. He wants a favour of them. Would they perform a rendering of the "Prodigal Son" story for Lent? "Priests will visit from all over the world during this sacred time. They will come for study and prayer. I want to show them how theatre and religion can work together."

Charles finds in the parable, the story of their own loss and abandonment. He speaks in favour. All agree.

Slowly, fitfully, the company struggles to reclaim its voice. They vocalize their grief in a traditional Ugandan song of loss and regret, a song of bewilderment emphasized by the knocking and clicking of calabashes, the rhythmic humming of the lyre.

Abafumi's *Prodigal Son* becomes the Easter hit of the Catholic churches of Rome. Father William brings in all the major congregations during Lent, providing Abafumi with full houses, some extra financial support and an extended run. Charles co-opts priests in their lavish cassocks to play the forgiving father, while he himself plays the errant son.

For the reduced company, *Prodigal Son* is the story of modern Africa, sold out by ruthless dictators.

Following this triumph, they are invited by Italian Tourism to help open a major resort in Calabria. They take up temporary residence at the luxurious Casa Rossano along the Gulf of Taranto, where, blatantly billed as "primitive dancers," they present cut-down versions of their repertoire. Every evening at sundown, crowds and cars crawl towards them under lights along the beach road in excited anticipation of performances.

In this context, Abafumi is hardly distinguishable from the later fireworks display exploding at midnight over the heads of spectators. In fact, while they drum and chant after each show, the hot black sky blooms into light, with flares and spirals, arcs and fans, into spluttering suns and hissing silver moons.

But each morning, the bright blue whispering sea tortures them with what they have become.

The struggle is hard, like a body that has been pulled apart too many times and carelessly reassembled in the wrong shape, with the wrong parts. Nothing fits or functions properly. The heart of Abafumi beats feebly here. Its agile limbs are atrophying. Its strength and grace fading daily.

Back in the crypt, back in Father William's care, Charles and Beth choreograph their private survival, perform their own drum and dance pieces on street corners for coins. Charles is humiliated, vows he will never let them be shamed like this again.

Months pass.

In a small restaurant that many from the crypt frequent, the name *Uganda* suddenly suffuses the air.

Kampala has been liberated.

The information is fragmented and confused but something seems to be happening, something major. Intimations of change have been filtering through for weeks, agitating everyone.

"What I have heard," says Kasa, "is that those against Amin have met in Tanzania."

"But who?" Joseph asks sharply. "Everybody must be against that bastard by now."

"Of course," says Charles, "but they're terrified to show it."

"No, I mean some powerful people," Kasa retorts. "Apparently representatives of twenty-two Ugandan civilian and military groups are meeting to try and agree on a government in exile, an interim government if and when Amin is removed."

"Do you think Robert is part of it?" asks Beth.

"It wouldn't surprise me," says Charles.

"That's good, isn't it?" Monday, like everyone else, is trying to penetrate the political fog.

Anything is good that will oppose Amin, they all agree.

The television report drifts on. Five of them sit tensely watching as beer bottles sweat on square-tiles and warm honeyed light floods the interior walls. They are oblivious to everything except the unrelenting drama taking place over their heads. The plummy tones of the BBC reassure them.

Former President Idi Amin — a man who has been accused of cannibalism while in office — has apparently fled Uganda. An interim government is expected to be announced shortly according to....

That evening, in Father William's apartment, they watch a thirty-minute special on Uganda from London, seeking assurance and details.

"Look, it's Robert!" shouts Charles, with a leap that sends his wooden chair skittering along the polished floor. The five of them gawk, open-mouthed, at their director in full commando attire, a rifle in one hand and a pistol in the other, being jostled by bodyguards and hoisted victoriously on shoulders.

Robert is mentioned for a cabinet position.

They hear how Robert and most other interim government members have been moving into and out of Uganda secretly from bases in Kenya. They also hear that there has been American involvement in what is now being called a coup. Direct CIA involvement.

"He is a genius," shouts Charles. "If he believes in something he can make it happen. The way he did with us and this company."

"What company?" says Kiri drily. Charles glares at her.

Over the next weeks, five of them divide their time between the crypt and what they have come to call the Green Room Café. Back home, Robert has been appointed Minister of Commerce and Industry, his training as an economist clearly standing him in good stead with the new government.

Robert seems to flit like a firefly in the news, aggravating their fears and hopes into frenzy. Robert is in Kampala. He is in Nairobi. One day he is in a suit making a speech about building a new Uganda. The next he is in casuals at the busy port in Mombasa overseeing crucial cargo imported from Germany and other parts of Europe for the great reconstruction.

The following week, he appears before a United Nations group at the Intercontinental Hotel in Mombasa to urge international reconstruction efforts.

More than once they hear him refer in interviews to his old "theatre family." He tells the world that he left them abroad and must work to bring them back. "Part of me is still with them."

They cheer. So he has not forgotten them.

Now he is seen with his wife and children in Kampala starting them all on a new life.

Charles and the others wait anxiously for his call.

But months after the new government is sworn in, there is still nothing from him. Leader after political leader is replaced. Still no word. Then to everyone's shock, Milton Obote once again takes over after a much-disputed election.

Rumours continue to fly. The one they hear most clearly has Robert himself leading a new revolution against Obote who dropped him from the cabinet post he occupied, thereby creating an instant and furious enemy.

With every successive political change in Kampala, Charles is asked by Father William if he wants to go home. His answer is always the same. "Home is what I built with Abafumi. It no longer exists in Uganda."

Only Beth has remained with him at the crypt. The others have fled. Abafumi is no more and Uganda still seems a death sentence.

Beth and Charles can barely keep themselves alive, much less the artistic dream that threw them together. Beth suggests they separate for a while. Just to survive. "But we are a couple," retorts Charles indignantly.

"We were, Charles, and it was good. But what drew us together is gone."

"I'm going to apply for a visa to Canada," she tells him. "Perhaps you should too."

"Canada," says Charles with a laugh. "It's as cold as Stockholm. And none of us wanted to go there. Remember?"

Father William believes her decision is a good one because he is sure she can easily find work in domestic service, if nothing else. About Charles, he is not so sure. Possibly once Beth is there, she can send for him.

Secretly, Charles still favours Sweden. It was a tempting refuge once. He thought he could shine there, his difference, his talent marking him out. He feels excited considering it, even though, without anyone as a reference, an official visa would be almost impossible to acquire. But if Beth really is leaving perhaps his Swedish dream is possible. On the street he manages to find someone who knows someone who knows someone who can get him the necessary documents. For cash.

Should he tell Father William? He decides not to. He will write once he is in Stockholm. And why get Father William into any trouble if the visa turns out to be less than legal.

Charles takes two hundred dollars, his life savings, buys the visa, then goes to a bucket shop where he trades in his watch for an amazingly cheap air ticket.

Beth is shocked when he tells her he is leaving. He will go the next day. She is sure he will be arrested.

In Rome, his papers are barely examined. On the SAS flight he is full of anticipation, convinced he will be comfortable in Sweden among people who are practical and straightforward. He will be well-fed and will bundle up against the chill. He will breathe salty sea air and warm himself in a snug bar with a beautiful woman who will ply him with strong drink. He will, most of all, function again as a dancer in the clear cold north.

On arrival, he hands his travel documents to an immigration officer who examines them in great detail. After some time, another official materializes and waves Charles out of the immigration line into a small office. Questions and more questions about the visa, about his temporary passport, about his sponsors in Stockholm.

Charles senses that something has gone wrong.

"These documents have been forged," he is told by the police. "Where did you get them?"

After several hours of futile explanation, Charles is told that he could be arrested but might instead just be returned to Italy if he can prove residence there. He asks to claim refugee status.

"Not with illegal travel documents," he is told. The debate is fruitless. "You will stay here overnight and leave in the morning."

Charles is led away. The suspicious eyes of strangers bore into his back.

He feels like a miscreant child, helpless, ashamed and stupid. But most most damningly he feels he has betrayed some vague higher purpose. He is taken, under guard, up an escalator, disappears through an unmarked door behind a partition of frosted glass that makes him yearn for the dark architecture of the crypt and its labyrinthine freedoms far underground where even the scorpions run loose.

He is left alone for hours. A sandwich is brought in. Juice. But he cannot keep his mind clear. Cannot follow the logic that put him here. He is a theatre artist whose company is dissolving. He is a Ugandan whose country is disappearing. He is an unemployed political refugee.

Those whom he trusted are gone. Those who inspired him, have abandoned him.

He stands and slowly begins to sway, singing softly. He will dance himself free. Alone if he has to.

After an hour, a policeman enters and orders him to empty his pockets. Wallet, comb, papers, change. Small diary. He pulls it all across the table towards him and begins to flip the pages of the tiny blue plastic notebook, glancing at the entries: Villa Gloria Hotel. Hotel Cavour. Pensione Rossi.

"I see you do not have a permanent address in Italy," he says with minimal emotion.

"I am in artist in exile from Uganda. I am temporarily homeless. I was hoping to live here."

"Why?"

"I told you, I am a political refugee. I am part of a theatre company with many members missing. Our director is not with us because he is helping the new government in Uganda. My position is very difficult."

The policeman has just read an entry that notes an invitation to the German Embassy, following remarks about getting drunk, following the comment, "a good supper and a good sleep, alone in my own bed on the occasion of my birthday."

"But you can afford to go to parties and celebrate in restaurants."

"I am no risk to you. I have broken no law," Charles declares, his face thorny with indignation.

"That may be so but I determine whether you constitute a political or a criminal threat. For all we know, you are a drug mule." And then he says, "Take off your clothes."

Images of Father Castelli pollute his imaginings. "Why?"

"I have orders to check you for illegal substances. It is not my choice."

Charles is mortified. Even the Rwandese did not humiliate him like this. He has sunk to the level of slaves. Nevertheless, he does what he is told, finding pride, in his strong glistening body mutely displayed. No beast of burden but a warrior king before this pale balding policeman in paunchy middle age.

Not impressed, the guard rises lethargically and, breathing hotly into Charles' face makes him open his mouth. Then he runs round his gums with a rubber-gloved finger, causing Charles to gag. He feels like an animal, slow moving, mute as Suna, mechanically prodded this way and that.

"Turn around. Bend over and hold your buttocks apart."

Aware of the flashlight's close heat, Charles burns with indignation, could burst into flame as the guard examines his rectum, pressing and poking with a stumpy thumb.

He is given back his clothes, led away to a holding cell and kept overnight. Next morning a different guard wakes him with a plastic cup of watery orange juice and instructs him to get ready to leave.

"Can I at least have some breakfast?" The guard, whose English is no doubt perfect, mumbles something brusque in Swedish and leaves him. He is finally given a full meal after which papers are signed under the supervision of two officers who now escort him everywhere.

"Where is my suitcase?" He is told not to worry. It is already on the plane. Soon, he is shepherded towards the SAS departure gate where a plane for Rome awaits him.

When he gets off, he is met by an Italian immigration officer and marched yet again into police custody amidst a barrage of curiosity seekers. One passenger from the plane, an elderly lady with a small powdery face wrinkled up like a question mark, keeps asking Charles, "What did you do? What did you do?"

The police in Rome are very upset with him. They seem to have taken it as a personal insult that a foreigner, a guest in their country — indeed, a refugee seeking shelter — should prefer Sweden to Italy, should risk so much for a cold dispassionate Scandinavian place that cannot compare with the myriad Italian flavours in which they, themselves, so happily swirl.

"You don't like Italian food? You don't like espresso? You are crazy. You had a good life. Now you have messed everything up." The police stand around him performing theatre, Italian style. Charles recognizes it immediately, having seen love spats on buses, pasta pots flung at husbands' heads from loggia railings, smiling pickpockets caught red-handed, and beautiful women outraged at the wandering fingers of gentlemen in a crowded market.

Masters of the grand gesture, the police too grunt and gesticulate, nod and shake, dramatizing all the emotion they feel, bringing it into the public arena so that everyone can emphatically assert what sheer folly it is to have turned one's back on the life force that is Italy!

"Please," says Charles clearly and slowly, "may I make a telephone call?"

He dials Beth's number.

"I knew it," she says. "I told you not to go."

He expects her to help him. She is angry and hurt. Why didn't he listen to her? Why did he take this risk alone? Doesn't he trust her at all? Don't they still care for one another?

He knows she is right. "I'm not perfect," he says. "I had to try this. I had to do something."

Finally she says she will get Father William to phone back. Minutes later, he does.

The priest hadn't even known Charles was gone. "My dear boy. Stay there. I am coming to get you. Now put on the chief officer."

"Thank God," says Charles, handing the phone to his somewhat affronted captor.

An hour later, in the upstairs offices of the police station, terms are negotiated. Papers signed. The Prodigal Son is finally embraced back at St. Paul's by Beth, Father William, and an official from the American Church in Rome. God has welcomed him back into the fold. He is forgiven, not forsaken.

In their rooms at the crypt, Beth faces him. She is in a black-and-white waitress uniform, looking more like an Italian maid than an African dancer. Ready for her first day, Charles tells her, as a servant. "Is this our destiny, Beth?"

"For now, it is," she says simply. "We did not choose ordinary lives, Charles. Or safe lives. Or secure lives. Our existence is not routine."

"But even when we do nothing, disaster happens."

"You did something. Something stupid."

"Will you still go to Canada?"

"Yes," says Beth.

She is strong. Standing so straight in her starched squares against the cold dim stone of the crypt, a fierce cat dazzling in sunlight. As strong as he needs her to be.

"Okay," he says. "I will find a job here. I'll become truly Italian."

Father William helps Charles get work at the Nigerian Embassy. His new role? A guard on the Ambassador's personal staff, he will occupy an easy and comparatively lucrative position. Indeed, almost everything at the Nigerian Embassy is lucrative, given that the country seems to be floating on wells of oil. The Embassy adds new staff weekly. Africans are their obvious first choice for employment.

Charles is to arrive every day at six a.m. Wear a uniform.

He spends most of his days sitting on a chair outside one office or another reading. No one can get into these offices without walking by Charles and no one walks by Charles without clearance in advance. If someone in the office he is guarding wants something, they buzz and Charles answers over the intercom. When they go out, Charles opens and closes the doors. He plays this role with detachment, indolently sampling its pleasures.

He luxuriates in the soft muted pinks and blues of the Embassy. To him, these colours are the essence of light, the evidence of life. Colours from the time of his childhood when women were wrapped in rainbows. The Embassy's arches enchant him and he grows to appreciate the lavish rooms and their luminous glow.

The Ambassador himself occupies a large pink room with blue brocade curtains, pale seashell tiles and blue satin couches, while the Cultural Attaché — someone Charles is trying to get to know — lounges calmly in creamy caramel.

He finds himself dreaming often of home. But not today. As he begins his fifth week on the job, he is roused from his seat by unusual noises downstairs. He stands, riveted by the sounds of files overturned, emptied, drawers ripped open.

He leaps to his feet. No longer merely playing soldier.

The scale of this destruction is large. Fine things seem to be breaking everywhere. Charles moves quietly along the Renaissance railing that marks the musician's gallery for evening parties, and peers carefully down. Through the thick plaster pillars, carved capitals and niches of tile and stone, past a black Madonna smiling serenely aloft, he sees huge potted plants being smashed, crockery shattering onto stone floors, and the large patio windows splintering.

He watches as four young men and two women, about his own age, shout in unison with each new attack on some exquisite item in the room. The vandals are Africans, not Italians. Nigerian students demanding to see the man in charge of educational grants. When the attaché opens his office door, the students stop their rampage and let loose a volley of vituperation.

"We are hungry. We are broke," they are saying. "We were promised grants for study abroad. But the grants have stopped and we can't live anymore. No one will listen to us."

"The government that promised you money," says the attaché, "did not get re-elected. The new government is not honouring previous promises. I am sorry about that but your actions are not going to help you. This is no way to communicate. We have already called the police."

"What are we supposed to do? We cannot live this way."

"I have no instructions from our government about this. I am only a civil servant."

Sirens scream around the building.

Charles unlocks an office and looks out the window to see what is going on in the street. *Carabinieri* have surrounded the embassy. He watches them storm in (grateful they are not on his floor) with sub-machine guns and tear gas. He hears them shouting to one another something about "*terroristi.*" Their compatriots outside are trying to tell the police that this is a legitimate protest.

In the next moment, the students in the Embassy all drop to their knees and do not move. One by one, they are handcuffed and led away. Everyone is arrested. As they are shoved out, they can be heard imploring the attaché to help them.

Charles tries to make sense of the situation. They have been brave, if more than a bit foolhardy, in their quest. He admires their boldness and determination, the way they have taken it upon themselves to correct an injustice.

But it is not his fight. He has deserted his fight.

Robert remains among the missing. No doubt, thinks Charles, the man is still moving in circles of power and pleasure for political ends. Organizing parties. Spending his time impressing people, elegantly sporting new clothes, nibbling finger foods, sipping fine wines, nudging beautiful women. Or waging war against corruption.

While Charles tortures his own head with images of himself, playfully flexing his muscles for photos with beautiful women in his starched embassy uniform.

But when he looks in the mirror, he sees a ghost. Drifting. If he looks long enough there is nothing but vapour. He has begun to disappear.

When he looks again he sees a very different Charles dancing out of the blankness.

The worst news is sudden. On the Spanish Steps. Late one night where he sits arm in arm with Beth. Inventing a future.

"Robert is dead." Kiri arrives in near hysteria.

"Not true." Charles' statement is absolute.

"He is dead," says Kiri through tears. "In Kenya."

Charles watches her dazed, traversing the full width of each step, struggling, as she climbs, with words. "He is gone. I heard it on the radio. The reports were unclear but he is dead...."

"How?"

"They think he was poisoned. In his hotel room. They found him dead. A woman followed him upstairs. An hour later, someone called, asked them to investigate. He's dead. He's dead."

Charles folds up inside. Grinds to a halt. Robert. The Priest. Trapped, burnt out, ravaged by visions. And a woman.

The three of them make their way awkwardly down the steps, clattering like spilled marbles. Weaving and swaying in sorrow, barely holding each other up. Then stop at a fountain. Incredulous.

"He loved his lives. All of them," says Beth.

"He loved us." Kiri barely whispers the words.

"And he died for all his lives," murmurs Charles.

Collecting themselves, they hurry back to St. Paul's.

The next day, still dazed, he knocks quietly on Father William's door. Inside, among the painted china cups, behind a thick wall of brocade curtain, he tells the priest that he must leave.

"You have a good life in Rome and a safe one," says Father William.

"I need to start again."

"So will you go with Beth to Canada?"

Father William is convincing with his descriptions of a land that is a gentler version of America, a land with fewer politics to worry about. "And employment opportunities falling from the sky like snowflakes."

Charles begins to think more and more of Canada. He looks through library books and tourist guides. He and Beth discuss a joint move. She would love him to be with her. A land without political upheaval. A stable place. No more embassy work.

Father William has agreed to check into the forms, the interviews, the complications.

"I will go to Canada," Charles finally decides.

Robert, he recalls, had spoken once of Canada. A summer festival. A few of the company had done a very truncated version of *Renga Moi* in a place called Edmonton.

Charles would ask to go to Edmonton. A city obviously interested in African theatre. He applies for a visa to Canada. "I have always wanted to go to Edmonton," he tells the surprised immigration officer at the Canadian Embassy.

He and Beth will formally become a couple, at least for visa purposes.

Beth's visa comes first. Clearly they have nothing against African women in Canada. When the two inquire about employment, they are told that she can always go into domestic service.

"Ah," says Charles knowingly, though he is not quite sure what that would involve in Canada. However, the Canadians remain unconvinced that he — listed for visa purposes as a dancer with some drumming skills — will find work as easily as this young woman will. "But she can ultimately help sponsor you," he is told.

At the airport twelve weeks later, they are both tearful. "I will do anything to join you in Canada," he tells her. "Wait for me."

"We are together now Charles. I trust you. And because I trust you I will wait. We really will be a couple."

With fear and sadness, he watches her disappear into the departure lounge. He knows she is frightened. He realizes he has come to love her. He is also her brother, her protector and shield. Together, he consoles himself, they will start their own small village among giant trees, a garden off the dirt track that disappears into the warm midday bush.

Letters from Edmonton begin to arrive. In the beginning they arrive regularly. Letters detailing how strange she feels on her own. How strange her life seems without him. How polite Canadians are. How comfortably hot it is in August. How she is searching for work. How she has found a job as housekeeper. Then as a waitress.

Eventually, the letters stretch from daily to weekly. Ultimately, he is surprised when they come at all. She has met someone Charles thinks.

One humid afternoon in the chilly crypt, Father William approaches him. He asks Charles to rethink his plans. Once more. To help a young lady named Christina. A Swede as it turns out. A careful chiseller of ecclesiastical song. Christina. She is stuck in a convent in frosty Stockholm and yearns to melt her voice and expand her art in the warmth of operatic Italy.

"The Vatican organization that sponsors this congregation has offered her board and lodging but she needs a sponsor here. A sort of family here. You could be that family."

"Family?"

"She needs a husband, Charles. At least on paper."

Charles is now beginning to see what Father William is really saying. "You mean marry her?"

"You could see where it leads. Perhaps it could lead back

to Sweden. She is a Swedish citizen. If you married her, you would be eligible for Swedish citizenship as well. You could get a proper passport. You could travel more easily...."

Since Beth's departure, Father William has watched his loneliness grow. His own inquiries to the Canadian Embassy have confirmed that Charles' refugee status is far down the immigration list. The only way Christina could stay in Italy for any length of time would be to have a relative here. Perhaps, thinks Father William ... perhaps he can help them help each other.

Charles begins to see possibilities. There is virtually no one left in Rome of the original Abafumi company now. Everyone has moved off. He has become a solitary musical note looking for its own special tune in a city flooded with sculpture.

Charles keeps returning to the Spanish Steps to speak to Robert there, a ghost in the night. They linger together watching couples cupped in one another. Robert whispers devilishly in his ear something about white women who let you make them laugh.

A Swedish wife? Well, maybe.

Yes. He'll do it.

Six weeks later, Christina arrives. Charles follows the priest through buttery sun slabs on the church floor, groomed and shiny as a colt in his new church-bought suit.

"Come and meet your bride."

In the dim recesses of the cloister, he sees her. Still as prayer, she twines among slender stone stems, a pale green vine stretching from its root. Bleached to crystal by a life of nuns and sacred music. Christina, the Lord's snowy sister.

They meet. They talk.

For days on end, they whisper and grow to know one another. Gradually, they accept the proposition. Each has an agenda. Unspoken. They wander together. Innocently and unwittingly, they allow each other perilous freedom.

A week later, they marry in Father William's study.

Charles borrows money from the priest to book a honey-moon night at a large hotel. Christina tiptoes into the room, like an angel trying new wings. Birdlike and ready to pounce, she perches on the edge of a chair surveying, her eyes berry bright. Delicate as alabaster, a butterfly from a dark chrysalis, she understands his need this night.

On the big blue bed of a suite in the Albernini, over a mirror of blood red tiles they allow themselves to drift in a shallow lake of love.

Six weeks later, Christina announces to Charles that she is pregnant.

"Wha-a-at?" he stammers. "You didn't fix anything?"

"Fix anything? Isn't that up to the man?"

Charles suddenly realizes how innocent she really is.

"I didn't know. The nuns didn't tell me anything about that. Except that I must be married if I wanted to come to Italy."

Charles is in shock. This marriage was just a temporary thing. But a child! He is confounded. He sees his dilemma clearly. He has begun an entirely new life.

Even Robert clucks in his ear. "How can you spend your-self so carelessly, scatter yourself this way? Soon there will be nothing left."

Charles smoulders. Christina slowly turns to ice, a frosty madonna singing over her immaculate conception, glass hard-ening around the divine spark she carries inside.

In her sixth month, she tells him that she will return to Swe-den. Alone. They sit on narrow sun-drenched stone steps. "I will take care of the child," she says simply. "Father William assured me that the marriage shouldn't cause you any problems in Canada. It was never registered in a civil court. Only God knows that we were married. I will agree to say whatever you need me to say."

They sit silent for a long time. Charles takes her hand — a

wayward flake of snow — and touches her swollen belly. He feels proud and unnerved that this was so easy to do, begin another being, some version of himself that will go on and on now. With or without him.

They know that whatever brief moment they had here in Rome ended as quickly as it began. She stands and Charles lets her go. Watches her walk up the shadowed steps, out the door under the winged angels of a yellow street lamp. Back into her world.

To have his child.

Alone again, he has returned to the Canadian Embassy several times pushing for permission to emigrate. To join Beth. Telling her of Christina but not of the child. Will she take him back?

He learns three months later that he is a father. Of a child he will never see. A little boy he will not be able to name.

The next day, his visa to Canada is approved. He will see Beth again.

Through Father William, the congregation in Rome offers him the plane ticket for Canada. A United Nations agency lends him three hundred dollars. The Nigerian Embassy gives him another two hundred dollars as a gift. He has saved four hundred more. How far will his money stretch in Canada? He has no idea.

But the puppet master yanking the cords of his fate is also a trickster artist whose deft, quick brushstrokes can fill in a bright life on a huge canvas, where nothing bad happens.

Beth knows from the Canadian government that she must be his official sponsor. She tells him that she has signed the papers. Everything is waiting for him.

He sits alongside Father William and a few friends for a fare-well dinner. Ravenously, he eats his way towards a new life. At meal's end, with the tang of bittersweet limoncello on his lips, he has consumed all the reasons to leave.

Dreaming sweet dreams of snow and mountains, cowboy hats and Indian feathers, red-coated police on horseback, a nameless baby boy.

Beth.

Robert.

Oh Canada.

7. CANADA

A WINDLESS DAY. JULY. 1987. Two rescue workers poke timidly around the twisted metal of a wrecked car. In a field, nearly a mile away from the nearest mountain road.

Devastation in clear light.

"How does a big old Ford, the size of a small tank, get squashed flat as a bug like this," asks one of the men, in dazed denial of the destruction that was a tornado. He wants not to know the dreadful details his eyes are delivering.

"It's like something just picked it up and squeezed the life out of it, vacuumed out all the life," says the other.

"I think I've found a body."

They walk over and stare down. Exchange hushed horror. "He's completely purple. Every blood vessel must be broken."

They move closer. Peer into the face of a black man.

"Is he alive?"

"Don't think so." A slight moan. A wheeze. Almost a rattle.

"He is still alive. Get on the two-way. We need an ambulance here quickly. Say it's urgent."

The call is made. Then they find another body nearby. A woman. Nearly naked. The clothes ripped from her body. Also unconscious but breathing. Clutching a purse. Open.

"I guess the two of them were at it," says the first man. "Or else it was a hell of a storm."

"It was a hell of a storm. Worst tornado in the Rockies for four years."

"Look in her bag. Maybe there's ID." They pick at the contents. Find her driver's licence.

"Angela. Her name is Angela. Looks oriental."

"Angela, can you hear me? Angela?"

"She's going to need all the angels she can get to save her."

The ambulance arrives. She might make it. The prognosis is not so good for him.

For Charles.

Not so good.

"Unknown black male," the ambulance records say.

Dreaming of angels.

"Angel Lady and The Miracle Man" reads the Edmonton newspaper headline next day. "Two Survive Tornado in Critical Condition."

But Miracle Man is still in a coma. Lost. Floating through images only he sees. Disconnected. An exhibit on view before anonymous spectators. Behind glass. Exposed to the curious gaze of medical onlookers who read the label on his bed: "Tornado Victim No. 6: No Name."

In dream he is still a soccer player — dribbling the ball with flashing feet, nimble as a top, flying free and scoring for his team. It is the version of himself he needs.

Slowly, he begins to wake. To speak. But he cannot remember who he is.

"Your name. What is your name?"

"Kampala ... Pele...."

Days pass. Moments of semi-consciousness. Hours of confusion. And as Charles starts to wake from this dream, the pain sets in. Intense pain. Excruciating pain. He cannot feel parts of himself.

Doctors intrude on his awareness.

Has he lost his fingers? No feeling. His legs?

He remembers. His sister sliced his finger. He shouts in his head that it was Debra.

Can anyone hear?

He explains the tale of *Renga Moi*. Then he explains the plot of *Amarykiti*. But they are not listening. They are circling around him. Ignoring him.

"Can you hear me?" comes the whisper.

Someone's voice. A woman's voice. He loves her.

But his wife is Christina, not Beth.

Why can he not speak? Why can he only dream? His wife is Christina. Not Beth.

Edmonton journalists inquire about him regularly. They dub him "Tornado Man," and "Miracle Man." Theirs is a morbid, nagging insistence, demanding photos, visual proof that he has survived. Like doubting apostles with fingers in the wounds of some crucified black Christ who has been sliced from neck to navel.

They know he has defied death and want to explore his secret.

He lapses back into coma. And out.

Charles, "Who stands for the Lord," lies unconscious in a hospital bed.

More than two months pass. During this time he dreams his own legend. A world-class dancer and director of the restored Abafumi Theatre Company. Telling their powerful stories around the globe — of a new Uganda, Africa's enlightened republic, its political and artistic leader.

Slowly awakening, he gradually sees, can follow simple commands, can hear but he cannot easily move. Nor can he easily recognize people.

An unknown population wanders continuously in and out of his room — rehabilitators of various kinds, occupational therapists, physiotherapists. He lies still in his bed waiting for some moment of recognition that does not come.

He drifts on the soothing sound of voices calling him home.

He hears words now. Coma. Amnesia.

Beth sits vigil beside him, moving when the doctors insist, as they test and re-test a body hung in suspended animation, rigged with tubes and sacks, sucking out and forcing in, collecting. His left leg and right arm hoisted in casts. Head injuries seep.

She watches his beard grow — a heavy black sprouting fed by morphine. She watches her lithe dancing partner swell with body fluids.

"Remember, Charles. Remember the great adventures we had?" she whispers, trying to coax him out of his dream world.

His mind skips easily back in time. Arriving in Canada. Excited. New beginnings.

"Passports please." Canadian officials in Montreal are polite and efficient. They seem determined to ask the same question over and over. Repetition does not amuse him. Eventually his passport is stamped.

In Canada at last. In the middle of winter.

Charles is travelling with a dozen sponsored refugees on the long flight from Rome. Mostly Africans and Asians, all are bound for Edmonton. Rome to Paris to Montreal. Sixteen hours. They arrive exhausted but exhilarated.

He follows his group onto a bus. Overnight in downtown Montreal and then another plane to Edmonton — four hours further to the west — in the morning.

The bus chugs through the city. Charles is amused at how fluently the driver curses in both French and English. The volubility of life on the streets — the amicable congestion so typical of a port city jostling in high-spirited commercialism — reminds Charles of Mombasa, the noise of market and crate, watery light and movement.

They are deposited at a Holiday Inn. That sounds right. He needs a vacation and Canada is kindly accommodating him. The group is told that because their stay is on the government, they can charge coffee shop meals to their rooms. They are also allowed one phone call anywhere in Canada using a special telephone code. Charles phones Beth in Edmonton.

Beth is pleased to hear that he has at last arrived. But the distance between them has also translated into strangeness. Their voices barely know each other after so long apart. They have lost their intimacy in this new world.

Restless in his room, too tired to sleep, he watches television all night, willing himself into this other life. He finds *Three's Company,* a show he has seen in Rome in clumsily dubbed Italian. The crispness of the program's humour in its native English wakes him up to its real comedy, the hero's stunned ineptitude, living with two female roommates and pretending to be some sort of homosexual. Jack is always in trouble but he merely needs to smile and people instantly forgive him.

Soon, thinks Charles cynically, there will be nothing left of him but the smile.

The next morning, in the harsh echoing light of the airport, Charles walks past a black man sweeping the floor. He tries to speak to him but the cleaner knows only French. Drawing down an accustomed cloak of invisibility, the sweeper turns away from this inquiring intruder and resumes his task.

He reads Hollywood gossip headlines in the bookshop. Women and sex scandals. Men and betrayals. He reads that John Wayne has died. His image of the rough, gun-slinging hero. How can John Wayne be dead? He is America.

"Where are you from?" asks the white man seated next to him on the plane bound to Edmonton.

"Uganda."

A blank response.

"And when did you arrive in Canada?"

"Yesterday. I came from Rome. I am moving to Edmonton. My wife is waiting for me there."

"Welcome to Canada," says the man. "I hope it's not going to be too cold for you. But it's all part of God's country."

God's country. A strange concept. Uganda was God's country. Rome was God's permanent residence. Canada too? Or perhaps God occasionally leaves his home countries, settling where he is needed. God now is apparently resident in western Canada.

His self-appointed welcoming committee buys Charles a beer from the stewardess.

"Tell me about the cold," he asks.

"You'll get used to it," comes the reply.

"I don't think so," Charles says with genuine trepidation. "But at least there is no dictator here, no bombs, no torture. And no war."

Lunch comes, prompting Charles to add, "You know, the food is better than on most of the other airlines."

He watches a Hollywood comedy on the screen to pass the hours. When it is time to land and he begins to feel the plane level down through the atmosphere, he pushes up his window shade and peers out incredulously. They are flying through swirling snow.

"How is this possible?" he asks, full of awe and alarm. "How can we land in snow? I thought March was spring."

"Ah, but it is also Alberta," chuckles his travelling companion through a beery haze. "This is a land of endless winter."

"Charles. Charles. Here. Here I am." Beth's voice greets him as he skips through the gate swinging his luggage and grinning. He peers into the crowd, not recognizing her at first. She is bundled up in a puffy green coat, still furred with snow.

"Welcome to Canada," she smiles, politely extending her hand.

This is not the Beth he protected in Rome, the girl child who snuggled in bed with him like a quivering new chick through one disaster after another, whose eyes widened like black moons over every grand glory and hidden pleasure of the eternal city.

This is the protective Beth who first led him through the amazing toy town of Amsterdam. He thought he had grown up since then. And this is the scolding Beth, furious with him after his fiasco in Sweden.

He takes her hand and then hugs her very tightly.

Beth kisses him in sisterly fashion, both of them aware of change — invisible as the wind yet palpable. She also knows exactly what to do in this massive airport and where to go. She has become part of this practical, efficient place with its pleasant people who all seem to play their roles, thinks Charles, in some huge unwritten script they carry around in their heads. No one looks lost. Or angry. Or scared. No one seems to be complaining. Not seriously. Everyone has something to do. Things function smoothly.

"Do you like it here?" he asks her, as they wheel the baggage cart past counters of rental cars and hotel kiosks, out into the chill white air.

"It is good here, Charles. You will see. It is safe."

"Let's take a limo," he suggests as they stand shivering at the airport bus stop. "I have money to pay for it."

"Save your money. You will need it."

As they board the airport bus and pull out onto the highway, Charles scans the frozen horizon, stares up through the falling snow, feeling as though he might vanish right into it. "It comes down so quietly," he says. "And the road is so flat,"

"Yes," she says. "It's flat around here. But you can get into the mountains pretty quickly. The Rocky Mountains are not far.

"The Rocky Mountains," he repeats, thinking of what they must look like. After a long and sometimes awkward while, he asks her if she has discovered where the theatre is in Edmonton.

"No," she says simply. "I have not paid any attention to theatre here. But I hear on the radio about a folk music festival that has free events. There is also a ski festival but I can barely imagine what that involves."

"We can start a theatre group here," he says. "We can perform in the summer here and tour in the winter to warmer places. We can make a lot of money."

"First we should learn to ski," she tells him. "That may be more useful."

It is a physical place, he realizes, thinking how Robert might have jogged them through a white freezing wilderness every day, tuning their bodies for performance. "But in the winter, if you want to stay warm, you just have to stay in the underground shopping malls."

"Oh, that's very good," he jokes, giving her a little squeeze. Not sure if she is kidding. And then, as though needing reassurance against the dizzying snow, he says in a serious tone, "Beth, you have changed."

"I promised I would help you in Canada, Charles, and I will. I am not the same person you knew in Rome. I am not star struck anymore. I work as a cashier now. I am not an actress. That is all in the past. My life is different now. You need to understand that."

The bus pulls to a stop in front of a huge hotel near the Provincial Legislature. He gazes at buildings perfectly frozen in architectural time, so different from those in Rome, where the new is polished to a high shine and the old is left to crumble and show character. It is dusk now and Edmonton's buildings glow in amber light. Fields of snow in front of them glittering green and yellow and red from the tiny coloured bulbs wound like ribbon around the sharp needles of pointed fir trees.

They take a taxi to Beth's apartment, bouncing together on seats that slope toward the centre with the heater at full blast. Charles puts his arm around her. At the first bump, she releases herself casually. The taxi makes an abrupt right from avenue to street and Charles is against her once again.

She looks at him. "Please, Charles. Don't."

He moves away.

The taxi stops at 95th Street.

"A very imaginative name," he says as he struggles out.

It is a squat, square building, neutral grey in the speckling snow, a blurred outline under blank sky. They climb steel stairs to the fourth floor and stop before beige doors.

They enter her small sitting room containing only a sofa and two chrome chairs. Charles sees the door to the bathroom, looks at a corner of the space that could barely contain the two of them, noticing how slyly it slides into what she calls a kitchenette. Then he spots a tiny hallway leading to the bedroom with its single bed. On the walls, Beth has placed a weaving of long-horned Ankole cattle stooping to drink under hills and clouds beside men in big brimmed hats with tall staffs who tend them.

"You can sleep on the sofa," she says.

"I thought…"

"No, Charles," she says

He looks out the window, feels mountains massing against them at the far edge of the land, rumbling up from a wild west coast. They are part of a frightened city huddled close for warmth and visibility in a vast empty landscape.

He has never been able to see so far. Nor felt so blind.

Then he spies the small, still screen. "Oh, you have TV."

"Not working."

"Then I will get it fixed."

They talk into the night. Charles falls asleep on the sofa.

The next morning, Beth is off to work before he wakes. She leaves him instant coffee and a spicy soup. When he wakes, he studies every item in the apartment. An African mask that she has bought in Edmonton. A creaky stove. Refrigerator. Her bed. The small table.

He eats, takes the key she has left him and heads out, the heavy broken television in his arms. She has told him to take it to a store called The Brick where she bought it. He walks out onto the wide, windswept street and hails a taxi. "The Brick," he says with authority.

"Only one block away," the Russian accented driver says in a thick deep voice. "Better to walk."

"I cannot walk in the freezing cold with this." The taxi driver shakes his head and tells him to get in.

Charles sits in the back seat hugging the set. He cannot believe how cold it is in spring. The cabbie drives the block and refuses the money Charles offers him.

"I was an immigrant too. You need your money more than me. So save up and maybe next time, you call a limo."

In the store, he is directed to a repair section. Someone checks it and tells him that there is nothing wrong with it.

"The wiring must have been connected wrong in the house." He is shown which wire goes into the cable outlet and which into the back of the television. In minutes, again without charge, he heads back out into the cold air. This time he walks back to the apartment stoically carrying his newly guaranteed appliance.

The television is coaxed into releasing its treasures. Mostly, he watches soap operas — *Days of Our Lives, Tomorrow's Children* — the unfolding of birth and death, betrayal and passion. All without a drop of sweat or blood, or a hair out of place. All with polished nails and immaculate clothes.

When Beth returns, they eat. She has bought a bottle of wine for them.

The silences are awkward.

While Beth sleeps, he watches *Three's Company*, along with Merv Griffin and Johnny Carson. America flickers at him in black and white through a seventeen-inch box. Late night America with its easy charm and its cool swagger. Maybe he can be a black Johnny Carson. Talk to people about their lives, make people laugh.

At the end of a week, Beth announces that he must find work.

"You can't lie around here all day watching TV."

"I'm studying my craft," he tells her.

"Study it at night. You have to support yourself. I can't do it for us both."

"I'll cook the meals and keep this place clean. I don't mind."

He has already begun shopping and making dinners. Aromatic African food awaits her most evenings. He also does some minimal housework.

Beth knows that as his sponsor, she has signed a multi-year agreement. The possibility of him lying on her sofa watching television for a decade depresses her. She wonders whether she really can persuade him to find paid employment. Or go back.

"Back to where?" he demands, deeply hurt.

Her words have catapulted him into darkness. In Canada for only two weeks and already he is to be exiled. He is also indignant and offended.

The next afternoon, he decides to call Immigration and informs them that his wife-to-be is refusing marriage. He asks if that happened, would he have to return to Rome? He is told that his refugee status is unconditional, not dependent on a marriage.

Relieved, he keeps this information from Beth. Knowing he can stay in Canada, he becomes more conciliatory, trying to comply with her wishes, trying not to upset her.

She helps him get a job as a waiter at the hotel where she works.

It reminds him of the Nigerian Embassy in Rome, breezily conveying trays of coffee and drinks with a flourish and a flair through the chatty posturing of official gatherings. Again, he embraces the role with joy, wheeling a dazzling white cart along carpeted hotel halls, listening to life in the rooms, behind doors: a football game, a quarrel, the giggle of love.

He knocks on those doors. With a flutter of clothing and limbs, the weekend lovers welcome him shyly in, past rumpled beds exuding sweat and perfume, to a window, pale with morning cloud.

He relishes his part in these little drawing room comedies from which Robert tried so passionately to rescue them. But he is good at enlightened subservience. He is paid to entertain this couple. Or that official. He plays for them and with them.

With easy aplomb, he becomes the butler in some British TV comedy who knows what is hidden from the protagonists. His speech is full of theatrical double meaning. The stage story is transparent to him though his own high drama remains opaque.

Unspoken in his mind and heart.

Stopped and mute.

After six months, he and Beth have grown to care enough about one another again to share the warmth of a bed once more. Charles, pushing for Canadian security, has asked Beth to marry him.

"If it becomes a problem for you," he tells her seriously, "we can separate. We can divorce. I need you to give me this security."

They both know it will not be a marriage of profound love and lifetime commitment, but it could be a marriage of convenience. Eventually Beth, against her better judgement, agrees.

They pick a date and marry in a judge's office without religious ceremony or significant celebration. It is a sleety afternoon in early winter. As they leave the room, Beth takes Charles' hand and thanks him for her flowers.

"You are safe now, Charles. You can live whatever life you want. You can make your own life in Canada. I will let you go whenever you ask."

This is his second empty marriage. The first was merely civilian; this one merely civil. Why, he thinks bitterly, is he denied the fulfilment of real union? He and Beth both know that their original infatuation was deeper — born in the sparking electricity of collective creation — and this new-world love, merely a sad echo of their Roman holiday. Now they are both so grown up and responsible in a cold world where the future somehow feels like eternal winter.

It is the inhospitableness of the climate that numbs his bones. He longs for pure African light, a warm radiance melting ice.

Wants again to be a small boy nuzzling a mother's breast, a son on a bicycle with his father, tearing along bush tracks, lifetimes away.

"Let's at least have a special lunch," says Charles, needing to flee from the pain of memory. Beth knows a good restaurant nearby.

"The food isn't African, but it's spicey. And the room is warm."

Shelter. It is what he needs. What she offers him. And he lets himself be taken. After food and warmth, on a long walk through the city's dark drizzle, needling his skin and stinging his eyes.

To their place of love. Sneaking into the city greenhouse.

In dreams, he is a child again, cooling his feet in a trickling river bed. A green dome rustling far above him. Rocks in the imaginary stream, tawny in filtered light. Behind him, long yellow grasses curl up to meet the sun. He gathers fine strong leaves on long thick stems to bring to Mother, bobbing through the water with them, in a little victory march home, anticipating her smile when he offers them up, his shiny flags of health and pleasure. Vital leaves grow from one deep root, in the forest. Just for him.

"Charles."

She is calling him back.

"Mother, I am so glad to be home."

"I've missed you, Charles."

Her arms wind around him. Back and forth they rock together, just as they used to under the banana plants in the village garden. When he was one with her, when she was his whole world.

Beth whispers. "Look. Rows and rows of African violets." And he sees silky star bursts of purple and mauve around tiny yellow beads, spidery filaments on furry leaves, soft honey-coloured stems.

He is alone with Beth. In a place where their dreams and longing can take root.

They make love in their minds among petals and stalks, on beds of sweet moist soil. Crying and sighing. Gazing up through windows, while lazy flakes hover down, winking at them through rags of cloud, sticking onto the sloping glass walls of this flower house until the lovers are covered with immaculate frozen air.

When Charles finally wakes from his two-month coma in the hospital, he does not recognize his own body. It is huge. And alien. Like a ship upon which his consciousness rocks precariously, far up in the crow's nest, occasionally spying a bit of land — a mirage, a trick of wave and sky — then subsiding again in the endless blue.

Charles is a vessel full of complicated rigging, piloted by others.

He is a wrecked whale inching through ocean.

There is pain everywhere. It is all he knows. Some tiny and acute, jabbing away on the hide of the stunned animal he has become. But there is another pain that throbs deep inside his mind, beating at him where nothing should, in a place he takes for granted, that always worked magically and perfectly, never bothering him, an internal place that has always functioned silently, invisibly, superbly on its own.

Now, it has been invaded by all the drums he has ever heard, using him as their instrument. Banging out a language he cannot understand.

"Jonah and the whale," he cries to a startled figure at the foot of the hospital bed, the one who has waited for this moment, willed it to happen.

"No," she cries joyfully. "You are *Makonde*. And you have come back."

Charles wails from deep inside. "I have been in the huge black belly of the whale. Punished by God." He does not recognize the woman speaking to him so gently, patiently.

"For what?" she weeps softly.

"I left her. They all died."

His eyes — the only part of him that can move — punctuate this declaration, jabbing at this soft figure before him, come at last to absolve him of guilt. "I am the only survivor. I am responsible for all their suffering." He stops, startled, stranded between his own hell and some immaculate place that invites him, with quietly humming machines, small red and green lights blinking wisely. This is not heaven because there is no joy. Perhaps the waiting room before heaven.

"Who are you?" he asks Beth, whose face he knows from some distant past.

"Angela did not die," Beth whispers reassuringly. "Angela is okay. She is at home with her children.

But the Angel Lady will always blame him, already telling people it was his fault.

The vivid stillness of coma, the belly of a whale, a hot suffocating cave, moves the sinner slowly and painfully through boundless waters of his semi-consciousness.

As the cave mouth opens, an ocean roars out hurling him onto dry land, thrusting him into painful light, where he squirms at every searing sensation, the very air rending his skin, slicing like a knife.

Makonde. Carvings. From the dark wood of the Makonde tree. The workers in wood tell their story from the images they create. The Makonde Theatre Company.

The word wanders through his gradual awakening.

Charles and Beth want to try. Send a tender root down into the packed soil of this difficult place. A little transplanted part of their authentic selves, to take hold, grow. Oh, grow into whatever it can.

"We will call it Makonde," says Charles. "It will be Edmonton's first African theatre troupe."

It has been so long since she's looked at him without pity or resentment. He has excited her. "Now you are Robert." Her voice is like honey.

He resists its thick sweetness. "No, I am myself, what he made me. His work has become my work."

They find their people. Some are Asian. Some are white. They all think they know theatre and want an opportunity to practice it. On wintry days in the vast cobwebby basement of a school he's found they can use, Charles inspires them. They've never heard the things he's saying they can do, this dancelike way of performing.

"Your body is your instrument. It's your language. It will take you beyond words but it will give voice to your own culture."

Far underground, among the pipes and vents, the cylinders and scrap lumber, this largely immigrant population will tell its stories. Edmonton will celebrate them. All Canada will celebrate them. Perhaps....

Charles loves the preparation, the rehearsal. Drums playing behind them, stretching and straining into rhythmic complication, the asymmetricality they are starting to feel, slightly askew from the prevailing order.

Up from the deep wells of their own past and pain the images come tumbling in pieces, hard minerals buried so long that even in the forced light of this cavernous cellar they can find rainbows, colours connecting over their heads and under their feet.

More and more people come to see the work, myriad reflections of self, the shattering and scattering of mirrors through which identity is puzzled out.

But Makonde does not pay salaries. And Charles knows he cannot continue being a dumb waiter in a Noel Coward play. He needs a job. A member of the group tells him there are jobs available in a meat-packing plant where pay is good and no experience necessary.

He is hired. He will work in the Ice House.

Charles soon realizes he has hired himself out to a death house for animals where workers wring the necks of chickens and butcher cows.

Even here, Charles finds a way to use his theatre skills. He becomes spokesman for the many immigrants employed there, speechifying at union meetings about the callous abuse of rights and privileges rampant in the company.

Strikes are discussed.

"But if we lose our jobs, then our families will really suffer."

"You will gain nothing without risk," says Charles, interrupted for a moment by the memory of a child in Sweden, the lead weight of responsibility.

"They can't hire replacements for everyone," he tells them. "We'll close down the whole operation."

His conviction is palpable. Endurance speaks through him. He is the living embodiment of suffering and survival.

Resurrecting so many dead selves, Charles also becomes a star of the company soccer team. Beth watches him on the field, his prancing feet propelling him like a comet, scorching earth everywhere he stops — mid-flight — then breaking into a solo run, arcing the ball hard, angling it into it to the net.

She is amused by his quick rise to fame with the Canada Packers Pirates, composed as it is mostly of Asians, Africans, and South Americans he has come to know during this time in Edmonton. New friends who represent distant cultures to one another.

"We'll win Saturday," says Mr. Uruguay to Charles, whom he affectionately refers to as Mr. Uganda. "Yes, we will," says Charles. "See you at the club tonight."

Charles often goes to the club alone but rarely stays single for long. Beth can smell women and whiskey on his breath when he finally comes home but says nothing. She knows she is losing him again, popular man-about-town prancing in and out of his various worlds.

Charles moves seductively with his dance partners far into the morning. Sometimes with Beth. Sometimes with Chantal or Jia or Consuela. Laughing as they are swung through the air by this always mysterious African who never fails to tell them of the royal kabaka and his beloved cow Suna.

During Makonde's increasingly popular public rehearsals, Charles puts on another self with the traditional garb of his people, trimmed around arms and neck, accentuating the smooth dark skin it softly drapes. Gazing into the mirror, thinking himself into something else, an ancestor's story he makes his own. Embodying another image to project, something from his ancestral past: with candles and gleaming water, a shaman raising up or the flame tree with its hard bark and crown of red flowers triumphing in dry savannah lands, channelling lightning. *Amarykiti.*

But non-theatre audiences misunderstand most of these attempts. As Beth knew they would. Even when he personally invites some of the so-called professional theatre reviewers, they only write about exoticism and difference. About Beth's bare breasts and the drumming that compels.

They stop at what startles them.

Why is he unable to take them further?

Makonde eventually raises enough money to stage a full production. This one, he tells Beth, will be both celebratory and doom-laden. He barrages the press with descriptions, calling his play a tale that weeps inconsolably, a play that will cause reluctant membranes to wrinkle up over stinging flesh wounds, a performance that will gleam pink under rough scabs, a myth that is sensitive and tentative.

And *Namanve* is like that. Charles and his cast re-create the grim forest where a man wanders to the plaintive cries of the dead. Namanve. Calling through the trees, filled with people lost to one another. A deep wound.

In the dark forest of Namanve, Charles and his tiny company sing, cry, and dance the atrocities they have seen. They struggle and suffer. They fight and die. In the blackness. Yet from harrowing agony emerges a tongue of fire that will not go out. The stage flickers with flame as the play ends.

Namanve sets Edmonton's Fringe Festival ablaze. In his press interviews, Charles speaks often of Abafumi and Robert although no one has really heard of either. He realizes, though, how much effect they have had, here where audiences are beginning to understand the high calling of theatre.

Robert would certainly have approved of Old Strathcona, a curious space where Makonde performs. Funky and historic, the festival puts on a special trolley car to get audiences there, a trolley provided by something called the Radial Railway Society. You climb aboard with your "Fringe Friendly" button and join a happy throng, rumbling through Edmonton's Old Town with its upright Victorian Post Office, its brick Farmers' Market, its shops and boutiques, nineteenth-century lamp standards and elegant memories, now extended as far as Yardbird Suite and TransAlta Power.

"Visceral and primeval" rave the reviews.

They are responding largely to Charles himself, the tightly tuned actor "whose every muscle registers emotion." He emerges alone from the total darkness of the stage carrying candles, singing his way through, singing his dead friends back from the depths. Slowly, he resurrects them all — Mr. Makuba, Robert, Byron, Willy, and Susi — into the dream of life.

The reviewers vie with one another to say what they've seen and felt. "It will rip you apart," one writer tells her readers.

For the next few months Charles builds his new company, around the stories that brought them to Canada, stories of persecution, escape, and diaspora. Not actors in any traditional sense, these new Canadians speak with their bodies and faces, with drums and stringed instruments.

Coaxed and encouraged by Charles, they strip themselves raw, trying to recapture the spirit of Abafumi.

They are hurt and they cry; they resist and are murdered. They pray and chant, find joy in the frenzy of dance. Devastating those who see their performances. Earning over and over again their reputation of being "a company without fear."

Charles talks to reporters, tells them that Makonde Total Theatre is the new Abafumi. When he says this, his eyes burn, "and he glows," as one writer puts it, "like the candles that light up the darkness of Namanve."

"Why don't you let some of the others do the interviews?" demands Beth, now concerned with his growing ego. "Share the spotlight."

The remark stings him. The interviews happen so quickly. He cannot control those who pounce on him after a performance.

Charles is defensive. "Because of *my* efforts with this company," he tells her, "you can practise your art again. I am sorry if they want to speak to me but I think I have earned that right."

"You have earned nothing. You are as self-centred as ever. As self-centred as your holy Robert."

Charles turns without saying anything and walks away.

During the remaining performances of *Namanve* — when Makonde calls upon the spirits of the dead — Charles insists only one name be used. Robert's name. Over and over as the drums thunder. He wants them to feel Robert's strength. Especially Beth. And to understand that he embodies it.

At every performance, Charles senses him hovering there, just beyond the lights, in the thick darkness, waiting in the wings. They have only to say his name.

Robert.

Charles.

Reporters continue to show up at the hospital seeking "Tornado Man." Though out of danger, he is too feeble to talk. And still confused.

"How did he survive?" they ask the doctors again and again. They want to see him even if they can't speak to him. Just one photo. The doctors refuse to allow the circus. "He is too weak."

The medical glare, however, is relentless. In the searchlight of physical inquiry, Charles is completely exposed. A child again, he now belongs to everyone in white. He worries in his pain. Feels guilty in his memories. Knows there are secrets he must keep but he can't remember what they are.

Knows they will hunt him down, these jackals who surge back again and again, tenacious, close to their quarry. His rational mind pins them to the ground: they are eager to touch this phenomenon of resurrection, share in the miracle.

But his body rebels, still a wounded flesh full of flaming torches that scorch, waking and sleeping.

Gradually, he begins to recall more and more. Arguments. Bitterness with Beth. What did they fight about? Why?

In the hospital he can only stare at her. She feels affronted, angered by his helplessness, his simple need of her. "One day we will dance together again," he tells her.

"Impossible, Charles," she tells him. "You won't ever dance again. They don't allow wheelchairs in discos."

In tears, Beth turns away. Leaving Charles to sleep, to dream.

Sleep is the most dangerous time. Unable to escape his dreams, he is beaten, punched, slapped. Wakes in pain. Cuts and bruises everywhere. Now his accosters descend on him in their white robes, disguising the night's assault with bandages. But he knows he cannot let his guard down.

They hover close, the nurses, never missing an opportunity. In the small cramped hours, against his struggles to stay awake, they tuck him in. Securely. "Angels all around you," they mur-

mur. His lacerated, broken body stranded on a strange white shore. Trapped and strapped, hoiked, wrapped and raised, angled to allow close scrutiny.

Some tiny speck of himself, though, hides deep inside. Buried beneath a monster, a wounded animal scraped raw.

Hands slather him thickly with creams, layer him in grease. Relentlessly under bright lights. Cold fingers prodding, arms rocking him slowly on the bed. Rumpled with every physical battle he wages.

"You're fighting, Charles. It's good. That's good."

Angel voices.

Now slouching in a wheelchair. A rag doll. Once as playful as a feather in air, he has deflated to limp skin and shrunken muscle, his face covered in rough beard. He stares into the blank mirror. Life has almost completely vanished. He is on an empty stage. Deserted. Dark and silent. A tiny light signifying nothing.

Was it for this he survived Amin?

Rubber wheels roll over polished tile, past nursing stations and oblivious clerks, past sinks and waiting rooms where people sit in gowns looking lost, looking like him. He is unseeing and unseen.

Was it for this he endured and overcame and began again in a new world?

Beth urges the clumsy cart of his life along a road full of turns to nowhere. How changed she is from the sweet-faced girl he scooped into his own fine chariot to whip through the streets of the Eternal City. Her face is stoic under big horn-rimmed glasses and close-cropped hair.

She stands unsmiling behind his wheelchair, her eyes gone. Replaced by points of silver light. She is not here either. All mask now, this string of a woman confronts him with her own suffering. Horizontal stripes hold her together like a stick figure in a funeral dance.

Could he stay with her the way she stays with him?
He looks at her and knows his sad answer.

Six months into recovery, he is brought to the Rehabilitation
Centre, a cross between Catholic heaven and a torture chamber.
A place of misery and humiliation.

Here he must learn how to live again. How to eat — with
the left hand now. How to move in a wheelchair.

He relaxes. Eventually he moves to muscular re-training and
coordination exercises. Becomes adept at the stacking of small
cups. Like a baby playing among Mother's pots, banging out
his first rhythms with a stick. Learning to move all over again.

Natasha is his favourite therapist. She sits with him day
after day trying to induce movement in his fingers, the nerves
of which have been disconnected from his arm. She pulls on
a strap that tells the muscles of his hand to do their job. Up,
down. Flex, relax. Make a fist. He cannot. She squeezes his
hand for him.

Raises his besieged limb on a pulley. And lowers it again and
again until he believes he can fly.

Natasha massages muscle and tendon while his hand rests.
It is enough that she is there now. With the raising of an arm,
he hears an audience applaud.

Nurse Cynthia is more serious and serene. She is in charge
of his lower mobility. With her, he climbs up three wooden
steps. Where he stands before her. Holds the balancing belt
they have strapped around his waist. She is ready to catch him
if he tumbles. With her he moves uncertainly.

After almost forever, his body cast is removed. Relief spreads
over him like warm water. Now he must learn control and
balance. Remember what it was like to take his first step. A
child finally standing on his own. Grinning.

With Cynthia steady beside him, quietly voicing encour-
agement, he wobbles each day from step to step. Her arm
inadvertently strays between his legs and he awkwardly inches

forward. They both stop. Discreetly, she ignores his unexpected erection. Slowly, they continue the exercise.

So, he thinks, I am not totally dead.

After a year in hospital, he still never knows which nights will rattle him awake, which storms will assault him all over again. There are no doctors for some of these pains. The blood that is taken cannot reveal all the causes of his suffering.

They encourage him to try living at home for a few days. He is reluctant but Beth is there, mechanically now, yet his constant companion. She nurses him like a professional, doing and saying all the right things. She has been told he requires mostly patience and love, so she rehearses her lines. He sees through her acting though, mocking moments of clarity.

"Beth, you are faking it."

The days she has off, he stays at her apartment. She sleeps when he sleeps, wakes when he wakes. He is her only life on this strange planet. His eyes search every dark corner for answers.

She studies his body. A lunar landscape, it is skin puckering over flat surfaces cratered from inactivity and reconstruction. No invisible mending here, no seamless repair. She cringes at his skin, squares of pink and red, orange and black. Incongruous. Odd.

He is a broken statue that someone has put back the wrong way. A scrappy patchwork of spare parts. Nothing quite right nor straight, nor fitting exactly. An upper inner thigh with flesh gouged to graft to his leg, now permanently out of alignment.

Saving the leg at all was the miracle, the doctors tell her, beginning with only bare bone, a crude outline of the man who once danced her through life.

Swaying slightly on the edge of her pull-out couch — a little smile playing at his lips, a crumpled quilt draped casually over his shoulder — he is now her deeply wounded warrior, a carved statue in a book, suddenly come to fractured life. Renga Moi in old age.

Occasionally, Beth brings some of his friends over. When she thinks he is up to it, she calls a football team member or an actor from Makonde. Charles believes they have come to gloat at his misfortune. In his heart, he is not convinced they want to help or sympathize.

At these times, he turns, imperious and angry, a relentless old testament prophet, demanding of one friend whether he is still cheating on his wife.

"I know what went on that night," he rails, waving an accusing finger wildly, his voice trembling.

"You are a pickpocket and a cheat," he harangues another.

"And you. You are a murderer," he declares before a well-wisher from Kenya who knew Robert.

He aims his violence at them all, a spotlight stabbing dark. He is the self-appointed judge and jury of everyone in exile. His brain screams "stop" but his voice rails on.

He has become one man dancing, a puppet, a ventriloquist's dummy.

He reserves the worst for his Makonde actors. Towards them, he is merciless. He knows that without his guidance, any hope of artistic truth is gone. He is surely Robert's artistic son, chosen to keep the vision, imbue Makonde with the fervour of the founder. He tosses his fury in their faces like acid.

When finally left alone, he fills with remorse. Cast brutally into his own personal Namanve.

Little rays of hope penetrate the density of his despair. He is finally allowed to stay permanently at Beth's. She agrees to take him four times each week for physiotherapy and X-rays, treatments, medications, and tests.

But he is also spiteful with her. Beth, his Lady of Perpetual Help; spiteful with the white nurses, his Sisters of Mercy; with the doctors, self-proclaimed Jehovahs, full of anger and jealousy.

He is the star of his own private disability drama, unable

to do the simplest things for himself, confined to Beth's living room with a pull-out bed, an armchair, a television.

Alone in the dark, he watches the weather channel until he falls asleep to the harshness of the flickering screen.

Each new day, he is in the forecaster's charge. He rises and falls with reports of barometric pressure, with big maps that tell what's on the way and how long it will stay. With every prediction of rain, he remembers the tornado and closes himself in behind curtains or simply wheels his throbbing body in the "crippled chair" through closet doors so that he can neither see nor hear, staying there until the "weather" is over, groping in an endless stage blackout for the flash of an exit.

The first time Beth sees him shake at the weather forecast, she throws her arms around him and holds on. He vibrates wildly against her, light as dry twigs in windstorm, snapping. On this day, however, he shouts at her. "Let me go," he begs, tears running down his face.

When she looks at him, she realizes that the trembling has been laughter. "What's so funny, Charles?"

"Nothing. Nothing," he assures her. "Everything is quite terrible. But I did this even in hospital. They called it my laughing sickness. There's no cure."

"Perhaps you just have no tears left. This is the result."

"The worst is that it reminds me of him."

"Who?"

"Amin. Do you remember? They used to call him 'the laughing one.' He would hack people to death with a grin on his face. Now I'm becoming like him. I am the destroyer now. And I laugh."

Charles is also convinced he has become impotent. Feels nothing there. Sees women in his mind, in his memory, but his instincts are now inert. Flaccid flesh in a wheelchair.

Distraught, he reveals his fears to the doctors. They try to explain how much shock his body has received, how the coma and drugs are doing this to him. Then they prescribe more drugs. He refuses the chemicals. A surgical procedure is also possible. But the physical aberrations of his body under siege are what he has left. He needs every one of its pleadings and complaints.

He will not go under again. His must stay awake now.

With what little remaining love she holds for him, Beth tries to fan the sexual flame. But he fails her as well. He is shamed in their room, shamed to be with her, to insult her this way.

"I am a drum without sound," he tells her.

She tries to console him but she too is drained. Run out of energy for even the simplest rationalization. "Maybe you're right," she says dully. "Maybe we should have given up when they killed Robert. Our lives were all but gone then anyway."

He throws his cane pathetically through the air, missing her by half the room.

She hates his eruptions. She has had enough. "I have as much right to reject this life as you do Charles. As much right to anger. If you want to live, you do it without me from now on. Charles, if we stay together neither of us will survive."

The next day, Beth packs her bags. And leaves.

He has no choice but to accept, adjust. Burying his anger deep inside — live coals that never stop burning — time drags him, battered in body and spirit, doggedly forward. Though he still cannot work, he is finally able to move without the wheelchair. He visits the rehab clinic once each week, a short taxi ride away.

Welfare now pays for his life.

He frequents a nearby church, its regular invalid. Imploring any force out there for help. Wants to be born again.

With a telephone call from Nairobi, he is. He can barely believe his ears. Samuel is coming to visit. Samuel, now a businessman, is going to be in Europe and then Chicago. He will arrive from Chicago.

"Will you be around?" he asks.

"I am always around," says Charles.

Three weeks later, Samuel walks in the door. So much older. But now he is important and important people need to look old. He will stay with Charles for three days, wheeling him outside for walks and sweet confections in donut shops and talk.

So much talk between them. Everyone back home has heard. Beth assured them all he was alive. But barely moving.

In the tiny apartment, Samuel sprawls on the scatter mats covering the scuffed parquet floors and talks, perches on collapsible canvas stools propped against the walls and talks, bumps against limp rubber plants and talks. Nothing matters but their being together again.

Charles speaks of former glories on the stages of the world. Aches to show this new city of Edmonton to his childhood friend but loathes being stared at. They study press photos and albums Charles has made of the life he once had.

"You have had many privileges," Samuel tells him. "God is just testing you one more time."

"God," says Charles ruefully. "I am his puppet. But let's not speak of that. Tell me why you have moved to Nairobi. Why did you leave Uganda?"

"Business was bad in Kampala and hopeless at home. I had to leave. I've been in Nairobi nearly ten years now. When I discovered I was coming this way, I knew we would meet. So I went back home. I saw your Mother and Father. And Debra."

Charles is hungry for details.

"Uganda is sick," says Samuel. "Everyone was damaged by Amin. He destroyed all the business communities. It will take another decade to heal. And Amin himself is now living in luxury in Saudi Arabia on the money he stole."

"Kampala? Our village?"

"Everything everywhere is in disrepair. Crime is rampant. Riots always over food or prices or electricity. Wherever you go there are military roadblocks. You don't know who is real military and who are criminals stopping people to rob them. People are accosted on the streets for hand-outs. These are not Muslims. These are Christians who are begging. Anyone who looks like they might have money is surrounded. You can't walk without beggars crawling all over you."

Charles listens with longing and horror. "And at home?"

"A taxi driver took me to our village from Kampala. I swear he was driving with his eyes shut. He looked like a starved dog and he smelled of liquor."

"There is a curse on our country, Samuel. Amin set us all against each other."

"Even the police are corrupt," Samuel continues. "I was told that they are often threatened at gunpoint until they promise to join the criminals. I knew that I could not go home with anything of value because I would be killed. Or the family would be robbed."

"So the village is also at the mercy of criminals? And we can do nothing about it."

"You are better off here, Charles. Believe me. Anyway, in your physical state, how could you possibly help?"

Charles says nothing.

"When I reached the village, I was shocked even more. I could not believe in what poor shape the roads were. Pits and potholes. And lining the roads everywhere, small coffins. God is pulling young people up to heaven each day."

"Samuel, is that really happening?"

"It is really happening. Chaos. God has punished all of us in Africa. Coffin makers are doing a booming business because of AIDS, Charles. Empty wooden boxes lined up waiting to be bought and filled."

Somewhere in Samuel's words Charles senses the emptiness of home.

"Uganda is being tested, Charles. Like Job. Punished like Lot's wicked wife. Scourged by God. There is no reason to return. Stay in Canada. And I will stay in Nairobi."

Samuel slowly begins a dirge of sorts, a mournful list of names — friends and family, known to them both — who have died.

"Why do you not speak of my mother?" asks Charles finally. It is for Kekinoni and Debra that he feels most concern.

And most responsible.

"She looks so old, Charles. And her mind is not always clear. But she recognized me. After so long, she recognized me. Jumped up and began to sing. Praising the Lord. You know how she is."

Charles pictures her, arms swaying over her head, dancing towards Samuel, gathering him in. And singing. As she would for him. Then they would hold and hug and laugh and cry together. And she would never stop singing salvation. Kekinoni knows God. Sees Him in her children. Her reason for living and her special route to heaven.

"We spoke of my life in Kenya. And I have a good life there. I asked her why Debra was still not married. She told me that Debra has never been comfortable with men since..."

Charles nods.

"Mostly, she wanted me to bring her back photos of you. She spoke of you a lot. She can barely walk now. She needs a good wheelchair."

"You must buy her one."

"I would but the ones made at home are junk. And a new one from abroad, well, the problem is getting it to her. It would be stolen and sold before she ever saw it."

Samuel continues. "She asked when I had last seen you. I told her it had been a very long time, that I had only received some newspaper clippings you sent me about the tours and that Beth had sent about the tornado.

Charles saddens visibly. "I sent Mother several letters with clippings and photos, Samuel. When I called, I could only get through to the village shop. They told me that they hadn't seen any post from me. Who knows what happened."

"She still wants a grandson from you, Charles. She always

expected you to return in triumph one day. She wanted you to marry at home, give her lots of grandchildren. She never stopped believing in you. Even now.

"I took her to the health centre for a kind of massage," continues Samuel. "She's got pain everywhere. Her whole body is separating, each part going a different way."

"You have pictures of her?" asks Charles.

Samuel hands him some photographs. Charles studies them intently travelling back with each one.

A grey-haired Kekinoni looks directly out at him. This once stately woman, now so small. Seated on a covered divan, wearing a long green checked cotton dress. Coolly and sedately she stares, speaking to him forcefully with her whole demeanour, focused on him. She smiles bravely through her toothless mouth because she knows her son will soon see.

"Be strong," she tells him in pictures. "Be my strong son."

"Her eyes are troubled," he says softly. "She is holding back so much."

He flips through the other pictures quickly and returns once more to the first.

He studies it again, noticing how tightly the dark headband wraps a few stray wisps of hair. Then his eyes fall on her hands, cupped carefully around a polished milk bowl. An offering to him. Of love. Of continuity.

"I have kept my bowl too," he tells her.

"What kind of life does Debra have now?"

"She has been so damaged, Charles. She stays with a cousin and comes to help Mother as she can. She wants so much to see you. She hopes you will come home one day. When I left, I felt as if I was abandoning her."

"I abandoned her," says Charles. "I abandoned all of them. But one day I will go back. I will set it all straight again." His voice is suddenly urgent, cutting through the calm and tears like a sword.

"It is impossible Charles. Even I can just barely survive in

Uganda. You are on crutches. You wouldn't make it through the airport terminal. I saw them insist that someone with a broken leg prove he wasn't smuggling things inside his cast."

"They made him take it off?"

"Finally they settled for a bribe."

"I can get money, Samuel. I have been saving a little bit each month from what the welfare gives me."

"Forget Uganda, my brother. It is like a graveyard. I drove through so many villages we used to know. Remember all those lively places, people coming to greet us? Now there is no one. Just a scrawny cow or two wandering among dilapidated huts."

"How is he, Samuel?" The unspoken name suddenly spoken. "How is Father? It is so many years now that he stopped living with Mother. Is he okay?"

"I took the taxi to his village too. It is not so far from hers. When he left, he gave up his government job. Everyone in the village gathered around the taxi. Cars do not come there so often. I had sent a telephone message but I could not be sure he got it. I told him I would arrive in the afternoon.

"It was seven in the evening when I found his small house. He was already asleep."

"Already asleep," repeats Charles mechanically. A sort of rehearsal for death, a little sleep easing into a bigger one.

"He woke up when I came in. He was surprised. He had not received my message. I was shocked at how thin he was. I could feel his bones."

Charles recalled the weight of Kanyunya's authority, his years of ceremonial feasting. "He is very frail now. When I knelt before him, he could not bend to help me up."

"And how is he in his mind?"

"He is depressed. His income is low. He has nothing to do. He is not important anymore."

Then Samuel adds with difficulty, "Everything he owned disappeared. His land is long gone. All the politicians are corrupt. Not like your father was."

Charles feels his guts wrench. "I should be there. I should help him."

"It is not your fault, Charles. And it would be very difficult for you to go back. When I left, the whole village came and said goodbye. They all send you good wishes."

"They remember me?"

"Of course. You are a celebrity." Samuel pauses on a thought. "But for each person who asked, for each person I met, there was another who had died. Or who did not remember anything. There is so much death."

"And the new government?"

"The new government cannot change the past. Cannot disguise the body count. Yes, there has been some improvement since Amin left and they have given a bit of power back to the business people. But it will take a very long time to repair the destruction."

Images of friends scuttle past on the same dusty track of his familial guilt. "Once Father distributed land to the people so grandly. He could give a mountain. He could give anything."

"It is sad. Your father is dreaming of death."

Charles sees his old home in some of Samuel's other photos. The land, brown and dry. Buildings ramshackle, outhouses thrown together and balanced precariously, just sticks in the wind. He can hear the trees cracking in the arid air, their stripped bark flapping, yellow and useless.

"How long did you stay?"

"Just overnight. I had to get back to Kampala. I had some business meetings. Then I had to catch the plane."

"Does everyone still dream of living in Kampala?"

"Not as many. A great number of our old friends returned to their home villages when the country fell apart. They had to flee. But now they're stuck in those places. They wake up in the morning, watch their livestock graze. All their hopes of living and working in the big city are dead. They're back where they began as children and now they can't get out.

Their only choice is to join the army and wait.

"The clever ones, though, survive on black market business in Kampala. Money-changing. Exporting sculptures, masks. Small stuff. Just enough to get by. I deal with one or two middlemen there still."

"They have no future, do they?"

"A future?" Samuel sighs sadly. "When I left the village, everyone came out expecting me to give them something. I had a bottle of gin that I was going to leave for your father but he didn't want it. So I handed it to a man by the car and told him to share it with the others."

He pauses, looking at Charles with hooded eyes. "I felt such shame."

The next day, Samuel broaches yet another difficult subject. "I was in Stockholm about a year ago Charles. I was there for a gathering of import-export people. I took advantage of it to contact your wife."

"You saw Christina? You saw the baby?" Charles almost leaps up out of his chair.

"I spoke to her on the phone."

"Tell me Samuel. Tell me."

"She's remarried. She has other children now."

Wonder comes in waves. And doubt. Had they really loved one another? Could it have worked?

"And your son is no baby. He is six now. I spoke with him on the phone."

"You actually talked to him?" Charles is crying silent tears, his body gushing through his eyes. Samuel waits.

"I asked for his mother. He said she was out, but I could call back tomorrow. He sounded so confident, my brother. A child with the world before him. Not tainted by all our bloody history."

"Did you call back?"

"Yes, the next day.

"Charles who?" she asked rather rudely when I told her I was a friend.

"She must not have remembered."

"But she let me continue. Asked if we had met in Rome. Where I was living. It was like being interrogated by a lawyer. She had me on the stand, a witness for the prosecution."

"Then what?" asks Charles. "Then what?"

Samuel moves him closer and closer to it. "Then her voice changed, Charles. It softened. She said, 'Tell him I wanted him to find us. Tell him that, Samuel.'"

"I deserted them too."

"She forgives you Charles. She wishes you well."

"Christina," he whispers, as though in prayer. "My Lady of Mercy."

"She left a photo of your son at my hotel the next day." He hands it to Charles who is mesmerized at the round brown face of a little boy. Black eyes lit like candles. Black curls forming an opaque crown. Smiling fondly at him.

"She calls him Kiti, Charles. Just as your father used to call you."

"He has her look," whispers Charles. "Full of hope and trust." He stops as though searching.

"And need," he says eventually, turning to Samuel, as though understanding at last. "She believed nobody could ever hurt her." Charles cries yet again under his own revelation. "But I did. I did."

"They are safe now, Charles. I'm telling you they are safe and well. Do not stress yourself any further over them."

Charles agonizes. As the son, he was supposed to be caring for Father, and for Mother, in their age and difficulty. As a husband, he was supposed to be responsible for his wife and child. He abandoned them all.

Charles already hears in his mind the voices of everyone who knew him.

"Where is the son who should fix this?"

They will, of course all blame him for leaving, will say he destroyed his family.

Charles knows he is no a prodigal son. He is no son at all.

After their time of difficult revelations, the two friends hug urgently, knotting themselves together so they will never come undone, as if letting go meant losing everything all over again.

Samuel leaves for the airport and the long trip back to Kenya.

Charles continues his slow circular spin. A torn solitary leaf swirling in autumn winds. A random flake of snow. Almost invisible against the sky. A man dancing. Without music.

A month later, his doctor recommends reconstructive surgery. It can only be done in Toronto, followed by extended physiotherapy. Beth urges him to go. There is nothing holding him in Edmonton any longer. Or anywhere.

Toronto appals him. Cautiously he ventures out with a walking stick and is lost. In alien territory. Buildings squeeze his head tight. The sun bores a hole through his skull and pours in fire. The edges of leaves scissor his brain.

In his tiny downtown apartment on rainy days, he lies staring out the window and listens to bullets drop, waiting for the roof to crash in. Watching the wind's giant hand swoop down and scoop him away, spinning the world again into cloud.

There are iron bars on his windows and delinquents have destroyed much of the lobby.

In a coffee shop, a woman moves menacingly toward him. She is nearly naked and whips her icy hair back and forth across his startled face before she is taken away.

"Your mind is retreating," say doctors in the hospital where he has checked himself in after many sleepless nights. "Your red cell count is low. Your immune system is not coping."

He sings himself to sleep. "Lullaby and goodnight. May the angels caress you."

The angels. How he longs for them. To dance with them. To dance with the ancestors. He is almost there.

What stops him is a play.

Although he cannot see it, he recognizes part of his story. Drifting back to him on rumour and speculation. Toronto audiences and theatre critics have raved over the play, *Come Good Rain*. They respond eagerly, compassionately to George Seremba's story of survival in Amin's Uganda.

A story owned by so many. Seldom told. Perhaps now for the first time.

"You can believe me. I stayed still as a stone, Charles. It was my only chance."

Charles knows Seremba. Has invited the actor to his tiny basement apartment. Downtown commotion swirls around them. Oblivious to all externals — yellow leaves flapping against the window's high hooded eye, slithering off — the two sit, glued thickly together by George's relentless recollections.

Charles is once more excited by possibility.

"I think of the things that Abafumi might have done with it, what my Makonde group did with some of the same material. Namanve. You said you were 'sinking' in the forest. That is absolutely the right image."

"I was being slowly swallowed by marsh mud. All but my head."

George stands, then begins physically, to drop down as though pulled into the ground. It is unbearable. Charles feels the panic. Cannot breathe.

"They must have lost sight of me and decided not to waste another bullet. After that, such agony. The ground wanted to suck me into its grave. So many souls already there. Then the rain."

"I can't imagine how I survived. Charles, really I can't. Or how you survived the tornado. And Amin."

A long pause.

"We both remain guilty of survival," says Charles.

"I suppose we were somehow meant to be here," Seremba responds. "Perhaps to bear witness. We were meant to tell others what we lived through. Maybe the talent God gave us is for that purpose alone. Maybe … but I'm no longer certain of anything.

"When I realized what you were doing with Makonde at the Fringe in Edmonton, Charles, I knew I had to tell my story too. You inspired me. Perhaps one day we can start a company together here. Reach other Africans. Others who care."

"My body is broken, George. I cannot work with people the way I used to. I can't even keep my concentration for very long."

"But you can coach younger artists — actors, musicians and dancers. You would be wonderful."

Charles wants to believe him.

But his reality is different now.

At his lowest moment, he meets God. Or rather, he meets David. David has read of the tornado disaster. An anniversary story about it appeared in a Toronto paper. Charles' name is mentioned. The Miracle Man again, living in Toronto. But did they have to reveal he was alone?

David has sought him out, inviting him to the non-denominational Brethren Church where Charles agrees to join the congregation and pray. Suddenly feels pure.

David and his wife spend hours discussing the Old and New Testament with Charles.

The Brethren's New Year's service lasts twelve hours. Charles is again loved and fed. In this Theatre of God, the congregation reads the Bible together, repeating the ten commandments over and over. He repents years' worth of sin, stands and renounces evil. And is forgiven. Publicly. Once more, born again.

Is it possible?

"No, not Robert Seremba," Charles corrects politely, "Robert Serumaga."

A Toronto theatre professor has phoned Charles. He is in need of material on theatre in Uganda and has found Charles' name. He has never heard of Serumaga, dead now for more than ten years. They arrange to meet a few streets from Charles' apartment. Charles brings his scrapbooks and limps slowly towards this academic who is curious about his old theatre life.

The professor had called George Seremba earlier (by now Mr. Uganda in Toronto) but Seremba was about to go on tour and suggested he speak to Charles.

So Charles and Prof. Don talk, the latter learning in detail of Abafumi and Robert Serumaga. He asks Charles about pictures for inclusion in his epic theatre encyclopedia, wants to bring Abafumi's reputation back to light, wants Charles to be his source. Prof. Don seems willing to learn. And genuinely interested.

The two spend many hours hunched like conspirators together in a tiny Lebanese café. The owner, a welcoming all-mother named Josie, reigns over the small kitchen and several plastic tables like royalty, hands on hips, black hair cascading, suggesting secret items from the menu along with yoga tips for physical and mental improvement.

She is fascinated to overhear their conversation. She regards her establishment as a refuge for intellectuals and artists and she is always pleased when she believes creativity is being nourished with her baklava and Turkish coffees. She is impressed when the professor, seeing her interest in their conversation, tells her that Charles is a major African theatre artist and shows her a photo.

"Is that a picture of you?" she asks Charles, marvelling at the face from *Renga Moi* slanted dramatically between crossed swords.

"It's who I was," he says slowly.

After three meetings with Prof. Don over the next month to discuss Ugandan theatre, Charles is asked, carefully and courteously, why he limps and what brought him to Toronto.

An innocent query, without pressure or accusation.

"How long do you have to listen?" laughs Charles.

Prof. Don hears the outlines of Charles' story. Wants to hear more.

But Charles is now thinking theatre again, wondering if he could teach a class for the Professor's students. The Professor agrees to have Charles speak to one of his classes. A visit is set for the following week.

The day before the visit, however, Charles panics. All his guilt and fear, his sorrow and sadness, his anger and despair rise up in attack.

Spears rattle the ravaged masks of everyone he has loved and lost. Dry stalks rasping, dead bones clacking in the wastes of Namanve

The visit is postponed.

Some days later, they are back at the Lebanese café. Prof. Don has brought a woman this time.

"Charles, this is my wife. This is Pat. She is a writer. I told her part of your story."

"It is a great pleasure to meet you Mrs. Pat."

He is like a tortoise in its shell, she thinks.

"Just 'Pat' is good enough Charles," Prof. Don says. "And please, I'm just Don.

"Yes sir," says Charles," always concerned with propriety.

They speak of Charles' former life, of Uganda, of his theatre.

Prof. Don also has a new idea for Charles. And Charles is staggered by it. A conference is being planned in Africa sponsored by the theatre encyclopedia he is editing. He wants Charles to attend and speak about Abafumi and Robert Serumaga. Don will try to get him a travel grant and a place on the program.

Charles is tempted by this opportunity — the first connection with his former life in so long — but he can't grasp enough of it to convince himself he should get involved. How, after all this time and all these assaults on his past and his pride, can he trust this renewed interest? His own body?

What do they really want?

How will they use him and Robert's memory?

How can he control things, protect what must be protected?

He has no right to resurrect what is finally at rest.

And he is very sceptical about speaking to academics who will analyze and judge and make pronouncements. Who will sentence him all over again — publicly, in the eyes of a whole new generation of theatre professionals — to the punishment he has been living. Rationalize it. Prolong it. Justify it.

After weeks of indecision, he reluctantly agrees. He will go back. Will attend a theatre conference: four days in Senegal for preliminary meetings and four days in Cameroon. Will give his paper at the University of Yaounde.

"It's good that it is not taking place in Kampala," Charles tells Pat in a phone call. "I couldn't go back to Uganda yet."

Because Don is not at home, he talks freely to Pat of his concerns and fears: of returning to Africa after so many years away, of flying so far by himself in his current state of disrepair.

"Prof. Don," he continues nervously, "said that you and he will be going early to set up the meetings. That means I must fly alone."

"Maybe we can find someone to travel with you," she suggests. "Did Don mention to you that our son is also going? He's a sports journalist. He has arranged to cover some soccer stories on a freelance basis while we're there. Cameroon is apparently a great soccer country."

"Oh yes," says Charles. "They have one of the best football clubs in Africa." His mind is now racing.

"The African Cup is going on in Cameroon then," adds Charles. "A perfect time to be there. I would like to make the trip with your son and show him African football."

A weight lifts. For Charles, there will be a companion, a sports writer who will talk football with him. Not theatre. Take his mind off fear. If the academics are too overbearing, he can escape their authority and see a match.

So it is settled. He will really go.

The decision brings warm relief. Chilled by a sense of new forces being unleashed, forces that could save or destroy him. He wonders in what disguises they will come. Is he really going back to face them?

Home? To Africa?

8. AFRICA

JASON, THE YOUNG SPORTS JOURNALIST, is affable and kind. Genuinely interested in Charles. A talker and a drinker, a buddy who enthusiastically embraces the most accessible pleasures. A devotee of the senses, of information in every form. And anything that could be construed as entertainment. A little like Charles on his first trip to Amsterdam when the world was a candy box crammed full.

They spend the Air Afrique flight to Dakar intensely exchanging views on African football. And women.

Humidity flaps wetly at them upon arrival. In the customs hall, distracted by electric fans, they take their jackets off as the line moves forward through immigration. Now in a tee shirt, Charles is proud of his red, white, and blue flag, with dollar signs all over it.

"I bought it for a laugh in a close-out shop. It's funny, isn't it?" he asks Jason.

But his good humour shrivels away the moment they approach the immigration booth. The officers on duty seem provoked. They see an African who has become rich while in America. Surely you will share your wealth a bit, they are thinking as they study this tall black man walking with a cane beside his white friend.

It takes Charles hours to convince them he is not rich. Jason looks on in total amazement.

"Welcome to Africa," says Charles as soon as they are allowed to leave the airport. Eventually, the two weary travellers struggle to Cheik Anta Diop University downtown, wet with sweat. Jason has added a fold-up cap to protect his head from the sun. Packed pockets with huge pads, pens sticking out from every angle and many rolls of film bulking up the rest of him.

Once settled down in their dorm, they go for a short slow walk. Charles feels calm for the first time, happily joining Jason in his concentrated search for a bar. On the way, they discover a carton of condoms on the ground, inadvertently dropped. They pick up the unopened box and notice that there is a stamp across the top indicating that the expiry date has passed by some six months.

"You are in the Third World now," says Charles. "Nothing is wasted. Even if no one will buy them in Europe or Canada, there is always a market for such things in Africa."

Jason makes a note for his story.

Then they have some beers and talk until sleep overwhelms them both. From this point on, they are inseparable. Charles begins to introduce Jason as his brother.

They meet up with Prof. Don and Mrs. Pat. Still somewhat hesitant around the scholar, Charles is easier in his talk with Don's writer wife. He loves her smile. Other theatre people and academics drop by to say hello. It has been so long since Charles was active this way — physically and mentally — that he fights back his urge to just cry.

The next day is official sightseeing. Charles is deeply grateful for this casual time before the meetings begin. A group from the conference gathers for lunch on the beach side of the grandest hotel in Dakar, lazily snacking by a shimmering sea that gurgles around black volcanic rock.

"I just know nothing else matters when I can look out at that scene," says Sylvia — an African born and American bred scholar now teaching in Dakar. "It returns me to my childhood."

Her talk is like a seductive weave of sun and water. When Charles asks her about her work, she declares simply that she teaches women to write.

"My mother also has stories to tell," Charles says. "You should meet my mother. But you would have to come to Uganda."

"It would be a pleasure," she says sincerely.

How different Sylvia is from Kekinoni. He studies her. Thinks her a monarch butterfly in her voluminous sun dress, tipped with colour at the ends of delicate veined hands. Her painted nails pluck at dangly earrings. She absently touches the tops of her full breasts. She is all secret swelling bounty. Poised somewhere between past and future, there is something sacred for him about this black woman.

They watch as the bright ocean boils up, white and dangerous, like a pot frothing over fire. "Sand blows into Senegal from the Sahara," Sylvia tells him. "This humid heat haze is always a sign. Feels like a sauna."

For Charles it is the finger of African divinity.

"But," she concludes, "as fast as the wave swirls in, it is over."

Huge pelicans flock and swoop, animating the gigantic trees behind them. A quick tropical sun makes every colour quiver across the sky. Charles takes a deep breath.

That evening, they are all invited to Sylvia's home. Charles is fascinated by the Frenchness he feels all around him. So different from living under the English at home. Jason wants to know about Senegal's past as a major slave port. Prof. Don wants to know conference details while Pat studies Charles studying this new place.

"We Africans are merely different pieces of the same puzzle," Sylvia says mysteriously. "You know that."

Her home is filled with dazzling silver gift-wrap cushions that remind Charles of crêpey Christmas windows in Toronto. Her furniture, though, is soft white leather. African leather. There is an open-air court at the heart of the house with a huge palm tree. They are always outside even when inside. As it should be.

For Charles, Sylvia is the new African woman, cosmopolitan, vibrant in her traditions, open to ideas, generous and confident. This is what Robert foresaw, Charles realizes. Robert and all of Abafumi. Such wondrous people.

At the official opening of the Senegalese portion of the conference, the assembly waits for the Minister of Culture to arrive. He is so late that they begin to doze in the comfortable armchairs placed for them under awnings outside the conference hall. Charles hopes that this minister will actually know something about culture, unlike the ignorant flunkies appointed by Amin and so many other world leaders.

Finally, the charming and knowledgeable minister arrives, apologizes, and speaks gracefully of politics and art. He stays on, in fact, to hear the papers. At various points, he even intervenes to discuss griotic tradition, the theatre of the concert party, the myth of Spider Anansi, and the various fables that so many of the continent's women playwrights have drawn upon. Charles is impressed. These experts seem to know something.

Two days later, the minister also leads them on a tour of an "Artisan Village" created by a multi-form artist with significant support from the Senegalese government.

After an interminable bus ride, the international assembly of scholars wanders straight into a vision. One created by painters and poets, by marble carvers, chipping and scraping at huge raw blocks, by potters at wheels, ironsmiths at a foundry glowing from its belly, by workers of miniature crafts. Charles meanders through elaborately chiselled doors, stands under shell-studded ceilings as though in a sea king's palace, gazes past abstractions gracefully curled into air by workers of ivory and stone.

The courtyard reminds Charles of his Indian house in Kampala, all enclosed and decorated space, except that this village

looks out to sea, opens its rounded rooms through bougain-
villea and oleander onto whispering ocean, rocks its residents
in airy hammocks, gently over foam, between walls that roll
and dart, that angle and curve with whimsical design, catching
every shudder of wind and gleam of wave.

Later, Charles walks the coarse sand alone. Raking his heels
across it. Shedding his old skin, he thinks. Avoiding the jellyfish,
each a shard of misty mauve glass tossed up and stranded,
hardening and drying.

Except the ones still straining towards the water. Graceful
arcs aching to complete themselves.

The next day Charles and Jason arrive from their university
dorm to a commotion in the lobby of the hotel where Pat and
Prof. Don are staying. Pat is upset. Their room has been robbed.

"It was so strange," she says, her voice strained. "I couldn't
see what was missing at first. Then I realized my sunglasses and
pen were gone. They were not really expensive. Just glittery. "

"Anything that looked like gold was taken," says Prof. Don.

"Well, they got lucky when they found my wedding ring,"
Pat adds sadly.

"How did they know you were out of the room?" Jason is
ever hungry for news.

"Africa has not changed," says Charles. "Especially in good
hotels that they know are filled with jewellery. You go out.
The elevator man sees you. Someone is signalled to. The room
is scoured for valuables. You have a right to be angry, Pat."

"I think I'm more disappointed than anything."

They all traipse disconsolately to the police station with
Sylvia. It is no more than a hot tin box, rusting on the outside,
paint-chipped inside, with two kitchen chairs, and a scratched
desk. Behind this sits a severe young man in full uniform peering
through his glasses, slowly reading the prescribed questions he
must fill out laboriously in longhand. His stubby pencil races
across the page.

This official is terrified before a group of foreigners, thinks Charles. The officer is peremptory with Sylvia.

"Here," she says to him as they leave, handing him twenty U.S. dollars. "And thank you."

She winks at Pat.

In the glare of a hot afternoon, in dusty, downtown Dakar with its clamour, its begging, and its raucous ostentation, she says, "At least the theft is on record. It is good that they know. But of course, nothing further will be done."

Charles is impressed by how long academics can sit without a break. He begins to understand why he is a performer. He must put his ideas into action, not pit them against one another in the rarefied air of intellectual inquiry, of debates over "dictionaries" vs. "encyclopedias," francophone issues vs. anglophone ones.

More interesting, he feels, are the student performances in the evenings, when he is able to hunker forward in concentration, captivated by music theatre, dance theatre, spoken play performances. With these young artists, he feels at home, remembering what he was, who his real people are.

Yet they are nothing like Abafumi. Will he say this to them in a few days when the conference moves to Cameroon? When he has his chance to speak?

The afternoon before they leave, they are taken to the old slave port at Gorée Island, a fifteen-minute ferry ride from downtown Dakar. Gorée. With its horrific holding cells and colonial sandstone buildings. A place of French prosperity built blandly over the slave bones it broke and buried so deep, over the African spirits it exiled.

Fort Jesus again. Charles burrows down inside himself.

They plod slowly along the Gorée beach to the main dock. Sharks can still be seen guarding this area. But it is bright this day. Warm and clear.

"Evil has a history," he finally says.

The group is silent. There is talk of African complicity. There is palpable white guilt.

The return ferry cleaves the sea and they move away. Charles strains his eyes, holding the dark island steady in his vision.

Remembering such similar moments in Kenya. Remembering Headmaster Hermitage. His daughters.

Remembering.

Charles talks easily with his journalist travel mate, Jason. "I've seen more of Europe and South America than I have of Africa," Charles says peering out the plane window on their way to Yaounde, Cameroon's capital, a thousand miles distant. Their plane will stop three times: in Abidjan, in the Ivory Coast; in Cotonou, in Benin; and finally in Douala, along the Cameroon coast. From there, they will go by bus up-river to Yaounde, several hours to the northeast.

A dozen scholars from francophone Africa travel with them.

Prof. Hansel is their Cameroonian host, a Professor of Literature at the University of Yaounde, fluent, like so many Cameroonians, in French, English, and his own tribal language. He is also working with the government as a national cultural advisor.

He welcomes them all and shepherds everyone onto the bus for Yaounde, some thirty anglophone scholars having now joined them.

Douala seems an overgrown shanty town of rain-slicked ruts offering bolts of tired cotton and grimy futons. Their bus snorts and snarls like an irritable animal onto Douala's main highway, heading north. A decrepit rusting hulk of a vehicle, it spews out fumes, and rocks precariously over the rutted road. With no river in sight, they soon sink into a drowse of green forest and palm trees, broken only by the clacking of crickets, tin roof shacks, and dangling bare bulbs that glare along the wayside.

"It must be endless, the bush," says Pat.

"You can easily get lost," Charles tells her. "I have."

Yaounde, the capital looms. Creeps up on them. Appears from a distance an improvement over Douala. Eventually, they arrive at the Mount Febe Hotel, perched on a mountainside above the city that sprawls steaming white below them.

Charles remembers royal palaces in the hills. Cooler. Away from the people. Aloof. And he remembers Abafumi's running track set calmly in the heights above Kampala where they used to race around the university. Robert and the rest of them. Through the gardens of paradise.

The hotel impresses everyone.

"Like the Hilton," Charles murmurs to no one in particular as they wander through the vast lobby past sundecks and restaurants. Laid out in swirls of concrete with balconies and curved wading pools. Striped parasols shade lacy white tables.

Pennants fluttering everywhere.

The German and French theatre scholars — European contributors to Prof. Don's theatre encyclopedia — greet Charles courteously and with interest. They regard him as a true theatre innovator. He is not being rated for charismatic stage presence, or being fawned over by fans with stars in their eyes, as in the days of Abafumi. He is being respectfully consulted. There are things only he can reveal about a company for whose pioneering work he has become the new spokesperson.

"We must talk soon," the scholars say.

He meets an attractive young female director from Nigeria who runs a Children's Theatre. And dreams of her at night. He meets others who perform social action drama on topics such as birth control. Here is a new African theatre world that believes in itself, that questions and examines and experiments, that interacts with its respective communities to make change. He longs to learn more of it.

He feels the spirit of Robert, trying to awaken a new generation of artists, many of them serious women artists.

But Charles must also keep an eye on the wayward Jason who has already been in the gift shop with its jostled display of masks and carvings. Discovering goddess images with curls snaking around their heads.

"Like Medusa," he raves to Charles. "And I thought that figure only existed in Greek mythology. This is all so interesting."

Jason chatters on about animism, how the gods need people in order to exist. About the village justice figure who bristles with nails.

"You feel them only if you are guilty," says Charles, realizing how much he himself has absorbed, of the old ways. How much he has rejected.

At the beginning of the conference next day, Jason — now garbed in newly-purchased traditional African cottons — is off to see a soccer match. Studying his crisp purple and white outfit over breakfast, Charles remarks, "My brother, you look like a prince. Be careful that people don't insist on royal tips from you."

"Really?" asks Jason. "I don't just look like a stupid white person trying to be African?"

Charles is both amused and gratified by Jason's genuine interest in his culture. They have already eaten crocodile meat and chewed kola nuts together. Pulled along by Jason's insatiable curiosity, Charles knows he is alive again, wants things again.

He appraises his younger white brother with an affectionate eye. In his Cameroonian costume, it isn't Jason's pale face that startles Charles. It is something about the way he walks. As though the body wanted jeans and a shirt, not this bright loose flapping fabric.

"You don't quite have the swing that goes with these clothes," says Charles, finally, putting his arm around him. "Come on, I'll show you how to walk African. I can do it even with a cane."

And off they saunter together.

Outside the university, a crowd has gathered. Local officials, the Cameroonian Minister of Culture. Delegates from various countries. Photographers with huge cameras squat or stretch to catch these exalted guests who stand politely around not quite knowing what is expected of them, except that they must look as though they are exalted for these picture takers who will eventually try to sell them back their own awkward images.

Everyone stands for Cameroon's national anthem and for the rector's prayer. Then high-pitched female voices fill the auditorium. Young voices, a sunny throng of shiny dresses wound around with festive red sashes, chanting welcome. One of them stops at each guest to present a small crépe paper rosette.

Charles holds his flower tightly. He is genuinely moved by the ceremonial speeches that say how gratifying for Cameroon to have such esteemed artists and academics gathered from so many important theatre cultures. He doesn't look up. His eyes are on the paper plant, its crinkly petals, its folds and angles, its secret centre holding everything together.

He hears the Nigerian delegation whispering. Complaining about too much money being spent on their lavish hotel rooms. Femi Osofisan, one of the continent's most important playwrights, leads the revolt. They believe they could have organized the event better. Should have. The presence of Osofisan deeply impresses Charles.

His mind drifts back to the previous night — an evening at the hotel bar — really just a small alcove set against badly painted jungle walls. He and Jason listening to a lone Zimbabwean guitarist dressed in white jeans and blue T-shirt play Bob Marley — his dreads shaking, his forehead smooth as moon on water. Charles can neither shake the image nor understand why it continues to haunt him.

He focuses on the speakers once again. Now it is the turn of the Minister of Education to sing their praises. Charles stares up above the politician's head, above ribbon and floral excesses to a latticework opening high on the plain white wall, letting in leafy breezes, and thinks of the National Theatre in Kampala, the big rehearsal room upstairs. Structured with the same strong delicate sky eyes. Weaving threads from the air, a lacy coolness beginning somewhere far-off and pure. Like this room.

How do they really see him? he wonders. This select group: African or foreigner? Broken theatre relic? Refugee?

The electric fans creak slowly, endlessly. He hears Robert's voice whispering through them. And Mr. Makuba's.

A short coffee break and the conference resumes. Papers. So many papers. African culture and politics. Social life and education. Theories, analyses, proposals and programs for the arts. Will they really care about Abafumi's now ancient history, the blood-soaked tragedy that stopped its life?

Charles sits through it all, his tense wooden body hunched over a stalled soul. Rigid with memory. Clutching a wrinkled rosette.

They eat lunch in a campus restaurant festooned with calendars of semi-naked girls. Charles enjoys the tang of genuine African food once again: yassa chicken, okra and fish over dense, starchy cassava. Open Cross Wines and sharp beer stacked against wide wooden shutters and giant green fronds.

That evening, they see a play. *The Battle of Tankriti*. Delegates are told it is an important event. The first time in six years a production has been allowed at the university campus. So even censorship is being relaxed for them.

Charles is one with the actors, deep in their joy and sorrow, fear and need. Singing and dancing the range of their feelings — shaping, shading, beating down, ringing out.

When the king receives a gift, Charles too, signals pleasure — a small stately movement, restraining ecstasy.

He watches the enactment of a people's moral code, the foundation myth of Cameroon.

He knows he has come home. Robert has finally brought him home.

"We must cultivate subtlety in our theatre for social action," says Mariya, a Zambian director, a young woman whose outspoken ideas have intrigued Charles. "Our theatre uses no texts. We improvise around a theme. Debate issues with the audience."

It is day two of the conference.

Charles quizzes her over lunch about the difference between politics and theatre. How far does theatre for social action move toward the directly political?

"Politics is so complicated," she says. "A government censor wrote a report against one of our plays that got him a promotion. At the same time, he told me personally that he liked the work. Ultimately, although the official system cannot support an aggressive theatre of opposition, in the laboratory of experiment, we can do almost anything."

"So," says Charles, "if you stay at the level of a work-in-progress, you're safe." She nods assent.

"It wasn't like that in Uganda for us under Amin," says Charles. "If the censors did not understand, we were told it had to stop. Close down."

But the talk charges on. The energy of argument among artists does not stop.

"If you write, produce, and perform your own piece," he hears himself saying, "then you can improvise dangerous material into a safe form. Those who know how to read it, will. The others will leave you alone. That's what Serumaga did."

"Exactly so," says Mariya. "It is a form of subtlety we all practise. But there also exists a subversive kind of censorship. If I am not mistaken, Charles, Abafumi toured extensively but played only rarely in Kampala."

"It's true and when we did…"

"It was the beginning of the end, wasn't it?"

Charles smiles grimly.

"Try to remember we are artists, not politicians," Mariya adds. "We all start with the same story, the human story that begins in the womb of woman."

As she makes her statement, she picks up a steaming yam with her fork. "And this is also what unites us."

"And this," says Dickson, a smiling Zambian playwright with thick glasses and a twinkle in his eye, hoisting high his frosty bottle of Flagg beer, glistening cold from the cooler. Adding, "I, for one, want to drink to the metaphor. We are, after all, poets of the theatre. Metaphor keeps us in the domain of art. Diatribe turns us into bullies and tyrants."

"Robert used to say," says Charles, "that the language of the oppressed was a silent language, spoken by the image."

They nod agreement. He is being listened to. Those around him hear him, react to the hard-won wisdom of his words. He is acknowledged here as a veteran of Africa's theatre wars. Fate has blasted apart, ripped open, exposed and re-arranged him in every way. But he has endured and they sense it. He is still dancing and they see it.

Mariya reminds them that in Zambia now, there is so much job training for women that men are starting to hang back.

"That's not good either," says Charles.

"We need a man's movement," asserts Dickson with a sly wink.

"You've had one," retorts Mariya. "For centuries."

Did men really have their way? Charles wonders. Did he? Was it the old way? Father's way?

Memories pour in.

And what is the new way?

"Nowadays," continues Mariya, "a wife can even take her husband to court. Can charge him with rape."

The heat of their talk cools with the setting sun. Evening scents deepen gold and green. Returning Charles to where he began.

Now it is his turn to address the delegates. He has asked Prof.

Don to walk with him to the podium, stand beside him while he speaks, artist and scholar together, mutually reinforcing.

Don smiles and takes Charles' arm, walks with him towards the stage. Charles is introduced to earnest applause. He turns, puts his papers on the lectern. Looks out.

Feels so strongly the weight of lives lived and stopped. Lives in triumph and ruin. Lives of song and story and dance. Wandering lives. Lives of passion and pain. Innocent lives. Doomed lives.

An inner script scrolls before his eyes. They wait for him to begin. For many, perhaps most, Abafumi is a vague but legendary memory. As is Robert.

Charles knows what he is supposed to say. What he wants to say. The words are written before him. But he stands in silence.

Finally beginning in a fierce whisper, as though telling them a secret intended only for private, sympathetic ears. He is testing his audience, assessing their worthiness to hear what he has to say.

They lean forward, straining to catch his words.

"I would like to begin by expressing the gratitude, joy and privilege of being on African soil once more...." He pauses and adds, "in the name of theatre."

Slowly, his life unfolds. His own creation story.

"In 1971, a school of theatre was begun in Uganda and a group of young men and women assembled, after rigorous search and auditions."

A strong confident stage voice begins to pull him along, take him back. Into his life. Into legend, myth.

"For Robert Serumaga, Abafumi was to deal fearlessly with the problems of contemporary Africa. We would be African in both form and content."

The memories flow. Father. Mother. A white man in a car. But his words are on target.

"Abafumi, The Storytellers. Ours was to be an actor's theatre. The actor's body and soul was the centre of it. Its language would connect to rituals, movement, and stillness. Sounds and silence. Mime, visual symbols, and emotion. That is how we would communicate."

The audience is with him now. He knows it as an actor knows it. They are brothers and sisters in the art of in his words.

"The training was intense. We were so physically and psychologically conditioned that our sense of reality actually altered. We became hypnotized. Almost possessed by the spirits of our ancestors whose legends and myths we were sharing. This company, this commune became a family, embodying past and future. Time and location never separated us. We were blood."

Charles is wound tight in the telling, his tension felt throughout the space.

"The hero, Renga Moi, had to spill blood to save his village. But the sacrifice was terrible."

Charles stops. Takes a deep breath.

"I want you to know that the warrior hero, Renga Moi was Robert Serumaga who gave us his vision, his blood, and his life. The seventies was a Golden Age for African theatre, for Ugandan theatre, thanks largely to him. We must acknowledge his great gift."

Charles' emotional tribute cracks open his audience like fissures in a volcano.

"Our next play, *Amarykiti,* took the flame tree for its symbol, a tree where, in some Ugandan communities, dogs are brought when they die. You drop the animal off and walk away. You don't look back."

Charles stops, deeply emotional now. There are tears in his eyes. A minute passes. Prof. Don puts an arm round him and whispers something in his ear. But he shakes his head, collects himself and continues.

"At the beginning of that play," he goes on haltingly, "a figure appears in the forest and lights a candle. He is giving the gift of life to the people. At the end of the play, the candle is extinguished. As Robert's life was."

Charles pauses a long time before adding, "The mythical

world of that play was the nightmare we were living in Uganda under Idi Amin. I see that so clearly now."

"It was the hero of *Renga Moi* who changed our lives. In 1976, we were asked to perform the play for assembled heads of state at a meeting in Kampala. The show we put on that night was not simply theatre; it was a cry for freedom. None of us knew whether we would ever get off the stage alive.

"After the performance a colleague told us that Amin was planning our deaths. We escaped to Kenya, were arrested on the way, released and finally we flew to Europe where we honoured a few bookings that Robert had arranged for us.

"We lost Robert in Rome. He disappeared for months. Not even his family knew where he was. The last time we saw him was on television, in combat uniform, as a field commander among exiled groups waging war against Amin. He was playing his last — maybe his most important — role in an effort to liberate his beloved country."

A long pause.

In the thick silence that fills the auditiorium, his heroism is finally recognized. Applause begins. Slowly. Each clap shattering. Exploding.

Charles walks back to his seat, thunder building around him. He is now in the embrace of his large theatre family. Passion streams down his face.

For some moments, he floats on sweet waters that carry him up and over the difficult terrain of his life, milky clouds filtering out all harshness. There is no pain.

Next day, the conference visits the village of Kribe where the group of academics and theatre people will picnic by the sea. Kribe is a long drive from Yaounde along an ancient lurching road. Charles watches, amused, as, en route, their rusty bus wheezes up to a gaggle of university students flapping and chattering by the side of the road like large birds, their white shirts and blouses snapping in the sunny breeze. Box lunches, once stiff and spotless, now limp and grey with chicken grease, are loaded on by the students. Then heavy drink coolers into what remains of the aisle. The student helpers finally sprawl over makeshift seats, their spirits high and their songs shrill, for the rest of the journey.

The bus stops for petrol. It stops to take on board an old Singer sewing machine from a large woman yelling something about her sister in Kribe. It stops to let some of them relieve themselves in the long grass.

Charles recognizes these arrangements, the chaos and exuberance. He recalls the many bus rides with Abafumi, the receptions, the excursions with dignitaries to local sites.

For a moment, he is there again.

Passing countless shacks of mud and wood, some with Fanta signs set in little clearings on powdery brown soil. Public bathing spots where clothes and bodies slither in lather. Roadside booths of copiers with typewriters, pecking away at the spoken letters for those who cannot read or write. All this along dirt roads that suddenly plunge into dense palm forests, meeting one another in the bush.

"Life makes different routes for each of us," Charles says to Pat.

Humidity smothers them as they approach the coast. Trees hang in heavy liquid silence. This is the climate Charles remembers. Wet. Close. Soft as Suna. They stop to watch water crash down from high rock and a dugout canoe paddling over shining sea. Where the jungle pours out, flowering in sun and blood.

Journalist Jason and playwright Dickson discuss prostitutes in the town. Who was and who wasn't. Overhearing them, Mariya chides them for being interested in lust not love. They see nothing wrong with that.

Charles smiles, recalling his own wars.

Long lazy hours on the beach. A break from serious things. Later, the bus — carrying a sleeping throng now, undisturbed by clacking crickets and lulled by quenching breezes, hurtling

past a blur of gleaming night market bulbs that rival the looming moon — shoots quickly, precipitously, back to the capital.

The closing day of the conference and Charles' final few hours
in Africa, delegates are gathered for lunch at the high white
house of their host, in the hills above Yaounde. They have
travelled there again by the bus they now affectionately call
Bumpity through the dust of lurching roads to Prof. Hansel's
gracious home.

At tables under the trees, guests dressed in dazzling white
and throbbing reds, greens and blues, swoop over a brilliant
array of food, picking and savouring with obvious pleasure.
Then plump down beside one another to drink and chat.

"You'll need the five stomachs of a cow to digest it all,"
laughs Hansel. "But it will keep you going for days."

Delegates and guests share succulent peanut chicken and
hot plums in tangy sauce and then return to the unbroken
threads of their conversations. Randomly they pull filaments
of African theatre out of the air, not greatly caring which seeds
float down and pollinate.

Charles is thinking how unsubtle censorship can be, almost
at the same moment as Maryia comes forward with her painful
reminder of direct government intervention. "I saw students
taken," she says without expression. "Their heads were shaved.
They were pushed onto the ground and forced to roll around
in the mud simply for performing publicly."

"Theatre," says Hansel, wanting to move them from violent strategies to artistic ones, "is an inter-medium where the
audience is invited to participate in its resolution, in closure."

"That is what Robert believed," says Charles eagerly. "It is
what he tried to do with Abafumi. Losing nothing, neither the
old way or the new, but fusing them in forms that we invented
together, that the power of the stories revealed to us."

The day also offers a few quiet hours. Several of them have

climbed up a hill behind the Mount Febe Hotel to discover an exquisite garden, a small peaceful paradise, a jungle of moss arching high into trees, fastened to earth by old round stone.

Charles and Pat sit calmly talking. "It's beautiful here. The rain cools off the bush."

"Pounds it into submission," Charles agrees. "Lets us breathe."

"It was difficult wasn't it, giving your speech."

"Yes, but it was my duty. I know Robert heard me. And others."

"I'm sure, he did Charles. Many heard you."

Together, they drift into a small museum behind the garden where she watches him finger pipes and tabourets in fine carved wood, calabashes and flasks, braziers and oil lamps. His attention is careful, loving. They stop at a decorated throne composed of abstract frogs, a chorus of thrumming fertility, surrounded by monkeys whose kindly duty is to help the dead rest.

"Everything has a purpose," she muses admiringly.

"Including me."

Puzzled, she takes refuge in the obvious. "Robert and Abafumi gave you your purpose."

"But they are gone now."

"Unless you keep them alive."

"It is what I want," he says. "To tell their story. Robert's."

"Do it," she urges him.

"I am not a writer."

"But you must do it."

He hears but does not look at her. Turning away, he studies spider designs etched on the walls, spiders regenerating, individually and painstakingly, ensuring the continuity of their species by attending to their own programmed complexities.

"I wish I could be as subtle as spiders," he says. "With every new pattern, they reveal a secret. Language is so intricate."

"You have the language to tell your story."

"I don't"

"You can spin the right words."

Charles stares into the flooding bush a long time before finally turning back to her.

"No. Once I could have danced it. But not now. I can only describe the steps. I can only speak from the darkness. Someone else has to choreograph the words. Maybe you," he suddenly says. "You could write my story."

"Me?"

"I will talk and you can write."

The thought sinks in. They gaze out at the gleaming green around them. Rain rinsing the world to deep new colours.

Slowly the project takes shape. Over weeks, months and ultimately years of conversation.

Charles' obsession is magnificent.

He and Pat agree to go beyond the facts, to create and dramatize as they recreate. His life, so much more than mere document will be the life of a hero, an African hero, filled with song and legend. Myth. His story must move from ice to fire, from tornado to torture, from here to there and back.

After many discussions, they are as ready as they can be.

Where shall we begin?" Pat asks, when they both feel right.

"In the rain. That terrible day. In the wind and the rain. In the eye of the tornado."

He pauses. Then changes his mind.

"No," he says "Let's start just before the storm. In the ice house.

Smiling broadly at her, he finishes his thought. "At the top of that mountain."

IN FACT: **SOME NOTES ON REALITIES**

As stated at the beginning of this book, Charles is a very real person. His full name is Charles Tumwesigye and he lives today in Toronto. Unable to work because of the injuries he sustained in the devastating Edmonton tornado of 1987, he has visited his native Uganda only once since giving his talk on Robert Serumaga in Cameroon in 1996.

It may be of interest here for readers to understand that Serumaga's theatrical aesthetic — Artaudian in its reliance on what has been called "total theatre" — has never been duplicated in Africa and has never been significantly documented anywhere in any public way. It is very much a myth still in the making. And for the record, the Robert Serumaga, who for parts of recent decades ran the National Theatre of Uganda, is actually Robert Serumaga Jr. whose father founded the Abafumi troupe at the centre of this book.

As for Charles' family, his father and mother in this book are based on the lives of the real Kanyunya and the real Kekinoni. One difference between this version and their reality is that they had eight children, not two. The eldest was named Mary and the second was named Wilson. Charles was the third to be born and he was followed by Betty, Stephen, Robert, John, and Herbert. For narrative and dramatic purposes, I have combined the real Mary and the real Betty into a single elder sister called here Debra. The real Betty now also lives in Toronto, having moved there to help Charles after his horrific accident. Charles' best friend Samuel is a composite of his brothers and friends.

Abafumi's reality is even more complicated than one finds in this narrative. While the essential facts are based on the realities of the company founded by Robert Serumaga, names have been changed throughout to protect the identities and lives of almost everyone involved. At its height, Abafumi had an acting company of twelve to fourteen plus six trainees. Some of its shows utilized all of the actors plus Serumaga himself who, for example, really did play the Priest in Abafumi's most famous production, *Renga Moi*, which really did tour to rave reviews world-wide in the early and mid-seventies. The actors named in my version are, in fact, composites, their circumstances based on reality but not necessarily on specific individuals.

For the sake of historical recognition, I think it is important here to name the members of the real Abafumi as Charles recalled them and to recognize their unique contributions to theatrical art. All were trained by Robert Serumaga as actors, dancers, drummers, and musicians, and all contributed collectively to the creation of Abafumi's extraordinary non-verbal, myth-based works.

They included: Alice Bitamba, Charles Buyondo, William Ddumba, Friday Kibombo, Marie Kirindi, Jones Kiwanuka, Jane Kobusingye, Stephen Lwanga, Rwandan-born Jane and Dede Majoro, Frank Mbaziira, Paul Mukasa, Victoria Nakazaana, Sarah Ntambi, Geoffrey and Margaret Oryema, Agnes Sabune, Deborah Sentongo, Richard Sseruwagi and, of course, Charles Tumwesigye. Sara Kibirige served as company secretary.

One more real character who makes some brief appearances in this novel is the playwright Byron Kawadwa who was the

Artistic Director of the National Theatre in Kampala for a time and who was, in fact, also executed on Idi Amin's direct orders. Kawadwa was not the first artist to die under this regime nor was he the last. His plays, too, remain an important part of modern Ugandan dramatic literature.

The character of Mr. Makuba is a composite based on several real characters Charles discussed over our extensive two-year-period of interviews. These included his female drama teacher at Mengo Collegiate and several others who led him both into Abafumi and into the world around it.

In attempting to make decisions about whether or not to use real names or to create pseudonyms and/or composites, I tried to read Charles' sensitivities as well as my own sense of clarity and effective storytelling. When in doubt, I asked myself what would most be in the spirit of Abafumi with its mythic sensibilities. Charles' goal and mine have been to recognize how profoundly this story is connected to myth. Having spent an extended period of time in probing conversation with Charles about his life, both personal and artistic, I apologize to any who might feel there is even the slightest injustice done to their memories or failures of understanding around this amazing, complicated and often contradictory story of extraordinary survival. Charles Tumwesigye, an artist all his life, has consistently encouraged me in this process and I thank him heartily for trusting me.

Another choice I felt I had to make concerns the play put on before the infamous gathering of African heads of state in Kampala. It was not in fact *Renga Moi* done that day but *Amyrikiti*. The latter play had a scene in it involving security guards throwing someone in the trunk of a car and driving away. Set in South Africa, Idi Amin took this "South Africa" at face value. It was only later when he realized it was intended to reflect Uganda's own situation that he issued the order to wipe out Abafumi. Because *Renga Moi* is treated more significantly in the novel, I opted to use it rather than *Amyrikiti* for dramatic effect.

One final word on reality. The CIA really was, in fact, all over Africa during this period of time. It is documented that it funded numerous African cultural activities both inside Uganda and out. Was Abafumi on the CIA payroll? Despite research, I have not been able to prove this for certain. And, to the best of my knowledge, Robert Serumaga never admitted it. Yet there is enough circumstantial evidence about this issue that I feel comfortable including it as an assumable fact in this novel.

Whatever the ultimate truth here, the real miracle is that Charles is still alive to tell his story and Abafumi's. Both are stories of artistic risk, endurance, courage, faith, and the bearing of witness. Such risk creates powerful images of pain and joy, fate and truth. Such risk affords us all a glimpse of the madness inherent in both a capricious universe and the political world. Charles and the spirit of Abafumi have been my own inspiration in the writing of this book. Hopefully their realities will inspire others to dance their own dance in the face of direst adversity.

ACKNOWLEDGEMENTS

This story first came to me some years ago when my husband and creative partner, York University theatre professor, Don Rubin arrived home from a lunch meeting with the Ugandan actor-dancer, Charles Tumwesigye. They had been discussing the Ugandan article for Routledge's six-volume *World Encyclopedia of Contemporary Theatre*, a project that Don was in the long process of editing and in which I, as a theatre critic and editor, was also actively involved.

We had encountered problems getting material about the fabled Abafumi company. Charles, a former member of the troupe who was now living in Toronto, promised to be the best lead. Don was excited. During that conversation, Abafumi sprang to life for him along with the international journey that brought Charles from Uganda to Canada.

"You must meet Charles," Don said to me after that lunch. "His story is incredible." A week later I did. And it was.

Over the next month or so, Charles continued to share his extraordinary artistic and personal wanderings. We soon became friends and sometime later, at an African symposium in Cameroon, Charles asked me to tell his astonishing story. There had been earlier journalistic attempts. Charles was dissatisfied with them all. Most seemed more interested in the sensational elements surrounding his survival of the Edmonton tornado than anything else.

After two years of interviewing him, my first attempts at writing Charles' story were straightforward and documentary. But I found I could not get at the dramatic truth of events in that format so I turned, with Charles' blessing, to another form, the novel, where I found the freedom to draw much closer to the story he wanted to tell. It was an approach that recognized more dramatically his passion for dance and theatre, an approach that stayed true to his faith in ultimate good, an approach that built a "Charles" myth evolving naturally out of the Abafumi context.

Charles has been puzzled at many points about what to make of this new version of his life. This is, no doubt, an occupational hazard of bio-fiction. But from the beginning we built trust and for that I am hugely indebted to him. This book truly belongs to him just as it also belongs to the brave, creative, and iconoclastic Robert Serumaga and to everyone else who was ever a member of Abafumi. I am sure that ultimately there will be many versions of the Abafumi story. I am honoured that I have been given the opportunity of writing the first.

I also want to give great thanks to those friends and colleagues who, having heard a piece of the adventure, have thought this book important to complete. And once I began working on the narrative, everyone — in and out of Africa, in and out of the theatre world — encouraged me to finish it, insisting that it needed to be told not just as a theatre story but also as a political story, an African story, a story of human endurance. A story about the power and importance of art in times of political repression.

Over several years, I have also read excerpts from the manuscript to audiences, sometimes with Charles present, sometimes when he was unable to be there. Often, people in those audiences were more expert than I was about specific things African. To them and to all who made suggestions and corrected my errors, I say thank you sincerely. You know who you are.

From time to time, I have also shared the process of this book with my Creative Writing students at York University and they too have made important comments that have helped me with what was always a sensitive and challenging manuscript.

One Man Dancing owes its final realization to the ongoing support of Luciana Ricciutelli and her team at Inanna Publications who have cared deeply about it. I cannot express enough gratitude to Luciana for believing in this project, for being absolutely true to her word on matters large and small, and for providing her special brand of publishing imagination, dedication, and enthusiasm.

Patricia Keeney is an award-winning poet, novelist, theatre and literary critic. Born in the UK, she moved to Canada with her parents and grew up in Ottawa and Montreal. A graduate of McGill University, she later completed doctoral studies in the UK, subsequently returning to Canada where she began teaching Creative Writing and English at Toronto's York University. A well-known arts writer for many years for CBC Radio, *Canadian Forum, Scene Changes, Canadian Theatre Review* and *Canadian Literature,* she continues this work in such publications as *Arc,* and the online journals *Critical Stages* and *Critically Speaking.* In 1989, her first collection of poetry, *Swimming Alone,* appeared and attracted serious critical attention. British poet Ted Hughes said he saw "real life burning way" in her poems and praised her "very natural voice." Now the author of ten books of poetry and two novels, her poetry has been translated and published in French (winning the Prix Jean Paris in 2003), Spanish, Bulgarian, Chinese, and Hindi, while her *Selected Poems* carries an introduction by the distinguished Russian poet Yevgeny Yevtushenko. Keeney's *Orpheus in Our World*—poetry and dialogues based on the oldest of Greek songs in verse, the *Orphic Hymns*—will also be released in the fall of 2016. An avid traveller, Keeney has taught and lectured in Europe, Africa, and Asia. For additional information, see her website: Wapitiwords.ca.